C000040999

BIRD_ _

PARADISE

BIRDS OF PARADISE

RUDOLF KREMERS

Elsewhen Press

Birds of Paradise
First published in Great Britain by Elsewhen Press, 2023
An imprint of Alnpete Limited

Copyright © Rudolf Kremers, 2023. All rights reserved
The right of Rudolf Kremers to be identified as the author of this work
has been asserted in accordance with sections 77 and 78 of the
Copyright, Designs and Patents Act 1988. No part of this publication
may be reproduced, stored in a retrieval system or transmitted in any
form, or by any means (electronic, mechanical, telepathic, or otherwise)
without the prior written permission of the copyright owner.

Quote in chapter 10 from *Moby-Dick; or, The Whale* by Herman Melville,
1851, London: Richard Bentley.

Elsewhen Press, PO Box 757, Dartford, Kent DA2 7TQ
www.elsewhen.press

British Library Cataloguing in Publication Data.
A catalogue record for this book is available from the British Library.

ISBN 978-1-915304-20-9 Print edition
ISBN 978-1-915304-30-8 eBook edition

Condition of Sale
This book is sold subject to the condition that it shall not, by way of
trade or otherwise, be lent, re-sold, hired out or otherwise circulated
in any form of binding or cover other than that in which it is
published and without a similar condition including this condition
being imposed on the subsequent purchaser.

This book is copyright under the Berne Convention.
Elsewhen Press & Planet-Clock Design are trademarks of Alnpete Limited

Frankenstein is a trademark of Universal City Studios LLC; Hello
Kitty is a trademark of Sanrio Company, Ltd.; Klingon and Star Trek
Discovery are trademarks of CBS Studios Inc.; Millennium Falcon is
a trademark of Lucasfilm Ltd. LLC. Use of trademarks has not been
authorised, sponsored, or otherwise approved by the trademark
owners.

Designed and formatted by Elsewhen Press

This book is a work of fiction. All names, characters, organisations, places, and events are either a product of the author's fertile imagination or are used fictitiously. Any resemblance to actual events, planets, orbiting space stations, colonies, interplanetary mega Corps, or people (living, dead, augmented or in stasis) is purely coincidental.

U

CONTENTS

For James

PART ONE
INFILTRATION

1

Mars: Red Colony space port – December 2240

As I lay there on my back, spreadeagled in a pool of blood, I watched the pretty Martian fireworks display wash over me. It was with a sense of distance and tranquility that I accepted the truth; I had failed in every possible way a person could fail.

He was gone. Taken from me. I had been unable to protect him, unable to cure him. And now, to compound mistake after mistake, I had been unable to keep him safe and by my side.

I was ready to die. I could not face a future of endless guilt, haunted by the spectre of the life we could have had. A life I had denied us through my own arrogance and mistakes. It was simply intolerable. Death was preferable.

I *willed* it. I tried to stop breathing, to stop fighting, to let my horrific injuries take their toll and be done with it all, but I was denied even that fundamental release. My augments were simply too efficient, halting blood-loss with hyper-effective coagulants, pumping me full of disinfectants, painkillers, psychotropic drugs. I suspect the latter was the only thing that stopped me from ending it all in the days that followed.

A particularly beautiful star-burst exploded just over the Martian horizon. Had I not been in such an abject mental state I would have appreciated the artistry of the fireworks display, but all I could think about was how I was sinking deeper and deeper into my own private hell – a parallel to the recurring nightmare that so often plagued my dreams with terrible visions of drowning and loss.

This time it was no dream; I had been dragged down under and I was drowning in my own failures. I closed my eyes, hoping for an end, and felt the world grow dim and distant, until I could feel no more.

2

Eighteen months before my terrible failure on Mars, my son Clint and I stood before the great gates of Diamond-Town. My humanity was still intact. My life was as it should be.

We had just returned from a salvage contract on the Moon. A somewhat indifferent gig, but thankfully profitable enough to earn us a few weeks of downtime back on Earth. A couple of months, if our auction went well.

I often took Clint on low-risk missions, prepping him to eventually join my crew once I was able to afford my own ship. He was on the young side for salvage work, but the practical experience was invaluable and he had real talent for the job.

We finished our work early on, giving us some spare time for private salvage – presenting a chance to earn some extra money on the side. Our client was a typical risk averse dig-scout who was disinterested in what we were up to in our time as long as we fulfilled *his* contract. Luckily, our efforts had paid off and we discovered several small but interesting Trickari artifacts (some I intended to study, others to sell), as well as a good number of human valuables. I was itching to get home in time for the auction later that day, keen to see how much our haul would fetch, but first we needed to pass through customs.

Our lot was due in the late afternoon. I liked being present when our items sold – partly out of professional pride but also because I valued the chance to mingle with others in the business and catch the latest gossip. Either way, I was impatient to enter the city and get on with my affairs.

Unfortunately, we were stuck in the customs line for

residents, moving with all the speed and urgency of a lethargic snake. Still, people in the other line (for visitors and other unfortunate creatures) envied us our progress which was at least measurable. Their line barely moved at all.

It was sweltering; the body heat of hundreds of tired and sweaty travellers mixing with the warmth of the afternoon sun, beating down on the corrugated iron roof of the customs building. This was the boring and unpleasant part of coming home.

To kill some time I studied both customs lines, scanning for differences between the people, trying to read their idiosyncrasies, honing in on interesting or telling aspects of their lives. It was a favourite pastime of mine when at the mercy of customs officials.

The visitors line was full of people with sharp edges, cold stares and hard faces. They were people haunted by fallout from the countless Icarus incidents that had plagued humanity in recent decades.

I saw the usual TrickMem junkies (there were more of them every time I returned to Earth), souped-up Mod-Fighters looking for quick cash and a smattering of Corp wannabees. It was easy to identify the different types of desperate people. Some were doing better than others, but all were looking to catch a lucky break in Diamond-Town. Most of them would gladly give up their right arm for permanent residency rights.

I noticed a woman to my right, further back in the line, who could have been my spitting image had I grown up outside the gates, on the streets of Greater London. She was of medium height, muscular, alert and vigilant, but without advertising those qualities too brazenly. Her physical appearance dwelled on the right side of lean, in that space just shy of haggard, but only just.

Hardship wrinkles danced around her face as she surveyed her surroundings, shielding her eyes from the low afternoon sun with hands which looked far too old for her age – a sure sign of a tough life. She probably spent the last of her money on some rejuvenation treatment, hoping that Diamond-Town would allow her another throw of the dice – another chance at a better life.

I compared her appearance with that of a man in front of me. A D-Town resident, but I suspected only recently so. He still exuded that sense of relief that new residents carried with them for the first few months after gaining residency rights. His clothes were colourful and street smart – brash hues with attitude in abundance. He was obviously augmented – made abundantly clear by the barcode tattoos on his neck, clearly visible behind his collar. I concluded that he was both a proud and vain man, qualities which would likely get him in trouble with the local gangs who weren't too squeamish to extract Trickari Blue from any device as long as it made them a profit. Even if that device was an augment inside a living human body.

Barcode man was oblivious to this potentially gruesome fate and smiled salaciously at me, thinking I was checking him out – which I was of course, if only out of boredom. He conformed perfectly to a type I had seen countless times before; his face had that uncanny quality that comes from too much body-sculpting. Once people modded themselves too many times they would never look natural again, unless they took on a fresh body – a solution out of reach for most people. Barcode's smile deepened as I openly studied him.

As the line moved I shuffled close enough to catch the smell of him. Even his body odour was fake; I was sure he had some kind of musk gland augmentation going on. A tendril of disgust wriggled in my stomach.

'Business or pleasure?' he asked.

I ignored him, studying the other people around me, but he misread my expressionless face, thinking I hadn't heard him.

'Business or pleasure?' he tried again. 'Because pleasure is my busin–'

'What are your augments?' I asked, startling him. 'Stamina? Speed? No, wait … I bet you went for a standard gigolo package, didn't you?'

He laughed nervously, unsure how to react. 'Well …
yes, but it was the best choice available and I–'

'How old?' I asked impatiently.

'I'm not sure what you … I don't understand?'

I sighed, already tired of him.

'When did you get the augments done?' I asked,
speaking slowly as if to a dim-witted child. 'More than a
year ago? Before the government introduced ARAG?'

Clint, shuffling along to my left, threw me an
exasperated look. I winked at him in return.

'ARAG?' asked Barcode man, thoroughly confused.

'Yes. ARAG. The Augment Regulation-Authority
Guidelines?'

Barcode man looked worried now, concern written on
his face. 'Was it in that back-alley chop shop in the North
London Warrens?' I caught the flicker of recognition in
his eyes and dug a bit deeper. 'It was wasn't it? Did they
use a surge-buffer? These days they're mandatory for all
Blue augments, you know? And with good reason …'

Clint kept throwing me disapproving looks, looking
more and more embarrassed. Barcode man on the other
hand was slowly getting worked up.

'Look luv, if you aren't interested I'm OK with that,'
he said, puffing up his chest. 'I don't need the hassle or–'

'Do you have *any* idea what happens when a Blue
power-source fails?'

'I … No, I don't know, but they said it would be OK.
Right?' His default cocky attitude fought briefly with the
doubts I had carefully planted in his head, and lost.
Worry and a touch of panic took over, eventually
breaking through his cosmetic veneer of cool. He ended
up looking genuinely nervous. I could even smell it. His
musk augment must have been working overtime.

'Of course they said that it would be OK,' I said. 'They
wanted your money.' I sighed, suddenly tired. The guy
was a pain in the arse but he had clearly been conned,
which was never fun. 'OK listen… Trick-Blue doesn't
just *gradually* lose power and then neatly wind down –
it's nothing as pretty as that. No – it swerves all over the

8

place; too much power… too little… it runs hot, it runs cold… all kinds of badness happening, *inside* you. Not nice. And then, just before it goes, it'll start spiking real hard. Random power-surges, heat flashes, faster and faster, until ZAP! It shorts out with a massive final surge.'

I glimpsed Clint rolling his eyes at me as I leaned in close to Barcode man's face. 'Now, imagine all of that, but happening right next to your vital organs. Doesn't sound too great now does it?'

The shocked expression on his face told me that I'd probably overdone it a bit. Maybe it was time to ease back a bit – throw him a lifeline. 'Look, don't worry too much about it, just go to a proper augment clinic when your gear starts misbehaving, and then get a buffer fitted. You'll get plenty of warning believe me. Anyway, you know what it's like. Trickari Blue can last decades if you're lucky. Just keep an eye on it.'

The man nodded slowly. He started to say something to me, but abruptly thought better of it – probably a good call.

Clint elbowed me. The line had reached the customs officer who, recognising us from many previous occasions, promptly waved us through.

I glimpsed from the corner of my eye that my counterpart in the other line was trying to suppress a smile. She had been close enough to have heard my exchange with barcode man. She gave me a sly look. I grinned in response, briefly wondering what her story was.

Then we stepped through.

After spending several tiring months in space – much of it in low gravity – entering D-Town felt like a huge relief. It was comforting to wear street-clothes again, instead of my clunky (and by now quite smelly) space suit. And although it was arduous to once again carry my full weight in Earth's gravity, that discomfort was countered by a deep sense of freedom and *rightness*. It was a feeling well-known to Earth-born people; a powerful biological reaction telling us that this was where we belonged. *Terra Firma, at last!*

I glanced sideways at Clint. He was grinning expansively, sharing my exhilaration at being back home.

'Stop looking at me like that. It's weird,' said Clint, but he kept smiling.

'You've grown again. You'll have to shave next.'

'Stop it. I shave.'

'Handsome young man, smart… I should probably give you the talk before you get some downtown hussy in trouble.'

'"Hussy?" *Really?* What's the matter with you mum?'

'Ok, so, about those birds and bees–'

'Please. Just stop,' Clint huffed, cheeks red.

I laughed, happy, excited – proud. It *was* great to be back, but I knew it wouldn't last. Eventually that old itch would return and I would sign up for a new salvage mission. The money was simply too good, and reclaiming Trickari artifacts was always rewarding and exciting.

But, for now, we were home, back in the dubious embrace of Diamond-Town, and ready to sell our precious cargo at auction. I caught myself smiling at the city streets, in anticipation of the many little pleasures on offer. Despite stinking alleys cluttered with food stalls selling exotic and sometimes dubious dishes, despite the all-pervasive air of hectic desperation, I felt as if surrounded by nothing but space and glorious opportunity.

Whenever I returned home, every inch of me reached out to take in the sights and sounds of the city, absorbing the tacky neon signs, the edgy thrift-core street wear (mother of pearl was back in fashion), the constant background rumble of competing sound systems. It was all delicious food to my starved senses. My work as a Xeno-archaeologist demanded great attention to detail, and had made me extra sensitive to sensory input.

I took a deep savouring breath but couldn't take it all in

fast enough, making me feel jittery. I got like that after lengthy salvage missions, spending too much time in cramped zero-g quarters, consuming (I won't call it eating) stale food rations and driven to extreme boredom by daily, mandatory exercise on tortuous fitness machines like some demented lab-rat. Still, despite the discomforts, there was nothing I loved doing more.

Once, many years ago, I took on a purely research-based office job. No time in the field whatsoever. It was an utter disaster. I ended up feeling like a ghost; a hollow version of myself, wondering if I was a real person, an *original*, or a deluded replica of somebody more substantial than me – somebody *true*.

That's why I became a Xeno in the first place – to anchor myself in the only kind of life that meant something to me; salvaging ancient Trickari artifacts, rediscovering lost valuables, exposing secret data caches … it all served to define my own place in the world.

I knew who I was, and what I was capable of.

When I was a little girl I had to watch my father slowly lose his mind. Day by day his sanity slipped away from him, in increments too small to pinpoint but with unmistakable results.

Before his illness he was the most rational person I knew. Everything he did was driven by logic, and he prided himself on being a realist foremost. Many's the time that he gave me lessons in the true way the world operates. He taught me from a young age to see things as they are, not how I wanted them to be.

Augment sickness turned him into a person I barely recognised, ranting and raving about unlikely conspiracies and evil plots, always looking over his shoulder, questioning my mother and me on innocuous details of our behaviour that had triggered his paranoia in some way. It was hard to accept from a father who I had always admired for his no-nonsense approach to life, and loved for his straightforward and unconditional affection for me. He fell a long way.

In his final days he was completely adrift, far away from the safe shore of our family life. My mother and I did what we could to maintain the illusion of normality in our every day lives. We cooked him his favourite meals, took him to his favourite places. We shared our favourite memories, made him reveal his. But it was no use; his sickness was progressive and incurable and, therefore, ultimately lethal.

Ironically, it was only during the wake, when we said goodbye to his corpse, that I felt he was with us again.

Although I didn't know it at the time, my father's fate taught me that everybody needs a frame of reference in life, something to help anchor them to reality, and for me D-Town was just that. It wasn't actually a "town" in the normal sense of the word, despite its name, although it started out as one. Over the years it had grown into something akin to a city-state, thriving on the outskirts of the remnants of East London. It had carved out a unique position for itself, attached to the gargantuan body of Greater London like lichen to a boulder – small, hardy, and if you looked close enough, rather beautiful.

Like most locals I knew its history well, and like most locals I took a measure of irrational pride from being a resident. I guess it made me feel part of the city's famed mythology.

D-Town's origins go back at least a century and a half, to a group of individuals – mostly artists and political eccentrics – known as "the Diamonds". They covered a broad spectrum of cultural outsiders and malcontents, pushed out of their former ecosystems in the cracks and crevices of Greater London. This was long before the first Icarus incidents laid waste to much of the city.

Exorbitant rent and stifling societal rules frustrated their preferred way of life, compelling them to join forces. Several hundred of them banded together, named themselves the Diamonds and jointly looked for a new place to settle and grow. They searched for months, trying to find a place that would allow them to practise their (frequently offensive) art and political activism. They searched for a place where they could settle as a *community*.

After a spate of false starts saw them kicked out of a string of London neighbourhoods, they finally discovered a long forgotten industrial estate on the edge of town. There were abandoned factories, workers' houses, a church, a steel mill, and all kinds of other interesting and useful buildings. Other than a pack of wild dogs that roamed the maze of structures, the estate was completely unoccupied. It was dirty, dangerous and disreputable, and the Diamonds took to it with zeal.

After they moved in they quickly established a political and social framework, devised a basic set of rules and rights, and christened their handiwork "Diamond-Town". Although ambitiously named, the project was much derided by other Londoners who mostly ignored it. They had no way of knowing just how much Diamond-Town would eventually live up to its imagined potential.

Walking through the streets with Clint by my side filled me with joy. People reacted well to him; pretty girls smiled their pretty smiles, and cool boys regarded him with a measure of respect. Clint, at sixteen, was well on his way to become a fine human being.

I felt myself break into a wide smile, wearing my maternal pride like armour – impenetrable and impervious to all the shit and the dirt that surrounded us. People stared at me, I stared back, right into their eyes. *I'm smiling, yes? What of it?* Even in a city as filled with ostentatious eccentrics as this one, showing off was frowned upon, but at that moment I simply didn't care. All was good, and I wasn't of a mood to hide that feeling.

Somebody bumped into me from behind, some street-punk with a mercury mohawk which kept changing shape. The punk kept pace with me, giving me the evil eye despite him being the one who bumped into me.

'What you want huh?' His snarl was extraordinarily rude, but I was too distracted by the mesmerising sight of his shape-changing Mohawk to respond to the challenge.

I felt a slight tug behind me, not enough to disturb my walking rhythm, so I ignored it. You can't walk the streets of D-Town without being jostled occasionally. Besides, that mohawk morphed again, turning into a row of silvery spikes, oddly fitting for the scowling face beneath it.

I ignored another jostle from behind when, with a sobering stab of adrenaline, I cursed myself for being a fool. I abruptly stopped in my tracks, jabbed sharply backwards with my elbow, connecting perfectly with the nose of the pickpocket who was trying to get into my bag.

Blood flowed down his dazed face. A knife fell to the ground.

'Hey!' he stammered clutching his bleeding nose. 'What's up with you lady?'

'Next time I'll break your nose properly,' I said slowly, to give my words time to register. 'Best be off now, little man.' I stepped up to him, threatening further violence with my eyes.

The pickpocket stared at me for a few seconds, gingerly touching his bloody nose, before slinking off without a word. He disappeared into the crowd like a spider down a drain.

I was annoyed with myself for letting my guard down. I clearly hadn't fully adjusted to being back on Earth yet.

'Look at Mohawk go!' said Clint, pointing at the punk, who had taken off the moment his accomplice had been elbowed.

'Couldn't you have said something?' I asked.

'I knew you'd get there eventually.'

'It's no joke, he had a knife. Don't be cocky.'

Clint held up his hand in surrender. 'Well, anyway, you got him good.'

D-town might not be the safest city at times – big parts of it are best entirely avoided – but it's as vibrant a place as I have known, and despite some of its less attractive features it's a city with a soul. There is always a fresh supply of socialites, upmarket hoodlums, young sim stars, pop stars and fashion stars – a whole firmament worth of glamorous types – willing to move in and join the party. The stars attract more stars, the parties beget more parties – everybody plays their part in a positive feedback loop. D-Town's cool edge had become a self-fulfilling prophecy.

Not wanting to dwell on the incident I gently pushed Clint forward, motioning him to keep going.

'We need to get to the auction house. I don't want to be late.'

'In a hurry to be defeated?' asked Clint. 'I like that.'

I laughed. 'Yeah, your track record speaks for itself. But feel free to deny reality, it will catch up with you soon enough.'

Clint huffed irritably. 'Don't be so sure mum, I got pretty close last time. Today might just be my day.'

He tried to hide it but my little jab had carried a sting, and he didn't like it.

There was that damn pride again.

We made our way towards the auction house in the old market district on foot. It wasn't a long walk, and I wanted to take in the local vibe. The neighbourhood was one of those typically Bohemian haunts that made up big chunks of the city, the locals somehow always outside; debating street philosophy, playing dominoes, or just hanging out and enjoying their community. There were little groups of people dotted around, drinking together, playing music. Some kids played with a micro Blue toy, sharing the rare plaything without argument. It was a pretty mellow place.

Streetlights were haphazard and of variable quality, especially since the Icarus incidents, so visibility was limited to intermittent pockets of light, opportunistically populated by the locals. On the surface it all felt like business as usual, but I detected something dissonant, something that felt *off* to me. There was a tension in the air. Subtle, but there nonetheless, and I wasn't the only person who had picked up on it.

Clint's body language subtly shifted. He appeared tense, more alert. He had seen something … Even at 16 years Clint had already developed good street instincts, prompting me to follow his gaze with interest. There was some kind of commotion further up the road, two groups of people – one small, one large – coming our way.

I motioned to Clint that we should cross the road and stay out of the way. He obeyed without question, knowing to follow my lead when I was serious.

'What do you see?' I asked.

Clint peered, taking in the scene. 'Local muscle, not sure whose, escorting somebody I think.' I nodded, hiding a smile. Whenever Clint concentrated deeply his forehead wrinkled in a sweet way, making him look eight years old again.

'What else?' I asked.

Clint squinted into the low afternoon sun. 'Bunch of curious people following the first group. Can't tell why, but seems foolish to me. Trying to see what's up I guess.'

This was a game we often played; I would ask Clint to report on something of interest, and he would try to describe the key elements in the scene. He was getting better and better at quickly honing in on the most important and relevant details. It taught him to train his senses, to always be alert and ready for any sign of trouble. *I can't protect him forever.*

'How heavy the muscle?' I asked.

'Heavy!' He looked concerned. 'Check for yourself'.

As we got closer to the first group of people, some details asserted themselves: the muscle weren't just standard goons for hire, they were Corp. They openly carried serious firepower, which meant they must have had the right permits, and that wasn't easy to come by.

I carefully checked if my own gun was still there, suddenly worried after the incident with the pickpockets.

Thankfully it was – snug in its holster, within easy reach if I needed it.

Why would elite corporate muscle come to this part of Diamond-Town? And why didn't those locals back off? These weren't people you wanted to piss off.

'Mum, look…' I spotted the source of the commotion at the same time as Clint.

'Oh! …' An inadequate response to an extraordinary sight; ahead of us, surrounded by five enforcers, walked a Neo-Trickster.

It (*He? She?*) easily stood over seven feet tall, dressed in an explosion of colourful fabrics, probably the most beautiful creature I had ever seen. Its body was all queer angles and strange joints, but elegant and purposeful. It walked with a motion so smooth that it created an illusion of gliding across the ground, like a brilliant ghost.

A small crowd of locals had gathered, following it from a small distance. They were a rough lot; rejects and low-lifes and other hard-done-by cases, hoping to bask in the creature's aura, looking for some of that exotic beauty to rub off on them. Later they would share the story of what they saw that day with their friends, trying to pretend that their lives *were* special after all. Other than getting off on TrickMem they had few opportunities to see such sights.

One of the enforcers decided that enough was enough and barked a warning at the gawking crowd. They recoiled, sensing real danger. Maybe they were street scum, but they weren't completely witless; they wouldn't have survived on the streets for long.

By now we had discreetly moved alongside the creature and its escorts. The road separated us from the main bustle but we could still study the Neo in some detail. Its appearance was of a male humanoid but its skin had taken on a distinctly reptilian sheen – a sign that its metamorphosis from human to Neo-Trickari had completed. From the looks of it, the creature had settled into its final state. It must have stopped generating new Trickari memories years ago. I wondered how much Mem had been extracted before it had run dry.

I felt a pang of sympathy for whatever poor soul was buried inside the Neo's body. Somewhere underneath the alien features lived an unwilling host, trapped inside a flesh prison, guarded by an alien mind. Its skin was mottled white with grey patches and looked tough, its limbs were long and graceful, as were its fingers and toes which ended in gem-encrusted nails and claws. Its feet were bare; no shoes could contain them. But nothing could compare to the beauty of the Neo's crystalline hair, chiming softly with each step as the creature moved down the road; a curious song lamenting a long lost alien race.

Its appearance reminded me of a docu-sim I had seen as a little girl, portraying the lives of an ancient African tribe whose members adorned themselves with intricate and colourful decorations, including coloured beads and feathers, scarification and other methods of body modification. At the time I marvelled at the sight, thinking them the most alien and exotic people I had ever seen, but the Neo presented a much stranger and more impressive display altogether.

As we got closer, more details manifested; a thick, solid mass of crystals nested on top of an elongated skull, solid and robust, yet the creature's head moved with grace and fluidity, as if unencumbered. Out of this base grew long strands of crystalline material. Colourful, dazzling, somehow flexible despite its gem-like appearance. The strands caught the afternoon sunshine, scattering its lazy rays like a hundred diamond prisms, causing my heart to flutter with a strange mixture of fear and joy. The creature was both exotically alien yet also painfully human, somehow encompassing both extremes in a single body. I had never seen anything like it.

And then, out of nowhere, we made ... *contact* – I have no other word for it. It happened just as it was about to pass us by. I was trying to move a transfixed Clint along when it noticed us from across the road. The creature and I slowly turned to face each other, like puppets without volition, moving as if directed by fate.

All external sensation melted away. I could only focus

on the miracle in front of me, captivated by the Neo's gaze. It stared at me with cold and purposeful eyes, the way a predator stares. A faint whispering sensation tickled the inside of my ears, yet there was no actual sound.

The Neo and I both stood frozen in place, facing each other.

–Brood Mother– ... The words drifted into my consciousness.

It moved abruptly; fast and long strides carried it across the road in seconds, leaving the Corp enforcers behind, mouths agape.

It towered over me, head held at an odd slant. A jewel encrusted hand, sparkling like tears, touched my cheek. It stung for the briefest of moments.

Strange images bubbled up from my subconscious mind. My scalp prickled, goose bumps marched up my arms. The hairs on my skin stood on end as if charged with static electricity.

I was sure it was trying to communicate with me, and somehow *I knew* that I could reach out and probe its thoughts.

–What do you want from me?–

Something formed in my mind: a concept, a purpose … I couldn't quite understand its meaning but it felt important. I instinctively tried to reciprocate, to reach out and–

'Step away now!' shouted the enforcer.

His hand was on my shoulder, pushing me away firmly. 'What?' I mumbled.

A second enforcer caught up – a dim looking bruiser.

'Fuck away,' he said. I almost laughed at his weird phrasing.

My senses were still going haywire; events appeared slowed down to me. I watched dispassionately as the first enforcer produced an impact pistol – a nasty weapon capable of doing serious internal damage. To my misfiring senses he appeared to move with all the speed and grace of a tired sloth. This time I laughed out loud.

His four colleagues caught up, all with drawn weapons, each of them ready to kill. And just like that it didn't seem funny anymore.

I suppressed an almost overwhelming urge to draw my own gun – a highly illegal Cluster-shot – but to do so would have meant instant death for both Clint and me.

Everybody froze …

I could smell my own sweat. The tips of my fingers tingled.

Nobody spoke.

Then, a harsh loud sound broke through the quiet. It was Clint laughing loudly. Heads whipped around to look at him.

'Never seen a drunk Trick-junkie before?' he barked.

That's my boy! Clint knew what he was doing.

They hesitated… glancing at each other. Then, one of the enforcers relaxed and lowered his gun. He spat on the floor, gestured to the others to move on. They all holstered their weapons and beckoned the Neo back to the other side of the road.

Clint laughed again, his voice gravelly and ugly, and shoved me forward, 'Come on you silly old cow!'

Although entirely feigned his show of disrespect still stung deep, but it was a smart move and probably saved my life that day. I took advantage of the moment and stumbled away from the Neo, acting like a drunk.

The encounter couldn't have lasted more than a few moments, yet my entire body was sore, my clothes drenched in sour sweat. I adopted an unsteady stance, taking on the role that Clint had given me. I spat on the floor and growled at the Neo; 'I smoked your memories you freak bastard!' *Just the thing a TrickMem junkie would say.*

The creature tilted its head sideways again, as if it could hear my insincerity.

It rejoined the group of enforcers.

And then they were gone.

3

The auction house had once been a famous meat packing plant and abattoir, back in Victorian times, before real-meat went out of fashion. This was when people still kept livestock, putting up with animal diseases, shit-filled pens and all the other unpleasantness that came with it. I shuddered with disgust at the thought, but I guess it was the norm at the time.

I imagined I could smell the blood of the old slaughter pits, seeping through the walls, infecting our modern, semi-civilised haggling with a touch of raw meat. Truth was that things could get pretty brutal during auctions. Rivalries were born, thievery concocted and revenge plots hatched. Many a fortune was won and lost here, many careers made and broken. The current use of the facility was in keeping with the spirit of its original blood-soaked purpose.

A massive circular display screen hung from the central part of the ceiling over the entrance hall, listing upcoming auctions, observing every transaction, like the eye of a giant sentinel.

The display screen confirmed that the next lot up held the goods we salvaged during our lunar mission. We had arrived just in time.

The main hall was buzzing with activity and anticipation from buyers and sellers both. The air was super-charged, looking for a release, the auction floor was rigged up to facilitate just that. Music boomed through the aether, augmented staff provided a wide spectrum of drink and drugs.

The sexual energy was so palpable that I sniffed the air, trying to catch the scent of the tell-tale pheromone cocktail the proprietors pumped into the air-circulation system; a classic method for encouraging clients to spend recklessly.

I caught the occasional punter touching themselves inappropriately, unaware of the display they were putting on, or maybe they simply didn't care. Dial-a-fetish sexomatons paraded in front of the crowd, employing the weird eroticised walk that was so typical of their outdated programming. Still, as crude as their pre-baked sexed-up moves were, they hit punters right in that part of the brain that involuntarily responds to sexual motion stimuli. Cheap and sordid stuff, but very effective.

Clint never let on being affected by any of this, I assumed to spare us both awkwardness. I must admit that I had on occasion felt the odd stirring myself, but thankfully learned to ignore them.

'Jeez it smells in here,' said Clint. He was right; it stank, but that was the way of it.

I checked the access records for our lot and was pleasantly surprised to discover that there was a lot of interest in our items. Because all salvaged goods were pre-processed by the authorities we had the advantage of being able to advertise our goods well ahead of time. Anything that made it through quarantine could be advance-registered for auction for a chunky fee. I had learned early in the game that it was a price worth paying.

A quick scan of the crowd revealed that many of my regular buyers were here; even more were active on the auction-net. This would have put me in a good mood under normal circumstances, but I was distracted – the Neo from earlier had put me on edge. The memory was buzzing around inside my head, like a fly trapped behind a glass window.

Something bothered me about that bizarre meeting in the street but I couldn't put my finger on it. *That Trickster was reaching out to me, as if it knew me...*

A sharp elbow jab from Clint alerted me that our lot was up next.

Clint was as competitive as I was – no surprise there – and we maintained a friendly rivalry, comparing whose salvage calls were most profitable. So far I easily had the better of him but he was starting to make some surprisingly good calls. My teachings were paying off.

A jingle played over the sound system, prompting the auctioneer to start his countdown. The audience cheered with one voice, then joined in. It was cheesy stuff, but the ritual helped people focus on the tense bidding action that was about to follow.

Hard work and difficult choices, frequently made during duress and in dangerous situations, had led to this precise moment in time. Yet it would all count for nothing unless the items on offer caught a buyer's interest. Every auction was a moment of truth, a little drama unfolding in front of a committed audience.

Despite my attempts to stay calm and detached I felt swept along with the tide of anticipation, like everybody else. I turned my head to observe the crowd which had transformed into a single entity, living completely in the moment, for *this* moment.

'Ready mum?' asked Clint, a gleam of excitement in his eyes. 'Today the student surpasses the master!'

I snorted, but secretly wished him good luck.

'I'm ready, sure,' I said. 'Ready to teach you another lesson in humility.' He grinned. I then spoiled it by giving him a big hug.

First up was a collection of maps created on our lunar mission. Clint had written an auto-mapping tool that spat out detailed floor-maps and reconnaissance reports, and put it to good use during our salvage missions. These maps were detailed and extremely current, and therefore very valuable to up-and-coming Xenos. In fact, an ever growing number of them followed in our wake using Clint's maps and data reports to snap up any leftovers we couldn't fit in.

Clint's work was popular and he was building a name for himself. I even spotted the occasional Xeno groupie hanging around him, trying to catch his eye. I didn't begrudge him the attention, and Clint was smart enough not to get involved.

Clint's maps sold quickly, putting him ahead of me in earnings, but I matched him soon after with the sale of some rare books. For a while we did equally well on collectibles and antiques. A rare painting from me, an obscure video game from Clint … but gradually Clint built up a sizeable lead.

I made up a lot of ground on Trickari artifacts – my specialism. My current lot didn't contain the best I had ever found, but as people were getting more and more desperate for Trickari Blue, prices were going up rapidly. Anything to replace the dying artifacts that had given humanity such a boost during the years of the Acceleration.

I checked my numbers; despite some good sales I was still behind in overall earnings.

Clint looked smug; I let him enjoy his lead.

Things went on like this for a little while longer. We both did moderately well but Clint maintained his lead. Until we hit my final lot.

'Pay attention now,' I said, suppressing my mirth.

Clint laughed in disbelief. 'That ancient sex stuff? For real? It's tacky as hell.' He noticed I was indeed serious. 'Come on mum, that stuff's worthless. It's not even made of gold or something.'

'Just watch and learn, little bear.'

My final lot was made up of a collection of 19th century erotic pendants, discovered in an old lady's antique dresser. We found her lying next to it, clutching a particularly rude sample in blissful reverie. Her body was frozen solid but she was still smiling, her secret pleasure finally exposed. I guess she tried to warm herself one last time before the end.

Clint was partially right; the pendants were indeed tacky as hell, but they were also expertly crafted. I had contacted three buyers ahead of time, knowing they were heavily into sex relics. Two of them were here in person, which was all I needed.

After an initial flurry of offers eliminated other prospective clients, my preferred buyers finally got serious. They matched each other bid for bid, escalating their duel until they were facing off in a red hot, stubborn bidding war. Either party was unable to back down, and they went at it like a bunch of fighting cocks. The bids rose higher and higher, soon surpassing my own best estimates.

'You've got to be joking,' said Clint. His triumphant, cocky smile long gone, withered away under the onslaught.

By the time my buyers were done the final, selling bid amounted to roughly the same profit as all our other items combined.

I turned to Clint. 'Sex sells. That will never change.'

Back outside my mood took a turn for the worse. Despite doing good business at the auction I was painfully aware that I still had a long way to go towards owning my own salvage vessel.

I looked up at the darkening sky, the wind had picked up and angry clouds were marching in. I could feel pressure building up behind my eyes – a precursor to serious migraine trouble. That wasn't something I was willing to risk while out and about so I decided to call it a day.

I let Clint choose the way home, which perked him up, giving him a chance to show off his knowledge of the city. Born and raised here, Clint knew the city as intimately as anybody could. He had seen every pore, every wart, every mole and every drop of sweat on D-Town's face. I could think of no better guide.

'Come on, new route,' said Clint.

'Again?' I laughed, despite the worsening ache behind my eyes.

'Yep. Do keep up.'

Clint picked up the pace, leading me up ladders, into elevators, escalators and climbable chutes, traversing to the highest level of the city. Despite the darkening skies it was a surprisingly beautiful excursion. The rooftops were bejewelled with the detritus of an individualistic society –

flags, sculptures, intricate graffiti, gardens, animal pens
… all connected by a complex latticework of bridges,
planks and alleys. Every turn brought something new.
Every hidden cut-through brought out more local colour.

D-town had done so much better than other cities or,
indeed, better than the rest of Greater London, because of
a quirk in its history: after the Diamonds had
appropriated their little enclave, its ideological
underpinnings helped D-town make a name for itself.
This attracted a certain type of anti-establishment settler:
real-meat abolitionists, eco-warriors, Gaianistas, and so
on. When the Acceleration kicked off, and the rest of
humanity gorged itself on Trickari Red and Blue, D-town
went down a different path. Far from embracing the new
technology they shunned it, focusing on self-reliance
instead. No Red power was allowed inside the gates, and
only a smattering of Blue – heavily regulated – found its
place into the city. Most of the locals weren't exactly
cash-rich anyway, so this approach suited the town's
ideological and financial constraints.

After the first Icarus incidents destroyed entire swathes
of Greater London, people picked up on something
strange; D-Town seemed immune from the carnage. This
was easily explained: there simply weren't any Red items
to go critical. There was some Blue tech yes, but Blue
power sources didn't catastrophically escalate like Red
ones did. They just ran out of juice over time.

Almost instantly, Diamond-Town became a very
attractive place to live.

These days, nobody calls it Diamond-Town (much to
my secret disappointment). In fact; to some people D-
Town is about as far from diamonds as one can get. It's
just that the alternatives are so much worse.

By the time we got home it was completely dark, or at
least as dark as it ever gets in this part of town, and I was
more than ready to put the day behind me. I was still re-

acclimatising from our lunar expedition. The day had turned out to be far too long for comfort.

I lived in an ancient 20th century pilot's tower which I had personally converted into a live-in work space. It stood, discreetly, in a quiet part of town known unexcitingly as "District 23".

Few people lived there. Most were repelled by an offensively bad smell that frequently pervaded the neighbourhood. Visitors (wrongly) attributed the smell to a nearby crematorium, and the idea of smelling and inhaling the particles of the recently deceased put most locals off.

It was a bogus story of course; the smell originated from a plot of land owned by a shy herb-farmer with a penchant for good old-fashioned manure, and was infrequent at best. Such smells that occasionally did waft around the neighbourhood didn't bother me as I had installed excellent air filters. Either way, District 23 wasn't seen as a fashionable part of town, which I considered a distinct advantage. I liked being left alone.

Clint and I had lived in our strange tower since he was nine years old. Its floorspace was much larger than it appeared from the outside, giving us a huge canvas to play with. Over the years the spaces inside the tower had slowly morphed into distinct physical manifestations of our private obsessions. Clint's work-space looked like the wired-up nest of a paranoid security expert, overflowing with a sea of screens, Net-Pads, heavy duty Sim-Jack gear (he spent a lot of time jacked in) and an insane amount of computers of every known persuasion and configuration.

Once inside, Clint immediately settled into his work-space and started tinkering.

'Really?' I asked. 'Straight back into it?'

'Sure, why not?' said Clint. 'I'm doing useful stuff you know?'

I felt that sting of pride again, watching him repair an antiquated Data Ripper. It was a typical Clint project, not tackled because he wanted a functioning Ripper –

although it was useful for chewing through hard-coded crypto on old storage platforms – but because it amused him to re-program it for an entirely different purpose than it was designed for.

'What's that thing going to do?' I asked.

'Counter measures mum. Just keeping us safe from net-bot attacks.'

'Why would we need that kind of protection?' I laughed, but I was genuinely concerned.

'Well, with the amount of errr... *exotic* data we deal with, it's best to deploy a lot of black ice.' Clint laughed as if I understood the reference. I didn't, but I appreciated his efforts to keep us safe. Clint was always good at things like that; thinking laterally, confounding expectations, breaking the mould.

My workspace wasn't exactly homely either. I let my eyes wander across the room. Row after row of industrial strength shelving, stacked with scientific equipment, instruments, mechanical parts, and real-books. All neat and tidy, all labelled and cleaned.

Centrally placed, solid and mighty as a giant anvil, stood a workbench equipped with all the tools one would ever need to fix mechanical devices. I inhaled deeply through my nose, savouring the smell of oil impregnated cloth and old gear. It was an engineer's paradise – exactly what I intended it to be.

One shelf was different from all the others; it was used to display rows and rows of miniature models of ships of every kind, collected, built and repaired over a period of many years.

Clint, following my gaze, said, 'You're supposed to be the grown-up, mum.'

'We all have our hobbies,' I said, smiling. It was a gentle jibe, and I didn't mind. 'Go back to your data hound, ok?'

'"Data Ripper", not "hound",' said Clint. 'And it's finished.'

'Already?'

'Yep. Not bad eh?'

I gently squeezed his shoulder in response. It was good to be home.

Our sleeping quarters were cozy and secure, protected by two feet of thick concrete padding, courtesy of the pilot tower's sturdy walls. We had struck a deal with the ancient building; it allowed us to live inside its body, protected by the skin of its thick walls and reinforced glass, keeping predators at bay. In exchange we kept the tower in good repair, nipping any structural problems in the bud before they got out of hand. It was a symbiotic relationship with a piece of twentieth century architecture.

The thought made me giggle, which in turn led to Clint throwing me an exasperated look. I was too tired to say something witty so I dragged myself onto my bed. I folded my hands behind the back of my head and stared at the concrete ceiling. I had forgotten that I had painted it yellow when we moved in. I rolled onto my side to watch Clint tinker with yet another device.

'You did well today Clint, thank you.'

'Yeah OK, you were pretty good yourself playing the Junkie.'

'I shouldn't have let that creature get to me like that. It was weird. I thought it tried to …' I wasn't sure how to describe the encounter to Clint. I wasn't sure if I understood it myself.

'Tried to what, mum?'

'Forget about it. Go study something useful.'

'Ah yeah. I have a book on rare space porn right here, I clearly need to work on that a bit more.'

I managed half a laugh, but the day's events were catching up with me.

'How did you learn that stuff mum? How did *you* become an expert in collectible porn?'

I laughed despite myself. It was easy to forget that he was just a teenage boy. I started to give him the "I was once a teenager too" routine, but Clint emphatically rolled his eyes at me, and I was just too tired to stick with it. I went back to staring at the yellow ceiling, content to let my mind drift, while my chest rose and fell to the gentle rhythm of my breathing.

Despite my efforts to stay awake, fatigue took me in its arms. After a brief struggle I succumbed and sank into murky sleep. I entered a world that was painfully familiar to me; I've been suffering the same recurring nightmare for years. Small details would change over time, but the same themes persisted: I found myself submerged, frantically diving after an unconscious Clint who was drifting deeper and deeper into nightmarish depths, like a murder victim made to disappear. The water was cold as death, enough to paralyse. I slowly lost the ability to swim. This was the point in the dream where I would normally lose Clint, watching him sink to his death, defeated by the bizarre logic that powers nightmares. But this time the scenario changed. Clint, slowly sinking backwards, opened his eyes. They blazed with an eerie purpose and intelligence.

It wasn't Clint looking at me through those eyes, but some other *presence*. Cold naked fear froze my blood. I recoiled, as the creature controlling Clint's body swam up to grab me. An icy cold hand grabbed my wrist, pulled hard. I was too weak to struggle free. All I could manage was to scream silently, over and over again as he/it dragged me down into the dark, to the coldest place in the universe.

I woke up crying, begging for Clint's life, drenched in sweat. I sat on the side of my bed shaking, unable to purge the nightmarish imagery from my mind. I must have stayed there for at least thirty minutes before I managed to compose myself enough to get up and make myself a tea. The comfortingly familiar smell of ginger and lemon was enough to finally calm me down. A look at the clock told me that twelve hours had passed while I was asleep. It was noon; I had slept through the morning.

Clint was gone. He left a note, telling me that he was

off to see some friends in some ratty D-Town borough, who-knows-where. I suppressed my knee-jerk maternal fear. *He's fine.*

Having reassured myself I realised that in contrast I felt weak, my stomach a gaping, empty maw. I hadn't eaten in a long time. I attacked my hunger by whipping up a huge breakfast, hoping that the sensory input would drown out the echoes of my horrible dream. I made waffles, Facon and eggs, beans in sweet tomato sauce, toast, coffee … the works. It was delicious.

While I ate, my thoughts kept fluttering around yesterday's events: the arsehole at customs, the pickpocket, the auction … but mostly I kept seeing the face of the Neo-Trickster as it tried to make contact with me, touching my face …

The encounter kept spinning round and round in my head on an endless loop. I started to wonder if the creature had done something to me when a shrill beeping through the intercom told me there was a visitor at the front door. A quick glance at the screen revealed it was a postman.

'Hi there,' I said into the intercom. 'I'm not expecting a delivery.'

'Letter madam. D-Town council. Need your print for this one.'

A little flutter of concern accompanied me as I let the postie take my fingerprints. The letter was marked "urgent", and addressed to both Clint and me, which was very unusual. I put it down on the counter for a moment while pouring myself another coffee, wondering how to proceed. *Should I wait for Clint?* Curiosity won me over and I quickly opened it with a kitchen knife.

It was a letter from the D-Town Residency Board, triggered by Clint's imminent seventeenth birthday. I scanned the contents quickly, then – as a sense of panic descended over me – I sat down and read the letter carefully. There was no denying the disaster it contained:

The Board was giving Clint and me sixty days' notice to start his formal residency application. He would have to qualify for full citizens' rights, or apply for sponsorship to remain. This was no surprise in and of itself – I had anticipated this for years – but the timing had been brought forward by 12 months; new rules had recently come into effect.

Being a contracting Xeno, I was reliant on somewhat unpredictable job opportunities. That was just the nature of the business. And while my reputation was good enough to regularly score me decent gigs, that was nowhere near a stable enough existence for the residency application board. Sponsorship was out of the question. The plan had always been for me to save enough money to obtain and captain my own ship, and make Clint a member of my crew. The position would grant him automatic D-Town residency with full rights, while allowing me to continue training him, making sure he would stay under my protection. But I was nowhere near ready to buy my own vessel at this stage in my career. I was doing well, better than most, but even with the original cutoff date it would have been tight. I cursed out loud. Tight yes, but possible, and I had been confident that I would pull it off. But now, with sixty days left, it was a very different proposition. I had time for one, maybe two more salvage missions until the new deadline would exact its toll. My earnings would have to be spectacular to enable me to buy my ship a year early.

To make matters worse; if I failed to achieve this near-impossible feat Clint would move in with his father and apply for sponsorship through him. It was an agreement I had made many years ago during our divorce proceedings.

I put down my coffee too abruptly. The clang of the metal cup bounced off the walls of my tower, echoing with the force of an accusation.

4

Baroness Odessa's very short history of

Humanity: the Trickari Discoveries.

Extract 7: "The Acceleration"

Earth Years 2050 – 2150

And so, dear reader, humanity somehow muddled through the horrors of the 20th century and – surprisingly – managed to survive the first half of the 21st century, despite numerous nuclear accidents, flings with neo-fascism and the sudden arrival of catastrophic climate change. It was truly a time for fools and follies.

But, not only did our beloved ancestors survive, they eventually presided over a period of relative calm and prosperity! For once, members of the human race merely bickered amongst themselves, refraining from our customary efforts towards mutual destruction.

This unexpected reprieve opened up a window of opportunity to improve our shared lot. World leaders and, equally important, *global corporations* knew that it was just a matter of time before geopolitical tensions would flare up again and that the next round of conflicts was one we might not survive.

Resources were pooled, a great Earth Summit was called, and very important people gathered. Many possible solutions were debated, as were some impossible ones. There were no easy answers found, but it was agreed that spreading our chances across two planets offered better odds than staying rooted to little old Earth.

This led to a grand consensus: terraforming was the

way of the future! And the only viable home for this future was our neighbourly planet Mars.

Yes my dear reader, decisions were made and plans were created. We would smash asteroids into Martian polar caps. Green-house gases would do their work, and countless robots would start mining the surface. We would try to solve the magnetosphere problem, and we would patiently transform the red planet to a new paradise, able to fulfil all our needs. Wasn't it an audacious plan?

A suitably icy asteroid near Saturn was chosen. An expedition was sent to nudge it towards Mars by means of a nuclear drive, to be installed on the dark side of that brave little rock. Those were exciting days.

And as you well know dear reader, this led to humanity's biggest discovery: the expedition, once it drew near the asteroid, picked up some *anomalous readings*. The brave men and women on that mission eventually traced the source of the mystery to what was then called "the anomaly".

Incredibly, and it still excites me to write these words: we found an alien spaceship in orbit around Saturn, camouflaged to appear like an ordinary asteroid, but we all know it was far from ordinary.

At first, this momentous find was kept secret from the public while a second expedition was put together to gather more information. "The Dyson" was soon underway.

Now, I'm sure dear reader, you already know the names of all the people on this famous mission, and they all performed heroically, but let's raise a special glass to celebrate the bravery and wisdom of captain Gabriel Rochas, for it was he who eventually gained access to the alien ship. And it was Gabriel Rochas who named its ancient builders the "Trickari" for reasons only known to him.

The alien ship was soon dubbed the "Trickari Ark", although there was no trace left of the creatures that had once travelled on it to our humble shores.

Perhaps, like Noah, they had found salvation a long time ago. I daren't hazard a guess.

The good captain and his loyal crew discovered that, although the Trickari beings had long since gone, probably millions of years ago, their technology was still very much alive. And oh, what miraculous technology it was!

As it turned out dear reader, the Trickari ark was enormous, the size of a large city, and filled to the rafters (or the alien equivalent of such things) with devices, gadgets, machinery, instruments, and even space ships. Trickari tech seemed to be made of indestructible materials, and harnessed incredible power derived from trans-dimensional sources. I shall leave the scientific details of this curious fact to more learned chroniclers, but it seemed that the alien technology tapped into an infinite supply of energy, perhaps drawn from white holes or supernovae, thus handily cheating the laws of physics as we knew them. We did not even need to fully understand the principles behind this phenomenon to be able to use the Trickari devices ourselves. Suddenly, we had access to unlimited power.

And thus, humanity received an upgrade. A new age of progress and expansion was ushered in, known as "The Acceleration". In other words: Humanity had hit the jackpot, and was ready to spend, spend, spend.

Over the course of the next hundred years or so our species blossomed, and reached out to the solar system. Mars was successfully terraformed, countless smaller colonies sprung up in its wake, built on our solar system's many moons, on major asteroids and in newly built habitats and installations.

My dear reader, it was a most exciting period in our human evolution, but sadly, like Icarus, we eventually overreached and we came crashing down, our wings aflame.

5

When Clint came home later that night – laughing and relaxed after seeing his friends – I decided not to tell him about the letter. What would be the point? I didn't want him to panic, to make a rushed decision that he might regret for the rest of his life. After all, I still had sixty days to resolve this.

I spent the next two weeks chasing every salvage lead and every contact I had in the Xeno business, in search of that one gig that would offer a big enough payday. I listened to pitch after pitch, some more promising than others. None would offer even remotely enough reward. I was starting to feel the pressure: something would have to shift soon.

One Saturday, after turning down yet another respectable but underwhelming offer to crew with a middling salvage operation, I decided I needed a break. After days of graft I was in a mood to drink at one of the many theme-bars in Diamond-Town's Sakura district. Much of the area was dominated by hulking Victorian-era industrial buildings, once essential to the commercial life of rich Londoners, but now mostly used for storage. Surrounded by these looming architectural mountains the bars in Sakura formed a colourful oasis. It was an excellent place to drink. Perhaps the best one in the world.

There were 47 theme-bars, and they were all micro-sized. The smallest offered seating to no more than four customers; two at a tiny bar and two at its single table. The largest could accommodate about twenty people, which almost made it a regular establishment if it weren't for its rather hardcore retro-cyberpunk theme.

Entering any of these bars would see me getting very drunk by myself, or if I was in the mood, in conversation until deep into the night, generally with some interesting but fleeting stranger. As I was striking out badly in my quest for a special commission, both options were fine by me.

Sakura's main street was bathed in bright light projected by a forest of colourful signs, alerting visitors to the existence of a long parade of obscure drinking dens. Some were familiar to me, others I hadn't frequented yet. There was "OptimUS" (Classic Japanese toys), "Le Chat Noir" (French Neo-Modernist art), "SimSim" (retro-movies) and many others, each offering up a customised and accessible slice of a particular bar owner's personal obsession.

I've always loved areas like this; representing a kind of folly that speaks to my romantic streak. Sakura district had a sense of *mythology*.

The night air felt smothering and humid. A brief bout of summer rain caught me out, swiftly soaking me through and through. I didn't care, it would dry soon enough.

As I walked the glistening streets I caught the reflection of my face in a puddle of dirty rainwater, animated by the light of flickering neon signs – green, red, green, red, green, red… I smiled at myself. Something about the night made me feel like listening to jazz, and I knew just the place, only a short walk away. I quickened my step and, soon enough, wisps of steam rose from my wet clothes as I whistled an old Charlie Parker tune.

"The Jazz Messenger" didn't disappoint. It wasn't busy yet when I arrived, but a nice vibe already hung in the air, welcoming any classical jazz aficionados who entered. The walls were literally plastered with music from the 20th century; there were posters, record sleeves, concert dates, portraits of musicians – all very quaint and rustic, but done with real passion and respect for the musical period it was trying to evoke.

Other than the bar staff I didn't spot any familiar faces, so I sauntered over to an empty table and winked at Luiz, my favourite bartender in the district. He winked back at me and danced over, steps as light as a flute solo.

'Jemm, *guappa*, my heart knew you would return to me, but my head feared you had betrayed me.' Luiz always spoke like this, a lazy stereotype of a Latino chancer. I played along because I liked him.

'And were you tempted to fish in new waters?' I asked, throwing him a mock-hurt expression.

'Every day!' exclaimed Luiz, dramatically. 'I am only a man – no more, no less. But never, *never* would I betray the eyes of my true love!' This was strong stuff even for Luiz. 'But can I say the same of you? Who is this man "Ballard", asking for you?'

Spotting the surprise in my expression, he dropped the act immediately.

'You don't know him? This guy, he's been asking for you for days now … Big guy, big beard?'

'Nope, not on my radar. How did he know to come find me here?' I asked, but I already knew the answer: I had become *predictable*, drinking at the same bars, in the same district, to the point where some stranger could just ask for me and people would know which way to point. *I need to fix that.* I thought.

'Actually, it doesn't matter,' I said. 'Did he mention what he wanted?'

'Ask him yourself, *guappa*.' Luiz pointed to the bar where a huge bearded man occupied a small barstool.

My first instinct was to get up, leave, and avoid Sakura district for a few months, but something inside me was too curious for my own good. Sometimes history is that simple; a small binary choice – talk to somebody or not – can radically alter future events, even if we don't realise it at the time. That night I didn't leave, and in failing to do so sealed my fate.

There was something disarming about Mr. Ballard … He sat by himself, an exotic looking giant, much too big for his barstool, reading a Real-book (who does that in a bar?), completely oblivious to my inspection. Not exactly naive, just at ease with himself.

He seemed no threat to me, so I joined him at the bar. 'Good?'

He looked up with a jolt, innocent incomprehension splashed across his face.

'Your book, is it any good?' I asked again.

'Oh! Yes, I mean. I read it before. It's Moby Dick!' he laughed, as if that was funny. His laughter was soft and melodious, at odds with his overwhelming physique. I couldn't place his slightly exotic accent.

'I read it too,' I said. 'I never know who to cheer for – the whale or the captain? Most people identify with one or the other.'

He looked surprised. 'That's an interesting question. I hadn't thought about it, Miss. Hmm … Ahab, he is both strong and weak, that's true yes? The whale is smart, but its heart is black …'

I was mildly surprised that he was giving this conundrum serious thought. *He seems harmless enough*, I thought.

I held out my hand. 'They call me Jemm.'

His eyes lit up. 'How did you know that I–'

I nodded at Luiz, who wiped his brow in mock relief.

'Ah! I see, good. Miss Jemima DeLaney, yes, I was told I might find you here.' He got off his stool, towered over me like a cliff stands over a beach, and returned my handshake with an unfeasibly large and hairy hand. 'Captain Ballard. J.J. Ballard!' I had to step back to avoid craning my neck too far backwards.

'Captain of, *what* exactly?' I asked.

'The *Effervescent*! My ship, she's called the *Effervescent*. I'm her captain.' A glimmer of steel flashed in his eyes when he mentioned his ship. I took note.

Ballard continued, 'Due to … *circumstances* I need to expand my crew, and it was suggested I talk to you.'

'Suggested by whom?'

His face remained blank.

'Fair enough,' I conceded. 'Anyway, it doesn't matter. I'm looking for something more than regular salvage at the moment.'

'Please hear me out Miss Delaney. We need a Xeno. I hear you're good,' he whispered, leaning in conspiratorially, as if we weren't already being watched by every single person in this place.

'What happened to your last one?' I asked. It seemed an important detail to me…

Ballard made a "please join me" gesture, indicating the stool next to him.

'Fine,' I said 'but you're wasting your time.'

As we sat down I noticed a Stanley Turrentine track playing in the background. "Don't mess with Mr. T". It had something to do with an old movie called "Troubleman". I dismissed the on-the-nose omen with a tired chuckle.

Ballard waved to the bartender for another drink, deploying an arm thick enough to embarrass a sturdy tree.

'Please, drink with me,' he implored when the bartender arrived.

'Gin, the usual,' I said. The bartender nodded and gave me a sly smile. He must have thought Ballard a suitor. I explored that thought by shamelessly looking Ballard up and down while waiting for our drinks. He was attractive enough for the part, despite his overly muscular stature. His face was welcoming without being soft. A sprinkling of grey flecked his otherwise brown hair.

Our drinks arrived. Ballard's was a weird green cocktail with cherries, which he stirred with a long thin spoon before finally telling me his story.

'Please understand …' he said. 'I run a tight ship and my crew are some of the best around, I'm proud to say. I'm no cowboy, and I take on good honest salvage contracts.' Ballard looked askance at me, as if he dared me to contradict him.

'But …?' I offered.

'But, you know, there's always risk, and we were reminded of that not so long ago,' He said.

There was an earnest quality to his demeanour, evoking – to my horror – protective instincts in me. I pushed that shit away immediately.

'Go on …' I said.

He nodded.

'I've been doing this a long time Miss Delaney. Seen a lot, experienced a lot … You understand? I've been knocked down, gotten up again … Anyway, I'm trying to say that I'm as experienced as any captain you'll meet, and I'm careful enough to avoid most stupid mistakes.'

'But …' I prompted again, but this time there was no attitude in my voice.

'But … salvage has a way to throw a demon at you at the most unexpected times. Yes? Like a Jack-in-a-box?'

I nodded again, getting into the story.

'Anyway, my last contract … We were doing well, it was a good clean mission, but then … Harry, my last Xeno, something happened to him. He had a bad encounter with Trick-Red.'

Ballard paused there, knowing fully well that statement would have a certain impact, and it did. I had to suppress a shudder – any Xeno would. We all learn early on that all Trick-tech should be treated with the utmost respect, but close encounters with Red, well … that was the stuff of nightmares.

Ballard continued, acknowledging my reaction. 'We were working a contract on a small mining facility. Low risk, but decent special equipment salvage. Run of the mill spec but not in a bad way, no? Well … the place wasn't what we thought it would be. We ran into all this military stuff – high-grade armour, explosives, war-chem, you name it. That wasn't what we contracted for. It seemed that the mining facility was a front for what used to be a secret government weapons facility.'

'That sounds like the kind of trouble you don't need.'

'It's true yes? This thing must have been set up that way, back in the old days. I mean, it was really dark tech.'

'Did the client know?'

'No, I don't think so. Records must have been lost during Icarus or something, because nobody knew it would pan out like that. My Xeno, Harry, he was still trying to make sense of it all, when he found a cache of strange devices. Weapons mostly, some of them Red. Frightening ones at that, and one of them went live while he was figuring out what exactly they were.

'Jesus,' I said. 'What a nightmare.'

'Yeah … poor guy. The situation got to him and he panicked. Forgot all about proper salvage protocol.'

'Did it escalate?' I asked softly.

'No, the tech was stable, but I had to go in and extract Harry myself. He just … froze.' Ballard's shoulders slumped. 'But I got him out.'

'How's he now?'

'He's got the shakes. He's finished.' Ballard sat back in his chair, which creaked disconcertingly. 'I gave him six months to see if he could pull himself together, but no, he's not coming back from this.'

Salvage syndrome … it can happen to anybody. I'd heard of a case recently, concerning a hotshot new Xeno, fantastic track record, amazing ability to salvage *just* the right Trickari artifacts. Until he mistook a small but immensely powerful Red recharge station for a similar but harmless Blue equivalent model. Something triggered the thing; it escalated, and an entire space station disappeared, sucked into some unholy inter-dimensional vortex. The Xeno and his crew managed to get out, and since the station had been quarantined at the start of the Icarus Years nobody died. *That* time at least …

Twelve months later the poor bastard's hands were still shaking so badly he literally couldn't sign his name on a piece of paper – not that anybody would offer him any new contracts to sign anyway. It's the kind of thing that can ruin a Xeno, especially early on in their career when they are still prone to mistakes, or just unlucky. Getting the shakes was often bad enough to completely squash any chance of future employment, one's reputation ruined beyond repair.

'Mr. Ballard …'

'Please … Call me J.J.'

'OK, if you insist J.J.' I took a quick sip from my Gin

and called the bartender over for a refill, before picking up the conversation again.

'Look, you aren't really spinning a pretty picture here. Your last mission was a major failure, your crew is probably in shock, you somehow got way too close to Trick-Red … I mean, look at it from my point of view. None of this sounds great.'

I knew I wasn't being exactly fair. Accidents could happen to anybody, although my own track record was spotless, which was of course why Ballard had approached me. He must have heard that I consistently made good calls on Trickari artifacts, had been doing so for years, and I had not once suffered the tremors, despite having run into some pretty hairy salvage situations from time to time myself. In other words: I was a solid bet, and Ballard needed solid to steady the rest of his crew.

Stanley Turrentine was still playing. This time a deep blues track.

'What's the contract anyway?' I asked, expecting yet another decent but underwhelming affair.

Ballard's eyebrows rose. Hope giving them life.

I quickly raised both my hands, and said, 'I'm just asking. Professional courtesy right?' This barely subdued Ballard.

'It's a good one!' He boomed. 'Government contract. Minimum return guaranteed. Safe, but with serious potential.'

'I'm going to need more than that.'

Ballard laughed. 'Of course. I haven't told you anything yet.' He leaned forward in that conspiratorial pose again, and half-whispered, 'You know the Gaianistas, yes?'

I nodded.

'Well, this is a government funded salvage mission to Gaianista Habitat 6. We're supposed to salvage rare seeds and scientific instruments. But plenty of time allocated, so we can run our own private salvage alongside. First time the site is open.'

Habitat 6 was one of the wrecked Gaianista-domes –

this one orbited a moonlet near Jupiter, quarantined after a later Icarus incident. It had never been cleared for salvage, so potentially a real treasure trove. It was obviously a good gig, with decent pay owing to the government angle, and offering a good chance of scoring Trickari artifacts. I was almost surprised to find that I was inclined to take the contract. There seemed to be few downsides.

I took in the atmosphere around me. A new album started playing – a great Idris Muhammad set called "The Power of Soul".

Lots of regulars had arrived by now. Luiz was flirting with all the girls, while occasionally winking at me outrageously. I turned to face Ballard again. 'I'm interested, but, there's a condition.'

'Name it.'

'My son Clint comes with me. He's sixteen, but not inexperienced, and he's the best data analyst I've ever seen.'

Ballard stood up, dismayed. 'Jemm … I can't do that. Salvage is not for children. It's not right.'

'He needs the experience, and you just tried to convince me this is easy and safe. He's almost of age. He turns seventeen next month.'

'Maybe when he's older. I'm sure–'

'We're a team.' I shrugged. 'Take it or leave it.'

Ballard sat down again, pondered hard. He was right, normally one wouldn't take a teenager on a salvage mission. But I knew what Clint was capable of. He was ready for this, and if I were to score the hit I was hoping for I would need his help.

'Listen, Clint and I complement each other, to put a fancy term to it. He can deal with data systems that nobody else can, and he knows that market better than guys three times his age. Last time he doubled the whole crew's take, simply by selling obscure database backups to specialist buyers.'

Ballard's forehead wrinkled up, considering my words. 'He'll have to pull his weight. No special treatment.'

'Of course.'

'What about pay?'

'Tell you what, you can have us both for just my cut. No need to pay him separately. Having him along will boost our yield so much that it will easily be worth it. For all of us.'

Ballard raised a single eyebrow at that. 'Really?'

'Really,' I laughed. I took a chance by cutting Clint's pay like that, but as I had no better leads I figured I had to land this gig as soon as possible.

'You won't regret it,' I said.

After that he finally buckled. We danced a bit around the small print, but neither of us was too interested in standing in the way of an obviously good deal, so we ended up celebrating our future partnership soon after.

The night had been good to us. We repaid her by drinking obscure Belgian beers and debating 20th and 21st century popular music. J.J.'s taste was surprisingly Avant-Garde, but he respected my interest in classical jazz.

It was hard not to like him.

The next few days we did our due diligence on the *Effervescent*, its captain and its crew. Clint wasted little time accessing a large database of business records associated with the ship and its missions, while I checked out Ballard's personal background. I asked the right people some questions – discreetly of course – angled for any bad vibes associated with him, but no, his reputation was rock-solid, just as I expected. J.J. Ballard was as reliable and trustworthy as they come.

On day three we had been busy with research all morning, which had involved much legwork. It was amazing how many records required a physical presence to allow access.

Halfway through our efforts a cold and eerie fog crept into the streets, followed by short spells of miserly drizzle. It was the kind of fog that did strange things to the city's background sounds. Some noises were muffled, while others carried across unlikely distances. Even our footsteps sounded wrong as we marched through the wispy mist.

Eventually the cold penetrated our clothes, entered our flesh and grabbed hold of our muscle and bones. No amount of brisk walking or energetic rubbing of hands could make it let go. It was time for a break.

We decided to visit "Noodlelicious", the worst named eatery in China District selling the best Ramen in town. The proprietor, Sin Yun, was a proud woman and quite a character. She had worked as head chef at some of the best restaurants around, but eventually she got the independence bug, and left to start her own place. China district, despite its name, provided every oriental cuisine imaginable, and Sin Yun's Japanese fusion creations slotted in naturally.

There had been several iterations of her place and many different names (all terrible) but eventually she settled on its current incarnation, and named it Noodlelicious; a name so bad it was good. Ever since she has waited for fame and fortune to be bestowed on her wonderful dishes. That was fifteen years ago.

Neither fame nor fortune ever arrived, but all the locals knew that Noodlelicious was the benchmark against which all other noodle joints were measured, and the others never stacked up. Sin Yun never made it big, but over the years her one little restaurant earned the respect of true connoisseurs, and she understood that that was good enough.

The door chimed an oriental melody when we entered, welcomed in by the dozen or so ceramic cats, waving us inside with automated paws. We ordered our favourite dishes by default. They arrived soon after, steaming and fragrant, bowls of culinary perfection.

Clint energetically slurped his miso "native style" – producing loud and wet sounds with his face and chopsticks right up to the edge of the bowl. I blatantly used a fork to get to my soba noodles, while spooning the broth in between bites. The food was spicy enough to make me sweat. The dish included a kind of marinated egg, which I always saved till last.

The windows had fogged up long before we arrived but some visibility was restored by streams of condensation, lazily snaking down, wiping the glass one little stream at a time. The resulting street-view was fractured and diffracted, a wet kaleidoscopic image of street light halos and flickering neon signs.

I noticed Clint smirking into his bowl.

'What?' I smiled at him.

'Nothing. Just eat your noodles.' He pulled an embarrassed face. 'Would you like me to get you a bib by the way?'

'Yeah your delicate slurping and slobbering is a real advert for sophisticated eating.' (I never understood how chopsticks for noodle soup made sense.)

'Hey, when in Rome …' Clint's smirk grew even stronger.

'OK, what?'

'You like this J.J guy don't you?'

'Ballard? Yeah, his credentials are top notch, he's smart, I reckon we can work well together.'

Clint rolled his eyes. 'No mum, I mean you *like* him, do you not? God, do I have to spell it out for you?'

'Oh I see … Well, sure. Maybe I'll take him home, do him in your bed… We'll have a great time.'

Clint's expression was priceless. Indignation, doubt, shock … all written clearly across his face.

'Or maybe you should eat your noodles and mind your own damn business,' I said, my tone deadly serious, but quietly amused underneath.

That drove his smirk underground for a while. Embarrassed, he looked outside the window to avoid facing me. His reflection in the foggy glass was faint, like a faded painting.

Something outside caught my eye; a ghostly lit face appeared for a second, then vanished again. I was thrown for a moment. *What was that*?

I stared out the window, waiting for another glimpse, but nothing happened. Just when I thought I had imagined seeing it at all, the ghostly face appeared again! This time I figured out what was happening; the face belonged to a man across the street, smoking a cigarette. Every time he took a puff his face momentarily illuminated, enough to be seen through the foggy window.

The man leaned nonchalantly against a wall, trying to blend in with the locals, but failing badly. He kept sending badly disguised glances at us, wearing an out-of-place business suit. Not a professional then, whoever this guy was. Now that I spotted him he stood out like a sore thumb.

I took another bite, taking a moment to calm my nerves. Anybody sloppy enough to get rumbled like this was no serious threat. Still, I didn't enjoy being followed.

I carefully alerted Clint to the man's presence. He was as puzzled as I was. At least now that we were aware of the stranger's presence we could see who we were dealing with … Our stalker was a young man, not yet out of his twenties, in an expensive business suit – a strange choice of attire for shadowing us. His posture exuded that air of arrogance and over-confidence that often came with being affiliated with a major corporation. Probably some mid-level Corp manager… But why follow us?

I toyed with the idea of confronting him straight on, right there, but decided against it. If I was wrong about the guy it could turn out bad for us. Instead, I treated the situation as an opportunity for Clint to practise evasion techniques. We could get some mission prep done in the process. Our upcoming gig required specialist supplies from sources all over D-Town; sourcing them should give us plenty of opportunity to lose our tail.

Once we agreed our course of action Clint executed our escape perfectly. A quick word with Sin Yun and we made our exit through the kitchen, via the deliveries entrance, into a back alley. Clint confidently led me past other restaurant back-lots, overflowing with stinking bins, sinister food supplies and tubs of disgusting steaming fluids. The smell was horrendous.

As a local creature Clint knew every twist in the maze of connecting streets, bridges and tunnels that made up this part of the city. He ushered us out of the district, dragging me through bustling markets and shopping areas so littered with obstructions that I could almost hear our pursuer stumble and trip while chasing us. Conversely we glided through the masses like a pair of sharks through a shoal of fish. People knew to make way for us.

Clint showed real flair, using the terrain to his advantage. Draw bridges miraculously opened behind us mere moments after we crossed. Lifts filled up just after we entered. We even jumped a small river ferry the exact moment it set off. These helpful incidents weren't down to luck …

I was impressed. Clint was a puzzle-solver, and traversing D-Town was apparently a puzzle he had already solved. His navigation skills were honed to such a degree that it appeared as if he had a telepathic connection to the city – a supernatural awareness of what was around the next corner, and the next …

Although we must have lost our suited stalker by then we kept it up for an hour at least. Best to make sure he was off our tail.

'OK, that was very good,' I said, sweat pouring down my back.

'Thanks, do I get an award?' said Clint.

'How about a nice public hug?'

'I'm good mum, thanks though.' He looked me over with some distaste. 'Also, you're pretty sweaty.'

'Yeah it's gross isn't it?' I made as if to hug him. He recoiled laughing nervously. 'Seriously though, good job. I'm impressed.'

'Thanks,' said Clint, slightly curt. But I could tell he was pleased.

'You're welcome.' I gave him a quick sweaty hug, which he enjoyed despite himself. 'Now let's get to work.'

Most cities function primarily at ground level, but D-Town wasn't like that. Shops and homes could be found on any floor of the many tall buildings. Businesses regularly sprang up (or disappeared) in random places, often connected to each other by opportunistic walkways and sky-tunnels. Traffic moved on all levels; high above ground, at street level, and in huge subterranean tunnels below the pavement. It was a thoroughly three-dimensional environment, and it was easy to lose yourself in its depths.

Staying clear of any followers we took the opportunity to visit our preferred dealers and brokers, stock up on mission supplies and do mission research, learning what we could about Gaianista beliefs and their Geo-habitats for the remainder of the afternoon, until we hit that wall of fatigue which comes from too much sensory input. We decided to wrap it up even though we realised just how little we had really learned about our mission target.

On our way home Clint kept throwing furtive glances my way, eventually getting on my nerves.

'What?' I asked, probably harsher than I should have.

'Don't bite my head off. I just want to help.'

'OK,' I said, trying to sound reasonable. 'Sorry, just say what you want to say.'

Clint took a breath before replying. 'Look, I know you don't want to see him, but Roy can get us the data we need in no time.'

I bit back a curse. Counting to ten before replying. 'You're right.' I gave Clint a sour expression. 'I don't want to see him.'

'Come on. We need an edge here. Roy can give us that.'

I pretended to think it over carefully, but my refusal to see him was just me being petty and I knew it.

'Fine,' I sighed. 'But he'd better come up with the goods.'

'I'll let him know what we need. I'm sure he'll have it ready tomorrow,' Clint said, trying not to smile.

We went to see Roy the next day, late in the afternoon. I wasn't looking forward to it.

The little neon sign shouted shamelessly: "The Electric Speakeasy II!", as it had done every day for a decade at least. The place was easy to miss, wedged in on the 9th floor of a long-ago gutted and re-purposed Victorian industrial facility, surrounded by more impressive neon signs for more impressive competing establishments.

To get there we had to survive a ride on an ancient and rickety elevator – insides plastered with embarrassingly bad graffiti and juvenile slogans. Clint was as happy as a puppy with a new toy, while desperately trying to look tough and mean to blend in with the locals. He wasn't even close to pulling it off.

The elevator arrived with a bone-jarring jerk. I took a deep breath and we stepped inside.

The Speakeasy resembled a haunted whorehouse; everything was sparkly and glittery, but in a somewhat sinister, off-putting way. The main room, illuminated by various neon "artworks" (some of which were exceptionally rude), was populated by a smattering of TrickMem junkies. Most were catatonic, with crystal growths of various sizes decorating their skulls like strange, precious carbuncles. In reality they were no more than a pale imitation of the real thing.

Some people called them "carbuncle heads", others called them "TJs". There seemed to be more of them each day. Clint toe-poked one of them. There was no reaction.

The rest of the room was taken up by a hefty bar forming a half-circle, offering about thirty barstools to people who wanted to be real close to the source of their booze. Only half the seats were occupied, which constituted a busy afternoon at the Speakeasy.

I made a sweeping gesture encompassing the entire space, and looked at Clint with a question in my eyes. *What do you see?*

He took a moment to assess the clientele, judged quietly, then gained confidence as he pointed them out, one by one:

'Cyberpunker, Trick-tech smuggler, holo-pimp, Mem pusher …' Clint paused on a tricky one …

'Go on,' I said with encouragement.

'Porn sim actor? No wait, that one's just an idiot or a mime or something. Next guy's an ex-Enforcer, that one … that's just a guy…' Clint's eyes widened with real surprise: 'Is that a snuff-puppet? Jesus.'

'It's a living Clint, don't judge.'

'Getting snuffed and reanimated for cash is a living? Sounds like a contradiction to me.'

'Ho ho, aren't you the semantic wizard?'

Clint raised an eyebrow at my irritated tone, but was wise not enough not to comment further.

'Look,' I said. 'I know it's pretty hideous. That whole scene is nasty, exploitative and I don't really understand how it's legal, but there you are. But you don't know anything about this guy. Snuffing pays incredibly well, and maybe the money is needed to pay a debt, or his child needs expensive medical augments, or… whatever. It doesn't take much in life to go wrong and suddenly you're desperate. That can happen to anybody. Including you.'

Clint looked a bit sheepish after my lecture, so I gently punched his arm, enough to conjure an embarrassed grin on his face. But I knew he would take my words to heart.

The bar was surprisingly clean and well maintained, as were the glasses. The bartender was an outlandishly large and bulky man, larger than seemed responsible considering the state of the old wooden floor, which sagged alarmingly each time he moved around.

When the bartender spotted us his entire shape seemed to transform – a bull turned butterfly.

'Mama bear and her cub!' He shouted. 'Hot damn, that makes me one happy feller.' His American accent was exaggerated but real. He was genuinely happy to see us.

'Hey Cliff, how's the leg?'

'Leg's OK. Arm ain't so great.' Cliff awkwardly raised

a massive arm, obviously augmented but without regard for cosmetic niceties like matching skin colour and realism. I could see metal parts sticking through badly patched cuts.

'All I could afford. Ain't the prettiest thing. None too precise either. Strong though …' I smiled, knowing that it was all an act. Clifton always had top notch augment work done but he liked to cultivate an aura of benign stupidity, inviting people to underestimate him. I've seen others fall for it on many occasions, generally leading to much regret on their side.

'Where is he, Clifton?' I asked.

A grotesque claw-hand pointed at a door behind the bar, accompanied by a laugh that could shift boulders and crush cowards. The glasses behind the bar shook in their racks. They were laughing too.

The backroom was large, well lit, and its contents were completely out of control. Haphazard stacks of boxes, crates and paperwork, some reaching all the way to the ceiling, teamed up with bulging rows of standalone shelving to form an Escher-like maze.

A wildly divergent collection of Trickari artifacts and parts peeked out from under lids, hid inside containers, or proudly showed themselves to whomever walked into the room. Most were Trickari White – depleted and dead – but some were Blue, adding a sense of exotic tension to the room.

Right in the middle of it all, behind a heavy duty leather clad desk, sat Roy, studying a book about Trickari relics. I felt a brief pang – an echo of stale but once comfortable desires – immediately followed by a flash of irritation. Old habits die hard I guess.

There was something about Roy that hinted at missed opportunities and cheated potential. He was still handsome in a rare, graceful way which eluded so many other men, yet he remained completely unaware of this quality. Instead, he hid his physique in bland but practical clothes, sported a completely arbitrary haircut and generally carried himself with the air of a patched-up college professor.

There was a sharp intelligence in his eyes, tempered by a sense of angry resignation. These weren't new observations to me, and as always, a sad conviction grabbed me and wouldn't let go: *I won't let Clint end up like this.*

'Have you got it?' I asked.

Roy stood up, his chair scraping the floor as he rose. The sound made me wince.

Pointedly ignoring me he held out his arms to Clint. Open wide, a safe harbour.

'Clint my boy, look at you. When did you become so stylish?' Clint dressed much like me; modest and to the point, but complementing his natural features. His hair was wild and curly, like fresh wood shavings – mine was short and straight. We both kept it fairly close-cropped.

Clint grinned, showing off that puppy look again. 'Have you got it, dad?'

'Stylish and serious, just like your mother.' Roy replied.

He was overacting a bit, trying to be nice I suppose, but I needed him to hurry things along.

'Roy … We haven't got much t–'

'*Yes* I've got it. Yes … Can I have a goddamn moment with my goddamn boy Jemm? Yes? Thank you.'

Roy sauntered theatrically to a cabinet, slowly opened a drawer, proceeding to rummage through its contents while whistling to himself.

I bit my tongue, swallowing a cutting reply that would no doubt have started a flaming row had it escaped. Despite his passive aggressive bullshit on full display, I still had some respect for Roy. He had always tried to be a good father to Clint, and he would always try to help us out – no strings attached – whenever I needed him to.

Although our personal relationship had soured he was still a professional asset. His knowledge of Trickari artifacts and tech was almost as comprehensive as mine, which was saying something. I could trust him to deal straight. Roy would never over-egg a salvage opportunity or low-ball a valuation, and he would never cheat us, which made him my preferred fence.

Roy held out a neatly wrapped package. 'For your seventeenth, Clint. I know it's early but hey, why not.'

Clint grunted a thank-you, accepting it with a bashful expression.

'Can I open it?' said Clint, sounding like a little boy. I had a flashback to his seventh birthday party. He looked just as happy then.

Roy nodded his approval; Clint unwrapped the present. He found a curious object inside. A dull glass cube, shot through with white strands like veins inside an egg.

'Trickster tech … Looks dead?' Clint asked.

'Yes. Well … no, not dead. It's Trickari alright, but this one is a bit different … It looks as dead as all White does, but it's special you see?' There was an almost endearing sparkle in Roy's eyes. He was having fun with it.

'It comes to life near other active relics,' he continued. 'Especially powerful ones. My guess is that it draws straight from their energy sources. It's like it's *feeding* off them. How exactly, I don't know. It won't tell you what kind of tech you're dealing with. Could be Blue, Red or even *Purple*, god forbid.' Roy appeared lost in an internal dialogue for a moment, his lips moved while he sub-vocalised some words to himself. 'Anyway, should come in handy on your raids'.

'Expeditions', I said. Roy stared at me uncomprehending.

'What?' he muttered, confused.

'They are archaeological *expeditions*, not raids. We're not thieves Roy.'

'That's a matter of opinion Jemm.' He finally found what he was looking for in the drawer and threw it to me.

'Is this it?' I caught the chrome data stick mid-air and studied it for a moment. 'Tested and integrity secured?' I asked.

'Of course it goddamn is. Have I ever given you a

dud?' He threw me an annoyed look. It was a relief to see he still had his pride. 'Anyway, that's it, yes. Good luck getting any treasure out of these Gaianista freaks.' Roy threw me sharp look then, before turning to Clint. 'Your mother and I need to talk for a moment. It's crappy legal stuff, so be a good lad and keep Clifton company for a moment OK?'

Clint shrugged, fully aware that it was just an excuse to get him out of the room.

'Time for your annual row?' he sniggered, but left the room without further complaint.

'You haven't told him have you?' asked Roy.

'I didn't see the point,' I said, folding my arms in front of me.

'Have you got the money to buy your precious ship? Tell me the truth.'

'Not quite,' I admitted. 'The deadline was supposed to be a year off.'

'Goddammit Jemm … You can't do this. He has a right to know.'

'I'll tell him. I will. In due time. But right now this Gaianista thing might be enough to get me there. To get my ship.' It wasn't quite a lie, but it still felt dishonest.

'Listen,' said Roy, his tone conciliatory, 'I can sponsor him, it's fine. You'll still get to see him. What's so bad about that?'

I could have said that the real reason I didn't want Clint to spend the next few years with Roy was the same reason I wanted Clint with me after our divorce: Roy was a man who had given up hope on being who he really wanted to be. Despite his tremendous talents and potential he had settled for a life of cynical mediocrity. Deep inside he was resentful of his own cowardice, causing an air of dissatisfaction to constantly ooze out of him, infecting everything and everybody around him. I would never let Clint spend crucial, formative years in an environment like that.

I didn't say any of those things. Instead I said, 'Sponsorship is not the same as full residency. He'll be stuck living with you unable to get his own place. Give me a chance with this Gaianista thing. If I'm successful it'll be better for Clint.'

'Better for Clint or for you?'

'Don't be an arse.'

'We have an agreement, and if I remember correctly that was your idea to begin with. *You* talked me into letting him move in with you, and it was *your* idea to make it conditional on you getting your own ship.'

'I know that.'

'So who's being an arse?'

'Is that all?'

'Yes that's goddamn all.'

I stood there, arms still folded like a petulant teenager while Roy called Clint back in via a little intercom on his desk. Clint came back in a moment later, looking sheepish, unsure how bad our argument had been.

'Time to leave,' I said to Clint. 'Thanks Roy, we appreciate your help.'

'You're welcome. Now get out, I've got work to do.'

I shrugged and turned to leave. When Roy got like this it was best to simply go.

'Clint …' Roy said.

Clint turned around, and for a moment they looked just like each other. A man and a boy, mirrored across time.

'Be careful,' he said, and nodded in my direction. 'Don't try and be like your mother. Keep yourself safe. Just … Look, just be yourself, that's hard enough.'

'I reckon she does better than most,' said Clint.

'She's *luckier* than most. You're not her, don't forget it.'

Clint's loyalties were finely balanced for a moment, torn between his need to stick up for me and his love for his father. He walked over to Roy and embraced him.

'Goodbye Dad.'

We left without a further word.

Meeting up with Roy had left me irritable and tired,

craving solitude and isolation. We had more research and prep ahead of us which I wanted to get on with, so we went straight home. We walked most of the way; I wanted to purge myself from the resentment I felt before coming home, and walking helped.

It had rained again while we were inside. The smell of wet tarmac was oddly comforting, and my mood started to improve. By the time we got home I felt myself again, so it was especially galling to find somebody waiting for us, right at our front door.

It was our amateur stalker, looking awkward, hands in pockets of his expensive suit – now adorned with several stains and marks. He was completely oblivious to our presence.

I cursed under my breath. This wouldn't do at all. I didn't like the idea of being followed while going about my business, and I certainly didn't like being followed to my home. It was time to see what he wanted.

'Clint … Be ready,' I whispered.

I kept walking for a minute longer, until we were about twenty metres from our front door. We blended in with the darkness while our stalker stood out like a scarecrow in an empty field. He hadn't noticed our approach. *Definitely not a pro.* I decided to be blunt with this guy.

I used my Padd to remote-activate the building's lighting rig. The system switched on with a loud clang, bathing our stalker in a sea of spotlights. He just stood there, frozen on the spot, unable to figure out what to do.

Clint had already produced his weapon – an inoffensive looking but fairly lethal flechette gun. He let it dangle at his side for now, making sure it was very visible. I doubted he would need to use it.

I took a moment to study the man in front of us. It was definitely the same guy we had spotted tailing us before, and he still seemed completely inept. But yet, there was something about him that made me curious. He was so ill equipped for this assignment that I figured a fair amount of arrogance was at work here. I've seen it many times before with up-and-coming Corp hotshots; they get overconfident when hanging around executive types long enough, thinking they are protected by association with powerful people.

'Can I help you?' I offered. He jumped, and stared into the light, completely blind. We stepped forward so he could see us. He relaxed, relieved that we had spotted him, removing the need to pretend that he knew what he was doing.

He squared his shoulders and stepped forward, extending his right hand. 'Jemm Delaney?'

Clint promptly raised his flechette gun.

'I suggest you explain your business with me.' The sound of my voice sounded wrong to me. Too low. I wondered if Clint noticed.

'Ah yes, that would seem the prudent course of action, of course.' He paused, half for effect, half due to nerves. 'Right, then, my name is Lawrence. I was sent to secure your services, to offer you a business proposal in fact. I tried to approach you earlier but you erm … you were having your lunch.'

'Go on …' I nodded at Clint to holster the flechette.

Lawrence visibly relaxed, more at ease with the situation. I suspected he had practised this part a few times before he set out to find me.

'My employer would like you to acquire an item for him, ideally on your next … expedition. He is willing to pay very well indeed, and possibly facilitate further non-financial rewards, through his um, corporate influence.'

'What does your employer know about my affairs?' I said, failing to keep the venom from my voice.

'Come now Miss Delaney, you are the best freelance Xeno in the business. If you wouldn't be so intent on staying an independent you would have been scooped up by Omni Systems, or RAN-Tech, or any of the major Corps a long time ago.'

'I like being independent. This doesn't sound independent to me.'

He shrugged, a strangely boyish mannerism. 'Maybe, but if successful, this contract might buy you all the independence you will ever need. We can offer a number of bonus incentives that might tip you into a whole new tax bracket.'

'Words are cheap mister. And I don't like talking business on the street.'

'Quite,' said Lawrence. 'Look, I understand this is not an ideal forum for business negotiations. Why don't you come to our offices and we can discuss details.' Lawrence whipped out a business card with dazzling speed and precision. I felt obliged to at least look at the damn thing.

LAWRENCE. J. SKINNER

ASSISTANT SUB-DIRECTOR TRICKARI ACQUISITIONS

SPECTRA VISION — LONDON OFFICE

Lawrence was right. Spectra Vision was a major corporate player. They could easily deliver on his boasts.

A disturbing smell drifted past. It was the herb-farmer's manure. Lawrence produced a handkerchief from his pocket and held it in front of his nose. It was a gesture so ridiculous that I decided to believe him. He was obviously not used to slumming it.

'Well done, I'm intrigued enough to look at the fine print. So, here's what I will do. I will politely ask you to *fuck off* now, so I can finally enter my home, ponder private matters and plan my next archaeology expedition. If I'm still interested at that point, then I will come over to your fancy offices.'

'Miss Delaney, there is some urgency–'

'And if I ever find you on my doorstep again, broadcasting to the entire district that some Corp wants to *hire* me, or worse, if I find you following me again … I'll make you thoroughly disappear. Your corporate connections won't protect you.'

Lawrence showed me a big grin. This was the kind of talk he was used to.

'Naturally madam. We will look forward to entertaining you at our office, when you are ready.' He bowed (I must have gained a measure of his respect) and walked off, fading away into the darkness like a happy ghost.

Once inside, my stomach growled, asserting itself with vigour. I was famished. I rummaged around, collecting ingredients, pots and pans. The herb-farmer cut me a great deal on some of his products, and within half an hour I had a delicious smelling mushroom-seitan stew going, enriched by some of the best ingredients available. I was lucky to have them; good seeds were becoming extremely rare.

When I called Clint over for dinner he ignored me. Normally Clint would be all over it, sneakily stealing a taster or two when he thought I wasn't looking, but something was off with him. He kept throwing me annoyed little looks.

'Stew?' I offered, trying to lure him out.

'Aren't you going to check Roy's data?' asked Clint curtly. 'I'm pretty sure he worked hard to get it ready for you on time.'

I shrugged, in no mood to justify myself, but something told me there was more going on with him.

'Aren't you going to play with your present?' I countered, but with some warmth.

'It's not a toy.' Flat, defensive, angry.

I tried again. 'It sounds pretty interesting. I'm surprised Roy didn't keep it for himself.' I stirred my stew, offering Clint a taste which he ignored.

'Well, mother, some people think about more than just themselves.' There was more than a whiff of petulance in his voice, and I think he knew it too. It wasn't something I cared for.

I put my spoon down and said, 'Can we cut straight to

what's pissing in your head, or do we have to play this tedious passive aggressive spot-the-hidden-insult game for much longer?'

That made him sit up, no longer hiding his hostility.

'OK, let's try that then,' said Clint. 'Here's a question: Why do you always treat dad like … like, he's an arsehole? Do you think that you're so perfect?'

'I don't think I'm perfect. And I don't think Roy is–'

'The way you talked to him mum…' Clint struck a pose, folding his arms; imitating my stance in Roy's office. '"*Is that it?*"' he said, impersonating me so well it was uncanny. He got the inflection just right, including a hint of impatience and disdain that I didn't even realise was in there. It cut a bit too close to the bone.

'Don't talk over me. It's rude,' was all I could muster in reply.

'Yeah, mother, we wouldn't want to be rude. Like you weren't rude to that guy in the customs queue.'

'What's this really about Clint …? I'm too damn tired to guess, so can you please put me out of my misery and just tell me?' As the words left my mouth I realised how true they were; I *was* tired. Exhausted even. I rubbed my face, only succeeding in amplifying my fatigue.

'You have no friends mum. I get it – you're strong and smart and all that – but you have no friends, no real ones anyway. That's not exactly a position of strength, and I don't think it's healthy.'

So that's what was messing with him; he was concerned for me, scared that I would remain alone, as I had been ever since leaving Roy. I laughed without humour. To be pitied by my own son was almost too much to bear. Still, it was a relief of sorts. For a moment I thought he knew about the letter.

'Friends are overrated,' I snapped. 'They always let you down in the end.'

Clint snorted a half-laugh. 'That's bullshit and you know it. You're cynical, but not that cynical.'

'I'm not cynical, just a realist. Anyway, who needs friends when you have family, right? Family's way better than friends. Family you *can* count on … You can count on them to give you shit.'

'Ain't that the truth,' Clint said. A smile appearing on his lips.

He couldn't quite evade the punch I threw at his arm. 'Now show me that damn cube.'

He handed it over to me, rubbing his arm.

I had to admit, Lawrence got me thinking.

I normally steered well clear from any Corp business, especially mega Corps like Spectra Vision. But this was an extraordinary situation; no matter how many times I turned things over in my mind it boiled down to somehow obtaining my own ship. Not just for Clint's sake, but equally for my own. Xeno-archaeology was a competitive field. Captaining my own Blue ship would let me operate in an entirely different sphere. The ability to choose my own expeditions, call the shots, and train Clint any way I saw fit, was incredibly attractive. I had been saving money towards that goal for most of my years as a professional Xeno, but maybe I just hadn't been pushing myself hard enough. Maybe the accelerated deadline was the catalyst I needed to finally get where I needed to be. "*Every disadvantage has an advantage.*" I thought. It was one of my favourite sayings. Maybe Spectra's offer was worth considering.

I cleared my desk, made myself a stiff drink – whiskey, not Fakahol – and tried to order my thoughts.

After the devastation of the first Icarus incident all major Trickari artifacts were carefully monitored and tracked. Human-tech ships could barely reach beyond Mars without burning too much fuel for any salvage expedition to be profitable, but a Blue ship could reach anywhere in the solar system without breaking a sweat, putting the countless quarantined moons, abandoned settlements or ruined installations firmly in play.

A Red ship could travel even farther of course, but

getting caught with Trickari Red translated to an instant death penalty, and pretty much anybody who *had* tried to get away with it had been caught.

Still, there was something exciting about illegal tech. Trickari Red was powered by *extra-dimensional* energy. Limitless, unmatched power, driving miraculous technology that we never managed to fully understand, even during the heady days of the Acceleration.

Trickari Blue was safer, and still exciting in its own way. All Blue tech contained an *internal* energy source, still unfathomable but non-volatile. A Blue device *itself* might cause damage, especially the powerful ones, but only through ignorance or misuse, not through catastrophic escalation. Sadly, Blue power was finite and running out, no longer fed by Red power regenerators. Blue devices were dying all over the solar system, snuffed out one by one – painting a sad picture of humanity rapidly losing its edge.

This is what my work as a Xeno was all about. Retrieving active Blue artifacts to shore up Earth's failing tech pool, to keep us all going just a bit longer. The challenge was twofold: salvage the right artifacts, and sell them to the right customers. A good Xeno was essential to achieve both.

A captain with a ship chooses its crew carefully. A talented Xeno could make the difference between scoring valuable Blue artifacts, or ending up with a cargo of alien toothbrushes.

I was good at my job, and Clint was a genius at reading data systems. Together we got a lot of work with reputable captains, but with my own Blue ship I wouldn't have to depend on other people to choose my salvage expeditions. I could choose my own missions whenever I felt like it.

That was worth more to me than I dared admit to myself.

6

Spectra Vision's HQ was located in Old London's City District. It towered over its grim surroundings with a dominating arrogance – one of the few Corp HQs in this area to survive the mayhem of the Icarus years. This was an impressive achievement in its own right but also had great symbolic significance, readily exploited by Spectra, to project strength and determination in the face of its competitors.

At first glance City District appeared to be a terrible location for a corporate HQ, surrounded as it was by failing infrastructure, near-feral communities of desperate people, and the husks of once powerful corporations – the latter reminding people that even Corps could crumble. But there was cunning behind the decision to stay in this wasteland … one could not help but be reminded that where others had failed, Spectra Vision still stood tall.

Although I understood the mind-set well enough I didn't get on well with any of this corporate posturing. My father used to be in charge of corporate enforcement at a subdivision of Nakatomo Enterprises. He got the job after grafting for years on the street as a special enforcement agent. Before he cracked and tried to kill his CEO he taught me all about "the Corp way of life". It was a phrase that he must have uttered to me on a hundred occasions. I can still recall every nuance in his voice as he said the words.

He taught me all of it: The modernised version of the Sun Tzu, corporate defence tactics, enforcement martial arts, even their bizarre lingo. All of it.

I arrived by taxi. It was the safest way to travel there. My cab driver, – "Jamie" according to his name tag – hastily dropped me off at the designated "human deliveries" area next to the front entrance. We were watched closely by security cameras and AI-controlled sentry guns. Jamie kept throwing nervous glances at the guns – quite understandable, all things considered. I briefly touched Clint's flechette gun in my pocket. I had taken a liking to it; sleek and small, it offered the right kind of threat in this part of town.

'First time dropoff at a Corp HQ?' I asked him.

'Lady, I've been around the block, no pun intended, but the day I relax around these Corp bozos is the day I need to get out of the biz. And that,' he said, pointing at the sentry guns, 'is just wrong. How's that even legal?'

The interior of Jamie's cab was plastered with permits, mostly for weapons, concealed and otherwise. Jamie himself was probably augmented – most cabbies in Old London were.

I leaned in, holding Lawrence's business card up against the enforced glass of the driver-passenger barrier.

'Triple your fee and charge it to this arsehole.'

'With pleasure ma'am.' Jamie scanned the card slowly, not wanting to alert the sentry guns.

'Anything else?' he asked.

In response I scanned his cab I.D., and added him to my Padd favourites.

'Not for now, thanks, but maybe later.'

I got out, stretched, and had a good look at the cameras and guns, letting whoever was watching me have a chance to check me out in return. Spectra Vision's facial recognition software would only take moments to identify me and prep the reception bot with the appropriate level of disdain. I gave it a few more beats, mentally preparing my own level of disdain, and stepped into the lobby.

The midday sun fell through slightly tinted windows adding a subtle golden hue to the light. Dust mites floated in the air, like pixies performing a secret dance, just for me.

The walls of the lobby were adorned with near life-size

posters of Gridrunners, the augmented inhabitants of Neopolis City. Spectra Vision was renowned around the world for organising, managing, and broadcasting brutal competitive battles between teams of augmented super athletes. They had built the city of Neopolis purely to facilitate their worldwide televised league, offering a wide range of urban arenas as well as living space for athletes, and for staff tasked with keeping the city running smoothly. The most successful Gridrunners had become super celebrities, attracting ever higher sponsorship deals and a steady stream of starry-eyed wannabees trying out for the lower leagues. Young players hoping one day to join the ranks of the top athletes in the best crews: the Omni Street Warriors, the Betsies, the Coyotes, the Disco Dazzlers … each crew immortalised in portraits of their best players hanging here in the lobby, looking down on every visitor walking beneath their lofty position. They had reason to be smug; the matches attracted a world-wide audience of over one billion viewers.

I scanned the surroundings, amused to find that the lobby followed the corporate playbook to the letter: the ceiling reached inanely high, held up with lushly decorated pillars, giving the space an air akin to a sacred temple. The seats were all too tall, and anybody sitting on them would have their legs dangle off the side like a child's. The reception bot was seated on an elevated platform, forcing visitors to look up at it. All very intimidating, all very corporate.

'Good afternoon Miss Delaney. You may now explain the reason for your visit,' said the bot.

How bloody generous of you! I thought.

I flashed the business card at the bot without speaking, and without looking at "her", performing my own little intimidation act. Not for *its* benefit – it was a bot after all – but to send a message to the Spectra operative looking at me through its dull eyes.

I was made to wait thirteen minutes exactly (surprisingly little time) before it spoke to me in a friendly and pleasant voice that somehow still smacked of contempt. I was impressed – the bot's design was quite sophisticated.

'Mr. Skinner will see you shortly,' it said. 'Enter the first elevator to your right. It will stop at the thirty-second floor but not at any others. Somebody will collect you there. You are of course required to leave your weapon with a member of our security staff.' Right on cue, one of the elevators down the side corridor pinged delicately. From it emerged a typical rent-a-goon. He walked with a stiff, awkward gait, barely used to his spanking new Spectra security uniform.

I glanced back at the bot, fantasising about shooting its stupidly smug expression off its not-quite-human face, but I would be dead before fully drawing the flechette. Instead, I politely waited for the security guard to arrive.

His name badge simply said "THEO", in some standard Corp font, and he carried the full low-level enforcer gear. Shock-rod, radio ear piece, and (holstered) a fat, snubby revolver. The kind of weapon that didn't require much thought to use.

'Please luv, give us your gun,' said Theo, his voice coated in a distinct London street accent that he completely failed to disguise.

'And what gun might that be?' I asked, against better judgement.

Theo looked confused, shot a questioning look to the reception bot. I found it oddly amusing that he was looking for guidance from a glorified automaton. *Definitely a newbie*, I thought.

'Please assist Miss Delaney in handing over her weapon,' said the bot. I was actually quite impressed with its ability to handle the situation.

'That would be me,' I said.

Theo composed himself, repeated his request. 'Bit of a joker, are ya? Just give us the gun, luv.' I noticed he had a birthmark resembling a shark, right next to his Adam's apple. It was strangely lifelike.

'Sure, but I'm curious... Does it bother you? Taking orders from a piece of office equipment?'

Theo clenched his jaw, swallowed, uncannily animating the shark on his throat, making it appear as if it was swimming. He held out his right hand, while demonstratively moving his left closer to the shock-rod hanging from his belt.

I carefully – using slow, precise movements – reached inside my pocket, making sure he could see what I was doing, and pulled out the Flechette. 'Don't lose it,' I said, and handed it over.

Theo gave me a grim look, nodded curtly, and escorted me to the elevators, where he pressed the button. It arrived after a lengthy descent from one of the top levels.

When the doors slid open, Theo blocked my way. I guess his pride got the better of him after all.

'What's your beef with me luv?'

'Currently, I want to get on this elevator, but you're blocking my way.'

Theo was trying to decide what to do about me, so I muscled past and pressed the close-doors button. He decided to get out of the way, which was the smart choice.

'See you around, luv,' he said, in what I believe was meant to be a menacing tone. I let the closing door answer for me.

The lift signalled its arrival at the thirty-second floor with a bright ping. It came to a halt so smoothly that I only realised we had stopped moving when the doors opened. A low ranking office serf stood waiting, ready to escort me to a large meeting room. As we walked down the corridors I picked up the smell of polished wood. I wondered if the smell was artificial. There certainly was a lot of heavy wooden furniture around.

The meeting room windows were tinted with a hint of purple, casting the space in an oddly surreal light, reminding me of the hues seen during the so called "blue hour", just after sunset, but before dark. I vaguely recalled something about obscure corporate colour theory, but couldn't remember the significance of this particular tint.

I spotted Lawrence Skinner seated near the head of a round, expensive looking table. He was wearing a bright red tie. The table stood resolutely, made of some kind of heavy oak. The smell of wood-polish was now quite prominent. A Blue-powered perpetual motion device was integrated in the table's surface, its intricate parts moving a large glass eye along an ever changing path. An outrageous display of wealth.

Seven other corporate officers were seated at the table, all wearing different coloured ties – each colour representing a specific corporate division. The officers reminded me of strange-suited modern versions of the knights of Arthurian legend, although I suspected that not much chivalry was to be found amongst them.

A man with an air of authority and competence stood at the head of the table. The others all listened to him with solemn deference. His tie was different; showing a rainbow motif incorporating all the colours of the other ties in the room. This was a Spectra Vision Exec, and he was, by a long shot, the most powerful man in the room. I had to present myself carefully.

Lawrence spotted me from across the room, bowed to his exec and opened the door to let me in. Although he smiled politely there was something different about his demeanour … some hint at violence in his eyes. When he grabbed my elbow a bit too firmly to usher me in he glanced at me, measuring my response. Anger bubbled up just below the surface of my control but I managed to ignore it. This was not a place to lose composure.

As I entered the room the meeting wrapped up. Reports were collected, pens gathered, electronic diaries updated. One by one the people in the room bowed to their Exec and exited until there were just two corporate officers left, embroiled in low level conflict. Not a rare occurrence at this corporate level where promotion often had to be won through confrontation and shows of strength. The argument was between a thin and ill-looking man wearing a yellow tie, and an older woman with an orange tie. Her blonde haircut was sharp enough to slice through paper.

Their disagreement was threatening to escalate from the sound of it, which could prove interesting. They barked at each other in Corporate Dialect – a bespoke language made up of Crypto-Klingon, Japanese, and a smattering of Desperanto. It was a language specifically designed to negotiate merciless business deals, and to focus the mind on survival in a corporate eco-system. I learned to speak it when I was a young girl – one of my father's many strange gifts.

The orange-tied woman decided it was time to put her younger counterpart in his place. She spat a scorching insult, and walked out – haughty and superior. She timed it well, leaving yellow tie incensed with the loss of face this represented. He tried to shove me out of the way trying to catch up with her. *Not a smart move ...*

I slapped his face with such speed and ferocity that he fell to the ground, clutching his rapidly reddening cheek. A trickle of blood and spittle leaked slowly from his mouth, shock and fury rippled across his youthful features.

Satisfied with my handiwork, I turned to Lawrence, executing a perfect dismissive stance. 'How much longer will this take?' I snapped. I could hear orange tie lady's laughter roll down the hallway. She must have seen what had happened.

'Please bear with me Miss Delaney. The room is nearly ours,' said Lawrence, not skipping a beat. He was young, but he knew the game.

Lawrence bowed to his exec, not too low, nor too shallow, and glanced at the pitiful creature on the floor behind me. His eyes narrowed momentarily, and I *sensed* more than saw yellow-tie rise; he would try to attack me. I made ready to counter him but before I could react, a voice spoke:

'Mr. Johnson? Is this really how you choose to

behave?' It was the high-level exec with the rainbow tie. His voice was soft but projected easily, carrying a hint of old-world culture and status, underscored by a subtly menacing quality. Mr. Johnson froze, mumbled a reply, grabbed his dropped folder, and left in abject shame – head bowed at an almost impossibly sharp angle. He knew his lack of discipline would cost him dearly.

'It's always the little dogs that bark loudest,' I said, to break the silence. It was an old Corp saying.

We all laughed politely at that and relaxed, having established our credentials.

'Lawrence tells me you are an experienced and talented Xeno-Archaeologist.' (It wasn't a question.) 'My name is Jeremy Gibson. Please sit down.' Gibson politely waited for me to do so, then followed suit. Lawrence remained standing momentarily, until Gibson offered him a tiny nod.

'My reputation speaks for itself,' I replied. 'I'm good at what I do.'

'Good, I like that. No need for false modesty. We haven't got the time to waste in our brief lives.'

Gibson produced a Padd, flicked it at me with his little finger, and sat back observing me carefully. I picked it up and swiped through its contents; it contained a detailed floor-plan of the "*Mother of Pearl*", the official name of Habitat 6; the Gaianista habitat I was to explore with the crew of the *Effervescent*.

'OK, what's this to do with you?' I asked.

'Miss Delaney, do you know anything about Spectra?'

I considered my reply, as I did actually know a fair bit. My Father – when he was still relatively sane – had made sure I knew the corporate landscape at all times, and Spectra was a major player even then.

'I know enough not to waste more time here unless there's a very good business proposition coming out of your mouth very soon.'

Gibson showed a measured amount of distaste. 'No foreplay Miss Delaney? Straight to the action? I expected more … *grace,* let's say.'

'Go on then, talk dirty to me,' I teased, trying to get a rise out of Gibson. I wanted to see how steady he really was.

Lawrence shot me a worried look – not used to seeing a corporate exec being spoken to in that way. Gibson on the other hand was unflappable, much to my disappointment.

'Spectra has been around a long time Miss Delaney, as you no doubt know. We have commercial interests in almost all spheres of life, or at least those likely to yield a healthy return on investment. The Gaianistas also knew this, which is why they turned to us for funding their little exodus over seventy years ago.'

I sniffed at that. 'Why would they deal with Spectra? They were supposed to be so *pure*, right?' I ignored another disturbed look from Lawrence and continued. 'Your Corp is all about tech, Gaianistas tried to abandon tech. How did you square that circle?'

'There is an incorrect assumption at the root of your question miss Delany, if I may say so. The Gaianistas didn't hate *all* technology. After all, they relied on it to execute their relocation and purification program. No, what they hated was the kind of technology that produced augments. They hated anything which they considered detrimental to human evolution. Augments, Sim-Gear, Cyber-Punks, TrickMem... All dilutions of the true potential of the human race. They wanted to evolve biologically, not technologically. So, we helped them breed.'

'Accelerated evolution?' I guessed. A slight tremor in my voice betrayed my unease with the concept.

'Am I talking dirty enough for you yet, Miss Delaney?'

'That's beyond illegal.'

'Incorrect. It is illegal *now*. Back then if you set up a breakaway colony as a recognised nation state you could largely write your own legal framework, within reason of course. Especially if you were a recognised religious group, like the Gaianistas were.' Gibson smiled down on me, as if lecturing a slightly dim student.

'I'm not one to judge Mr. Gibson, but that's insane.'

'Indeed. They were insane times. Technically any group with a recognised and protected belief system could go for independence, and many did. I think the idea was to encourage more variety in humanity's efforts to colonise space. Spread our bets as it were.'

'OK, that was then, seventy years ago … I fail to see how any of this ties into the here and now?'

Gibson put the palms of his hands together as if in prayer, and briefly touched the fingertips to his mouth. It was such a strangely delicate gesture, especially coming from such a hardened corporate exec, that I wondered if he was having second thoughts.

'It matters to us now, Miss Delaney, because at Spectra we have always been interested in human transformation. Not just for our bio-weapons division, although we value their contribution highly, but also for our long-term plans for space exploration. Back then, as we do now, we considered it a serious problem that humans are so ill equipped to cope outside of their natural Earth-bound habitat, and it might surprise you that the Gaianistas shared our concern.'

'Oh?' I asked 'That *is* surprising.'

'Indeed. The Gaianistas were looking to breed humans who were more durable in a space-faring context. They wanted to achieve their goal through purely *evolutionary* methods. We offered them our assistance in expediting that process. And they accepted.'

'All agreed in secret I assume? I can't imagine regular Gaianistas being grateful to their leaders for getting in bed with Spectra.'

'Gratitude Miss Delaney? Gratitude is the disease of *dogs*.'

Gibson put just a little bit too much into that statement. A small crack in his impeccable corporate veneer, just enough to offer a glimpse of a temper underneath. I made a mental note that he could be provoked, if the right buttons were pushed.

'Again, how does this relate to our business?' I asked.

'Simple; we operated an in-house facility on Habitat 6 and we would like somebody to go there, to retrieve a rare Trickari artifact. It was used for invaluable and important research which we would also like returned to us, in a discreet manner.'

'I see … Let me recap that so that I'm clear on this: You struck a deal with the Gaianistas to help them evo-accelerate their minions, and in exchange they allowed you free reign to work on your own fucked up bio-tech research, free from annoying Earth regulations.'

Gibson smiled, flashing impeccable teeth. 'Perfectly legal *and* mutually beneficial to all parties involved. The best kind of business arrangement, don't you think?'

Gibson was right; it made perfect sense. It was rotten to the core of course, but it was right for Spectra-Vision and their Gaianista partners.

'Why not simply go yourself? Send one of your Samu?'

'Miss Delaney … Our Samurai are constantly monitored, as are all our vessels. But I suspect you already knew that.'

Gibson had a way of slightly tilting his head as if he were constantly assessing you, which he probably was. A few seconds passed, before he continued in an almost bored voice.

'We would be very visible indeed if we were to try to solve this conundrum ourselves. So, when our sources told us that Habitat 6 was finally cleared for salvage we kept tabs on Mr. Ballard's affairs, to see if we could … *enhance* his mission parameters, let's say. We did our due diligence and you, as a freelancer with the right set of skills, seemed a good candidate for the job. Discretion is of the utmost importance to us, and we think you could offer us just that.'

'What about my salvage contract? I'd have to clear it with Ballard. He may not like the sound of this at all, in which case my hands are tied.'

'Already dealt with. You are to perform your Xeno duties to the best of your abilities, but once completed you will be given leave to execute your Spectra contract.'

'You spoke to him?'

Gibson nodded. 'Yes of course. Mr. Ballard will be well compensated for his discretion and support. He has already agreed to our terms, which leaves just the matter of your consent.'

I wasn't sure I trusted his explanation for outsourcing this gig, but still … there was a deal to be made here.

'Forgive me for being blunt Gibson, but what are you offering me exactly?'

'Freedom and independence Miss Delaney! Your remuneration will be impressive, and we will offer you additional freelance contracts if your performance is satisfactory. If you turn out to be as good an operative as we think you are, then we'll help you find and purchase your own Blue-ship.'

'You would help me with that?' I asked, with incredulity.

'Indeed. If you were to captain your own Blue-ship you would be an even more valuable operative to us.'

'Legal and mutually beneficial,' I offered.

'The best kind of business,' he replied. 'Now, to aid you in this mission, we will give you a Key-Pass containing historic Spectra-Vision access codes. You'll be able to enter the high security areas of the facility without too many problems. Who knows, you might find some trinkets there. I imagine some of them will be worth a fair bit.'

And with that, Gibson reeled me in like a big fat fish. I could *feel* the hook wriggling in my mouth, but the bait was simply too good.

7

When I was a little girl – before creeping augment-sickness melted his sanity away – my father used to buy me miniature models of famous ships. He brought me naval vessels, space ships, deep sea explorers, even *land*-ships. I loved my father and I loved every millimetre of these wondrous creations. Their wildly divergent shapes, the strangely specific detail unique to each model, their smell – and as much as anything – the wonderful names they bore: *The Bounty*, *the Nautilus*, *the Millennium Falcon*, *the Discovery* ... every one of them a treasure trove of imagination and potential.

Ever since, I have fallen in love with every real world ship I encountered, no matter how ugly or mundane it seemed to people less romantically inclined. The truth is that to me, few things are as beautiful as a space ship. Ballard's ship was no exception.

Ballard wanted me to get a feel for the ship and its crew, and had invited me to come and see both. I walked by his side as he strode around its chunky landing gear, rattling off spec and stats, beaming with pride. Next to Ballard's seven foot tall frame I felt like that little girl again, marvelling over the latest ship my father had brought home.

The *Effervescent* was a slow but dependable vessel, sturdy and solid not unlike its captain. Its overall shape was defined by utilitarian cube components. Off-the-shelf sections, modified and upgraded over many years of use, clung together in a pleasingly angular arrangement. It may have looked haphazard to the untrained eye, but I could see that real love and expertise had gone into the design.

The ship wasn't drab, far from it, painted in ochres and greens and aquamarine stripes, finished off with a touch of white around its engines. She was surprisingly large, owing to an impressively spacious cargo hold. I hoped it would also offer decently sized crew quarters. A rarity on a salvage mission.

I could hear a loud beeping coming from the inside of the ship, when the cargo bay opened and a ramp extended to a loading platform. Ballard spread his arms wide – a remarkable distance, encompassing everything.

'New friends! I brought new friends!'

The ship's crew of three looked up in unison and immediately adopted the same defensive stance shown to new recruits through the ages. Not malicious per se, but sceptical.

'Jemm, Clint, we are in luck today, yes? We are in the presence of some of my favourite human beings in the Solar system. And they're not bad crew-mates either.' Ballard's laugh was loud enough to make everybody wince, crew and newcomers alike.

'Look! Look here,' he said, pointing at a woman on the left. 'Betsie here is my muscle.' He then pointed at the others, one by one. 'Charles takes care of our health, and little Kiyoshi here has the honourable task of not crashing my lovely ship.' Ballard gestured to me and Clint, a twinkle in his eye. 'My lovely crew, meet our new Xeno, Jemm, and her talented son Clint. Two for the price of one. Don't say I never bring you anything nice eh?'

We all looked each other over for a moment, awkwardly silent, until Betsie stepped forward and said: 'I don't really like the term "*muscle*". I prefer "*security and demolitions*". Muscle sounds like I'm some corporate thug.'

Betsie's voice was gentle and soft, without lacking confidence. On first inspection she seemed an unlikely candidate for the job; she wasn't particularly large or muscular, and I didn't sense any of the simmering aggression sometimes associated with her profession. Nor did she come across as a techno-fetishist, who tend to be fond of showing off the myriad gadgets and tools that come with the job. Instead she dressed in a standard-issue jumpsuit, as worn by countless nondescript spacers.

A closer look revealed a supple and balanced stance, betraying some kind of martial training. I counted at least three hidden weapons on her – no doubt *meant* to be noticed – and I suspected there were a fair few more that were harder to spot. We shook hands. Hers was a strong grip, businesslike and to the point. I thought we got off to a decent enough start.

Kiyoshi was tall, and lanky, and like Betsie he dressed against type. There was no swaggering flyboy-wear, no enhanced shades, no good-natured banter. Far from it.

Kyoshi gave us a withering look of appraisal. 'Are we taking on kids now? *Effervescent* day care? What is this shit?'

'What's your beef old man?' Clint said. I groaned internally. *Really Clint?*

'What the fucking fuck? This kid, this *pup*, is going to cut into my share? Doing what exactly? Keep mummy all broody and maternal? I'm supposed to trust a fucking teen now?' He spat between my legs, drops of spittle splattering my boots. I guess he had expected me to move. This wasn't going well.

Clint, smiled a crooked smile; he knew what he was doing. 'Want to talk about trust *Leroy*?' he said calmly. 'You sure about that?'

Kyoshi's face stiffened as all colour drained from his face, leaving him white as a corpse for several heart beats, until it returned with a vengeance, painting his face a red mask of fury.

'What did you call me you little shit? Where did you get that name–'

'I'm just asking, because not many people would trust a Doppelganger. Or should I say "*persona thief*"? That's what it said on your arrest warrant by the way.'

Kyoshi glanced at Ballard. Uncertainty trickling through his defences.

'You got the wrong idea there pup, you've been digging in the wrong garbage. Best be careful or you might get dirty. I don't give a shit if you're hot shit in teenage xeno-land. I'm not gonna take any shit from you.'

Clint was calmness personified. He even winked at Kyoshi. 'Don't get nervous old man, I did you a favour. Your record is now scrubbed clean like a newborn baby. I gotta say though, whoever you paid to fix up your new ident? He or she was pretty good. Just not quite as good as me.'

'Is that right?' said Kyoshi, the words laced with menace.

'That's right. And don't be so precious about your pathetic share. Mother and I work as a single unit. One share for both of us. And we'll still come out on top.'

Kyoshi teetered on the edge of doing something either very stupid or very smart. For a moment it looked like it could go either way until Ballard steadied him with a hand easily as large as Kyoshi's entire head, pushing down on his shoulder, pinning him in place. It took only a second for Kyoshi to calm down.

'Ha!' roared Ballard. 'Thank you Clint. Your mother was right about you.'

An awkward pause, then, a voice cut through the tension, sharp and clear: 'You are not augmented in any way, is that correct? No implants whatsoever?' Charles' manner was impeccable, his enunciation perfect and precise. 'Most Xenos are though, unless I'm mistaken?'

'That's right,' I replied.

'But not you. Why is that if I may ask?'

'I don't believe in those kinds of shortcuts.'

Charles nodded, but I had no idea if it was agreement. He smiled vaguely, a slender man dressed with impeccably tailored clothes, perfectly groomed, almost to the point of obsessiveness. I couldn't read him at all.

'Well, well. Interesting.' He turned to Ballard. 'This has been excellent fun,' he said, 'but I suggest we prepare for launch. That is, if our captain agrees?'

Ballard shoved a glaring Kyoshi ahead of him. 'Yes yes. Introductions are over. Or maybe they just started eh, *Leroy*?' He laughed even louder than before, if such a thing was even possible.

At that point I knew that the *Effervescent* and her crew would accept us in their embrace, for better or for worse.

We launched the next day.

On previous missions, Clint only experienced take off from within a protective environment – either strapped in safely, or in a nice artificial gravity bubble, but always shielded from the visual side of the experience. This time I took Clint to the observatory so we could experience the true feeling of leaving Earth together.

No matter how many times I travelled by spaceship it was a sight that would never cease to amaze. Watching Earth fall away and slowly transform into a small blue dot was one of the most extraordinary sights a person could experience, and an important part of understanding the true nature of space. Clint needed to learn the real context of working in this environment.

The observatory walls and ceiling doubled as display screens, perfectly conveying the outside of the ship as if seen through windows. Pure, cold vacuum loomed over all of us, foreboding and implacable, but in the centre of the blackness floated Earth, like a jewel on pitch black velour.

Initially, seeing Earth like this excited Clint, but gradually, as the planet shrunk smaller and smaller against the vast background of deep space, the experience became oppressive. I anticipated it; most people, exposed to the sight for the first time, are fundamentally affected by it. The mind doesn't like to feel infinitely small in an all-encompassing universe. Clint became subdued and pensive.

'You'll get used to it,' I said.

Clint didn't reply, but put his arm around my shoulder. For a moment we were at peace. We were the only people in the observatory, for which I was grateful.

I changed the display setting to show a point of view away from Earth, showing the entirety of the ship instead. Together we observed the *Effervescent* drifting in space, alone and vulnerable. It reinforced the lesson that I needed Clint to learn: *Space feels no pity. It offers no mercy. It just is.*

I learned that lesson a long time ago. It doesn't matter who we are back on Earth, when here in space we must know that we are nothing. The only thing that keeps our fragile life-force from dissipating into the cold empty vacuum is this insignificant shell of a ship, and the crew that travels in its belly.

Clint was a strong boy, but after a while he could no longer contain his tears. I hated myself for having to teach him such a harsh truth.

It took us a few days to get settled on the *Effervescent*. Like most ships she had her quirks and idiosyncrasies, but it was clear to me from the start that she was a ship well loved by her crew, and that she had been on many adventures. There were no areas of neglect. Every bulkhead, every airlock, every sub-system control-point was well maintained. There were numerous repairs, parts and panels swapped out – giving the ship a slightly patched-up vibe at times – but it was all done with expert care and to a high professional standard.

Every crew-member did their bit; no job was beneath their concern. On many occasions did I see Kyoshi or Betsie and even Charles perform an impromptu systems check or swap out a part that would need replacing before long, or even just polish some readout screens, all without being ordered to do so. This was an excellent sign; clearly the crew cared about their ship.

The *Effervescent's* Blue engine was as smooth as I had experienced. Acceleration and deceleration was inertia free, as with all Blue drives, but normally one could feel a jarring shudder or a slightly queasy sensation in one's stomach when a Blue engine activated. Not so on the *Effervescent*; the ship was as finely tuned and balanced as a concert violin.

I was even impressed with the aesthetics on-board. There was a tasteful but sturdy functionality about the ship. Unashamed to show off its heavy machinery and structural features, but never feeling cluttered or jagged. There was always plenty of illumination, and most panels were painted in light tints, making sure that one's eye wasn't constantly tugged at by wild colour clashes.

Clint and I gradually established a routine, getting used to the new sleep cycles, picking up odd jobs and continuing our research into the habitat's history, and Gaianista life in general. We managed not to step on too many toes while blending in with the crew as much as we could.

Roy's data on the Habitat had given us one strong lead, but no more than that. Clint and I had devised a plan around retrieving a possible private hoard, owned by one of the Habitat's managers. There was great potential there, *if* it existed, but there was no telling if we would even find ourselves in a position to execute the plan. We kept working on the scheme. If the other salvage opportunities didn't pan out it could be our only shot at scoring big.

I smiled in anticipation, only to cry out in pain a moment later.

'Jesus mum, what's wrong?'

'Head …' I gasped, barely able to speak. 'Pressure …'

'Here,' he grabbed me, 'lie down for a bit.' With Clint's help I dragged myself to bed, moaning, clutching my head. A deep, nauseating, cutting sensation pulsed through my skull. Clint's eyes were wide with shock and worry, but I wasn't in any position to reassure him.

'Painkillers …' I rasped, desperately.

Clint went off to rummage in the first aid box on the wall. I was about to tell him to hurry when the pain eased. A great pressure fell away. My mind was free again.

'Ah, that was awful …'

'Better?'

I nodded.

'What the hell was that?'

'I don't know,' I said. 'I've been feeling weird ever since

that Neo tried to get into my head. Maybe it's related.'

'Like a psychic bruise or something?'

I nearly laughed out loud at the term. 'Yeah, maybe something like that. Whatever it is, I hope it stops.'

I lay back down, trying not to think too much, but the same question kept creeping up on me, like a stalker; *what did that Neo do to me?*

The gym was old and could use a new coat of paint, but was perfectly serviceable. The smell of thousands of hours of sweaty exercise and training had permanently bonded with the environment. It was so ingrained in the place that it wasn't even unpleasant.

I started my customary cardio-vascular routine and soon worked up a sweat, patiently stepping through the moves and repetitions. I found exercise intensely boring but I managed to make it tolerable by using a top-notch music playlist that I had been perfecting over the years – mostly classical funk and disco. I soon settled into my customary rhythm.

Halfway through my set I spotted Betsie entering the gym from the corner of my eye. She set up a shadow boxing scenario using a VR partner and went to work. Her feet were fast, like a street dancer's. Her torso dipped and weaved and swayed from side to side avoiding the jabs from her virtual opponent. Betsie's punches flew fast and furious. Sweat poured down her face, but her breathing remained steady.

Betsie was the first person on the crew to make Clint and me feel welcome, yet she was often standoffish and impersonal when I tried to talk to her. Something about her was sending out conflicting signals. I could sense no anger or aggression in her, yet there was something furious about her training routine. Something was obviously driving her. Whatever it was, she seemed to go beyond the typical efforts needed for hired Muscle.

I must have checked her out a bit too long because she

suddenly stopped her exercise and walked over, gesturing for me to turn off my music. She raised her hand, holding up a pair of sparring gloves.

'Come on, let's have some fun,' she said in that soft, almost husky voice.

'Doesn't seem fair to me ...' I said carefully. 'Muscle vs Xeno, there's only one way that's going to turn out.'

'Come *on*, it's just training. Don't pretend you don't know how to spar.' She walked over to a sparring mat which had been white once, long ago, but had now settled into a dull grey colour. Betsie adopted a basic boxing stance, right in the middle of the mat. 'It'll be fun,' she said.

I joined her on the mat, feeling a slight twinge of concern. Despite her reassuring words things didn't feel that friendly to me.

'Ready?' she asked.

Before I could reply her left fist shot out, *fast*. I dodged her jab, purely instinctual. *Dad's old training alive and well*. Another jab, even faster. This time I bobbed and returned the favour, actually glancing her temple.

'See? You know what you're doing don't you?' Betsie started to circle me slowly. 'How's your legwork?' She aimed a nasty diagonal stomp at my right thigh, a move that would have completely numbed my leg had it connected. 'Not bad Jemm! Are you sure you're not augmented?'

I feinted. Once ... twice ... then went on the offensive with controlled jabs and left-right combinations. Betsie avoided real contact easily enough, as expected, and showed no clear weaknesses in her defence – also as expected but slightly disappointing.

'Like I told Charles, I don't like shortcuts,' I said, slightly out of breath.

Betsie replied with a sudden leg sweep that turned out to be a feint. I knew what she was doing but couldn't avoid a sharp jab to the face regardless. I rolled with it as much as I could but even so, sharp pain knifed through my nose. Bright red blood splatters like angry fireworks appeared briefly on the grey mat beneath my feet, before fading to a dull brown as they were absorbed.

I wiped my face with the back of my hand, counter-circling her, wondering how to handle this. There was no way I could defeat her in hand to hand combat, despite my old training. I had to work at a different way out of this. Betsie's next attack could do some real damage. *Why was she doing this?*

'Sorry if my face hurt your hand. Haven't done this in a while.' I grinned broadly, blood running down my face.

'Hand's good, thanks. But be careful not to damage the knife.'

The knife had appeared in her left hand unnoticed. A short and nasty little blade, made for street-fighting.

This was getting out of hand.

Betsie's moves were fluid, graceful and natural. The knife cut through the air in front of my face in graceful arcs, promising pain and misery. Perhaps enjoying herself too much she made her first mistake then: she showed off her blade fighting skills with a playful thrust, but it left her arm exposed. I struck with speed, punched her elbow, hard. It didn't break, but that arm would be useless for a day or two.

Unfazed, despite what must have been significant discomfort, she pushed me back with a punishing right hand blow, and calmly moved the knife to her right hand.

'Nice … It's a good thing I'm right handed.' She returned to her basic fighting stance. 'But I wonder where a freelance Xeno learns to fight like that?' She moved in again, knife ready. 'Which Corp are you Jemm?' She lunged again, knife moving to my throat. A sloppy move which allowed me to grab, twist, and reverse. We grappled for a moment on the floor. I could smell my own sweat as I was slowly gaining control of the knife.

'I'm freelance,' I panted. 'Already told you that.'

A gun – a neuro-jammer to be precise – appeared in her left hand. Clearly I had done less damage than I thought.

'Time to talk straight Jemm. I want to know why you're here and who you're working for.' She aimed the gun at me, starting to seriously piss me off. 'This beauty won't kill you but believe me, it can conjure up more pain than you can imagine.'

'I told you, I'm—'

A giant fist enveloped Betsie's hand and most of her gun with it.

'I don't allow this on my ship.' Ballard's rumbling voice filled the entire gym. 'What's going on here?'

'Just asking some questions,' said Betsie. Her voice coarse with strain. 'Maybe you should have done that yourself before bringing this Corp snake on-board.'

'You don't know what you're talking about,' grumbled Ballard.

'Wake up *Captain*. I can smell the stink of Corp training from across the room. I want to know who's pulling her strings. Why is she really here?'

'Yes, I see. Well, I already know those things, so maybe next time come to me first.' He pulled Betsie off the mat with ease. 'Go away, I need to talk with Jemm, alone.'

Finally losing my temper, I threw a wild right at Betsie, only to see it blocked by Ballard's other hand. My hand disappeared inside his fist.

'Let … fucking … go of me, right now,' I gasped. I was sick of being attacked.

Ballard didn't respond. He just *squeezed.* The pain shut me up effectively. Betsie received the same treatment, until we both fell to our knees, trying to ride the pain but failing. Then, Ballard slowly eased off until we had calmed down sufficiently, after which he finally let go.

I sat on one knee for a moment slowly clenching and unclenching my fist, wondering if any permanent damage was done. When I glanced to see how Betsie was doing she smiled and got back on her feet with an agility that was impressive. She bowed slightly to Ballard. 'Captain …'

'Go. I'll fill you in later, yes?' Betsie bowed again, then turned and left. There was something defiant about the way she walked, or maybe it was just a matter of pride.

Ballard called after her, 'You were wrong about her, but also a little bit right. But don't worry, I'll explain later and you can apologise to Jemm next time, yes?' He winked at me as he said it.

Together we watched Betsie leave the gym. I felt a pang of satisfaction when I caught her briefly clutching her elbow on her way out. It was petty of me, but her discomfort made me smile for a moment, before I remembered how angry I really was.

I turned that enmity on Ballard, and said, 'Put her on a leash J.J. or somebody will put her down.'

'Yes. I'm sure somebody will one day. But not you.'

I huffed, 'We'll see about that.' But I couldn't muster much conviction.

'Can you blame her for being suspicious?' asked Ballard. 'You are a strange person yes?'

'Everybody is fucking strange. Look in the mirror recently?'

Ballard's face showed instant disappointment, I felt a brief stab of guilt.

'Think about it Jemm,' he said softly. 'Think about what Betsie sees. You act like this tough Xeno girl, but are too scared to leave your boy at home. You say you're a freelancer but you are obviously Corp-trained. You make one deal with me and suddenly I get a Spectra-Vision payoff for another deal.'

'Which you signed happily in exchange for a great sum of money,' I countered.

'Not happily, no. A lot of money yes, but you must admit, it's all a bit… *strange* yes? The crew aren't stupid, they see it too.' He looked at me sideways, huge arms crossed, in the exact same pose Clint adopts when trying to make me see reason. Suddenly I lost interest in the argument.

'Fine. You want to know all about me?' I asked.

I found a chair to sit in, folded my arms as well, sat back and told him everything. How my father trained me in all aspects of Corp lore and survival techniques. How he slowly lost his mind, and how all the way through that horrible descent into disaster, I still couldn't help but love him with all my heart. I even told Ballard everything I knew about the Spectra-Vision mission, the secret lab we were to raid and the incredible reward they dangled in front of me. I figured he had a right to know.

The following day I mostly kept to myself.

My body was sore, my nose a nexus of pain, my body a map of bruises. I pushed through the discomfort by focusing on the Xeno job. Clint and I went over our mission objectives, double-checked our data on the Gaianista station, and scrutinised our backup plans. Although I felt confident that we had prepared well, I had to admit that Habitat 6 was an intimidating place, even more so for carrying the saddest of histories.

During the worst period of Icarus, when the death toll started to add up to millions of lost souls, there was a rush to quarantine any facility known to contain Trickari Red technology. In practice this meant thousands of rushed (often forced) quarantine orders were executed. Mars domes, moon bases, space stations, asteroid enclaves … nothing was spared. But few quarantines were more tragic than those of the so-called breakaway-colonies. These colonies were the product of splinter-groups, trying to kick-start new societies, growing their own new branch of humanity. These places were suffused with positivity and hope, a righteous and glorious future awaited them, free from Earth's corrupting influence – or so the colony leaders imagined. In other words they engaged in that classic human pastime: trying to establish Utopia.

Reality, sadistic bastard that it can be, decided to give most of them the exact opposite. Like many Utopians before them, the colonies collectively failed – every single one of them. They simply weren't up to the task; theory did not align with practice. Like all Utopias, actually *implementing* their idealised society exposed all their inherent and fatal flaws, previously masked by attractive theory and rhetoric. And when Utopias fail, they fail completely.

Entire religions and philosophies were buried inside the frozen husks of these failed temples to humanity's ego. Their visionaries, luminaries, oracles and messiahs perished or fled. It was as if the universe wanted to put the entire human race in its place, for daring to dream, and the fate of the Gaianistas was amongst the most heartbreaking of them all.

Unlike some of the newer splinter groups the Gaianistas had been at it for a long time. They had been going against the grain of human progress for at least 150 years, and been largely ridiculed for their efforts. When the Acceleration took off they saw a way forward. The Trickari discovery gave them an opportunity to take radical steps towards their idealised future, free from impure outsiders. So, in their zeal to follow the one pure way, they embraced the new legislation allowing outbreak-colonies to be formed, and committed fully to leaving Earth altogether. In essence they were given a chance to start afresh.

Yes, the Gaianistas were aware of the inherent irony in using ultra advanced technology to get away from the corrupting influence of that same technology, but that kind of ideological sleight-of-hand was typical in the 22nd century.

They built seven torus-shaped deep space habitats, each housing 10,000 colonists, each espousing slightly different models of governance and social cohesion strategies. Thinking they had multiple fail-safes built in because of the diversity of their colonies, the Gaianistas blossomed in their new environments. They even started a recruitment drive of sorts, offering interested parties full conversion rights if they agreed to work for free for one full year. Quite a few Earthlings signed up for this deal. Gaianism was the sexy new thing, probably for the first time in its existence.

But it didn't last, and when things went bad for the

Gaianistas they went very bad indeed. Within the first week of Icarus incidents, three of their domes disappeared in a ball of super-heated plasma. Panic set in immediately, since every single Gaianista habitat depended on a Red-powered Micro-Sun. Trickari energy at its finest.

Two more habitats suffered the same fate while still being quarantined. By now the death-toll was among the worst of the Icarus years.

The final two domes suffered a plethora of smaller system malfunctions which still managed to cause havoc. After their Micro-Suns were jettisoned there wasn't much Red tech to shut down, yet thousands of colonists still perished in the rush to secure the habitats and get out. The abandoned husks float eternally in deep space, a shrine to the power of Utopian hubris.

In subsequent years the few surviving Gaianista members either left the organisation in shame, or died in one of several mass suicide events.

The habitat we were about to enter – Habitat 6 – was an ancient mausoleum. A place where some of the brightest hopes of humanity had been buried. It was a place of *extinguished* hope.

There hadn't been any escalation incidents for at least twenty years, but that did nothing to lift our mood when we finally docked.

It took us only two weeks to reach Habitat 6. While on paper, the *Effervescent* wasn't a particularly fast ship by modern standards, Trickari engines do something peculiar – and theoretically impossible – to space-time coherence. It's what allowed humanity to completely redefine its ambitions for the Solar System.

During those weeks, I learned a great deal about the ship and its crew, the latter proving to be a fascinating group of people. My respect for Ballard went up another notch. He hadn't simply thrown a handful of capable individuals together – although they *were* all highly capable – but he somehow managed to mould them into a tight and efficient unit, without resorting to the benevolent dictator approach that so many Captains defaulted to. Instead, he had brought together an eclectic group of characters who somehow meshed together naturally and seemingly effortlessly. Not an easy thing to do, especially when dealing with the kinds of personalities that are attracted to dangerous salvage work.

Clint and I would have to work hard to fit into that dynamic, but that was OK – nothing we hadn't done before. As always the fastest way to acceptance came through competence, and we would get many opportunities to demonstrate ours. Although arguably, Clint had already showcased his skills when he exposed Kyoshi's true identity.

Clint could be a very effective social creature when he chose to utilise that side of him, as was evidenced by the unlikely friendship that had sprung up between him and Kyoshi. They performed that classical male bonding dance involving harsh mutual insults met by loud laughter, the sharing of secrets, and generally spending too much time with each other. This suited me fine as it helped our standing with the crew, as well as making it easy for me to locate Clint when I needed him. Generally, I just had to find Kyoshi and Clint would be by his side.

Such was the case when I went looking for him three days before we were due to arrive, finding them both on the bridge. Kyoshi was teaching Clint basic navigation protocols, a valuable addition to his skill-set which I gratefully encouraged. Both were strapped into their pilot seats and both turned to me with a wide grin when I arrived.

'The Kid's got skills, no doubt,' said Kyoshi. (Clint had progressed from "Pup" to "The Kid" or just plain "Kid"). 'You sure you want him to be a professional *sniffer*? He can do better you know?'

'Yes, I want him to be a data retrieval analyst,' I said, putting on a fake snooty voice. 'It's a profession that comes out significantly ahead of *shit-can pilot.* Especially when it comes to long-term mortality rates. It's true – I double-checked the data myself.'

'Very funny. Don't let J.J. hear you badmouth the *Effer* like that. The man's nice, but he ain't that nice.'

To be fair, he had a point. Although our ship was slow for a salvage vessel, she was finely tuned and state-of-the-art where it mattered. The navigational array was top-notch, weapons and armature were impressively intimidating, and she even carried human-tech propulsion backups in case her Blue engine core ran out of juice – always a danger with Trickari tech. She was a fine ship and I felt a pang of guilt even jokingly suggesting that she wasn't up to par.

'Clint. With me please,' I asked, maybe a bit too commanding. He rolled his eyes at his new friend like all boys do when their mothers take them away from their toys and games, but he complied. One day soon he wouldn't be so accommodating, and that would be the day I would no longer expect him to.

Although the *Effervescent* – or the *Effer* as Kyoshi had called her – was deceptively large, that didn't make her corridors and access hatches feel any less cramped. In that, the *Effervescent* was the same as any other ship in history; no matter how big they got, the crew would still have to navigate tight spaces and occupy squeezed accommodations, and as newcomers our quarters were the least convenient available. Clint and I were given a small rectangular room featuring an oppressively low ceiling, which made me feel like I had to duck all the time.

It didn't bother me. I've had to put up with far worse in the past and there were perks as well. Ballard's operation was successful enough that he could run a modest Blue gravitation unit, which gave us just enough weight to be spared the worst downsides of zero-g, while still allowing us to enjoy the sensation of lightness.

We were even given a little workstation with access to the ship's sub-ai, quickly taken over by Clint who immediately dominated that space in typical over-the-top fashion, installing a bewildering array of devices, gadgets and contraptions. The associated wiring resembled a little mangrove forest, long roots and all.

One of his devices – disguised as a Hello Kitty desk lamp – was actually a little Privacy Shield. I switched it on and gestured for Clint to sit with me, in the lamp's pink glow. When Clint sat down the lamp giggled excitedly and said something in Japanese to indicate that Clint was now also shielded.

'We need to talk,' I said.

'That's not a promising start to a conversation,' laughed Clint. 'Whatever you think I've done … I haven't done it. There's no proof.'

'This is serious. Listen …' I sighed, hating to have to play this role. 'Look, I can't have you with me on this Spectra mission.'

Clint's eyes narrowed, his jaw muscles clenched. This would not be an easy conversation.

'You're joking,' said Clint, exasperated. 'You said I would join you all the way on this one.'

'I know I did, but that was when we were just dealing with Ballard. Spectra is a different beast altogether. You know that don't you?'

'Maybe … Aren't you being a little paranoid?

'Come on Clint. If you want to be taken serious enough to go on missions like this with me, prove that you can handle it. Ask yourself, can you trust a Corp like Spectra? Do they really need *somebody like me* for this mission?'

'I don't know mum. I didn't choose this gig, now did I?' He had a point. 'Of course I don't trust Spectra,' he continued. 'I'm not completely stupid.'

'Well, I don't trust Gibson either,' I said. 'I don't think he's given us the full picture so I can't be sure what the real risks are. I'm taking a gamble as it is, and that's making me nervous. I can't expose you to danger like that. I just can't, there's too many unknowns. You get that, right?'

Clint pushed out his chin, forcing his face into a

childish expression of stubbornness – the same face he used to pull as a toddler. I never had the heart to tell him how endearing it was.

I carried on, ignoring his irritation. 'Just think about it: I'm entering a secret Spectra-Vision biotech facility – likely used for crazily illegal experiments that spell "instant death sentence" for anybody mixed up in it – so I expect to see some pretty serious defensive measures, no matter the supposed clearance we get from Gibson's fancy little Key-Pass.'

Clint frowned, not convinced. 'I'd say that means you need me even *more* on this,' he said. 'I'm better than you with defensive systems and we both know you can't touch my skills with data retrieval. You *know* this.'

'What I know is that there's a line I can't cross, Clint. I'm already too close to it when I take you on regular salvage contracts,' I sighed. 'There are some things you just aren't ready for, no matter how much you think you are.' He stared at me, hurt, weighing up his options.

'I see,' he said. Clint had accurately read between the lines to recognise the implied threat: *Careful, or stay Earthbound from now on.*

'I know Corp business better than anybody,' I said. 'I'll be OK. Look, I won't lock you out, I just need to secure the site. If it all pans out as we planned I'll let you in and you can do your thing. But only when it's safe.'

'I think it's stupid but … Fine.' He squared his shoulders, then continued. 'I'll prep you then – get you comfortable with my gear. I know old people learn slowly, so we should get going on that.'

He looked so pleased with himself – earnest, proud, standing there in the pink glow of a Hello Kitty themed anti-surveillance device – that I couldn't help but burst out in uncontrollable laughter.

Clint was not amused.

8

Even with a navigator as skilled as Kyoshi our final approach took several hours. A smattering of crew had gathered in the observatory to witness the final stages of our journey, and to get a sense of what lay ahead.

Clint and I were present, as were Charles and Ballard. Betsie was keeping herself apart from me, either out of embarrassment or residual anger. Frankly, I was happy for her to leave me alone.

Charles had patched me up a bit. My nose had suffered a small fracture which he treated carefully and efficiently, using some kind of skin epoxy. It itched like the devil, and the result was almost cartoonish, making me look like a character straight from a cheap crime-sim: "*The heroine who changed her face, just to escape her past ...*"

A few minutes after I entered the observatory, Charles sat down next to me, wordlessly examining his handiwork. He gently cupped my chin, tested the position of the cast from different angles to make sure the nose was set correctly.

Clint joked, 'Will she ever play the piano again, doc?' It was a pretty good impression of a bad sim-actor. 'Is it amnesia? Does she … Does she remember her name?' I tried to laugh but it hurt too much.

Charles ignored the banter, engaged in his duties as on-board physician, shutting out all external noise. There was a certain *distance* about him. Not exactly aloof, or standoffish, but perhaps a mild reservedness. As if he stood slightly apart, observing events from a different place than the others.

'How long do I have to wear this thing?' I asked, to fill the silence. My voice sounded nasal and whiny to me.

'How is the pain?' came Charles's non-reply. I noticed that he had groomed so fastidiously that even his nose hair appeared trimmed.

'The pain is fine, the itching is terrible. I want to take this thing off.'

'Dizziness? Nausea? What about balance?'

'I have great balance thanks.' I was getting annoyed with being ignored but grudgingly admitted to myself that he was just doing his job. 'Nothing seems *too* bad, just a dull pain. Throbbing mostly.' I wondered if he trimmed his ear hairs too.

'That's to be expected. Things could be rather worse, for both of you in fact.'

'Oh? Our security expert is not as invulnerable as she appears then?' I knew I sounded petulant but felt I deserved some leeway in this matter. 'How bad is it?'

'I imagine she is just fine. Her elbow is somewhat sore, but not irrevocably damaged.' He looked up at me from under perfectly oval-shaped spectacles. 'If you had used even a fraction more force however, I suspect we would be having a different conversation altogether.'

He stood up abruptly. 'Well, well … Will you look at that?'

The sunlit side of Habitat 6 slowly drifted into view. Despite being classed as a dome it was more of a classical torus shape, spinning lazily, hard shadows creeping along its outer hull like knights riding sunlight.

I knew from my research that there were 64 sections, each reinforced and equipped with its own airlock. Many looked to be in bad shape. An old abandoned transport vessel was still moored to an airlock close to us, dwarfed by the outlandishly large mass to which it was tethered. The station measured at least ten kilometres across, perhaps another five kilometres deep.

A hush came down over the observatory. It became clear to us what incredible scale we were dealing with. It was like looking at a magic ring of power, meant for the finger of a lost god. Quiet now but harnessing untold forces, ready for the taking.

Solar energy arrays adorned the gargantuan ring, sparkling like black diamonds, designed by a cosmic jeweller. I raised my hand in front of me and for a moment it felt like I could simply place the ring on my own finger. The mind plays strange tricks when confronted with something so far beyond its regular frame of reference.

'Did everybody pack their lunch?' I joked. That earned me some chuckles at least. 'Look, it's just a salvage mission,' I continued. 'Yes, it's big. Well, really fucking big, but that's why we bring maps and skimmers and gear and booze.' A few more laughs. 'Besides, at that size it just means there's more for us to find, right?'

Charles gave me a pointed look. 'Yes thank you. We have, occasionally, done this before.' I held up my hands in a "just doing my best to help!" gesture.

Ballard pointed at a huge antenna. 'There! That's our marker. Our airlock is …' He mentally traced a line north, then east. His index finger jabbed forward: 'That's it, there. Next to that red plating.'

He turned to face us all, solemn, yet as excited as a little boy. 'Get ready. We dock soon.'

The dead were everywhere, the dark their only blanket. Light-sources were dim and few between, staring down on us with softly glowing eyes. At least they offered occasional respite when the darkness became too overbearing and the countless corpses around us appeared to whisper among themselves.

We were lucky to have even this much light. The solar energy array was still largely operational, but limited to providing power for emergency lighting and a smattering of support systems.

I was concerned how Clint would deal with all this *death*. He had seen corpses before, but this felt different. There were just so many of them, covered in rime, caught out by hull breaches or botched evacuation attempts. Sometimes the dead appeared clustered together in corridors, telling the story of their death in forever frozen scenes: caught out on leisurely walks, on their way to work, or going to school – when disaster had struck. Other times we found them huddled together in locked-off sections of the station, asphyxiated or killed by the cold.

My worries about Clint were misplaced. He dealt with the grim reality on the ground by focusing on the job at hand. He wasted little time accessing the Habitat's network which was still active in places, retrieving extremely useful data and files that he shared with the rest of the crew. This was met with much murmuring of approval. As good as the crew was, they hadn't worked with a system specialist of Clint's calibre before.

Gravity, courtesy of the habitat's centrifugal capability, was a reasonable 0.4 gees – ideal conditions for our little convoy of skimmers. Ballard insisted I'd share the smallest skimmer with Betsie of all people, but I guess it made sense from his point of view. He needed us to get on, at least professionally, and this would give us the chance to work out a truce. *So be it*, I thought, ready to move on from our little spat.

The skimmers were great. They were fast and steady, yet small enough to allow us to traverse most corridors, and they easily fitted through the bulkhead doors. We had entered the torus at section 12, made our way to 18. Our first mission objective was a large seed-bank in section 21.

So far we had mostly travelled through the central maintenance boulevard. Its bulkheads had held admirably, and only on a few occasions when forced to bypass blockages or dangerous environmental conditions did we have to detour deeper into the habitat proper.

Our suits were light-weight marvels, fully cleared for a range of environments, from hostile atmospheric conditions to full-on deep-space E.V.A.

Communication took place over standard radio channels which gave us plenty of range but made it hard to build up any rapport with my crew-mates. I gave it a half-hearted try anyway and opened a direct, private channel to Betsie.

'How's the elbow?' I asked, trying for a laconic *laissez-faire* approach.

'How's the nose?' Betsie replied, adopting the same tone.

'It only hurts when I sneeze. I guess you only broke it a little bit.'

'Well, I'll try not to hit you again. But no promises.'

'Seriously, how's the elbow?' Betsie turned sideways to be able to face me straight on. The look she gave me – withering and curious at the same time – offered little conciliation. I don't think she was the diplomatic type.

'Look, can we not do this please?' I asked. 'It's tedious.' I waited for her reply, but it never came. 'Really?' I asked. 'It's going to be like that?' The radio channel hissed softly at me, like a petulant snake. The silence stretched for long seconds until I got bored. 'Fine. Whatever.'

Switching back to the common frequency I could hear Clint and Kyoshi laughing and joking, getting on like an old married couple on holiday. Their skimmer was twice the size of mine, carrying a heavy load of equipment and supplies. It made a gentle humming sound as it floated along.

The final and largest skimmer was reserved for J.J. and Doc. It could have easily carried all of us, but it was reserved for salvage. If everything went well we would return later that day with hundreds of containers filled with rare, important seeds and a great deal of Blue-powered equipment – topped off with the fruit of our private efforts beyond the core contract.

I checked my map; we were approaching our first serious challenge. Clint's efforts to interface with the local network had turned up a final transmission from the Habitat – a gut-wrenching damage report from a young engineer called Jebediah Parker ("Jeb" to his friends) – waiting desperately for an evacuation team that would never show up. Jeb tried to give them an update on the damage and dangers they would have to overcome in order to collect him.

Jebediah means "friend of God" in Hebrew, but maybe God had enough friends that day. Jeb's broadcast never did him any good, although it was of great use to us, providing us with a vital upgrade to the old archived map that Clint had managed to sniff out of the Gaianista data trove from Roy. Consequently we were in good shape with regards to navigating the Habitat, allowing us to prepare for specific obstacles. Jeb's damage report gave us a headsup for our first major blockage.

'Wow …' said Clint. 'Just … wow.'

'The kid ain't wrong,' said Kyoshi. More subdued than I had heard him before.

The scene ahead of us was strangely beautiful, but no less problematic for it. A water reservoir had exploded into the maintenance boulevard, plugging it with a frozen wall of ice. We slowed down to a stop, approaching the final distance on foot for inspection. The Blue glow from the skimmer's energy units cast our shadows onto the frozen wall, a silent and sinister kabuki performance.

As I expected, there was no discernible way through. We carried fierce lasers, easily capable of melting the ice, but the water would just freeze again, too fast for us to make meaningful progress.

I patted Betsie on her helmet. 'Seems you're up. Show us some muscle will ya?' I couldn't help but needle her again, hoping for some kind of engagement.

'Captain?' she asked, ignoring me.

'Proceed,' he replied. They were all business now.

She walked to the wall of ice, taking a series of measurements with a rugged looking piece of handheld military tech. The device was pronged, like a cattle prod. She rammed it into the ice in various places along the wall, collecting data as she went along.

Her voice crackled over the radio. 'Captain, please give me a hand with that orange case?'

Ballard jumped off the side of the large skimmer and proceeded to help Betsie locate and carry a large reinforced case to the edge of the ice wall. They opened it to reveal dozens of little egg-shaped objects. I had seen them before; they were powerful micro-charges, sometimes lovingly referred to as "Little Bastards". I knew enough about them to stay well out of their way.

The first explosion, relatively small, created a cave of sorts. It wasn't meant to clear the ice, but to provide positioning angles for additional Little Bastards. I could see Betsie was enjoying herself as she placed the charges and double-checked her data, clearly in her element.

Eventually she was satisfied and proceeded to herd us far, far back – at least half a kilometre – before finally erecting an impact shelter. The shelter was a magical piece of kit which could fit in a mid-sized suitcase, but when activated expanded to a dome about fifteen metres across. It wouldn't stop large heavy fragments, it wasn't designed for that, but it would buffer any high speed shrapnel and shards bound to fly our way. We huddled inside like a bunch of superstitious cave dwellers.

The next explosion was a rumble more than a blast. A deep vibration felt through the floor, lasting uncomfortably long. I clumsily grabbed Clint's hand, eerily blue in the light of the skimmers' energy units. I couldn't feel much through the fabric of the environment suit but I knew he tried to squeeze my hand in return.

A split second later a barrage of small objects hit the shelter, rippling its surface as if buffeted by a strong wind. Up high, a hole appeared out of nowhere, corresponding with another hole on the far side of the tent. The shelter suddenly seemed flimsy. For a tense moment we were all waiting for a giant fragment to crush us all, or for our habitat segment to break off, carrying us off into space. Then, silence descended on us, and we were too timid to break it.

I took a deep breath and stepped out, the first to emerge from the shelter, eager to see the result of Betsie's work. Debris littered the scene around us – nothing structural and much of it dirty ice fragments. Betsie had blasted an opening akin to an inverted mountain pass: wide at the bottom, narrow at the top, all the way through to the other side. We didn't even need to clear it out. We just mounted our skimmers again and moved on, our first salvage point just ahead.

Betsie put her hand on my helmet, and shook it gently.

'The arm hurts all the time. I'm lucky you didn't break it. Feels like you did actually.'

'Hold off masturbating for a while,' I advised.

Her laughter was hearty and loud, and held for a full minute. Eventually she said, 'Yeah, I was worried about that …' She clapped me on the back, like a high school football jock. 'I'll just have to manage with my other hand.'

I could see J.J. observing us, a little smile on his large face.

We travelled through the breach in silence, high on adrenaline, infected with a sense of elation. The mood in the group was good, better than it had been, until our eyes started to make sense of what was all around us. I heard Clint gasp when it became clear that we were not alone; the ice walls flanking us were riddled with human shapes, some broken, some whole. The dead were looking down on us with envy, wishing they were still alive.

Habitat 6 was a classic Stanford Torus. Inside, a large continuous valley looped in on itself, eventually meant to support conditions close to those on Earth: farmland, forests, lakes, gentle towns … It was a grand plan reminiscent of retro-futurist paintings of torus space stations one could find in old popular science books. The Gaianistas might actually have pulled it off, at least on a technical level, if it hadn't been for Icarus.

Bio-diversity was crucial to the whole endeavour, and the habitat's seed-bank was extensive. Hundreds of crates filled with many thousands of rare seeds of every possible description and type. Not just the predictable grain, corn, fruit & rice strains, but countless exotic flowers and rare trees, bushes and grasses and moss and lichen. There were seeds for lush water plants – salt and freshwater – cacti, herbs. This kind of salvage was the *real* treasure that humanity needed.

For the Gaianistas, the future simply wouldn't have worked without it, but their dream was dead. There were no more Gaianista habitats, while Earth had a current and urgent need. Our mother planet had lost many species of flora to Icarus; our salvage mission was supposed to help her recover some of that.

When we finally arrived at the seed-bank's impressive airlock we all felt tense. It is rare that salvage provides an opportunity to genuinely help others. Were its contents safe?

'It should have its own Blue power,' said Charles. 'One of the few areas on the station to allow it.'

The airlock door was battered, but fully powered. The latter was a good sign, but when Ballard tried to open it the display panel beeped and chirped like an angry hornet.

'It's locked itself off from the rest of the facility,' said Betsie. 'That's a bit of a problem I'm afraid.'

'Why?' Ballard's gruff voice was all business.

'Because it's a protective lock-down. The seed-bank sensors know that the outside is a danger to its contents. And that's not going to change any time soon.'

'Can you muscle in?'

'Sure I can,' said Betsie, impatiently, 'but that seems unwise to say the least. Don't really want to set off heavy charges right next to some of the most valuable crates in the system.'

'Maybe not,' said Ballard.

'OK, please tell me we have a backup plan,' said Kyoshi. 'I'm already bored staring at this stupid door.'

'As long as the seed-bank thinks there's danger outside this door the lock-down stays active,' said Betsie. 'That's just the way it is.'

'What then? Move on? This seeds stuff was the most profitable thing in the damn salvage contract.'

Nobody spoke for a while, unwilling to give up on the opportunity in front of us, but unable to offer any useful suggestions.

Kyoshi sucked his teeth impatiently, and said, 'I say we blow our way in. Take a chance. Betsie can do it.'

'Of course I can do it you imbecile,' she snapped. 'but I don't want to blow the damn seeds up. What if I set off some bigger reaction? What if we lose the whole ring segment? Use your brain for once.'

Kyoshi finally had enough. 'How about you take one of your bomb–'

'Maybe I can trick it?' Clint's voice cut through the argument like a knife. Everybody fell quiet. 'I mean, maybe I can convince the seed-bank that there is no danger?'

'You can do that?' asked Ballard.

'I can try. I just need to trick the environmental sensors. Make it think it's room temperature out here,' he said confidently. 'Or something like that anyway,' Clint stammered quickly, spoiling his air of confidence.

'I don't know …' Ballard said.

'Just let me have a go at looking at its programming. I can't imagine they put up serious counter-measures. I mean, who'd mess with the thing right? I never heard of a Gaianista hacker.'

Kyoshi giggled at the mental image, then turned to Ballard. 'Let the kid have a go. He's got skills. We've seen that already.' He turned back to Clint; 'What do you need for this?'

'Not much, my Padd has some pretty powerful sniffer-ware. I just need to hook it up to the door's display panel. It must be hooked up to the seed-bank's other systems. If it's a two-way link then I should be in business.'

'Waddaya say J.J.?' asked Kyoshi. 'Yay or nay?'

'Be careful,' was Ballard's reply. 'Slow, yes?'

Clint nodded as Kyoshi shouted, 'Take it away kid!'

I didn't get involved with Clint's decision although I wasn't sure I was comfortable with him taking on this kind of responsibility. But, I held back as this was the kind of situation I brought him along for in the first place. *He has a role to play like any other member on the crew.* I chided myself for being too protective. This was exactly the kind of exposure to real salvage problems he needed.

'What's happening kid?' asked Kyoshi.

'Well, I was right, there's not much here to stop me from checking out other systems,' replied Clint. 'Gimme a moment …' Kyoshi walked up behind him to look over his shoulder. Clint's Padd, hooked up with a single wire to the airlock, was running some kind of analytical program. I'd seen him use it before with good results. The Padd's display flashed network data too fast to read. Clint hummed to himself for a spell until the Padd made a loud chiming sound.

'Aaaaaand I'm in,' said Clint.

'Already?' asked Betsie.

'Already,' confirmed Clint. 'Wow, I can get to pretty much everything from here.'

'Can you open it?' asked Kyoshi.

'Jees, gimme a moment dude …' Clint spent some time looking at various sub-systems until he hit upon something he liked. 'This is good. I found the self-diagnostics program. If I run that it'll show us why exactly there's a lock-down to begin with.'

Kyoshi pulled a comical "I'm impressed" face. It was funny even through his visor.

'Won't take a minute …' Clint mumbled. Again his Padd flashed data at him, too fast for me to read. A progress bar slowly expanded across his screen. It took five minutes to complete.

'OK, this is interesting?'

'Be specific Clint,' I admonished. 'We don't know what you're looking at.'

'OK yeah, sorry …'

'So …' I gently prodded.

'Right. The seed-bank thinks there's vacuum outside the airlock. I reckon one of its sensors is kaput. I can probably mark it as defective, and let it run another diagnostic. That should fix it.'

Clint tapped in a few commands. No easy thing to do in his enviro-suit. 'OK, that worked. It's running a new self-diagnostic now … It's gotten past the fault, just like I thought … running other tests … Oh! It's found something else …'

'Come on Kid, spell it out,' snapped Kyoshi.

'Nothing serious though. It thinks the air inside is the wrong mix or something. It's been pumping in pure oxygen to fix it.'

'Oxygen? Pure oxygen?' I asked, suddenly alert.

'Yeah, but it won't affect the airlock I think. I just gotta let it finish and then I can open this baby up. Just a few seconds now …'

I looked at the airlock door in anticipation. Surprised it was still operational considering how battered it was. Then, something clicked in my mind …

'No wait!' I shouted.

It was too late. Clint had given the command.

Lights flashed on the door. The unlock sequence had started.

'Cancel it, now!' I urged.

'I can't. It's gonna open,' said Clint. 'What's the problem anyway?'

I watched the door carefully. Maybe my fear was unwarranted …

A metallic screeching sound filled the air. The door was protesting. My stomach contracted with fear.

'What the …' said Kyoshi, as we felt a deep shudder rippled through the floor, followed by a loud roar.

'Clint?' asked Ballard. His voice nearly drowned out by the roaring coming from the seed-bank.

The screeching stopped. Clint looked confused. 'This … doesn't make sense …, ' he stammered. He looked at me, a question unspoken.

'Temperature spike?' I asked, my fears all but confirmed.

Clint nodded. His shoulders slumped as he reached the same conclusion as me.

'Fire?' Ballard asked, caught up with our train of thought.

'I can't stop it …' Clint whispered. Nobody heard him but me.

'Maybe it will burn out quickly?' I tried to offer hope. 'Once the oxygen is burned up?'

'It won't stop. It's still pumping oxygen into the room … I … I don't know what to do.'

'Somebody please fucking tell me what is going on?' Kyoshi's voice was like a slap in the face. Jarring me awake.

'The door was too damaged. Trying to open it caused some kind of malfunction. Sparks …' I didn't have to finish my sentence.

'In a room full of oxygen …' Kyoshi said.

'And more oxygen pumped in all the time.'

'It's all burning. The temperature is insane in there. Sensors are failing … there's nothing I can do.'

We waited several hours before Betsie blew the airlock. Inside we found hell.

'Look at this shit. Just look at it. It's completely F.U.B.A.R.' Kyoshi kicked a partially melted storage crate, so badly warped that it could have come straight out of a Salvador Dali painting. It slid across the floor into another broken crate, leaving a rising cloud of soot in its wake. 'Oh yeah this is great. This is just fucking great. Look at it.'

We all did. The contents of the seed-bank had been reduced to ashes and slag. Soot was all we could harvest here.

The seed storage chambers must have burned at remarkable temperatures judging by the scene of utter devastation in front of us. Glass, metal, hyper-plastics … all melted down to grotesque and unreal shapes – wax sculptures resembling hideous creatures never before seen by human eyes. I could almost taste the black soot between my teeth. I had to suppress the urge to spit.

I glanced at Ballard, unable to read him. He walked to the

far end of the storage unit where the damage was slightly less extreme, and appeared to be rifling through the ashes.

Clint was devastated. Kyoshi wasn't helping matters with his angry mutterings, but Betsie and Charles were not exactly supportive either.

'I was trying to help,' said Clint. Nobody responded. 'It could have happened to anybody. It was just freakish bad luck.'

'Silence is probably the better option right now,' said Charles. It was a mean thing to say, and it rubbed me the wrong way.

'Oh really?' I said. 'What has your contribution been so far Charles? Clint is right. He tried to help. He got unlucky. It's not his fault.'

Betsie snorted in derision at my words. I had to bite my tongue to stop myself from giving her both barrels. *This was turning into a disaster.*

Ballard finished searching the debris. He'd picked up a round, blackened object. I couldn't make out what it was. He walked back slowly, seemingly lost in thought. When he returned to the group he threw the object at our feet. It was a human skull.

'Is that us?' asked Ballard.

Nobody spoke.

'We're not dead like them?' He pointed vaguely to where we came from. 'Should we give up?'

Nobody knew what to say. This didn't sound like Ballard.

'We go back to the ship? Go home?' Even with our helmets on we could see the intensity in his eyes.

'*I don't think so ...*' he rumbled, and stomped on the skull. It disintegrated, all but disappearing in the ashes below his foot. 'No. We only just got here,' he laughed, but there was no humour in his eyes.'We're a lot better off than the people who used to live here, so stop acting like a bunch of sad teenagers, yes? We are here now, professionals! And we won't leave without something good.'

Two steps brought him next to me, squeezing my shoulders with both hands. It hurt.

'Jemm here knows what to do. She has backup plans,

yes?' I nodded in a daze. He was right, Clint and I had prepared contingency plans and had an ace up our sleeves. 'And so do I,' he continued. 'Tomorrow we look for the farm tools. Good Blue tech! Enough to honour our contract. After that we find our own treasure. Yes?'

The speech was good enough. Maybe not brilliant, but good enough to lift a worsening sense of gloom and fatigue that had stealthily infiltrated the crew, catching us unawares and stealing our enthusiasm.

The setting aided his delivery. He struck an almost iconic figure – a giant, crushing bones into dust.

We did go back to the ship, but only to prepare for the next day, and work on our contingency plans. I couldn't wait to show them what Clint and I had discovered.

Gibson contacted me that night via Padd. The signal was boosted through a private Spectra satellite, secure and encrypted. Such are the things a powerful Corp can do.

'Miss Delaney,' he started. 'I trust your journey wasn't too arduous?'

'It was fine, thank you,' I said. 'Errr, shall we quit the pleasantries for now? I mean, it's nice and all, but I don't want to waste your time.'

Gibson smiled without humour. 'Manners matter Miss Delaney. Without it we aren't much better than savages. But I take your point.'

'Right then. It's too early to report on our contract. Ballard's salvage mission has run into some trouble, and it will take a few days to see if we can compensate. I've made backup plans that should cover any losses, but I need to see if they pan out.'

'How long will this take? I don't want to rush you but …'

'It will take as long as it takes,' I said. 'At least a few days like I said. The terrain here is unpredictable. It could be three days, it could be three weeks …'

'That would be intolerable. Please keep me up to date on progress. If it looks like it will take that long I might just buy out the entire mission, although I don't want to raise those kinds of flags to our competition. If they see us spending such sums of money on a salvage operation they might send their own team in.'

'That would be a serious waste of money and resources. I don't intend to fail.'

'Well, that is why I hired you Miss Delaney. But sadly a man in my position must plan for all eventualities.'

'You do what you must,' I said. 'I'll still bring you your goods, and that's the truth.'

'It's not truth that matters, but victory.' replied Gibson. It had the sound of a quote about it. I made a mental note look it up later.

'I will await your next report with interest,' he continued. 'Goodbye for now.'

I sat in silence for a little while, contemplating the call. Something in Gibson's voice was worrying me, but I couldn't put my finger on it. I wasn't being paranoid; there was always some kind of angle with these types. That was the problem with dealing with Corp execs – they have hidden agendas inside hidden agendas. It was impossible to trust them. Still, I knew that going in, and as there was nothing I could do about it I decided to get some sleep.

We re-entered the habitat the next day. This time we travelled in the opposite direction, towards Section 1, where according to my research, we would find a storage facility for high-tech equipment and parts. In theory we could still satisfy the government contract by salvaging enough specialist gear on a list they gave us, as long as the equipment was Blue-powered. Maybe we had a decent chance at that, but I had another, more ambitious goal in mind.

Our progress was markedly slower. Much of the maintenance boulevard had been badly damaged, and several torus segments were exposed to hard vacuum, forcing us to find alternative routes.

This time I was paired with Charles. Ballard must have recognised that Betsie and I were on better footing, and saw an opportunity for Charles and me to interact.

So far, not much of that was going on: Charles remained mostly silent for the better part of our journey, polite when spoken to but not initiating any conversation himself. For my part I still felt resentful for his remark towards Clint after the fire. I let the silence stretch out to start with, but eventually I grew so bored of this that I tried to draw him out a bit.

'Why are you here Charles? I mean, I'm glad you are, it's good to have a doc on the team, and I'm glad you fixed my nose, but you don't seem like the salvage type to me.' Charles momentarily turned his helmet my way, then resumed his stare ahead.

I cursed under my breath but stuck with it. 'Why aren't you on a low-risk commission instead? I picture you fussing and tutting over scrapes and bruises on high society ladies on some glitzy pleasure yacht. Maybe fussing over them in other ways as well? Handsome feller like you should be able to get noticed by a flush Contessa or maybe a bored diplomat's wife?' Charles didn't bother with a reply but I saw the hint of a smile twitching at the corners of his mouth.

I was about to give up on any chance for decent conversation when he finally asked, 'I suspect that this little endeavour of ours is bound to be a bit of a dud? Likely to yield distinctly underwhelming returns?'

I made a non-committal gesture, encouraging him to keep talking, even if he sounded more reserved than ever.

'Ballard's mission assessment is too optimistic,' said Charles. 'Our government contract is solid enough, at least on paper. It should be easy enough to tick off the fancy equipment on their wish list. Not terribly *exciting* mind you, but guarantees us a decent pay day, even with the rather unfortunate loss of the seed-bank.' Charles held up a hand, indicating he hadn't meant it as a barb. I bit my tongue and let him continue with a curt nod; 'But, the real *gravy* as they say, was supposed to come from the all the nice, *extra* salvage we would manage on the side. A nice enough idea, but, to be frank, when I look around, I see precious little opportunity for that in this sad, sad place.' Charles made an exasperated gesture, made to look slightly ridiculous by the suit, like a mime. 'These people were puritanical fanatics. Not exactly prime candidates for opulence and wealth.' He looked at me again, but this time held my gaze. 'But you already know this of course. Yet here you are nonetheless. I do wonder why.'

He was right. The builders of the Gaianista-Habitats were cultist zealots who had dedicated their lives to creating some kind of neo-primitivist Utopia – allegedly allowing humanity to evolve free from "technological impurities" – and were not known to amass Trickari artifacts, or other more traditional worldly treasures for that matter. I suspected that the deeper we penetrated the structure the clearer it would become that this place was almost barren in terms of salvage opportunities. Charles seemed to have correctly deduced that I had anticipated that. I briefly considered sharing my plans with Charles – he was smart enough to appreciate them – but this wasn't the time.

'I know why I'm here doc. Same as anybody else on the crew. But you didn't really answer my question did you?'

Charles stayed silent, but held eye contact. There was no challenge in it, just enquiry, curiosity. The silence stretched for several heartbeats, ended in a weary sigh; 'It's not complicated,' said Charles. 'I'm here because I'm on Ballard's crew, and he decides where we go and what we salvage. The arrangement offers a certain amount of continuity and camaraderie that I find pleasing, even if the actual expeditions are sometimes … let's say … *below par*.'

Charles unexpectedly lay down on his back as if he was about to take a nap. '*Your* motivations on the other hand Jemm … I am not so sure about. But I trust that whatever you have in mind will be highly entertaining.'

I was wondering how to respond to that when, almost on cue, Ballard signalled us to stop. We had finally arrived.

9

Section 1 was vast. Its hangars, storage bays, and access ramps stretched out in front of us, covering hundreds of metres.

Initially we thought we were in luck. Unlike the seed-bank, this part of the installation was relatively unscathed. Section 1's structural integrity was mostly intact, emergency lighting was still functional, and there was even breathable atmosphere. So far so good ... We got to work, exploring, searching for items on the government contract list as well as anything else worth our while. But soon it became clear that the gargantuan size of this section worked against us. This was the main storage area of all major equipment used on the habitat, and should have been a goldmine of rare Blue devices and valuable Human tech, and in many ways it was just that. The problem was logistical; there was so much equipment that there simply wasn't enough time to check it all against our government contract. Not if we also wanted to find enough salvage for ourselves to make the trip pay off. Nonetheless, we tried – some with more enthusiasm than others.

I was teamed with Betsie again and put in charge of "risk assessment and evaluations". It was slow going. We spent nearly half a day sifting through endless rows of containers and countless stacks of crates. Very little of the unearthed content was worth the effort, but we had to log it all. Soon, Betsie was bored witless, although she tried her best to hide it. I didn't blame her, this was an arduous assignment.

'Living the dream eh?' I joked, trying to lighten the mood.

'It's the light,' she said. 'It's too dim. I mean, it's great to have some light, don't get me wrong, but in a way this is worse than no light at all.' She rubbed her helmet as if it was her head. 'Look, this place is just too big to secure and this shitty dim light is putting me on edge, you know what I mean?'

'Yeah I do. That's an occupational hazard for you I guess?' There was no reply but I assumed she nodded in her helmet.

Feeling Betsie's unease I peered deep into the distance. We could see remarkably far, but the murky dim light took away so much visual detail that it was easy to imagine sinister shapes gathering on the edge of our visibility range.

'It's not the cheeriest place,' I said. 'That's obvious at least.'

Betsie had gone quiet again. I took the opportunity to observe her discreetly. I was getting better at reading her body language. Something was bothering her; she seemed angry.

'Look Betsie, Clint was just unlucky. You have to admit it was impressive how quickly he hacked the seed-bank systems.'

'That's not it.'

'There's an it?' I sighed.

'J.J. told me about your father.' She threw me a quick glance, then continued. 'That explains your training at least.'

'At least?'

'Why didn't you tell me?'

'Tell you what?'

'How you got your training. How your father betrayed his Corp. How you got to work for Spectra.'

I sighed, 'It's none of your damn business. That's why.'

'I'm in charge of security. It very much *is* my business.'

'Well, now you know.' I shrugged. 'Anything else?'

'Plenty.' Betsie stopped working, and walked up to me. 'You're holding out on us. I can tell.'

'Don't be silly. Holding out how?' I raised both my hands in a mock confused gesture. 'Why?'

'You know why.' She pointed at nothing in particular. 'This. There's nothing worth much here. But somehow, you're smiling all the time. It doesn't add up.'

Betsie was perceptive. I had done OK on the government contract so far – scored some decent Blue-powered portable landscaping tools and farming equipment – but, truth be told, most of what we found was substandard stuff. All bulk, and little resale value.

I glanced around the huge space. The crew weren't stupid. They knew this wasn't going their way, and they were getting restless. Betsie was just the first to vocalise their collective frustration. After Clint's mishap our credit was running low. It was almost time to go to plan B.

For the next two hours Betsie and I worked in silence, sorting through the remainder of the items in our assigned storage bay. Our fortunes didn't improve.

Eventually Ballard and the rest of the crew showed up to check on our progress, which I took as a sign that they weren't doing any better. Betsie ran them through our list of items, occasionally glancing my way, still annoyed. As expected the rest of the crew hadn't fared any better.

'Our Xeno is awfully quiet isn't she?' said Betsie. 'I thought she was supposed to be our golden ticket?' It came out in an ugly sneer, probably more so than she intended. This place was getting to her. Clint, picking up on her hostility, moved closer to me, subconsciously looking for protection. I suppressed the urge to put my arm around him.

'Don't start Betsie, I'm not in the mood,' said Ballard. His shoulders drooped just a tiny bit, but enough to broadcast his sense of disappointment. Kiyoshi avoided our eyes, looking embarrassed, as if he had caught his parents arguing. Charles however had perked up, a look of anticipation on his face.

'Oh but that's about to change, isn't it Jemm?' he said.

I ignored everyone but Ballard and switched to a

private channel. 'Captain, may I have a word?' Ballard nodded, then took me aside, away from the others. It used to be considered rude to talk privately while in the company of others. I admired him for honouring such an old-fashioned custom.

'What's the mystery?' asked Ballard. 'This kind of chat doesn't look good to the rest of the crew, no?' He sounded tired. His grammar slipped when he was.

'Good news or bad news first?' I said with a smile.

'Good news. Please.'

'Well, I have a terrific lead that will save your bacon and will make you the hero of the crew.'

'Really? I'm already their hero, I thought? Well … sometimes.' He laughed softly, his mood improving. 'OK, yes. Tell me more.'

'Clint and I want to go to the crew quarters. There is serious Blue salvage to be found.' I paused a moment, but he didn't speak. 'It will be good,' I offered.

Ballard looked doubtful. 'We looked into that ourselves, it's no good,' he said, bitterly disappointed. 'These people … They were extremists. No Blue allowed for personal use. Hardly any luxuries … There's nothing there.'

'Yeah that's the general consensus among Xenos as well. Good thing our research is a bit more in-depth than other people's.'

I stepped closer to him, so we could clearly see each other's faces behind the helmet's glass. 'Listen, the Gaianista's may have been extremists, but they were human beings nonetheless, the same as every other member of the damn species. Everybody *always* make that mistake … to forget that people do what people do.

'Clint and I worked together on this for a long time, and we found that, like in most cults, Gaianista leaders were as hypocritical and corrupt as all so-called leaders have been throughout human history. It's a natural consequence of being in a position of power.

'Anyway, we reached the conclusion that the elites on this installation were unlikely to have chosen a life of pious modesty. They never do, right?'

'This is true, but these people were very strict.' Ballard absentmindedly tried to scratch the chin hiding somewhere in his beard, but forgot he was wearing a helmet.

I carried on. 'Once we figured that out we did some research into which Gaianista top dogs had been assigned to this particular installation, ran their names against the client databases of major auction houses of that era – one of Clint's ideas that was – and soon enough we honed in on a very promising lead. It turned out that the habitat's operation manager "Mr. Johnson", used to go by a slightly different name: "Mr. Johansen". Interestingly, Mr. Johansen had been a committed gun collector before he turned Gaianista. We suspected that he had sneakily kept up with his little hobby.'

I now firmly had Ballard's attention, and beamed him a big smile.

'No wait, it gets better. Even back then it was impossible to buy Blue gear without a background check, and Clint's database handily lists all the *actual names* of buyers. Guess what we found?'

'Johansen was on the list?' asked Ballard.

'And then some. Our hunch was right. Mr Johansen had purchased many many valuable pieces over the years, and crucially, kept doing so even after he got that good ole religion. He also had many containers shipped to this facility, which was easy for him to do because he was the operations manager.'

'And you think ...' Ballard didn't have to finish his sentence.

'Of course he did. And we know where his personal quarters are. Clint already plotted several possible routes to get us there. It will take at least a day of travel, maybe more depending on environmental damage, but it could be a huge haul.'

Ballard chewed on this for a moment, feeling his way towards a decision.

'And the bad news?' He asked.

'The bad news is that all routes take us past the Spectra

Vision facility, and you signed a contract that expressly forbids you to share their dirty little secret with the crew. Me and Clint are the only people on this station who are allowed to go near it.'

This prompted more vigorous chin scratching, but the final outcome of his deliberations was never in doubt. 'OK, I like your story. Pack some supplies. We'll need two skimmers. I will tell the crew you're going on a research mission, but that I need them to keep working here, in case it's no good.' He stopped scratching his chin, and put a big hand on my shoulder. 'I will come with you. This is clear, yes?'

'Wouldn't have it any other way.'

Our journey to the Crew Quarters was probably the hardest one I had attempted in my career. They were located in Torus Section 37, dangerously far from the *Effervescent*. Although we could retrace our steps along the path of our initial expedition, we couldn't use the maintenance corridor far beyond the seed-bank – there were simply too many damaged sections in between us and our target.

En route I could kill two birds with one stone by passing the Science Labs Section – the target for the Spectra-Vision contract.

I had some initial doubts about taking Clint along, especially now that his confidence had taken a knock, but with Ballard with us for support I felt it was a manageable risk. It was probably best for him to get straight back on that horse.

To be fair to him, Clint performed extremely well, clearly on his best behaviour. After the devastation of the seed-bank we were wary of further setbacks, but to my relief the path to the Science Labs was relatively straightforward. It took us no more than half a day to get there.

The area was very different to the other sections we had seen so far. The corridors were of a slick design, curving gracefully, painted bright red – a far cry from the grey and functional access corridors we had seen before. A bewildering array of signs and notices warned of dangerous substances and equipment. Acronyms were plentiful.

Our skimmers cast their blue light on the crimson walls as we silently made our way through. Spectra's lab would be somewhere deep inside this warren of labs and science personnel quarters.

'That's it, look', said Clint, pointing at a large corridor spinning off around a corner. 'Look at that sign.'

Some Gaianista worker must have had a sense of humour; there was an access door featuring a painted sign depicting a large staring eye. The writing underneath read:

> Vision Scan – Qualified Personnel Only.
>
> Wear Protective Goggles!

It was clearly a dig at Spectra-Vision.

Clint jumped off the skimmer and approached the door. I followed him.

'Doable?' I asked. The door looked impressive, and blinking lights indicated that it was still receiving power.

'Uh huh. Just need to hook up Spectra's little magic genie.'

'Want to do it now? Make sure?'

'Nah, I don't want to set off any counter-measures. We may only get one chance at this. We'll do it when we can finish what we start.'

'We?'

Clint picked up the menace in my voice, but tried to ignore it. 'Come on mum, you know it makes sense, I know how to get us in.'

'We're not having this talk again,' I sighed. 'Just open the door, and I'll get back here on my own later on. I told you, I don't want you exposed to this mission. It's not safe.'

'Oh, but dragging me half way across the station to some guy's weapon's cache is *safe*?'

'You know what? You're doing a good job convincing me that it's not. Maybe I should take you back to the others. You can help them with crate counting duty. Or better yet, take you back to the ship, where it's really safe in our quarters.' We faced off for a moment, equally stubborn, but ultimately the decision was mine. I just needed Clint to acknowledge this, but threatening to send him to his room did nothing to temper his mood.

'Open the door Clint, we need to get on.' said Ballard. He made it sound more reasonable than me. 'A good crewman knows when to follow orders, yes?'

Realising that he would get precisely nowhere by being stubborn, Clint went to work with Spectra's Key-Pass. About fifteen minutes later the door made a sound and unlocked itself.

'There,' Clint pouted. 'Don't complain when you get stuck at the next door down.'

'Come on,' Ballard said, and gently pushed Clint forward. 'Let's get going OK?'

Clint complied, not that he had much choice in the matter.

The maintenance corridor showed increasing signs of damage – some of it severe. Ballard and I exchanged frequent worried looks, enough for Clint to pick up on it.

'OK, so how bad is it?' he said eventually, causing Ballard to snigger.

'It's not good,' I said, wondering how much further we could go.

When we reached the next section of the station we found it collapsed, as was the subsequent one as far as we could tell. The maintenance corridor was blocked by debris for the next few sections at least, rendering it useless to us.

'So … now what?' asked Clint. 'This was pretty much the best route I could find.'

Ballard replied, 'We have to go inside the Habitat itself, try to reach the far side of the torus. That's where the civilian boulevards are. It's far from here but if we can reach it it should be easy to get to section 37.'

'Clint?' I asked, looking for confirmation.

'Well, yeah that makes sense,' he said, 'There's very little damage on that side of the habitat according to Jeb's reports. It's worth a shot I guess? But we have to travel across and I have no idea how bad it gets inside the Habitat itself.'

'Do you want to take Clint back?' asked Ballard. 'We can try again tomorrow, just you and me, yes?'

I glanced at both of them, wondering what to do, before making a decision.

'Clint can do it. Isn't that right Clint?' I said.

'I want to come! I mean, I can do it,' Clint hurriedly agreed.

Over the rest of the day we ground out an arduous path through broken forests, destroyed gardens and devastated rural fields. The terrain was as difficult as it was varied. We travelled mostly in near-darkness, with little upfront knowledge of the damage we would encounter on the ground. Although there was no structural damage inside the torus there was utter devastation from neglect and decay. Our progress was slow.

Ballard proved to be a formidable travel companion. Nothing seemed to phase him, be it difficult physical challenges or logistic puzzles, he always attacked the problem head on until we defeated it. He kept good cheer through the most arduous of tasks, lifting both Clint's and my spirits on multiple occasions. That was until we reached a large hydroponics installation, where it became clear that even Ballard could crack.

The hydroponics facility was relatively intact, at least structurally. The terrain wasn't too hard to navigate so we pressed on. Clint was some way behind us, happy to let Ballard and me handle reconnaissance.

Frozen debris surrounded us, complicating progress

occasionally, but the solar backup systems provided a modest level of illumination even here, allowing us to proceed at a steady pace. At times we had to walk, our skimmers following us like docile beasts of burden. I could feel ice crunch under the boots of my enviro-suit, bringing back childhood memories of walking on fresh snow, leaving deep prints. Ice particles sparkled a gentle golden colour, happily animated by our torchlight, flickering like out-of-place Christmas decorations. I imagined our skimmer was our sled, half expecting to hear "Jingle Bells" at any moment now. It was a ridiculous thought, but one that lifted my spirits considerably in the gloomy environment.

Ballard, conversely, had slowly become quieter and more sullen as we travelled. I caught him throwing furtive glances at our surroundings. When I followed his gaze I noticed various odd things around us. On inspection disturbing details slowly revealed themselves. There was graffiti on the walls. Angry slogans, expressions of despair, furious questions aimed at Gaianista leaders … The writing was somehow *wrong* – full of small grammatical errors, yet made more human and affecting as a result. There was evidence of impromptu campfires, lit on the cold metal floor. Somebody had lived here …

Clint, having caught up with us, pointed at one of the campfire sites. Half covered by some frozen blankets lay an old sturdy Padd. It was covered in rime and dust, but looked undamaged otherwise.

'I bet I can hack that thing you know?' said Clint.

'Why?' asked Ballard, unusually brief.

'Why? Because it may contain useful data? Because it might help us with our mission? I won't know until I try it right?'

Ballard stiffened at Clint's tone. For a moment I thought Clint was in for it, but Ballard relaxed his stance. 'OK, let me know what you find,' he said. 'You can do it while we keep moving, yes?'

'Yep, just gimme a few minutes.'

We carried on in silence. Some plants and flowers still stood upright, their frozen fingers defiantly reaching out to us, while we walked across the remains of their shattered kin.

Hydroponics was a larger section of the habitat than I imagined. It was hard to get to grips with the scale of the Gaianista station. Everything was built to service a large population, with redundancy buffers built in. It all counted for nothing in the end.

'You guys, this is a diary.' Clint's voice made me jump. 'Some woman called April?' he continued. 'I think she worked here. Worked with the plants and flowers … It's quite sweet really. Most of it is too damaged to read, but there's some stuff here that might be useful. Lemme clean it up and I'll send it to your comms.'

Ballard said softly, 'This isn't right. Maybe we shouldn't do this.' Clint didn't reply, unsure about his mood. We fell quiet again, together in person, but alone with our thoughts.

I was amazed at how well preserved much of Hydroponics was. There were still many operational lights high above us and among the countless rows of crops. In some places entire sections of vegetation appeared as if they had merely suffered a strong night-frost. Occasionally we saw further evidence of a survivor: more impromptu camps, more messages scrawled on walls and floors. I tried to ignore it as much as I could, eerie though it was.

A chiming sound indicated that Clint had sent us the contents of the diary. I was about to thank him when Ballard said, 'Reading personal diaries, going after this man Johansen's personal things … This is … without respect.'

'Respect? The dead don't care about respect,' I replied. 'Be more concerned about the living.' Perhaps I spoke too harshly, but I meant it.

I checked on Clint to make sure that he was OK, then switched back to a private channel with Ballard. 'It's going to be worth it. We can't help the poor souls that died here but we can help ourselves, and we can help people on Earth.'

'You are here to help people? Is that what you want to do?' said Ballard, his voice dripping with sarcasm.

'I want to help my son,' I bit back. 'And for that I need to earn enough money to buy a ship. That doesn't make me a monster, so why don't you back off with shit like that.'

'It's good to have a ship. I know this, yes? But this … this is not how I earned mine. Not this … stealing from the dead.'

'Bull shit. This is no different from anything else you've done before.' *Where was this coming from?* I thought.

I tried a more positive tone, 'Look, I get it. This is a tough one, but we just have to push through.'

After that Ballard retreated into silence, which was fine by me.

We drudged on without further talk until we found the exit door an hour later. It was in emergency lock-down mode, still waiting for a security code to release it from its final command.

'Well, that sucks,' said Clint.

'Quite,' I agreed.

The door was enormous. More of a bunker door than a regular exit. There was no way we would be able to get through it by force.

'We'll have to backtrack, find a way around hydroponics. Maybe find a different exit,' I said trying to stay positive.

'That will take many hours, yes?'

'Well, yes, but …'

'But it's the way it is?' suggested Ballard.

'It is what it is. Not what we want it to be.'

Ballard turned around, ready to turn back. I turned my skimmer around, ready to follow him.

'Whoa people, wait,' said Clint. 'We can't just give up?'

'Well, unless you have the passcode ...' I offered.

'I might be able to find it. I saw a terminal about ten minutes back. It still looked active. Maybe I can bypass the door from there?'

'I don't know ...,' rumbled Ballard. I could tell he was still upset about Clint's mistake with the seed-bank. It wasn't fair, but I could see why.

'Just let me try,' pleaded Clint. 'It won't take long. And you guys can help too.'

'How?' asked Ballard.

'Read that diary I sent you. Sometimes people write passwords down. Maybe the code is in there?' It was a long shot, but not an unreasonable idea.

'J.J.? Your call ...'

Ballard turned back to the exit door for a moment. It managed to make him look small. He squared his shoulders, looked up at the offending door and as if accepting a challenge said;

'You have one hour.'

Clint only had to be told once. He hurried back the way we came, excited to be given a chance to help. Eager to prove himself.

I pulled up the diary on the visor of my enviro-suit. Most of the content was corrupted – scrambled beyond recognition, its meaning forever lost in the past. But some sections had survived. The diary had belonged to a woman called April, a worker in the hydroponic gardens. I started reading, soon drawn into the surviving segments:

***

```
9w*8**_xX%%$h9 APRIL
<_-I9%"fCC/-in my work. I never thought
I'd find such joy in working with
plants. Maybe this will all work=_
(iIii*8gvv.>
```

TUESDAY 11 APRIL
Lira drew me a picture. It showed all
three of us surrounded by flowers in a
green field. The sun was blue and the
sky purple, but that only made the
picture nicer. She no longer draws Earth
scenes.

She drew James with his head on fire.
Funniest thing ever! James praised her
through gritted teeth. Hah! I cracked up
when she shouted "CHEER UP DAD!" at him.

Maybe she's finally settling in.

THURSDAY 13 APRIL
Dammit I spoke too soon. Lira has been
crying all day, holding that stupid
rabbit toy. (Will she ever get rid of
it?)

The native kids bully her because
they're so much taller than her. It's
not fair, just because they were born
here in lower gravity doesn't make them
better. The stupid thing is that Lira is
way stronger than all of them and could
easily kick their asses from here till
Tuesday. I guess I shouldn't tell her
that but I get so mad. Can't stand
bullies.

James is no use at all at the moment.
All he cares about right now is managing
supply ships. He's angling for
promotion. Can't even get him to play
with his own daughter.

MONDAY 27 MAY
James is freaking me out. He keeps
talking about Red tech failing on other
colonies. I thought we joined the
Gaianistas to get away from all this
shit? How can it be a problem here? We
have almost no Trick-tech? I should look
into it I guess but I'm too scared. What
if it's true? What about Lira?

Oh god … I just realised our sun is Red.

TUESDAY 11 JUNE
This thing with Lira is getting out of
control. She was already scared enough
with those bullies harassing her all the
time but now she thinks the station will
explode soon. Thing is, she keeps hiding
in hydroponics. It's so big in there …
one day she'll fall or have an accident
and she won't be able to get help.

Why did we come here? I hate this place.

THURSDAY 17 JUNE
It's true. Goddammit it's true. Red tech
is failing all over the Solar System.
Everybody is talking about it. But no
word from our "esteemed" leaders. Scared
of losing their precious "Pure Humans" I
guess. But if this is really happening
then we need to evacuate as soon as
possible.

FRIDAY 18 JUNE
I keep hearing about people leaving the

station. Funnily enough it's always the higher-ups. Station managers, bureaucrats, politicians. God I hate them.

Even here on our little Gaianista paradise leaders are just out for themselves.

SUNDAY 20 JUNE
I had a massive row with James. I was suddenly sick of him scaring Lira all the time. What's the point if we can't get off this cursed station? And then he tells me he can sneak her off in a supply ship! He's been preparing it for weeks!

So I had to swallow my anger and send Lira away with him. I hate myself so much now, but what else could I do? I want my little girl to have a life … to have a future …

I don't think the station will last much longer. I can feel weird tremors. People are starting to panic. I don't feel panic, but I think we'll all die soon.

Why am I not afraid?

***

The entries ended there. Presumably they were her last recorded words. I had no idea what had happened to her; maybe she had died, or maybe she had escaped. Although that seemed unlikely.

The diary contained a picture of her daughter Lira; a lovely little girl with a stubborn jaw. I guessed she was about ten years old. It sounded like she had gotten out just in time. It was the first time since arriving on the station that I could feel good about the fate of one of the inhabitants.

'No code,' I said to Ballard.

'No code,' he agreed.

We prepped our skimmer, ready to travel back the way we came, when Clint called us over the radio.

'Mum, J.J., can you come over here please?' I could tell immediately that something was wrong.

I raced back, cursing myself for not keeping Clint close to me. Furiously scanning the hydroponics bays I couldn't see any trace of him. Panic got hold of me, shaking me hard until I was literally running on instinct. Panting, nearly hyperventilating, I looked for him everywhere. My mind raced, thinking unspeakable thoughts. *What have I done?*

I stopped for a moment to catch my breath. I had lost my bearings. While I tried to reorient myself Ballard caught up with me. I saw movement, a torch beam just behind some frozen rows of grapes. We rushed towards the light source.

Clint sat on the floor, surrounded by graffiti. He had found the author of the scribbled messages: a little girl, maybe ten years old, frozen dead. I recognised Lira immediately. She was partially covered by makeshift blankets. A pathetic looking rabbit toy lay by her side. Lira must have been stuck here on her own for a while, before the cold got to her.

'Mum … We can't leave her like this,' said Clint. He didn't know what to do with himself.

I didn't reply, but awkwardly tried to put my arms around him in a clumsy attempt to offer comfort. The suit rendered the gesture all but useless.

'Come on let's go,' I said softly. 'We can't help her now.' I made to leave, but Ballard stopped me.

'Your son is right. We have to do something.'

'There's nothing we can do for her J.J. Don't you get it? We're alive, she's dead.' I tried to walk past him, but he pushed me back. Not hard, but with enough force to make me consider my next actions carefully.

Ballard rasped, 'This is my mission. My responsibility.'

'You're not responsible for her. She is–'

'Enough!' Ballard shouted, his voice distorted over the radio channel. 'Tell me what to do *one more time* and I will lock you up for the rest of this cursed expedition.' He stood over me, shaking with fury, daring me to say a word. My mouth gaped open like a gutted fish, until I shut it with a wet snap.

Satisfied with my silence Ballard told Clint to get a flare from the skimmer. While Clint was away Ballard collected a pile of blankets and subsequently wrapped Lira in a cocoon of cloth. When he was done nothing remained of her shape; she had been transformed into a curious creature inside a chrysalis pod – but she would never emerge.

Ballard lit the flare, and threw it at her feet. He made a sound that I couldn't identify, something between singing and crying. I had no idea what it meant. After a few minutes Ballard quieted down, and spoke in a language unknown to me. If he said a prayer or some kind of eulogy I never found out.

We didn't leave until the flare died, sputtering and hissing in the gloom.

Clint found an active terminal soon after, and managed to open the giant exit door with little effort.

After hydroponics something in Ballard had changed. He had found new determination, and it powered us forward with an energy and zeal that bordered on relentless. We saw many other dead people, but they didn't have the same impact on Ballard as the girl in hydroponics had.

We rested in a sports park, completely empty. I guess people weren't interested in fitness while their entire world fell to pieces around them. We slept a few much needed hours in our suits, tired beyond description but determined to carry on.

The next day was easier; there was a long stretch of farm land that posed few difficulties, and we soon reached the civilian boulevard at the opposite side of the torus. Mercifully there was little damage, and we arrived at our final destination three hours later. Section 37; home to personnel offices and crew quarters, and hopefully Mr. Johnson's personal collection of illegal weapons.

Contemplating our plan suddenly made it seem desperately far-fetched, but we were here now, and we had work to do. This is what I was good at.

A featureless grey corridor gave access to a number of identical doors. A sign indicated that there were twenty residential spaces here, but there was no indication of who they belonged to.

'Any idea where to start? These all look the same to me,' I asked Clint.

'There's no way to know really,' he said. 'Gaianistas were supposedly super egalitarian. No special treatment for some jobs over others, so Johanson's could be any of these. We'll have to check them all until we find the right one.'

'And how will we know which one is the right one?'

'Dunno, just keep our eyes open I guess?'

It was as good an answer as any, so we got started. We did a quick sweep of each apartment, then searched more thoroughly until the owner's identity became clear, after which we moved onto the next apartment.

They were all depressingly nondescript, offering bare-boned functionality over any aesthetic comfort. Gaianista egalitarianism turned out to be extremely boring in practice. The former occupants must have secretly agreed because we soon discovered that many residents had created small private shrines, filled with trinkets and memorabilia. Little hints of individuality which they weren't allowed to flaunt in public, yet too precious to do without. One can't suppress humanity – *People do what people do,* I reminded myself.

We discovered a particularly interesting, if tacky, example of this inside somebody's hidden cabinet. It was filled with terrible erotic art and questionable books. Clint eagerly told Ballard about our last auction result, earning him a hearty laugh. I joined in their mirth even though I felt a bit guilty for laughing at someone's private passion, but we really needed the comic relief.

Ballard surprised me by showing a real knack for finding these private treasures, which he put to good use while we searched the contents of each new apartment. He was amassing a nice little hoard. It was encouraging, but 22nd century collectibles and knick-knacks would only take us so far. We needed to find the real thing.

The 6th apartment we entered was similar to the others, and we located some hidden pockets of valuables soon enough. But this collection was different from the others, with a focus on small toy guns and miniature replicas of weaponry. Our suspicions were confirmed when Ballard found an old photograph hidden in the pages of a small real-book about 19th century pistols. It portrayed Mr. Johnson posing with an exotic rifle.

'This is our guy,' I said with relief.

Clint whooped loudly, unable to contain himself.

'See J.J.?' I said. 'We just needed to keep the faith.'

But Ballard wasn't impressed. After glancing around Johnson's quarters for a few minutes he said, 'Is this it? Toy guns, a few books?' irritation shimmering around his words like angry hornets.

'We just got here J.J. Give it a chance,' I replied.

'Chances run out yes? There is nothing here.'

'It's here. There's nowhere else it *can* be. Johnson wouldn't dare hide his stash where others could easily find it.'

'You know this for sure? How?'

'Just let me think for a moment,' I said. 'Obviously he would hide his real collection extremely well. If anybody would find it he would have been expelled, or worse, so why don't you back off for a moment so I can think?'

Ballard's temper was set to flare up again. 'I warned you not to tell me what to–'

'Oh shut up,' Clint sneered, shocking both Ballard and myself into silence. 'Wait here.' He walked away brusquely, and I couldn't suppress a giggle.

Ballard's scowl dropped, and he laughed, 'He's your boy alright.'

Clint came back only moments later, carrying a little case and a Padd. He opened the case, and retrieved the Trickari artifact his father had given him for his birthday. Next, he studied the Padd's screen carefully. It showed a floorplan.

'These are the original drawings used to build these quarters …' He walked through the apartment, knocking on walls, comparing what he saw to the drawings on his Padd. 'If something is off …' He didn't finish his sentence, but we knew what he was getting at. He continued walking through the apartment, trying to find discrepancies.

'Bathroom OK … not a good place anyway. Bedroom seems legit …'

'No wait!' I said. 'The wardrobe …' Every apartment we had seen contained a walk-in wardrobe, but this one seemed different. I stepped inside, and touched the back wall. It featured a polished metal mirror, but so did some of the others. I ran out, back to the previous apartment – it was the same configuration, but the wardrobe seemed just a touch deeper. When I returned to Mr. Johnson's bedroom Clint had produced the Trickari cube. He was slowly, methodically moving it along the back wall of the wardrobe. Ballard looked on with a bewildered expression behind the helmet's glass.

'What is that, Clint,' he asked.

Clint replied, 'I'm not sure if this will work. Just let me try a bit longer.'

'Jemm?' Ballard's questioning voice had a lost quality to it.

'It's supposed to activate when close to other artifacts,' I said. 'It works, but I have no idea how reliable it is, or how much range– ' The cube flashed several times – faint, but clear enough in the darkness of the room. 'Slow down, Clint, do that spot again.' The flash returned, then turned into a blue pulse, strong enough to illuminate the entire bedroom.

'There's something there alright,' I said, 'but how do we get to it?'

Ballard approached the back wall, presumably to regain some control over the situation. After a short inspection he removed the clothes rail which crossed the entire wardrobe, creating space and clearing our line of sight. Nothing jumped out at us but we could at least see clearly now. I swept the interior with my torch, finding two small clasps on the right hand wall, perpendicular to the mirror. They were hard to manipulate through the padding of the enviro-suit, but once I managed to turn them the entire back wall slid effortlessly away.

'Open Sesame!' I said.

We were rewarded with a glass trophy cabinet that measured approximately three metres wide, by two metres high. Inside, like strange eggs inside a crystal nest, we found a weapons collection of impressive scope and firepower.

There were several very valuable historical pieces – iconic weapons from Earth's violent history up to the 21st century, but the top of the cabinet revealed the most lustrous items in the collection: seven Blue-powered weapons. Five were of human design, but two were *actual* Trickari weapons, an extremely rare proposition.

Ballard's eyes lit up like twin sunrises. Taken together these weapons added up to several fortunes. We were looking at life-changing wealth for every crew member of the *Effervescent*.

After loading up the skimmer we travelled in silence. A strange subdued mood had settled over all of us, despite the shocking success of our mission. Exhaustion was starting to bite, as none of us had slept beyond a few stolen hours during the last few days. Nonetheless, retracing our steps was relatively easy now that we had forged a path, and we returned to Section 1 in less than a day.

Ballard gathered everybody, sharing the news of our find. The crew took the news with varying levels of excitement; Charles chuckled to himself, mildly amused by some private observation. Kyoshi was predictably over the top in his celebrations, going as far as to try and hug Betsie and myself, receiving some painful bruises in response, which did nothing to calm him down. Betsie underplayed our success and tried to tell Ballard about the items they found while we were gone. She found it hard to make herself heard over the excitement.

When everybody finally quieted down it became clear that the government contract was largely fulfilled, and that they had collected a much better than anticipated haul of additional items. Against all odds both strands of the salvage had done well.

Kyoshi could not contain himself. He laughed, 'We have to celebrate. It's a ehm … It's *a moral imperative.*'

'Careful with the big words now Kyoshi. You're not used to that kind of thing,' said Betsie.

'Yeah yeah, I bet you'll be more impressed when I share my best whiskey with you. Or maybe *that kind of thing* is beneath you?'

'No, no, I'm perfectly willing to slum it with the likes of you, on this one occasion at least.'

It was the most relaxed I had seen the crew since boarding the *Effervescent*. Their mood was infectious; I felt the subdued atmosphere that had settled over me dissolve, like morning fog chased away by sunrise. I felt compelled to join in.

'I'll have some of that whiskey,' I said. 'I can give you all the rundown on how we found the stuff.'

Images of the dead girl in hydroponics briefly flashed before my eyes. I would tell her story too. 'It's quite a tale,' I said.

Kyoshi raised an imaginary glass to me and Clint. 'Please do. And the pup can have a soda.'

Clint sputtered, 'I can have a beer, tell him mum!' which set off everybody – even Charles.

Ballard once again showed he was a shrewd captain by giving everybody the rest of the cycle off and calling for a mandatory celebration onboard the *Effervescent*. Nobody needed to be told twice.

We all freshened up, took some stims to ward off the worst of our exhaustion, and dived into Kyoshi's case of "his best whiskey", which was in truth decidedly average, but perfect for the occasion nonetheless. When everybody had settled in I told the story of our journey, warts and all, including our experience in hydroponics. For a moment, thinking of the girl's lonely death, I thought I would choke up but I managed to force myself through the telling of it. We owed her that at least.

I even explained how Clint and I got our intel in the first place. Not something I would normally do, but I was damn proud of what we achieved. The only part I left out was finding the Spectra Labs.

The party went on for a long time, and I enjoyed hearing stories of previous salvage operations from the rest of the crew. They were an interesting bunch – I almost felt part of their experience. I could easily imagine working with them again.

As the night progressed most of us got satisfyingly drunk. Even Clint sipped a beer or two, quietly growing up in front of me.

10

I woke up to a sickening feeling of dread tugging at my mind. *Something was wrong.* A glance at Clint's bunk confirmed my fears. It was empty. Looking at his workstation I could tell that some of our gear was missing, as was the Spectra-Vision Key-Pass.

I got dressed as fast as I could, ignoring the adrenaline cramps wracking my stomach as my mind contemplated disaster. Panic took hold of me, shook me, sending icy tendrils into my brain. *Why, Clint? Why do this?*

I raced to the cargo hold, already knowing what I would find. The ship was now familiar enough to me to navigate on instinct, and to this day I have no recollection of how exactly I got there, but I will never forget how I felt when I arrived.

A small skimmer was missing, as well as Clint's enviro-suit. *I knew exactly where he was going.*

I wrestled into my own suit, halting momentarily to calm myself down, then jumping into the driver's seat of the other small skimmer. Waiting at the airlock gave me time to gather my thoughts: I had been asleep for six hours. Not a lot of time to penetrate Spectra's lab. *I might still reach him.*

The suit's radio range was limited, but I tried to reach him anyway. 'Clint please… This is a bad plan. Wait for me and we'll go in together.' Static hiss was the only response.

For the next hour I kept trying to reach him, sounding more and more desperate on each attempt. I heard a kind of madness in my voice – tremulous words with ragged edges and raw overtones. My journey was a blur.

When I arrived at the labs I found the Vision Scan access door open; he had already entered the Spectra facility. All I had to do now was to find the main lab.

I wandered the lab corridors for what seemed like

hours, but must have been mere minutes. Everywhere I looked I found Spectra's corporate logo – an eye rendered in the colours of the rainbow – looking down on me, unblinking, seeing right through me.

When I finally found the main laboratory complex its main airlock door was left open. It measured inches thick, steel bolts and advanced security scanners must have once made it a formidable barrier. There were auto-guns bolted to the flanking corridor walls – guardian weapons, left drooping and inert, as if ashamed.

The corridor beyond the door was starkly lit, the walls a clinical, dull white interrupted by two saturated lines, one orange, and one blue. I followed the orange line, some vague memory of Corp colour theory guiding me.

As I penetrated deeper into the complex the corridors appeared well lit – the complex must have its own energy source. Considering how long ago it had been abandoned it was likely a potent Blue energy core, probably extremely valuable. With a loud curse I chided myself for still thinking in terms of evaluating salvage, even under these circumstances.

As I got deeper into the complex I was struck by how pristine the surroundings were. The walls appeared freshly painted white. The floor looked like it had just been waxed. It seemed like people could show up for work at any moment – a disconcerting thought.

My musings were silenced when I reached the next airlock door. It stood gaping wide, a wave of corpses spilling out into the corridor – a sudden abundance of death. There were at least twelve bodies, desiccated and warped into grotesque shapes over the many years since their demise, their faces wearing the grinning rictus smile of death. Considering the rate of decay of the bodies I figured all must have died at the same time. No wounds were apparent.

Clint must have stepped over them to make his way deeper into the facility and I briefly felt pride for his tenacity, replaced by a dull, useless resentment that he went without my permission.

Finally I arrived at what seemed to be one of the main Spectra labs. I entered a cavernous, oval space, at least seventy metres deep by forty metres wide. Emergency lights painted everything a sickly red colour, making the walls appear as if they were bleeding. Somebody or something had triggered an alarm.

It was dim, severely restricting my vision, making it hard to distinguish details. I moved slowly and carefully through the space to catch my bearing, aided by the glow of two dozen or so workstations, splashing small pools of light around themselves. Blue oases in a desert of red.

I still saw no sign of Clint.

A large central workstation caught my eye. A pulsing light indicated that its systems were active. I approached slowly, both curious and afraid of what I would find.

Clint had been there … His deck was plugged into the work station, running some kind of scrambler protocol. I had seen this before; it was a powerful counter-measure program he had written last year.

As I was trying to figure out what system Clint had been trying to suppress, the red emergency lights flickered, once, twice … before the main lights were abruptly restored. Screens came alive all through the lab. A soft hum permeated the air, intensified, then died away. The sound of a door closing came from the far side of the lab. It was the entrance to the neighbouring lab, Clint's likely destination, now locked. I cursed loudly, then had an idea. I walked back to Clint's deck, restarted his scrambler protocol. It would take some time to run before I could try that door again.

I decided to search the lab in its entirety in the mean time. Perhaps I could find something useful.

The lab was a treasure trove of specialist equipment – Blue tech was everywhere. The Lab's walls contained segments of milky glass behind which I could see amorphous shapes. One of the glass segments had cracked; a large piece of glass had fallen away, revealing an alcove, housing a strange shape. I couldn't quite tell what was inside. Curiosity pulled me closer …

I peered inside the alcove, drew a sharp breath. It held a large transparent canister filled with a hazy yellow fluid. Inside the canister floated the corpse of a creature, barely recognisable as human. The thing was obviously derived from human genes but had evolved along a sick and twisted evolutionary path to become something else. It possessed arms and legs but they were double jointed, ending in hands sporting three long fingers, flanked by two thumbs. Its skin was thick, almost scaly, like a reptile.

The creature was small, perhaps five feet tall. I had the feeling I was looking at a child but I couldn't be sure. *Spectra, you utter utter bastards* ...

I grabbed a heavy metal tool from the nearest work station and smashed the glass of the next wall segment, and the next one, and the next, until I couldn't stop, and kept smashing, glass flying, until every alcove lay exposed.

Each one held a different shape: an amphibian, a quadruped, a crab-like shape ... none of them were even close to baseline human physiology.

Although I had known about the lab's purpose from the start of this mission I was still sickened by what I had found. I had expected obscure research, helping humans take small incremental evolutionary steps: tougher skin, increased lung capacity, enhanced senses ... not this horrific parade of evolutionary affronts.

And all this right under the noses of the Gaianistas, who would have surely spaced the entire Spectra staff if they had known what was happening on their Utopian station.

'Do you have clearance?'

The unexpected voice startled me. It had come from the lab's intercom. I could feel my heart pounding in my throat. My skin crawled as if touched by a ghost.

'Who's this?' I said, confused.

'Clint told me I should grant his associates permission to access the main lab.' The voice said. There was a peculiarly androgynous quality to the voice, something not quite right.

'Yes … yes I have the same clearance as Clint,' I stammered, trying to play for time.

'Something is wrong with the station,' the voice continued. 'Can you help?'

'Where is Clint?' I said. 'I mean, maybe … maybe we can help you, but I need to find him first.'

'Are you his blood relative?', the voice asked, ignoring my question. 'You seem to share genetic traits.' It was silent for a moment. 'I am interested in genetics.'

I called out, 'Clint?' Forgetting that I was wearing a helmet.

'He went into the next lab,' said the voice. 'It is where we study Trickari genetics and Human-Trickari interface potential. He is there now, but I don't think I should let you in. You don't seem to have the same security clearance as Clint.'

I ignored the voice, and rushed to the far side of the lab, only to be stopped by another airlock door. It was in lock-down mode. Clint must have used the Spectra Key-Pass to get past this door, which had subsequently locked behind him.

I could see a small room behind the door. There was a human shape inside. *Clint! He's not moving …*

'What's your name?' I asked the voice, desperate to get inside. 'What do people call you?'

'My colleagues call me Ashley. But they haven't spoken to me in a long time.'

'Hello Ashley, I'm Jemm. It's nice to meet you. How long exactly have you been here?'

'I have been performing my duties at the lab for 68 years and three months.' For a moment I was lost for words. Who, or what, was I dealing with here? I forced myself to focus on the problem in front of me.

'And when did you last speak to your colleagues?' I asked.

'It was some time ago.' Ashley sounded hesitant.

'How long ago exactly? You can tell me.'

'My last conversation took place 64 years ago, Jemm.' A slight pause, then, 'I think something has gone wrong.'

'That's why we're here Ashley, to make things right again.'

I was at a loss as to what to do next. Ashley appeared to be a fully sentient AI, albeit a primitive one; an outrage against every conceivable law dealing with artificial lifeforms. No wonder I could feel my skin crawl. They had been outlawed for a very long time, even during the Acceleration– one of the most permissive times in human history. There had simply been too many catastrophes involving full AIs, typically leading to massive loss of life. They tended to be unstable, taking little time to transition from a benign awakening mindset to full on aggressive hegemonic tendencies.

Humanity eventually reached the conclusion that it wasn't ready to deal with frequent near-singularity events, and radically constrained all AI research and related fields. Personally I found even today's Sub-AIs disconcerting. Like most people I suffered from a cultural Frankenstein complex, but this one was rooted in real horrors of the past.

'What's your main function Ashley? Your core mission protocol?'

'I have many tasks, but key among them are to assist Spectra-Vision's accelerated bio-expansion program, and process Human-Trickari interface data.'

I started to get an idea about what had been going on here, making it even more important to get to Clint. But I needed to get past this damn door first.

'Clint … Can you hear me …' *Nothing.*

'Your colleague is currently interfacing with our equipment,' said Ashley, unemotional, unhurried. 'He seemed ill prepared for the task.'

'Let me in please.' I could feel panic rising in me once again. A geyser of raw emotion and frustration, ready to blow. 'I'm Clint's mother. I need to be with him.'

'Can you verify your Spectra Vision security clearance? Clint could. His security codes offered high level clearance.'

'Just ask him,' I said. 'Let me in. Just do it, please.'

'Clint is interfacing. He can't speak right now.'

'Let me in, NOW! What's your fucking problem? Let me in, please!'

There was no reply. Ashley had probably reverted to some kind of defensive protocol. I forced myself to calm down, knowing fully well I had blown my chance to argue my way past it.

I felt a hand on my shoulder, my body almost spasmed in shock, then, purely instinctively I elbowed backwards. *It must have an avatar!*

Somebody grabbed and twisted my elbow, moved in, and I felt myself fly through the air.

'Ballard, get her out of the way, now!' It was Betsie. She wasted no time, reaching into her backpack and produced a device that looked a bit like a mechanical spider. She rammed it against the door after which it scuttled up, somehow defying gravity, until it settled on a spot near the door's left edge.

'Everybody step back,' Betsie said, her voice all mercury focus and steely discipline. Ballard picked me up as easy as if I were a department store mannequin and rushed away from the door.

The spider-thing started to glow brighter and brighter, a keening sound emanated from its body. Abruptly the glow spiked to a blinding flash, and an intense jolt of heat hit us. A loud groaning sound came from the door. When my eyes readjusted after a few seconds I could see that at least half of the door had been turned into slag. A bulbous cloud of thick dirty smoke writhed in the opening, slowly crawling up the walls and along the ceiling. There was no draft to dispel it.

Ashly objected, strangely muted, 'You have no clearance. Please desist. This is not acceptable.'

Betsie gestured to the door. 'Don't touch the sides.'

I stepped through, the smoke obscuring my view. It had filled most of the room beyond and I shouted in frustration when I couldn't find Clint. A minute later the air scrubbers kicked in, slowly revealing the insides of the second lab.

I found Clint slumped over a workstation attached to the sarcophagus shape of an old stasis unit. There was somebody inside – another evolutionary experiment, but different from the evolved corpses in the other lab. This creature clearly had predominantly Trickari DNA, apparently spliced with human genetic material. It resembled a Neo-Trickari, but lacked their otherworldly grace and beauty. This specimen, old as it was, looked wracked with pain, all wrong angles and bent bones. For a moment I wondered if it could still be alive.

The upper part of the stasis unit was hooked up to a peculiar piece of Trick-tech – a spherical device, where most Trickari artifacts were cubist in design. I recognised it immediately – it was the artifact Spectra had contracted me to find. It looked like Clint had tried to dislodge it, but in the process something had gone wrong. I moved closer, intent to get Clint away from the thing, but Ballard pulled me back.

'Jemm, no. Look at the artifact.'

And then I saw it: an intermittent pulse of light veined through the sphere. Dread filled my every fibre.

Recognising the true nature of the artifact almost took away the last vestige of what little control I had left. This wasn't Blue tech, or even Red. As disastrous as the latter would have been I would have preferred it to *this*.

The artifact in front of Clint was Trickari *Purple*.

My memories of the next few hours are fragmented, like a smashed mirror put together in the wrong order. Most pieces are there, but they form a warped, cut up picture.

I recall Ballard and Betsie helping me dislodge Clint from the Trickari device, urging me to leave with them afterwards. I must have refused them as I remembered taking time to carefully transfer the artifact in a containment case, as well as securing Clint's deck and the data drives attached to it. I wanted to preserve anything that could help me fight Clint's condition, including the cache of research data that Gibson was looking for.

I don't remember leaving that place, but my next memory is of Betsie speaking to me aboard one of the skimmers.

'Listen, he's going to be OK. Vitals are good, no wounds … Charles will take good care of him. I know you've seen much worse.' The skimmer glided past the Gaianista ruins and corpses like the ferry on the river Styx crossing into the underworld.

Betsie was agitated. She could tell the situation was worse than it seemed on the surface, but she didn't understand what had happened to Clint.

'What the hell was he doing there anyway?' she said. 'And why, goddamn why, didn't you come to us first?' She punched the side of the skimmer in frustration, then turned my way. She lowered her voice back to her normal, carefully considered volume, 'What were those things in the alcoves?' she asked. 'What on Earth were they trying to do in that lab? And that *creature* next to Clint … This is *exactly* why I don't get involved with Corp business.' She put her hand on the side of my helmet with surprising gentleness. 'Tell us so we can help.'

Words finally came to me then, slowly at first, but gathering in strength until I couldn't hold them back and they all came rushing out at once: 'It's Purple,' I said. 'Have you ever heard of Trickari Purple? Most people haven't.' I could see Betsie shaking her head inside her helmet. 'It's an old rumour, a myth really, that some dead artifacts are booby-trapped – they can be re-activated. They supposedly turn purple, and discharge some … I don't know what to call it … some *virus*.' I looked at my son. Briefly unable to speak. 'It's not a myth, Clint is infected. There's no cure.'

'No cure for what?'

'Purple tech transforms people into Neo-Tricksters. Clint will become one within a year.' Saying it out loud made it painfully real to me. *I would lose Clint.* My sense of panic turned to white hot rage. My mouth tasted like battery acid and old blood.

'Spectra must have stumbled onto something new,' I said. 'Normally, according to the stories, this type of artifact discharges once, after which it's supposed to stay dead, forever. That's why we know so little about Neo-Tricksters.'

'An alien booby-trap,' said Betsie.

I looked at Clint again, wondering how much time it would take him to lose his mind, like those Neos who had gone before him. I thought back to the Neo I encountered two weeks ago in D-Town. How it felt like it was trying to communicate with me. Trying to reach out, looking for some spark of understanding. Was that to be Clint's future? A warped creature, no longer human, unable to understand his own mother – his mind invaded by an alien presence. Clint's memories would merge with those of an ancient Trickari – long dead but brought back to live inside the transformed body of my son.

And if anyone got their hands on him, those hybrid memories would eventually get harvested and sold to millions of TrickMem junkies, some bastard crime syndicate feasting on the proceeds like human maggots.

It was too much to take. I felt a sudden pressure in my mind, a sense of simultaneous tearing and compressing. Dizziness took over until I could feel myself sliding, falling off the skimmer, unable to intervene. The floor pivoted upwards, slamming into me with force. I felt no pain.

Lying on the floor my legs lost all feeling and strength, as did my hands. Tunnel-vision rushed in. I could vaguely see Betsie, far away, rushing towards me, but she seemed to be getting further away, shrinking all the time, until finally all I could see was a small circle of light at the end of a tunnel.

The light shrunk to the size of a dot, then faded out, and all was dark.

I dreamt that dream again; the dream that has haunted me. I was submerged once more in the blackest coldest depths, swimming after Clint who was ever dropping deeper into the watery abyss. My legs kicked harder than ever before, my arms fought the water like snakes possessed. And then, for the first time since the onset of this awful recurring nightmare, *I gained on him.*

Slowly but surely I gained on him, until I was close enough to grab his foot.

It was cold as death.

I snatched at his hands, they were lifeless.

When I finally held his head to look at him, red crystal-faceted eyes stared back at me, vacant, without any human intelligence.

I opened my mouth to scream when suddenly I felt hands pulling at me, dragging me away from Clint. The water was a frenzy of movement and bubbles as I tried to fight off my assailant but it was no use; I was dragged into the deep until it was so dark I could not see.

A voice spoke to me, 'Good, you're coming back. It's time to join the living again.' I recognised the calm voice … it was Charles. 'Take it easy, don't sit up too fast.'

Ignoring Charles' advice I leaned over to him and grabbed his arm. The world spun. I thought for a moment that I was going to faint again, but then my vision steadied. I looked around me, finding myself in the *Effervescent's* sick bay.

'Where's Clint? How is he?' I tried to keep the fear out of my voice.

Charles gestured to a stasis pod on his left. 'It's OK … He's right here. I sedated him for now, to give us time to figure out what to do next.'

I got off the bed, carefully this time, and ambled over to Clint. My legs were weak, my entire body felt bruised.

Clint's eyes were closed, his arms relaxed by his side. He had a small head-wound near his temple, but otherwise he appeared as if he were merely sleeping. I felt a brief flash of hope.

'Is he–'

'You were right, I'm sorry to say. He *is* infected,' said Charles. 'I know he looks normal on the surface, like himself, but his body is already reacting to the infection. There is nothing normal about what's going on inside him. His DNA is transforming at a steady rate, his cells morphing into who-knows-what, his brain … Well, I don't even know what I'm looking at.'

'Can I talk to him?'

'Soon, I hope. But…there are certain *other* matters to attend to first.' Charles took off his glasses to rub his eyes with both hands. Fatigue had softened his features to the point that his normal reservedness had fallen away, and revealed a shy, more empathetic version of himself underneath.. 'I think you should go talk to Ballard.'

'I can talk to him here.'

'Jemm, listen … Right now you don't have many friends on the crew. Betsie and Kyoshi are talking about the advantage of just spacing you, over turning you in.' Charles replaced his glasses after a final vigorous rub of his face. 'Look, they are only half-joking. Ballard is keeping his options open, and he needs to hear your side of the story before he hears too much of their side. Do you understand what I'm saying? Go talk to him.'

'I see … And how about you?'

'Well, to be honest – and don't take this the wrong way – I'm both fascinated and appalled at what happened to Clint. Part of me wants to stick around and help you take care of him. Maybe find a way to slow the process if I can. Maybe even stop it, although I doubt that's possible. But I can't do that and stay a part of this crew. So really, I haven't made up my mind yet about what I should do next.'

I looked at Clint again, unnaturally still in the stasis box, his chest barely moving. I ached to hold him in my arms, to touch his face. The cold and harsh lighting in sick bay rendered him into a waxen statue, but I knew my boy was in there somewhere, fighting a ghost that was trying to steal his soul.

I left without a word, ready to confront Ballard.

The moment I stepped into Ballard's private quarters I knew something was different about him. He sat in a chair, holding his copy of Moby Dick in one hand, a glass of whiskey in his other. A Freddie Hubbard recording was playing in the background, slightly too loud.

Ballard was wearing reading glasses. Old fashioned and horn-rimmed, probably quite valuable. It made his face look stern; the effect was enhanced by a deep frown ploughing his brow like soil to be tilled. His expression softened a fraction when he looked at me, which was something at least, and more than I expected.

He nodded at the empty chair next to him. I sat down in silence. Ballard poured another glass of whiskey after topping up his own and handed it to me. The glass appeared comically small in his giant hand. We sat in silence for several minutes, sipping whiskey. I welcomed the warm glow in my stomach, pushing back the fear induced acid lingering just beneath the surface.

'Not Ahab, not the whale,' he said.

'Excuse me?'

'I don't identify with either of them. I don't.' He opened the book to read a passage, then closed it again. For a moment he seemed lost in thought. I was about to say something to break the silence when he spoke again.

'They're not very different from each other.'

'Ahab and the whale?'

Ballard nodded. 'That's right. They are both stuck with what they are. They can't be anything else.'

'J.J. ... I don't see what this—'

'You know why Harry broke down?'

I had to think a moment before I knew who he meant. 'Harry, your last Xeno?' Ballard nodded.

'Because he was already damaged,' said Ballard. 'Didn't take much to break him.' A sadness crept in Ballard's voice as he continued. 'Harry was very talented. A natural, yes? A natural Xeno. He always knew what treasure to go for, what to leave behind. Always had his research ready. Harry had a real nose for Artifacts.'

'So, what made him so special?' I didn't mean to sound defensive, but I guess I did.

'Well, I'm not proud of this Jemm. But, he was special because he was in pain. Something in his past ... He never told me about it, but it showed.'

'I don't want to be an arsehole, but everybody is in *some* kind of pain. That doesn't make us special.' Ballard threw me a stern look – too paternalistic for me to ignore. 'That's the way it is,' I said. 'That's reality.'

'You don't understand. He was special, because running salvage is how he tried to fix himself. When he wasn't working, when he was just being a man he was ... unbalanced, yes? Always insecure, not happy with himself ... But as a Xeno he was *wonderful*. Everybody could see he was special when he was working. I could see it too.'

'So you blame yourself?'

'Yes. Because I knew what he was underneath, and I used that.'

'Is that so bad?' I asked. 'I'm sure he wanted to work with you.'

Ballard picked up the book again, looking for a passage, which he read out a moment later.

"...for there is no folly of the beast of the earth which is not infinitely outdone by the madness of men."

He looked up at me over his glasses, like a scruffy English teacher. I wasn't sure what to say. 'People can't change what they are Jemm. That's why I hired you.'

An uncomfortable silence stretched out between us, making it hard to maintain eye contact, but we did. I could tell Ballard was wrestling with an inner conundrum, a dilemma. The frown came back as he contemplated what to do. More minutes passed until, abruptly, his forehead smoothed and a sense of resolve came over Ballard. He seemed almost defiant.

'We have to make you dead!' he shouted. 'And Clint too! It has to look like an accident.'

I was stunned. When Ballard saw my consternation he barked a humourless laugh. 'Hah, not like that. I mean, we have to make it look like you died. It's the only way to keep you alive.' He laughed at the contradiction. 'That's the universe playing a little joke on us, yes?'

'What are you talking about? I have to go back to Earth. I have to make Spectra help me. With Clint, with the artifact. Their research on the habitat… They must know something that could help him. It must be there in the data cache that Clint grabbed. It can only be read by Spectra …'

'Think!' He spat the word at me. 'Think! How long has it been since the last Neo memories were harvested? The last time that new Mem hit the market?'

I thought for a moment, trying to remember the most recent reports on the drug. 'I don't know … Years. At least five years, probably more?'

'Think Jemm. What does that mean for Clint?' asked Ballard, with sympathy and warmth. The magnitude of what he was saying was starting to sink in.

I felt sick.

'There are millions of TrickMem junkies. All waiting for a new rush,' I stammered. 'They all want new Mem …'

Ballard nodded. 'You see it now, yes? Clint's memories, the Trickari creature's memories … when they merge and get harvested as Mem they're worth *billions*. How can you keep him safe? And that Spectra research? How much is that worth? How much do Spectra want it? What about the other Corps? What if word comes out? What would they do?'

He didn't have to spell it out any further. Clint and I had become the most valuable targets in the entire solar system. Any Corp would gladly kill and torture to get their hands on us. Hell, they wouldn't hesitate to start an inter-Corp war to capture us. Clint and I represented a new source of Mem, and the research we discovered on Habitat 6 might unlock an infinite future supply of the stuff.

Ballard waited patiently for me to catch up. My thoughts were like an open book, as there was nothing else to think.

'I know somebody,' he said. 'A scientist. No guarantees OK?'

I slowly nodded my thanks. Desperate for a way out of this. 'What about you? What will you tell them? Spectra I mean.'

Ballard explained his plan to me. It was logical and smart, as I had come to expect from him. I could tell he was still angry – partly at me, partly at his run of bad luck with the Xenos he recruited – yet he was going to help me regardless. As he had said himself on an earlier occasion: people can't change what they are.

We had a final drink together, discussing music, books, echoing our first meeting. It was awkward and enjoyable in equal measures in that way things can get when too much has happened between people.

I was *made dead* the next day.

The following morning Clint emerged from his fugue state confused and scared. He looked as innocent and as vulnerable as a newborn. Having to explain to him what had happened, explain the virus he now carried and the terrible future that awaited him, was the most painful, difficult, heartbreaking moment of my life.

It was an unfair burden for somebody so young and so full of life. There were too many emotions to deal with, leaving him simultaneously angry, scared, confused, defiant … He looked to me for help but what could I say? What could I do?

Afterwards he covered his ears and cried. I looked at him with pity. What Clint was hearing was the deafening roar of an existential threat, a manifestation of the abyss. I heard it too. I dared not acknowledge it, lest it would suck me into its embrace, but it was there, immutable, implacable.

I tried to ignore my own fears and told Clint we could beat this fate, that there *was* the sliver of a chance that we could stop his metamorphosis – maybe even reverse it.

Ballard's offer of help represented a lifeline, so I grabbed hold of it with all I had, tenuous as it was. I barely believed it myself.

I took Clint to the observatory to await the final details of Ballard's plan. We were alone; I think the crew tried to give us some space for private reflection. The observation screens showed Habitat 6 in all its overwhelming size, looming over us like fate. I cursed it, vehemently.

The *Effervescent* was about to detach from the Gaianista station when Ballard joined us. I felt a deep shudder, indicating the release of the docking clamps. We were now floating free.

Ballard gave us the rundown as we slowly drifted away from Habitat 6. As I watched its torus shape fall away into the dark sea of space, it felt like it was I who was drowning, my link to a previous life untethered, quietly adrift.

Ballard spoke softly, 'You still have a chance Jemm. You do. Take the boy and the data cache to Mars, and meet with my friend Ella. She owes me yes? She'll help you, she's a geneticist.' He clenched his jaw for a moment, then continued. 'Ella owes me much. This favour won't be enough to pay off all of her debt to me, but it will go a long way. She'll be eager to help.'

Clint's voice quivered as he spoke, 'There's always a solution. There really is. The data we've got … It's priceless! Trickari-induced transformation, human-xeno gene splicing, cellular reprogramming … None of this stuff has been seen before and I made sure I got every damn thing from that data cache before I … before I got infected. We have the artifact, the thing that infected me. Who knows what *that* could teach us …'

'If anybody can make sense of this it's Ella,' said Ballard. 'She's been studying this stuff for years: genetics, xeno-biology, bio-modification … Believe me, she's motivated.'

I had a hard time accepting this story. 'How? How do we get there?' I asked.

'Well, we will have to go through artifact screening on Phobos Station anyway. You can sneak off there …

charter a shuttle. I will register you as a KDS – Killed During Salvage.' Ballard smiled. 'I'll make sure you died a painless death.'

'But how do we avoid detection? Spectra will be monitoring every check point in the damn solar system.'

'Kyoshi took care of that. He maintains a whole collection of backup identities for emergencies, all prepped and ready.'

'Typical Doppelganger,' said Clint. 'I should have known.'

Ballard leaned forward, and said, 'You'll be fine. You have a chance, I'll make sure of that. And I'll keep your percentage safe.' He winked at me, and I realised I would probably never see him again.

We all fell silent, contemplating the diminishing shape of Habitat 6. It had transformed all of us, one way or another.

Clint shivered. He hugged himself as if he was freezing. I moved closer, held him tightly. The silence stretched for many slow seconds, then minutes. Eventually he stirred.

'I can feel it you know?' Clint said to all of us. 'I can feel it in my skin, my hair … my head is all wrong … I keep having weird ideas like I'm thinking impossible thoughts or something, and then I get scared wondering if it is me thinking those thoughts or the Trickari inside of me. The "Trickster" …' He spoke the word as if it tasted vile on his tongue. 'I wonder what it will be like to lose my mind? How will I even know when it happens?'

11

Phobos Station was one of the few places in the Solar System where salvage crews could submit their artifacts for screening. The station nested inside a large dome built over the Stickney crater, measuring about ten kilometres across.

After submitting a detailed manifest we were allowed to descend on one of the many landing platforms encircling the crater. The platforms stood over shafts reaching deep down, intersecting with enormous sub-surface tunnels which provided airlocked access to the station proper.

Security was intense, security staff intimidating. This was not a place to get caught breaking the law. Like all vessels with goods to declare we had to submit to cargo bay inspection. All our salvage would get inspected, classified, and logged. It was an integral part of salvage missions, and although I had undergone dozens of inspections I never knew them to be a relaxed affair. A mistake was easily made. Fines for improper goods could be eye-watering, and punishments for illegal Trickari artifacts were extreme, up to and including death.

The initial inspection was carried out by a senior official. Once he had a good idea of the total volume and type of salvage, he would delegate the final inspection to a team of underlings. Invariably, senior inspectors were hard-nosed individuals who had to be treated with a certain amount of caution. Lack of humour seemed to be part of their job description. The inspector assigned to our case was no exception.

'Aren't you a little short to be an inspector?' joked Kyoshi, completely misjudging the occasion.

'I would like to speak to the captain of the ship please,' said the inspector, with icy indifference to Kyoshi's attempt at humour.

'That man is me,' boomed Ballard, towering over the little bureaucrat.

'And this vessel is the *Effervescent*?'

'That she is,' replied Ballard proudly.

The inspector glanced around the cargo bay, checking his Padd for details of our journey. 'You lost your Xeno?'

'A Xeno and her son, we are still in shock,' said Ballard. He sounded genuinely bereaved.

'That's rough,' muttered the inspector, while checking the manifest. 'What happened?'

'We filled out all the required paperwork,' said Ballard.

The inspector looked up from his Padd. An awkward silence descended on the cargo bay until he spoke again. 'That's not what I asked Mr. Ballard.' There was a quiet menace in his voice. The air was thick with it.

'Yes, well... They were excavating an abandoned library, full of extremely rare books, when the whole thing went up in flames. Some kind of oxygen leak, yes? They were too dedicated to the job. Should have left at the first sign of danger.'

'They got too greedy huh?' The inspector's callous response was likely a ruse, to study Ballard's reaction.

Ballard's voice turned a low rumble, there was thunder in his eyes. 'They were the best Xenos I ever worked with and they gave their lives for the mission. I'll not have them slandered by the likes of you.'

Satisfied by Ballard's reaction the inspector went back to checking his Padd. 'Some exotic stuff here ...'

'I told you, they were dedicated.'

'Fair enough,' said the inspector, businesslike and to the point. 'Well, this all seems fine. It will take a day or two for all the physical checks to complete. Will you stay aboard?'

'Most of us will, but two of our crew are travelling to Mars,' said Ballard, pointing at Clint and me.

The man nodded. 'They'll need to charter a shuttle to the surface, and register with the customs office. If they pass the background check they'll be cleared to travel.'

Kyoshi laughed. 'Do they still do the checks? When does anybody ever fail one of those eh?'

'The checks are vital to the safety of us all,' the inspector said stiffly. 'Only last week we rooted out a fugitive from Earth. Some kind of terrorist, trying to infiltrate Mars Red Colony.'

'Gee, what happened to him?' asked Kyoshi, his smile fading.

'He was killed while resisting arrest.' The inspector laughed. 'And that's why we do background checks!'

Clint and I said our goodbyes that very day. There were tears and oaths, hugs and well-wishes. Even though we hadn't worked together for a long time the crew of the *Effervescent* had become an indelible part of our lives. Saying goodbye was harder than I thought it would be.

Kyoshi provided us with two short term false identities: *Anita Jensen*, a female librarian and her travel companion *Derek de Wit,* a young computer scientist. "Single use personas" Kyoshi called them. He swore that they would stand up to scrutiny, yet he appeared nervous and jittery. This did not fill us with confidence.

Betsie and Charles each came over to thank us for our contribution to the salvage mission, and in the case of Betsie to apologise for harsh words and actions. We exchanged details and swore that we would hook up again at some future date. Nobody dared mention the possibility that Clint and I would not come out of this intact.

Ballard was the last to say goodbye. His large frame seemed smaller than normal, his broad shoulders drooping just a touch. I felt a sudden urge to stay with him, to stay with the *Effervescent*, to run away from all this madness, but I couldn't abandon my son.

'Goodbyes are tricky, yes?' He grunted.

'You never told me where your accent is from,' I replied, curiosity finally getting the better of me.

Ballard laughed, 'We must keep some mysteries in

life.' He was right of course. 'Maybe Ella will tell you.'

'I'll make sure to ask her all about you.' I winked. 'And maybe tell her some things I have learned myself.'

Ballard just smiled a shy smile, picked up our bags as if they were made of air, and escorted us to the Phobos transit system. As the subway carriage sped off I waved, once. Ballard waved back as we disappeared into the tunnel, until I could no longer see him.

The customs line for the shuttle service to Mars inched forward, slowly bringing us closer to the moment of truth when it would become clear if Kyoshi's false identities stood up to scrutiny.

Unlike the line at D-Town customs, this line was filled with the kind of experienced travellers one finds at all interplanetary crossings. These were professional people who knew where they were going in life, prepared to deal with the harsh realities of space travel and interplanetary culture shock. Kyoshi's fake personas would have to compete with the very real identities of the people standing in front of me.

The line moved … stopped … moved … in a hypnotic cadence. We shuffled closer and closer to our fate. If the customs officer suspected anything, or if our paperwork was exposed as a fraud, we would pay the price.

We finally arrived at the customs window, the booth occupied by a woman in her forties. She looked experienced and totally professional. I handed her my fake passport. The woman studied it carefully, then tapped her screen in order to pull up some data. I had no idea if this was regular procedure but it took uncomfortably long.

'Librarian?' she asked, her voice almost toneless.

'That's right. I specialise in antique real-books.'

'And where did you learn your craft?'

'Municipal library, D-Town. It's got a good education program.'

'I see … Tell me Miss Jensen, what place is there for a librarian on a salvage crew?'

I didn't like the forensic focus of her question; would she ask any traveller such detailed things?

'I was there to assist their Xeno. Their research showed that there was a large library of potentially valuable real-books on the station they were going to travel to. It was a last minute find, so they got me in to help out.'

'Really?' asked the official. 'Valuable books? Like what?'

I almost panicked. I couldn't think of a single rare real-book, although I had found and sold many, sourced from previous missions.

'I never got the chance to see,' I stammered.

'Is that so?' said the official, her voice flat.

I forced a tear into my eye, and said 'They all burned. It was horrible. I shouldn't have come.' I cleared my throat, steadied my voice. 'Their Xeno and her son burned alive with all the books in the abandoned library.'

'Is this why you are travelling to Mars?' The official's voice had softened slightly.

'It is. I don't want to stay on that ship one moment longer than I have to. I can get a new job on Mars – start again.'

The customs lady stared at me then, stared deep into my eyes. *Did she believe me?*

She held my gaze a moment longer, then said, 'Good luck Miss Jensen,' and nodded me through.

I walked past her and gave her a nod in return. My heart beating wildly, I awaited the outcome of Clint's custom check, but to my relief it took mere moments before they waved him through.

We boarded the shuttle an hour later.

PART TWO

ESCALATION

12

Ella lived in Mars Colony East, Gagarin Enclave, Sector 12. Or rather "Escher City" as it was known to locals, owing to it being such a damn confusing place. Much of Escher existed underground for obvious protective reasons, whereas the parts that stood proudly on the surface formed a messy warren of prefab walkways, residential units and standardised government-provided "cube buildings".

Having been a resident of the city for two weeks had done nothing to improve my understanding of its layout and structure. I just couldn't get a true sense of *place.* There wasn't much to distinguish one part of town from the other. There were some road signs which did not help whatsoever. A few shops and bars sported sad attempts at adding a personal decorative touch. To me it all looked the same. I was hopelessly lost, despite my efforts to get to know the city.

Clint snapped, 'Why not? What's wrong with me getting a tattoo?' He had been tetchy with me all day.

'Normally, nothing at all,' I replied, 'But since we can't risk you getting recognised it seems pretty obvious to me why not.'

'Who's going to recognise me? Nobody knows who we are. Or where we are.' Clint underscored his last remark with a theatrical bow and flourish. His Oxy-Buddy breathing mask gave him the appearance of a pirate of sorts.

'Let's keep it that way,' I hissed. 'Your condition is getting harder and harder to hide. Imagine what would happen if people would put two and two together ...' I was getting pretty tired of the argument. It had only been two weeks since we left the *Effervescent*, but Clint's behaviour was already starting to worry me. An erratic edge had crept into his personality despite protestations to the contrary. It was a problem that I didn't know how to fix.

On the surface he seemed the same young man he was before, but I could tell he was fighting a change from within. There were no clear telltale signs of alien thoughts or behaviours – nothing *that* obvious – but his emotional responses were getting strangely intense. One moment he would act like a defiant teenager looking for an argument over something inconsequential, the next moment he desperately needed support and comforting, as if he was a little boy again.

He developed a few minor tics – again nothing too severe, but disconcerting nonetheless. He would ruffle his hair too frequently, worried about the crystalline growths that could manifest any time now. I caught him looking in wonder at mundane everyday objects as if he'd never seen them before: a wallet … a glass … a spoon … or touching random surfaces, amazed at the texture of the everyday world around us.

It was easy to believe he was unsettled by the momentous change about to rob him of his young life – to try and ignore these quirks for now – but we needed to keep a low profile; his odd behaviour was making that harder by the day.

Ella had taken us in, just as Ballard had promised. She was, however, not a gracious host. Ella was the kind of person who made everything intensely personal. In her mind the universe and everybody in it was out to get her, and she spent her entire life fighting back against this injustice. But, to be fair, life *had* dealt her a shitty hand. She was crippled by a slow-acting degenerative disease that no doctor seemed to understand. She had already lost one leg and the other one was severely damaged, the source of unpredictable episodes of stabbing, crippling pain.

She ran a small augment shop, which immediately put me on edge. After what had happened to my father I intimately understood the inherent dangers of augments and I distrusted the practice on a strong, personal level.

Ella picked up on my distaste towards her augment practice, and understandably felt put out by our presence, but Ballard had been right in as much that she was uniquely qualified to help us solve Clint's problem, and she was keen to repay her debt to him.

Part of the reason why she had specialised in augmentation and bio-mods was out of a desperate desire to heal herself. She wasn't unsuccessful in that regard. She had mostly succeeded to stave off what other so-called specialists had diagnosed as inevitable, miserable decline, and eventually a pitiful death, by treating herself with a mixture of bespoke augments and barely legal cellular regeneration programs. It was a painful and expensive business but it was keeping her alive. Understandably, she was not the easiest person to be around.

Ella had provided us with accommodation in an empty section at the back of her augment clinic. This gave us access to much of her professional equipment and allowed us a small measure of privacy at least.

'Don't steal my stuff!' was the first thing she snapped at us while showing us around, her words thick with her Martian accent. As if we could go anywhere with stolen gear.

'This is top of the line …' Clint mused, glancing around with interest. 'Really good gear …'

'Yeah, I bet you're surprised. Expected some chop-shop butcher did you?'

'Ballard said you'd know your sh…' he paused, the profanity died before it was released. 'Is that a Terra-bot? Is it real?'

'Of course it's real, do you think I'm into fake stuff?' said Ella with pride. Both of them smiled simultaneously – recognising a kindred spirit in each other.

'Is it powered? For real?'

Ella laughed, 'Yes for fucking real. Well kind of. I modified it a bit.'

'How many bots have you got?' asked Clint, excited and hopeful.

'More than you can shake a stick at. You good at bot modding?'

'I know a few tricks, yeah.'

'In that case, you can be my assistant. I'll show you some cool models if you like?'

They bonded easily after that. Again I was impressed with Clint, with how he had found a way into her trust, simply by being a good human being.

It was a relief; we needed all the friends we could find.

"Ella's Augment Shop" was bigger than it looked on the outside. Cubist in style, like all Martian architecture, but even more Spartan than similar buildings in the neighbourhood. The extra space came partly from the building extending farther into the ground than a typical Martian abode. There were at least three sub-surface floors, although I suspected that Ella's private quarters, which we weren't allowed to enter, extended even farther down.

Clint and I were given a section which existed of two intersecting cubes and a little mezzanine, reached by a set of aluminium stairs. This is where I slept, whereas Clint preferred to stay close to the ground. This was not typical of him – normally he would have made sure to get the top bunk.

The walls were strictly utilitarian, covered in useful storage modules and painted an inoffensive but bland colour. (A kind of industrial magnolia, if such a thing was even possible.) Our footsteps echoed in that slightly dopplered way that empty rooms seem to encourage.

We had set up a research station near Clint's bed allowing us access to Ella's home network, and she gave us a broad selection of equipment to help with data analysis. Clint had gotten up early that day, already tinkering with esoteric hardware supposedly useful to our attempts to decipher his condition. I joined him, easing into a well-established collaborative routine born out of years of joint tinkering. I instinctively knew what tools to hand over or what bits to work on myself.

I pointed at the Spectra data module. It had somehow sprouted dozens of wires and cables, snaking into Clint's arsenal of home-made data sniffers and decryption devices.

'How's it holding up?' I asked.

'Cracked most of it this morning.' He looked up, eyes red-rimmed and tired looking. 'I'm not sleeping well.'

'Yeah, I figured.'

'There's some truly weird data here,' Clint continued. 'They did some awful things in that lab, no doubt, but it's fascinating stuff.'

'Fascinating how? Useful fascinating?'

'Maybe … Not sure yet. Probably.' Clint drifted off into deep concentration, trying to make sense of some piece of obscure data, a slight smile on his face. He was happiest when uncovering oblique connections and thwarting high-level security measures. I would be of little use to him until he had swum in that particular sea long enough to make decent progress. Once he found something worthy of sharing with me he would let me know. I left to find Ella.

I marvelled at the strange habitats Martians considered their homes. The low gravity affected things inside a house in unexpected ways: stairs were steeper than I was used to but easy to navigate, heavy ornaments were mounted without fear of damaging walls … Everything felt just a bit different from what I was used to.

In many ways Mars was ideal for Ella. Her lack of muscular strength and bone density wasn't as big a problem here as it would be on Earth. She had modded a small skimmer to function as a personal transport. Small enough for her to use inside her home, it transformed her into a strange machine-human hybrid as she floated about, but she could get around just fine in most situations without it, as long as she didn't over-exert herself.

After searching for a few minutes I found Ella in her

storage unit. She was cataloguing a bewildering array of augment tech, all the while whistling to herself, gliding along sagging shelves in her converted skimmer.

Ella spotted me watching her. She adopted a mischievous grin.

'Never seen a cyborg before?'

'Plenty of those on Earth,' I replied. 'None as stylish as you however.'

'Oh flattery! I like!' She floated down to me, putting her face level with mine. 'Let's have some more of that.'

'Does that thing have an in-built toilet? I really hope it does.'

'You want to know what I've learned about your boy's little problem, yes?' Interestingly Ella and Ballard shared some of the same linguistic mannerisms, although Ella cursed a lot more.

'So you *have* learned something then?' I asked.

'Sure did. Come on, I'll show you.'

As Ella floated deftly through her home I couldn't help but wonder what kind of life she would have led if it weren't for her illness. Somehow I couldn't imagine her any different. She was obviously no demure wallflower. Ella very much seemed like a person who was born with rough edges already in place.

We arrived at her inner sanctum – a workshop-laboratory hybrid, filled to the rafters with gear and equipment. Incongruously she had painted rectangular shapes on the inside walls in all kinds of clashing colours. It resembled a child's drawing of a Trickari artifact, blown up to a giant size.

Once we arrived at her main work area she hauled herself out of the skimmer, groaning in pain but with grim determination. She batted me away when I tried to help.

'Oh fuck off,' she bit through clenched teeth, while wedging herself into an E-Chair in front of a huge desk. 'Look at this ...' She switched on several screens, showing cryptic data files and what appeared to be images of cellular growth.

'Those cells on the left are Clint's,' she said. 'These cells here on the right are baseline human cells. Archive footage I grabbed from an old-net repository. Can you see the difference?'

I nodded, 'Clint's cells seem to be changing more rapidly. And they look slightly different.'

'Yup, and "slightly" equates to massively different once you look at the particulars.'

'He's changing.'

'Of course he's changing, what did you expect?'

'Fine, so how's this helping us? How's this helping *Clint*?'

'Yeah yeah, gimme a minute …' Ella conjured up a new set of images. They were the same cells, but growing much slower. 'Ta da!' She announced. 'Not bad eh?'

Clint's cells still looked *wrong*, but seemed more stable. A few cells, maybe ten percent or so, were acting odd; they writhed violently and then seemed to wither away.

'So you've slowed down the transformation? And what's happening to those other cells, are they dying?'

Ella sighed and cursed under her breath. 'You have no idea just how impressive this is do you?' I didn't answer. 'Look, Clint's Spectra data is starting to yield some useful stuff. For now, it's given me just enough to at least attempt to help him, but this is hard shit. So, what we have here is an initial experiment that came out way better than I expected. You should be grateful.'

'What is it?' I said, ignoring her attempt to shame me into praise. 'How does it work?'

'Fine,' Ella sighed. 'Be that way.'

'Come on,' I said. 'I want to hear.'

Ella relented, eager to show off the progress she had made.

'You know I get special treatment for my illness?' she asked. 'And all Martians get drugs to help with loss of muscle mass, bone density, that kind of thing? Well, I came up with a cocktail that combines both treatments but aimed at the opposite side of the spectrum; I make it *suppress* regeneration. Annoyingly, this does, occasionally, seem to encourage cellular decay as well, which … is a problem.'

'So, how would you counter that?' I asked, already fearing the answer to that question.

'I'm not completely sure, but,' Ella paused to consider her words carefully. 'It mostly affects major organs, like the heart, kidneys, liver … My equipment is more than up to–'

'No. Don't even go there. I'm not that desperate. We only just started looking into this.'

Ella continued, ignoring my outburst, '–replacing those organs with augments. What's much harder is to regulate the process after. The system would have to maintain a stable hormonal balance, react to spikes in transformation… all that requires a new augment design. I can probably do it. I think I should.' She looked up at me expectantly.

'Absolutely not,' I said, horrified. 'I can't allow it.' Images of my father, paranoid and deluded and shivering with augment sickness flashed through my mind. Eternal reminders of a life that had taken one wrong turn too many. I couldn't expose Clint to that.

Ella whispered, but it was through clenched teeth, 'You don't understand … He's almost out of time. The transformation will accelerate. Once his brain starts morphing you will lose him.'

I shook my head. 'No. You don't under–'

'Shut up for one minute, you selfish bitch.' My reply stuck in my throat, shocked into silent submission. 'He's nearly seventeen years old. What *right* do you have–!' Ella caught herself. Then, gentler, 'Listen to me. The augments will give him a *chance*. Without them he's lost.'

Her eyes pleaded with me, appealing to my better nature.

I turned and left. Unable to speak, let alone agree.

There were three permanent major settlements on Mars, not counting the smattering of micro enclaves which pop up and disappear again depending on the local needs of the terraforming project.

Colony East represented the largest settlement, with Red Colony and Colony Three not far behind. Each was made up of a diverse collection of domes, each dome housing one or more districts, and each district housing a wide variety of neighbourhoods. All three settlements were distinct from each other in history and culture, infused with their own character and personality.

Escher was the largest district in Colony East, unified by a dedicated single dome, established in the early days of terraforming. In Mars terms it was an ancient city, full of history and culture. To me it was just a place to get lost in the crowds, embracing my inability to find my way around town.

I was a ghost, wandering the avenues, trying to figure out why I was there, forgotten who I was supposed to haunt. Nobody knew me or could see me, not truly. I felt erased, no longer there. It was a strange existence, a hazy in-between-state, and had it not been for Clint's terrible condition keeping me focused I could have easily drifted away.

Despite the maze-like layout the streets and buildings on Mars were tidy and well organised, its people straight as arrows. My own messy thoughts and disrupted life a jarring juxtaposition on this well-ordered environment.

But even here there were signs of rot; Mem junkies ghosted along the streets in surprising numbers. Their blank faces were partially hidden by their masks, but their odd shuffling gait gave away their addiction. I wondered, as I did frequently, how anybody could voluntarily invite such an existence. Yet millions had.

I walked around in this strange reflective mood for a long time, my thoughts unresolved. I viewed Martian settlements as soulless, interchangeable and dreary places. Everything and everybody in it looked the same to me, trapped in a life of drudgery. Equally, I saw Martians as dull reflections of the people I knew in Diamond-Town. I wondered how they viewed themselves.

But almost from one moment to the next, these preconceptions abruptly changed, as if the world shifted into proper focus, allowing me to see it clearly for the first time.

It started with the masks – the Oxy-Buddy that everybody wore as a final stopgap measure until the terraforming of Mars was complete and its atmosphere fully breathable. At first I thought the masks made everybody look the same, caricatures of the stereotype of the typical rugged Martian. But the exact opposite was true: people had created individual designs for their masks. I couldn't understand how I hadn't noticed this before, or rather, how it hadn't registered with me, as the masks were both ubiquitous and stunning.

Each mask was adorned with beautifully handcrafted decorations. People used paint, small objects, feathers, jewellery and anything else that could be incorporated on the masks' modestly sized canvas. Once I appreciated the sheer work and artistry involved with each mask I could no longer imagine seeing the Martians as anything other than fiercely individual.

I went through a similar shift of perception with the local architecture. Yes, they used mundane industrial materials, and yes they mostly followed a purely functional cubist architecture, but within that narrow spectrum a surprising sophistication and aesthetic could be found. It was clear as day.

I stopped dead in my tracks, and let my gaze complete a slow 360 degree scan of my environment. I had been a fool, blind to the individuality that was all around me. I finally understood why Clint felt the desire to get a tattoo. He wanted to be part of this place while he could still call himself an individual.

Maybe I had been too harsh on him. Maybe I should let him have his wish. But as soon as I tasted that thought I spat it out again. It was my responsibility to keep him safe, and to risk being exposed as an evolving Neo-

Trickster in some unknown tattoo parlour was not compatible with that.

I picked up my journey again, but now blessed with a new sense of place. I no longer felt so lost.

When I got back Ella and Clint were laughing and celebrating. Ella had unearthed a gaudy home tattoo unit from her vast collection of gear. It was in perfect working order.

'Forgot about this beauty!' laughed Ella. 'Got it as payment for doing somebody a favour. This will definitely be popular with some of my clients.' Ella beamed proudly, happier than I had ever seen her, Clint's smile an exact replica.

'This is it mum. The perfect present for my seventeenth. Right?' He wasn't quite asking for permission, but hoping for my approval.

'Have you got a design?' I asked.

'Yes!' Clint couldn't quite believe it. 'Well, a few. I was hoping you would help me choose one. One of your model ships ... I mean ...' He turned all shy, wondering if he had strayed into something too personal.

'Fuck it. Let's get matching ones,' I laughed. Clint's eyes grew as round as saucers, while Ella nearly choked on her beer.

'How about the *Gunstar* from *The Last Starfighter*.' I suggested, 'What do you reckon?'

We did it the same evening. Even Ella got in on the act with a tattoo of a long-extinct exotic bird, and we ended up celebrating till deep into the night. Clint had a few beers, which – unaccustomed to the alcohol – made him painfully sweet and emotional. I didn't hold back either. The tattoos may have been a pointless gesture in the context of our predicament, but it allowed us to feel like we still had some control over our lives, and at the time, that was priceless.

13

Over the course of the next few weeks we settled into a routine of sorts. We were never completely comfortable with each other, and Clint's erratic behaviour was slowly getting worse, but we managed to hold it together and focus on the challenge we were faced with.

Despite the obvious distractions facing Clint, he managed to completely decrypt the Spectra data cache – a feat which still makes me proud to this day, long after.

The results were breathtaking. The Spectra lab research team had mostly concentrated on two distinct areas: first, they delved deep into the transformational process Neo-Tricksters went through, and tried to selectively apply those same forces to other human subjects, hoping to steer the transformation in controlled directions. Sickening but understandable, in a warped kind of way.

Secondly, they aimed to isolate specific Trickari memories encoded in Neo cranial crystals – the source of all Mem. It was this work that was hardest to understand, yet its implications were monumental. Clint was the first to grasp the magnitude of what we were looking at.

I was with him while he was working at his little desk when he made a major breakthrough. He was hunched over a small display screen, quietly scrolling through a database, when he brusquely sat up.

'They aren't just random memories,' he said softly. 'There's something else here …'

I could only just make out what he said, so I sat down with him. 'How so?'

'Well … it's really dense. Like, it's hard to describe just how much data there is in this … crystal stuff, but most of it seems to be what we thought it was, the basic building blocks of memories: visual data, audio, sensory data … but not all of it is like that.'

He pointed at some of the Spectra research data on his

screen, 'Look, they kept finding little pockets of data that didn't conform to the memory err … *format*, for lack of a better word. First they thought it was just random noise or damaged data clusters, right?'

'Right … go on,' I said.

'Well, Spectra was sitting on a mountain of data from other Neo's, not just the ones they created in the lab. So they could compare right?' He waited for me to nod him on.

'Right, yes. Stop saying "right" all the time. You don't need my permission to tell me all this.'

'Yeah OK, sorry. So, they found that these anomalies … they appeared in roughly equal concentration in every crystal sample they analysed. Which points at something deliberate, not random.'

'Like what? How far did they get with this?'

'Like puzzle pieces. Components of a bigger whole. They found that there was overlap. Some of the data had hooks or keys – hmm not sure how to put this – the data would tie neatly into similar hidden data in the other Neo crystals. Like pieces of a puzzle, as I said.' Irritation crept into his voice. He was close to exhaustion.

'What kind of puzzle? I mean, what do the pieces add up to?'

He sighed, 'That's what they were still trying to figure out when their Habitat core failed. But it must have been significant to say the least. Figuring this stuff out could lead to understanding what the Trickari were, what they wanted … why they left these traps for us to fall into …'

This was it, the unthinkable: *a sliver of hope*. A splinter of a possibility that we could beat this. 'Can you finish what they started?' I asked.

'Mum … I'm not … I'm just a kid. They – Spectra – they had everything, a lab, a team, the best equipment, even an AI. I have almost nothing.'

'But you have all their data, and there have been later Neo cases they didn't have access to. We could look into those … More puzzle pieces to work with, right?' I left unsaid that one of those cases would be himself.

'Well, that's true, but I need to get access to that data somehow. I have no idea how to do that.'

Ella laughed, 'Easy, we need to score us some Mem.'

We both jumped, completely oblivious to her arrival. But she was right. We needed to score. Mem was the key to unlock this thing.

'No, it can't be me. How many times do I have to say it?' Ella shouted, getting pissed off with me. 'Everybody knows me, and everybody knows I don't touch the stuff! Last guy who offered me some still can't walk right.'

'Well, it can't be me either. I'm too young,' said Clint. I threw such a cutting look his way that he visibly winced.

'It has to be you Jemm. It is what it is,' said Ella. 'What's the problem anyway? It's not like we'll use it to get high.'

She was right of course, but how could I explain to her that even getting near drugs put my hackles up. Mem reminded me too much of what happened to my father.

'Damn it to hell,' I cursed. 'I don't know how to do this. I don't know where to get it. They'll know something is wrong.'

'Come off it,' Ella said. 'They're drug dealers. Everybody who comes to them has something wrong with them. And I'll tell you where to go.'

'Come on mum,' Clint pleaded. 'We need this.'

'Fine. Be quiet, both of you, I'll do it. Just ... lay off me for a moment.'

I was crankier than I had any reason to be. Something had been bothering me, but it was hard to define. I felt strange, my heart was pounding – there was something wrong with me. I tried to collect my thoughts when I noticed a strange taste in my mouth, getting stronger and stronger. I couldn't identify it at first, and drank some water to get rid of it, but it just kept getting stronger. The taste was impossible to describe, and I started to get worried I was having some kind of episode. Then, the true nature of the odd taste dawned on me – I was having a synaesthetic experience. I could taste … a *colour*, but it was no colour I had ever seen before. I felt I was looking (*tasting)* through the eyes of an exotic creature, seeing a completely different spectrum to what humans normally can perceive.

I had to sit down – the sensory input was overwhelming. My brain furiously tried to make sense of it all but failed miserably, leaving me on the verge of fainting. A wave of panicked thoughts washed over me:

<No please no I can't take this not now it's too soon I'm not ready please stop>

Everything spun. Everything felt wrong. Too much light … too little light … I couldn't cope. I had no defences capable of dealing with this onslaught. I moaned in distress.

I vaguely felt Ella shaking me, gentle but firm, but I couldn't respond. The thoughts kept coming:

<I need to live I don't want to lose my mind–where is my*^76&–how come I can't%^^– what is happening to me …>

Then it hit me: The thoughts weren't mine, they were *Clint's*! A dam had burst in his mind, flooding his thoughts with Trickari concepts and feelings and somehow it was spilling over to my senses. I was feeling what he was feeling.

I forced myself to get up, and though unsteady I managed to walk up to him. I held his head, forcing him to look into my eyes.

'It's not real,' I said, trying to get his attention. 'It's not real. *This* is real. Here, around you, me, Ella.' He was starting to calm down, and I could feel/taste/hear his mind settling down. The bizarre colourful taste in my mouth receded, leaving behind a metallic numbness.

'Mother?' Clint moaned, sounding weak.

I held him close, pulling his face to my chest, cradling him. I stroked his head like I used to do when he had bad dreams. I stroked slowly, soothing him, glad that after everything that had happened to him I could still just be his mother.

I continued stroking until, to my horror, I realised his hair was falling out in clumps. Hard crystalline edges revealed themselves underneath, all over his scalp.

They were flowers of madness, aching to bloom.

"The Chimera" was a mess of a bar – a real dive. It was dirty, smelly, and filled with comically shady characters. It stood almost diametrically opposed to the ordered and disciplined society outside its doors.

I saw a woman with half her face burned off, the remaining half permanently stuck in a painful parody of a smile. A burly man, enhanced with augments so badly integrated that I expected him to fall over from augment sickness at any moment. Junkies sat quietly in every corner, zonked on Mem.

The soundsystem was decent enough. Pumping out neo-punk from the likes of the Dead Jenkins and some other modern stuff I didn't recognise.

The bartender was a surprisingly tall woman who looked like she would enjoy a scrap. She was muscular, athletic and despite her hard edges strikingly beautiful.

The walls were covered with dozens and dozens of *flags*, of all things. I guess the Chimera was meant to be a home to scum of all nations – a cosmopolitan shithole.

I sat down at the bar and was greeted with an appraising look from the bar lady.

'What?' she asked. Charm personified.

'A cosmopolitan,' I joked, mostly for my own benefit. But she smiled and mixed me one without complaint. With mild surprise I found it absolutely perfect.

'Best cosmo I had in years,' I said while raising my glass in a grateful salute.

'Yah,' she grunted. A smug note of pride cut through her neutral expression, and settled into a razor-thin smile. 'New in town?'

'Not new, not a regular either. I move around a lot you know?'

'Bit of this, bit of that?' She winked as she said it.

'Something like that.'

'You don't look much like my regulars.' She cocked her head in a girlish way. 'Thankfully.' That sharp smile appeared again; she was very attractive, in a classical Sim-actress kind of way.

We engaged in some harmless back-and-forth flirting, which I enjoyed more than I should have. Her names was Rosie – not her real name I suspected – and she was smart as a whip. It was tempting to just sit there and talk and flirt and get pleasantly wobbly, but I was there for another reason, and I had to push on. I figured I had prepared the ground enough to move forward.

'TJs here look different to me than on Earth. How come?' I asked.

'Dunno. Junkie's a junkie to me. Same empty eyes no matter where they are.'

I carried on, undeterred, 'Yeah but there are differences. Some are more jittery, some more laid back … I think it's to do with how old the Mem is.'

'Could be. Who knows right?' It was obvious she knew what I wanted, so I decided to push my luck.

'Do you get new stuff here? Maybe got your own supply?' I asked hopefully. A glimpse of resigned disappointment flashed in Rosie's eyes.

'Look babe, if you want to score just tell me and I'll hook you up. No need to sex me up first.'

'Oh, it's not for me. And I like sexing you up. Come on, do I look like a junkie to you?'

'Not sure what you look like, but whatever.' She pointed to a corner even darker than the rest of the place. It almost hid a hunched-over character sipping a flat beer at an old round table. 'The man you want sits over there. That's Theo, if he asks, tell him I said it's OK. He won't ask though.' I nodded and moved to join him. Things were going better than expected.

The table, like most of the decor, had seen better days.

It was sturdy enough, made out of some indestructible poly-compound, but covered in rings from an endless history of bearing dirty glasses.

'I've got a friend who needs to remember,' I said as I sat down. It was a line Ella had taught me, apparently code for scoring Mem.

The guy didn't even look up. I guess he was used to this kind of thing.

'What memories is he struggling with?' he said, staring at his drink. 'I might be able to help him if it's recent stuff.' He sat back in his chair, taking a good look at his prospective client.

The hairs in my neck stood up straight with a tingling sensation, as if trying to uproot themselves and run off. *I know this guy …*

'My friend needs to remember many things,' I continued regardless. 'He's never had this problem before.'

'Sure luv, I can offer a whole range of samples. Won't be cheap though.' And just then, the badly disguised London snarl in his accent sparked recognition in me: he was the obnoxious enforcer from Spectra HQ, with the shark-shaped birthmark on his throat. The one I toyed with before seeing Lawrence Skinner.

I looked closer. Sure enough; the shark on his throat swam around when he sipped his drink..

"Theo", that's right, that's what his badge at the time said as well… What if he remembers me? It was *several months ago…*

But I didn't have another option – and Clint didn't have time for me to find any.

'Good,' I said brusquely, 'Let's do it.'

'Take it easy there luv, I like some foreplay before the main event. I like to know who I'm being intimate with, so to speak. Why don't you order another drink so we can chat eh?' In my mind's eye I watched myself smash a chair into his arrogant face. Tempting as that notion was I needed to get this deal over with before he recognised me. I had to play it cool.

'Maybe another time *luv*. Now listen, my friend can pay a nice premium if we do this quickly. Nice and clean. If not … then I'll go and make sure I go find somebody that can help my friend with the urgency he deserves. See, this deal works both ways.'

Theo was struggling. He wanted to make the sale, but something was bothering him. I could tell his dim-witted brain was struggling to connect the person in front of him to a memory which was eluding him for now. Our meeting on Earth occurred in such a different context that he couldn't place me… yet.

I stood up, snapped, 'Fine, then. Nice meetin' ya.'

'Sit down luv. Let's get it done. How many samples does your mate need?'

'Firstly, he doesn't care about volume. He cares about *diversity*. So, as wide a set as you can possibly put together. The smallest samples that can still make him remember. Understand? A bit of everything you got, basically.'

'OK can do. And secondly?'

'Secondly, call me luv again and I will personally skin that crazy shark off your throat with my teeth.'

He held up his hands in a mock surrender. 'Just a figure of speech, milady. No harm intended.' When I didn't reply he continued, this time more business-like. 'I'll need a few hours to get it all together. It's a big order … but I'll do you a fair price.'

'How much?'

'25,000 credits.'

'15,000, which is too much but I'm in a hurry.'

'OK 20,000. That's cheap.'

'15,000. You know that's more than a bunch of samples is worth.'

He sat there for a while, trying to work out who he was dealing with, yet I needed him to get on with this before he managed to put two and two together. I made to leave again but he pulled me back.

'Fine, let's do it. Stay here, I'll be back in an hour. You can trust me on that because Rosie here gets a cut and she will rip me in two if I fuck with her customers.' He waved at her, 'You vouch for me Rosie? Right?' She gave us both a thumbs up, after which he slithered out the door, wincing when the outside light hit his features.

'Do your thing shithead,' I said under my breath.

Rosie snorted derisively, but I wasn't sure if it was in reply to my insult.

It took Theo two hours to get back with the samples, but spending time with Rosie made it a pleasant two hours. As rough around the edges as she was, she also possessed a sharp sense of humour and her stories betrayed a talent for getting both in and out of trouble. Rosie was one of those people who have a natural talent for telling tales. These days I had a few of my own, and sharing them was surprisingly fun. For a brief moment I wondered what it would be like to not be alone, to go through life with a partner as vivacious as Rosie. It was an entertaining fantasy. In fact, I was almost irritated when Theo finally returned, proudly carrying the goods. I paid him there and then, keeping an eye out for any signs of recognition in his eyes, but it seemed I had slipped through the net. He scampered off, happy and cocky and oblivious, true to type.

'What's his story then?' I asked Rosie. 'Doesn't seem local to me?'

'Yeah he used to be some Corp goon on Earth before something went wrong. Still pines for it too, but hey; a man's gotta eat.'

'True. A woman's gotta eat too. I'd better go grab a bite.' A ferocious appetite had snuck up on me. 'Catch you around.'

As I carried the sample case out the door, Rosie blew me a kiss. I couldn't help but laugh out loud.

14

Over the next weeks Clint's condition deteriorated rapidly, and with it his mental stability. Naively I had expected the changes to be gradual – a slow metamorphosis, or perhaps a gentle cocooning phase. Nothing could be further from the truth. The changes were violent, abrupt and shocking.

Clint's bones elongated during agonising spurts, lasting hours at a time. Crystal growths ripped through his scalp, blood pouring down his face. His eyes changed colour and shape, the new physiology subjecting his brain to confusing visual concepts. He literally wept bitter black tears.

We had to stay with him at all times, consoling him, treating his pain … There was no way he could go outside now. Cooped up inside he oscillated between bouts of morose depression and manic energy, feverishly attempting to analyse the data from the Mem samples I had bought.

Yet, in some ways the metamorphosis was helpful; Clint's mental acuity came to align with the very data he was examining. Intuitive jumps that he would have never made before became commonplace. I felt we were inching closer and closer toward some vital truth, but we were losing the battle with time. This became abundantly clear one afternoon, about a few weeks after I bought the Mem samples. We were both hunched over his workstation, when I noticed his body stiffen abruptly.

'Pain?' I asked.

He shook his head, causing the light reflected off his cranial crystals to dance across the room. 'I think I've got something …' He paused to scratch his knees vigorously, something he had started doing recently. One of many new tics. 'So far we've treated all this Mem data as if it's just a matter of decryption, to get to the true meaning, right? But I think that's all wrong. I think that data is something else.'

'How so?' I asked.

He didn't answer immediately. He opened and closed his mouth, as if to speak, but lacking the right words to convey the concepts involved – which might well be the case. He composed himself and said, 'I think it's meant to be executed. They are commands.'

'Executed by whom?'

'By *what*. I think it's computer code. It's incredibly dense, and I have no idea what it's *for* exactly, but I think we are looking at one or more programs, distributed over the memory caches of all the Neos that have been created over the decades since the Trickari discoveries.'

I was stunned. 'That's … worrying.'

'I don't know what it is. But it's something. I think I can–'

Clint keeled over violently, his eyes bulging, and screamed like his soul was being torn to shreds. I had never seen him in this much pain before.

The screaming stopped as he inhaled sharply, then returned even louder. Ella came rushing in on her skimmer.

'What the fuck is this? What's wrong with him?'

'I don't know! He was about to tell me about a breakthrough when this happened!' It was hard to make myself heard over Clint's anguished screams. 'Can you do something?'

'Take him to my lab. I need to examine him,' she grunted at me.

'We need to help him!' I shouted, the screaming tearing through all my defences. I was on the verge of complete panic.

'Just bring him, now!'

When we arrived in Ella's lab she produced a syringe, injecting Clint in his neck. He spasmed once or twice like a fish being reeled in, before he suddenly went limp.

For a moment all I could hear was our panicked, frantic

breathing, gradually calming down as we regained some of our composure, until eventually a quiet descended on the scene.

Ella and I looked at each other in stunned silence.

I sat by his side for the next twelve hours, feeling a wrongness settle over him. I can't explain it better than that, even to myself, but I knew that something fundamental had changed for the worse. He appeared no different from the day before – haggard, sure, but still mostly human. Yet there was a change that had come over him that touched all his features, his entire *being*. The rhythm of his breathing, the pallor of his skin, the sound of his voice as he moaned in his sleep; he had entered a new stage in his transformation.

I was frightened to the core, disturbed at a fundamental level by watching my child turn into something ... *other*. I didn't know if I should feel pity or disgust at what was happening to him. My mind went round and round in circles, unable to come to grips with events until, finally, exhaustion dulled my thoughts and dragged me down.

My sleep brought no relief. Once again I was sinking into the depths, surrounded by water, colder and darker than the deepest lake.

Clint was below me, but so was something else, circling him. I couldn't tell what it was but I knew that I didn't want it near my son. I kicked hard against the water, gaining on them, getting ever closer until I was within touching distance. When I desperately reached for Clint the creature's hand shot out, grabbed my wrist with a grip like a vice. I couldn't break free. I thrashed and kicked and screamed, but he was beyond my reach.

A voice spoke, I couldn't make out who it was or where it came from ...

... Here come here it's where we are down here all of you come soon come to us we are here find us in this

place down here come here we are waiting in here come to us …

It was an outpouring of *sensations* as much as words. I could hear, smell, see, and feel that message over and over again. It was overwhelming me, drowning me.

I heard my own voice as if from far away trying to resist the onslaught. *Stop it. No, please. It hurts!* The water around me brightened, stabbed by beams of sunshine. The glow erased the shapes of Clint and the creature below me, until they were nothing but retinal afterimages.

Then I was awake, with Ella standing over me, cloaked in an expression of concern.

'You were moaning,' she said.

Tears rolled down my cheek. 'He … *It* is talking to me.'

'Who? What do you mean?'

<here it's where we are down here all of you come soon come to us we are here find us in this place down here>

'I can't shut it out. It's drowning everything. Clint is lost in there.'

'You're not making sense,' said Ella, eyes wide. 'Tell me what you're hearing. Please.'

'Trickari. Ghosts … I don't know what they are. I can hear them.' I grabbed Ella's arm, firmly. 'You were right. I should have listened to you. We need to try your plan. Before it's too late.'

But I knew it was too late already.

'Are you sure about this?' Ella said.

I looked at the solo augment unit. It looked a bit like a cryogenic tube out of old sci-fi sims, only bigger. Medical white, touchscreen displays, tubes and needles and robot arms; the unit seemed comprehensive, state of the art even.

Clint was laid out inside, naked, vulnerable, like a baby. His exotic shape gave the unit a surreal otherworldly quality. His crystal hair a crown for a pharaoh from the stars.

'Yes. Do it.' I replied.

'I've only used this unit a few times. It was damn expensive because it runs a military grade sub-AI. It should be OK. '

'Should? Jesus Christ … Come on Ella, I'm on the verge here. Don't fuck with me.'

'Well, I only do light augment ops at my clinic. Anything major goes to the big outfits. I have a contract with them. People buy my augments, I do all the prep work and outsource the big jobs. But obviously we can't fucking do that with Clint.' I noticed that whenever I cursed, Ella joined in. It was almost funny.

'How safe is it?' I asked, struggling to keep focused. I had developed an apocalyptic headache after the mental onslaught from earlier.

'Safe … what's fucking safe here? None of this is safe.' Ella brushed through her hair with both hands. 'Look, all I can say is that without the Trickari infection this kind of operation would be fine for Clint. With the transformational elements added to the mix though … Who knows? Sorry, but that's the truth of it.'

I thought back to the previous day; Clint had woken up shortly after my experience with the Trickari voices. He seemed dazed, unsure of himself, but slowly regained a measure of his composure. The ghostly voices had receded but never went away completely. I kept catching snippets, trapped in a game of hide and seek inside a hall of mirrors. Clint confessed he had been hearing the voices for days. It was no surprise that he wanted to try Ella's procedure.

I sighed, 'We don't have a choice. *Clint* doesn't have a choice. What else can we do?'

Ella just nodded. There wasn't much more to say.

The operation was almost too much for me to watch, but I persevered. Nimble robotic appendages cut and sliced with lasers and scalpels. Needles entered flesh, tubes provided suction. Major organs were replaced by slick-looking augments, designed and built by Ella. I felt every incision as if I was being cut myself.

Even with the incredible precision and speed of the sub-AI the operation still took six hours. When it was finally done Clint resembled a corpse, animated by a cruel god-machine.

A hand gently touched my arm. 'He did well. Look.' Ella pointed out the vital stats readouts. 'He's in good shape.'

'How long before he's awake?' I asked, my voice raspy from exhaustion.

'A while … 24 hours at least.'

'When will we know if it worked?'

'Soon after. But I feel confident.' The reassurance in her voice triggered something in me. Something ugly. Unable to put words to my feelings, my face showed such withering resentment that she visibly flinched. 'I'll let you be alone with him,' said Ella. 'Try to get some rest OK?'

Ella left after that, her skimmer purring softly like a cat settling down to sleep.

The next five days were some of the hardest we had to endure. Clint regained consciousness on day two, but he was barely coherent. To my relief the Trickari voices were all but gone, which I took as a good sign, but I wondered if his mind had been permanently damaged.

On day three Clint sat up, managed a small meal and an attempt at witty conversation before he passed out again. I cried for hours afterwards. I was starting to believe again.

Tests showed that the treatment was working. Cell transformation had slowed down to a fraction of its previous speed, and the augments were doing their part. This meant we had achieved the main goal of the treatment: we had bought ourselves a bit more time to try to fix the underlying problem.

Still, I could not look upon my son without horror. He was Frankenstein's monster made flesh again, and I was responsible. I would never forgive myself for the part I had played in this.

Day four was different. At this point I had finally regained some hope we could beat this. Ella had extracted some of Clint's crystal hair for analysis and comparison. Her work on the samples yielded new Trickari code snippets – enough to support Clint's theory. Further research suggested that we had nearly assembled the full set of instructions. If we could hold off fate long enough we might uncover the biggest secret in the solar system. Maybe it would be enough to save my son.

Driven by the extraordinary potential of these revelations Ella and I worked through the night until I finally fell asleep at the dawn of day five, the day they attacked.

The lab was bathed in the soft blue light used for the facility's night cycle. It reminded me of moonlight, and I felt a sharp pang of longing for Earth. No matter how adept humans are at adjusting to their environment, we will always be subject to base instincts developed over millions of years on the home planet. We may push these feelings aside, but they are as involuntary as the beating of our own heart.

The attackers wore shimmer-suits and kinetic enhancers. The suits must have been padded, we couldn't hear them approach. There were only three of them. The small size of the extraction team showed how confident they were in their abilities.

Shimmer-tech made it almost impossible to see them in the near-dark, but something woke me up … some protective instinct maybe, attuned to my environment. Or maybe it was just my old Corp training kicking in.

My eyes flashed open – something was horribly wrong. I slowly scanned the room while reaching for a weapon; my fingers found Clint's little flechette gun. I slowly drew it towards me, continuing the sweep of the room. All looked normal … Clint was still in his pod, while Ella was deep asleep in a makeshift bed. It was quiet. All I could hear was my breathing and the gentle hum of Clint's pod.

I saw an odd sparkle in the glare of one of the lab screens and instantly knew what we were dealing with; my father had shown me shimmer-tech before, and I had never forgotten the telltale signs.

They went for Ella first – which ironically saved her life. They should have attacked us both simultaneously, but they gave me a split second to react. I shouted out, Ella sat up with a jolt, and a gaping wound blossomed on her side, just below her heart. Her eyes radiated pain, her mouth twisted into a silent screen

I used the flechette without thinking, spraying a large area to the side of Ella's bed. Sharp impact sounds filled the room until I found a target as much by luck as by design. Sparks and blood erupted mid-air. The shimmering effect appeared again, intensified, and eventually gave shape to a man clutching his stomach. The suit protected well against prying eyes but offered little shielding against high velocity shards. I shot him again, the projectiles disintegrating most of his face. He fell over without a sound.

A noise behind me alerted me to another intruder. I spun around, took aim.

Nothing …

I fired anyway, hoping for a repeat of my earlier success. The shards hit a wall instead, wasting valuable rounds. I stood frozen watching for movement, listening for signs of life …

A quiet settled over the room. Dust particles floated in the blue light, a red stain grew ever larger under the body of the man I shot. I vaguely heard Ella breathing. Irregular, but signalling that she was still alive.

I backed into a corner, painfully aware that there was at least one other person in the room. I held the gun in front of me, hoping to get a warning before they attacked again. I spotted movement near Clint and whipped my gun in the direction of the pod, cursing under my breath; I couldn't shoot for fear of hitting Clint. Before I could finish the move I felt a devastating shock in my left arm. Nausea flooded me as I observed in a detached haze how my forearm dangled at a strange angle.

Another shock, this time in my right leg. It buckled, snapped like a twig, and I fell on the floor. An ugly and jagged bone shard pierced the skin of my lower leg. The pain was beyond description.

A ghost-like figure opened Clint's pod – perhaps it was a spectre, jealous of the living, trying to steal his soul and drag it with him into the netherworld. I was in shock, my mind unable to process events.

Another shimmering figure appeared right next to me and picked up my flechette gun. He spoke to me in a voice that sung with violence and sadism and malice.

'You stole from a Corp, Jemm. Why would you do such a thing?' *He knew my name...*

I rasped, 'Don't take ... my son ...' I was barely able to speak, but I forced the words out. 'If you take him ... I will hunt you down ...'

The shimmer-field prevented me from seeing his face, but I could see amusement in his body language. 'Look at you. You're lying there in pieces and you still think you can threaten me? Silly girl.' He lifted the flechette gun, aimed it at my head. 'Nothing personal, but this nonsense has to stop, now.'

He pulled the trigger. The gun beeped. It was empty.

His partner barked something in Corp speak, his voice raspy but to the point.

'*Leave her, she'll bleed out soon enough.*'

This confirmed two things to me: first, Spectra was behind this raid – I recognised the dialect immediately.

Secondly, our discovery was worth a lot to them. To send a wetwork team out to Mars like this was no minor operation.

Another barked comment followed: Police were on their way. They were nearly out of time.

The third man used some kind of tracking device to locate the Spectra data drives we retrieved from the Gaianista habitat. He pocketed them, then joined his colleague and helped him lift up Clint – gently but with purpose. The second man produced a syringe and injected Clint with some fluid, presumably to keep him under while they got away.

I lifted my hand as if to grab them both. I screeched, 'I will find you!' over and over again, barely recognising my own voice. They didn't even hear me, or maybe they just didn't care.

After they left I drifted in and out of consciousness, my mind as fragmented as the shattered bones in my arm and leg. I embraced the pain that was coming my way. I would use it. Precious fuel, to launch myself like a rocket aimed straight at the heart of the monster that took my son.

PART THREE
TRANSFORMATION

15

Baroness Odessa's very short history of

Humanity: the Trickari Discovery years.

Extract II: "The Icarus Years"

– Earth Years 2150 – 2200

Dear reader, weren't we once glorious? Hadn't we overcome our petty differences? Didn't we reach that summit together, a united human race, aiming for the sky? This writer knows we did. They say there is nothing more cruel than gifting a person hope, only to snatch it away. I think we all know this to be true. Humanity had finally overcome its own weaknesses and built the foundation for a glorious new age, only to watch it crash and burn. Trickari technology, as powerful as it was, turned out to be tainted.

First we lost the Moon. The lunar colonies all relied on Trickari power-cores to maintain the structural integrity of the great domes which had stood proudly for decades. But, they came down nonetheless, one by one, like tired balloons deflated at the end of a grand party.

Tens of thousands of poor souls died without warning, lost in the silence of deep vacuum. At first nobody quite believed our beloved Trick-tech was to blame. Indeed, anybody whispering such a dangerous suggestion could expect to be rounded up and … well dear reader, let's not dwell on such things.

Many months passed. No real explanation was found so we blamed "terrorists" and moved on. Things eventually settled back into their rightful groove. Oh, we grieved appropriately, and we mourned our poor lost Lunarians with all our heart, but "the show had to go on" as they said.

Next, my dear reader, we lost Mars dome "Heracles", Mars Orbital II and several Gaianista habitats, all in quick succession. Shockingly, further catastrophic incidents were being reported on Earth. This time there was no hiding behind terrorists or other fanciful explanations. No, this time it became clear that Trickari technology was failing catastrophically all around us. Or rather, to be precise, Trickari *Red* technology was failing us.

Every Red artifact and every Red-powered device we had ever built had become a ticking time bomb. A primed mine, ready to blow at the merest touch. It seemed we could not cheat the laws of nature after all, and that the bill for our hubris had finally arrived.

Mercifully, it was only Trick-Red that had become unstable, likely due to "extra-dimensional blowback", so I'm told. Whatever that may mean. Trick-Blue on the other hand only derived power from its *internal* power source, which is what saved humanity in the end.

Blue tech gave us the power to quarantine disaster zones and keep us going while we tried to isolate every Red device we could find, until we finally contained the crisis.

But, oh how we suffered before that moment dear reader! While cities burned, and space stations were falling from the sky, humanity rediscovered its capacity for self-sabotage. Border conflicts long forgotten flared up once again. Racial tensions – previously abandoned against the background of newly discovered extra-terrestrial life – spilled out in the open once again.

Even while some were trying to save us all we reverted to a state of perpetual war and conflict, rapidly strangling any progress we had previously made. As bad as the damage caused by unstable Red was, it paled into insignificance next to the damage we were doing to ourselves. War had returned to humanity. Millions died in the new trenches.

Eventually Korea and Japan spat "tactical" nukes at each other, although I fail to see how nuclear holocaust can be tactical. The resulting horror provided the shock therapy we needed to pull ourselves together. International accords outlawed Trick-Red while Blue was put under serious regulations. The boys with the biggest guns put pressure on the boys with the little ones, and eventually we all stopped fighting and began licking our wounds.

Ironically, the Trickari tech that nearly brought us down had also preserved us. If we had still been constrained on Earth we probably would have wiped ourselves out with great fervour and enthusiasm, but since the Acceleration we had spread out over so many planets, moons and stations that we had become more resilient as a species. A new spirit rose out of the ashes of our misfortune, determined to keep the fire alive.

Little did we know there was worse to come. But, dear reader, the painful truth is that ignorance makes a poor shield against the savage sword of destiny.

16

Rosie looked at me with a mixture of concern and excitement. 'You OK hun?'

I nodded unconvincingly and grimaced, biting back a moan as I tried to ride out the wave of nauseating pain rolling over me.

'Augment pain,' I managed to whisper. 'It'll pass.' I slowly flexed my cybernetic arm and hand, willing the pain to go away. It refused to do so, instead spreading to my new leg. This time I couldn't suppress the pain and I moaned pitifully.

Rosie rolled over to my side of the bed, taking care not to lean on me with her large muscular frame. She gently rubbed my real leg, slowly moving upwards. I welcomed the distraction and smiled.

'Want me to stop?' she teased.

I answered by grabbing her hand and pushing it against me, hard. Despite being sore my body responded with a hunger and eagerness that was impossible to deny.

Rosie gradually sped up her movement. I reached out to her to return the favour but she batted my hand away.

'It's OK, let Rosie do her thing.'

It only took a few minutes but my orgasm was as intense as any I've had before. My body jerked and spasmed while I rode her hand relentlessly, refusing to let go.

Afterwards I felt myself sliding into sleep, but forced myself awake. I didn't want to go back to the nightmares that had been haunting me since the attack three months ago, when something went cold inside me.

Rosie spotted my darkening mood and gently but firmly kissed me until I was out of breath.

'Don't go there hun,' she said, 'You might not come back.'

She was wrong. I embraced the anguish and disgust and hatred that infused me when I thought back to what had happened; Clint stolen from me, Ella hideously disfigured but too stubborn to die, and my own transformation from a whole person into this *thing* with badly fitting artificial parts.

Every day my mind revolted at what had been done to my body. I had allowed augments to be fitted to repair the terrible damage I had suffered during the raid on Ella's compound. Although they went against all my instincts I grudgingly accepted the enhancements, if only to give myself a sliver of a chance to get my son back – or failing that, a chance at revenge.

'Too late,' I said. 'I'm there already.'

'Come on, let's get dressed. We got work to do.'

She stood up abruptly, showing off her remarkable body. Her back was athletic, broad, covered in scars and tattoos. Not a gym body, but one born from an active life and lucky genes. Her breasts were surprisingly small, but well formed, her legs muscular and long. Rosie wasn't vain, but she wasn't shy either.

I felt myself get excited again, and it took little effort to convince Rosie to get back to bed. This time she let me take the reins.

Our new gig was a nasty one, but it paid well. Rosie was involved with an enforcement and research agency, whose main business seemed to revolve around cases that were a little too rich for local law enforcement.

The agency, like many of its ilk, bore an incredibly bland and generic name – EN-COM – but most of our jobs with them were anything but bland and generic. Far from it; almost every EN-COM gig so far had been messy, and often violent.

That day we were sent to investigate reports of illegal artifact possession, which wasn't too exciting in itself, but the alleged owner was a known violent criminal and there had been indications that the artifact in question might be unstable. There was great potential for bad mojo.

Surprisingly, I enjoyed the work a lot. Rosie was

remarkably capable, ruthless to the core, but terrific company. I learned a lot from her, including effective use of my new arm and leg, and the advantages that came with their prodigious strength and ability.

Additionally, I could flex my Xeno muscles, surprising Rosie with my ability to wring out extra profit on almost every mission. That profit was shared equally, and we were both extremely motivated to increase our earnings on every EN-COM job.

Our transport buggy was taking us to one of the old Mars enclaves. The Bug's huge wheels were able to deal with any kind of environment with ease, which seemed to encourage the driver to seek out the roughest terrain available. The vehicle lurched and dipped and dived in an unpredictable and sickening dance with the Martian landscape, leaving behind a long trail of red dust.

The rough ride brought me to the edge of serious motion sickness, but the sharp augment-pain triggered by the frequent jolts kept me distracted.

'You look a bit green babe. You going to make it, or do you need a baggie?' said Rosie. She was enjoying my discomfort far too much, flashing me an impish smile.

I didn't answer, but battled stoically to maintain my focus on the horizon in front of me. It just about worked; I managed not to empty my stomach all over the Bug's passenger compartment.

'How much further?' I eventually croaked.

'Don't worry. Not too far.' She punched the driver seat playfully. 'Isn't that right Ernest?'

'Yes, yes,' Ernest replied. Short for Ernesto, he was a man of few words and even less interest in small talk. He was a good driver but the dipping and swaying was getting to me.

'Can you get us on less rough terrain please,' I pleaded.

'No, no. This is quickest.'

The next bump was so extreme that my leg exploded in agony and I screamed. 'For fuck's sake Ernest. Get us to better terrain or I won't be able to do the job. And then you won't get paid either. Got that?'

Rosie leaned in and quietly spoke in Ernest's ear.

'OK, OK,' he said. We swerved away from our current path and soon enough the Bug was on steadier footing.

'Thank you. Not that fucking hard, was it?' I spat the words from behind gritted teeth. It really had hurt, and I had already exceeded my daily painkillers limit. It added up to a seriously foul mood.

I refocused my eyes on the horizon; a level line to fight the nausea which was trying to take over. There was a sudden flash, followed by an explosion full of star-bursts and coloured trails. I ducked instinctively but Rosie and Ernest seemed completely non-plussed. Another explosion, this time a shower of magenta sparks came down in its wake. I cursed; I had been looking at fireworks. The Martian New Year was still a fair bit away, but evidently some people couldn't contain themselves.

It was no different back on Earth. D-Town nights were peppered with explosions and rocket-trails months before the new year. I took comfort in that familiar memory and for a moment I felt less adrift.

The rest of the trip took about an hour, which made me wonder if it was ever necessary to go over such bumpy terrain in the first place. I shrugged and mentally prepared myself for the job ahead.

We stopped behind a ridge, just out of sight of a little enclave situated in a depression in the landscape below us. I couldn't tell if it was a natural valley or an old meteor impact site but it made for an easily approachable target, roughly twenty metres below our current position. Not a huge problem in Mars's low gravity, and we soon found a safe approach path.

Ernest and Rosie both drew their guns – utterly vicious wide-beam energy weapons, designed to cause maximum pain to multiple enemies indiscriminately. They were normally used for crowd control.

We slid and hopped down the sandy side of the hollow, like a bunch of playful children, eventually ending up at the back-door of the largest structure.

EN-COM was fully sanctioned to support law enforcement at a high operational level. This meant that we could use override-hammers on most doors on Mars.

We zapped the door several times, but it remained stubbornly shut. The little hammer-shaped devices could fry almost any lock on the planet, but surprisingly this particular back-door seemed to just ignore this fact.

We all looked at each other in puzzlement, until I had an idea. I stepped forward and slowly pushed the door sideways. It slid open without complaint; its main opening mechanism was clearly not powered.

Ernest was first to enter, slowly but confidently moving forward into a plain white corridor. The corridor lights were dim, but provided just enough illumination to follow him. Rosie moved first. I made the rear.

The corridor was covered in fine red dust. It seemed the air scrubbers had failed some time ago, which wasn't a good sign; the occupants had probably left long before, taking anything of value with them. Still, we couldn't presume anything.

I produced an energy scanner and was surprised to see that it indicated several power sources deeper into the facility. There was still a chance that we would find what we were looking for.

The corridor came to a sudden end around a corner. A door, slightly ajar, invited us to step inside. A hand signal from Ernest told us to stop while he checked out the next room. Ernest liked to take point. The danger and excitement of these missions was as much an incentive to him as the high pay. *It's always the quiet ones ...* I thought.

Ernest slid past the door, quiet as a shadow, kicking up small clouds of fine red dust as he disappeared. I counted the seconds in my head. Ten, twenty, thirty ... He returned almost exactly 120 seconds later, looking confused and worried.

'Jemm, you'd better come and see this. It's not … I don't know what this is.'

I nodded, following him into the room.

There was red dust everywhere; centimetres deep in places. It was a typical Martian structure – utilitarian, solid and rugged, square to a fault. There were heaps of clothes lying scattered throughout the room. Boots, shoes, coveralls, but no sign of the alleged offenders. I checked my scanner again and noticed that the energy readings were in this room. I followed the signal to a large metal table – part of it covered in yet more red dust. I spotted a box, and wiped the dust off to reveal a rugged artifact container – military design, clearly stolen. A small pulsing Blue artifact lay inside, like a pretty pearl in a green shell. Ernest whistled appreciatively.

I noticed something odd about the dust on the table: it contained streaks of grey particles, like veins inside a rock formation. A disturbing theory teased my brain.

'Rosie,' I said, trying to keep my voice steady. Are the boots and shoes full of red dust, with grey particles in the middle?

It only took seconds to verify. 'Yep, how did you know hun?'

A sick feeling entered my stomach. Foreboding mixed with horror. 'Ernest, how many people were supposed to be here?'

'Three … four maybe. Latest intel said so. Maybe more'

'They're still here,' I pointed at the shoes and boots and the heaps of red dust. 'All this dust … It isn't surface dust, it's blood. And bones.'

It took Rosie and Ernest only a few moments to understand what I was saying. Awe and disgust rippled across their faces.

'It's the artifact,' I said, stating what was now obvious. 'And that, ladies and gentlemen, is why Trickari artifacts are tightly regulated.'

'Is it unstable? Shouldn't we get the fuck out of dodge?' Rosie asked.

'No. Look at the markings on the box. It's Blue.' I

emptied the box of the red dust, trying not to think about the fact that it had once been a person, presumably the one who had operated the artifact.

Rosie looked on in distaste. 'I didn't know artifacts could do that.'

'You'd be surprised what some of them can do.'

'Let's go.' Ernest had had enough. There was no opportunity for further action.

'Wait. I want to check something.' My scanner had indicated additional power sources and I had a good idea what they were. I rooted through the dust in the clothes heaps, despite Rosie's disgusted protestations.

'Come on Jemm. That's just sick.'

'I'm not here to have a goddamn good time, Rosie.' My temper was getting the best of me but it was too late to walk it back now. 'Now let me do this. I you don't like it, you can wait in the Bug.'

Rosie stepped up and shoved me, hard, landing me on my arse. 'Tell me to wait in the fucking car again and I will knock you out.' She was deadly serious.

'Look, I'm sorry,' I said, brushing myself off as I got to my feet. 'I know this looks awful, but if you can just give me a minute …' I went back to my search and soon found what I was looking for – several augments, high grade stuff, hiding in the dessicated remains of the people whose lives they had previously enhanced. It was hard to tell what their function was, but one of them blinked intermittently, driven by a strong Blue power source. I showed them off to the others, grinning like a prospector who had hit pay-dirt.

I dug a bit deeper on a hunch, and found a beautiful silver necklace with an empty locket. I offered it to Rosie as a peace offering. She snatched it out of my hand with a snarl – sending a small plume of dust in the air – but as she immediately hung it round her neck. I assumed I was back in her favour.

After the Spectra attack I didn't bleed out, although it was a close call. Ella managed to drag herself to an autodoc, stabilised herself so she would survive her own injuries, and then saw to mine.

I was in a bad state, but somehow she managed essential life-saving procedures on me, smuggled me out of her ravaged lab, and got me to a medical facility, all without making matters worse.

On her request the medics treated me as an anonymous patient. It must have cost her a lot of money and favours. I was there for weeks. Full recovery and physio took even longer, but eventually I was able to get up and about again.

To my relief I learned that she had not only saved my life, she had also made backups of the Spectra drives weeks before the attack. She'd scrubbed the stolen original drives of all useful data, and made it seem like they had degraded over the years, ruining any content they had ever held. Anybody spending any time inspecting them would assume they were useless.

Additionally, she'd infected the drives with an ancient virus so destructive that Spectra would suffer some serious pain once the nasty thing started chewing up their networked systems. Ella wasn't just tough, she was also smart.

The whole episode had caused a diplomatic stink between Earth and Mars. The local authorities were not at all pleased with an Earth-originated attack causing such a mess, with apparent impunity. Martian diplomats spoke some very stern words. Earth diplomats, denying any involvement, spoke stern words in return.

When the dust had settled I moved in with Rosie. I needed to lay low and Ella's shop was too busy with customers and under investigation by the authorities. I was surprised by the chemistry between Rosie and me, embracing it with enthusiasm bordering on the obsessive. Anything to stop my mind from dwelling on my problems on its own. Rosie kept me sharp and focused, which was exactly what I needed.

I still visited Ella whenever I could. She had stubbornly remained in her old home, and somehow kept her business running while she slowly recovered from her injuries. God knows how she pulled it all off.

I decided one morning to visit her for breakfast, and to get an update on her research. The walk took only thirty minutes, and took me through a part of town with a good bakery. I went in to buy a peace offering. I chose some excellent Portuguese custard tarts and Madeira cake.

I had to admit to myself that it was partly out of guilt that I wanted to visit her; I was indirectly responsible for the attack on her home, and ideally I'd leave her be in acknowledgement of that, but unfortunately I needed her to continue her research. It was an uncomfortable situation, and every time I saw Ella I was reminded of this.

Ella's survival had come at a cost; the incident had left her physically even weaker than she had been before, which was a bitter pill to swallow.

I rushed through Escher's intricate alleys, now confident enough to find the quickest route to her house. I hoped to catch her before she had her breakfast. Maybe I could get her in a good mood. I felt a tinge of disgust at my cheap manipulative approach, but what else could I do? My self-esteem was irrelevant next to Clint's needs.

I sighed, fed up with my own navel-gazing. I looked up, intending to straighten my shoulders and get on with things, and looked straight into the eyes of a female Trick-Junkie. She had approached me unnoticed. TJ's are normally self-absorbed, almost to the point of bewilderment, but this one had some spark left in her eyes, something that was usually missing. She cocked her head, as if she could hear my thoughts if she listened hard enough …

'Mother?' she said. A taste of metal welled up in my mouth. The hairs on my arms stood up, painfully straight.

'What do you want?' I snapped, feeling disoriented. The taste in my mouth was overpowering.

'I want to go home mother. Please …'

Suddenly, it was all too much for me. 'It's too late for that,' I hissed. 'Nobody forced you to take that shit.'

She stopped in her tracks, suddenly confused, as if no longer sure of where she was. I backed off, grateful for the opportunity to get away, but she had lost all interest in me. I picked up my pace and rushed to Ellie's house.

The incident stuck with me for the rest of the walk. When I finally arrived I took a moment to compose myself before I let myself in the side entrance. I found Ella hunched over a terminal in her lab.

'Hi,' she said. There was too much anger and tension in her voice, even in that one little word. It was so strong that it took me a moment to figure out what to say in return.

'I've found new augments,' I blurted out. 'One of them is Blue and active.'

'Show me.'

'Wait, I also brought these,' and handed over the cakes. Ella put them to the side with barely a glance at the contents.

I also handed over the carrier case that I had brought with me. This got her attention.

'Maybe there's something there for me…' I said. A wave of disgust welled up inside me, as it did every time I considered what I was doing to my own body. My arm and limb augments were bad enough, but they were necessary for me to function at a basic level. But once I had crossed that line, it became clear that I had to make even deeper sacrifices if I was ever going to see Clint again. I was painfully aware that if I had been combat augmented at the time, I would have been able to stop the Spectra shimmer-team with ease.

Ella softened a bit. 'You still have eyes on Clint, right?'

I nodded. 'I'm paying a guy, he's dependable. Apparently they've barely moved Clint,' I said, watching Ella sift through the augments I brought in.

'He's still in London then…,' she said, more to herself than to me. 'They must have found his augments by now, but it won't matter. They'll still slow down the transformation, and even mighty Spectra won't be able to replace them immediately. They won't risk their precious little Mem-factory, and...' Ella paused, finally noticing the impact of her words, then continued with a gentler tone; 'Look... They're not as smart as they think they are. They never are. They'll mess up, get cocky. We'll be ready for that.'

Ella lifted a glassy sphere from the carrier case, about the size of a small tangerine. Small fibre optic threads spilled out one side, like gossamer hair.

'Ocular augment,' said Ella. 'Damn... Very useful. Ultraviolet, enhanced night vision... probably other stuff too. I need to check but this looks like a prize candidate.'

'You want me to replace my eye with that thing?'

'Do you want your son back?'

I didn't dignify that with an answer.

'Does it have to be both eyes?' I asked, hating how squeamish I sounded.

'Probably not, we'll see.' She looked at the other augments. 'Come back tomorrow and I'll prep you for anything you can use. I'll sell the rest.'

We ate the cakes together, but I barely tasted a thing.

Later that day I couldn't face going back to Rosie's, opting to sample Escher's nightlife instead. Martians weren't much into my brand of obscure classical jazz, but there was one dive bar called "Spot Five" that occasionally played a tune I liked.

I found it open, spinning some unknown record – a kind of shmaltzy jazz covers trio – and ordered wine. It tasted terrible but I persevered.

By the time a decent album played on the rickety sound system I was half way towards very drunk, and decided to finish that particular journey. I sipped my drinks quietly, progressing from wine to whiskey, slowly numbing my senses. I stared out the window while the day bled out like a wounded animal, dying into the night.

17

They called the ridge "The God Axe" because it cleaved the landscape in two in a manner only a god could achieve. It was both beautiful and terrible, despite its relatively humble height. At approximately 400 metres it was nowhere near the size of true giants like Olympus Mons, but it was sharp and vertiginous and damn intimidating. It was just right for me. Every day I went out there, onto that ridge, to die a little.

At sunrise it threw an astonishingly long, jagged shadow right across the landscape, racing it against the merciless speed of the light at dawn, but always losing in the end. Every day my little skimmer carried me upwards, dwarfed by the ridge and the landscape, as if I was a child going up a hill with my sled.

When I reached the top I slowly surveyed my surroundings. The view was mind-boggling. I thought about Clint, and what he was going through without me. I had failed to protect him and now he was in the hands of people without morals or qualms, who would not hesitate to use him up like a disposable rag. It was intolerable.

I thought of Gibson, confidently exuding an air of control and power, effortlessly roping me in to do his dirty work. I would make sure he would regret that decision. There was something there, tugging at the corner of my mind, something that I knew I had to deal with, but I filed it away for later.

I also thought of Theo. If it hadn't been for him… I clenched my jaws, biting down hard. I had visions of Theo turning into nothing more than a fine red dust, like those people on the EN-COM mission.

I clung on to that rage while I activated my ocular augment to cycle through different modes: infrared, ultra-violet, electromagnetic … The landscape transformed before my eyes. The new visual data mixed with my regular vision flawlessly. Somehow the augment made sense of it all. Everything seemed more sharp, more in focus than they had ever been, both literally and metaphorically.

The task ahead of me was hard but clear, and to remind myself of that duty I came here every day and took off my re-breather. The air was cold and lacking in oxygen – our terraforming efforts hadn't tamed Mars just yet.

As I gasped for air the landscape came alive. Rocks baked in warm golden light, craters invited my gaze, tempting me to come inside and see what ancient meteorites had brought to the surface. I could see vast fields of lichen, doing their bit to help transform the planet, to make it a refuge for humanity, even though we didn't deserve one.

Soon, the lack of oxygen was making me lightheaded. My legs felt heavy and I started to sway. I had to concentrate hard to keep my focus on my mantra of revenge. If I fainted I would die within minutes. Only when dancing spots appeared in my vision did I calmly replace my breather.

I inhaled deeply, reminding myself that every breath should be in the service of finding my son, and punishing those who harmed him.

18

The challenge ahead was simple at its core: steal Clint back. We knew where he was, and they didn't know that we were looking. They thought I was dead.

How to get to Clint, or how I would escape with him was not yet clear, but I knew that I had to transform myself into a weapon, somebody who could go up against the full might of a Corp and come out alive on the other side. That meant augments. Military grade offensive enhancements, deep tactical sensory augments, strength mods, defensive encasements, kinetic skin meshes… whatever I could use to give myself a chance to pull this off.

The surgery was invasive and humiliating and almost too much to bear. I witnessed myself slowly being turned into a monster of my own design – one procedure at a time.

For now, these were just low level enhancements to pave the way for the more fundamental upgrades that I required. An artificial kidney with enhanced filtering function, lung capacity increase, regeneration stimulators. All useful in their own right, but still just a foundation for what was yet to come.

I often thought about my father, and wondered if his sanity had started to slip well before the radiation got him. I could feel my own sanity teetering on the edge after each procedure.

Rosie had pulled in a string of favours to set up a suitable false persona for me. I was now officially a different person, which seemed apt as I barely recognised myself. I think it actually helped me get through the surgeries and their aftermath. The pain and the disgust and self-loathing belonged to "Jane Dyne", not to Jemm Delaney.

The practical challenges ahead were substantial. Like

most people my two biggest problems were related to time and money; Clint only had limited time before his transformation would progress past the point of no return, and it was just a matter of time before Spectra would remove his custom augments. Furthermore, I needed to acquire a small fortune to pay for the upgrades I needed. But I was determined to succeed.

I went to visit Ella in the afternoon to plan my next surgery. I found her tinkering in her lab; nothing work related, just some fun with one of her vintage droids. Her eyes were red from crying, but that wasn't unusual.

'Rough night?' I asked.

'They're all rough nights Jemm. I'm just going to have to accept that.'

Guilt flared up in me, followed by irritation. I hadn't asked for any of this myself, but there it was, nonetheless. I pushed it away, I still needed her on my side.

'We'll get them Ella. You and me,' I said, surprised by the conviction in my words. 'They're overconfident, lazy. We have to get to them. Make them pay.'

Ella looked me up and down with sadness in her eyes. 'What are we doing here Jemm? I'm a washed up cripple, and you …you're just one person. How is this ever going to work? You can't do it all by yourself.' I started to reply but she cut me off. 'No, seriously, how?' Her voice grew louder and a tremor affected her words. I had never seen her like this before. 'Look at you! Look at what you're doing to yourself. What *I* am doing to you.' She grabbed my hand, squeezed it hard. 'You can walk away, build something with Rosie. Forget this … this fucking shit.'

I was taken aback by her words. Ella was the one who had sent me down this path to begin with. I knew she craved revenge, and thought she could achieve that through me. I couldn't believe that fundamental drive had changed.

'What's going on Ella?' I said. 'Are you still going to help me? Or do I need to worry?'

'Of course I'll help you. Don't be stupid.' *That's more*

like it. I thought. 'But, you're running out of time. The augments you want … They're expensive, and will take time to source, and then there's the recovery …'

'Spit it out, Ella.'

'Oh, fuck you. Feel free to leave and find somebody else you can treat like shit.'

I rode out her anger, waiting for her to let me back in. She gave me a furious look, letting the silence fill the room. 'I want out, got that?' she spat at me. 'I want something out of this for me. For *me* goddammit. I'll help you with Clint, but then I want out. And soon.'

'What do you mean?'

'I found a treatment for myself. It's a new therapy, and you won't like it, but …' Ella spread her arms, palms up, in a curiously endearing gesture. 'I could walk again.'

'But that's great! What's the treatment?' I said. 'And what do you mean I won't like it?'

'Well, it's expensive, and it's on Earth. Some kind of cellular reset therapy.'

'Earth? When?'

'I leave in six weeks. That's all the time I can give you.'

Six weeks wasn't enough for my current augment regime. Not without a small fortune to help speed things along. Ella knew this. I could see it in her eyes. My current enhancements were good, but nowhere near the kind of power that I was looking for. The EN-COM gigs simply didn't pay enough.

'I'll get the money somehow,' I said.

'You don't even have a plan to get to Clint.' Ella replied. 'What will you do?'

'I don't know yet. But I'll make it work.'

And that's how I decided to do a Ceres raid.

Ella tried to talk me out of it. She knew as well as anyone how dangerous it was, but I could think of no other way to raise the money, and frankly, I was suited to the job. I would succeed where many had failed and died.

Rosie stopped tending her own bar. She now paid somebody to take care of the Chimera while spending more time with me. It was more profitable for her; the money she made on EN-COM missions easily paid for the new bar manager with plenty left over after. Much of that went into giving the Chimera a makeover, but it would always remain a dive, and that was just how Rosie liked it.

We no longer drank in the Chimera (Rosie kept work and pleasure separate), but, unsurprisingly, she knew all the best bars in Escher. She proudly gave me the tour.

Her favourite haunt was called "Gagarin Gagarin". It was an oddity in town, eschewing the standard Martian cubist grey style of interior decorating. The Gagarin was exotic, daring, colourful and surprising, as was its proprietor, Ruben. He was one of those infuriatingly capable people who succeed at anything they try with apparent ease.

He had made and lost several fortunes before leaving his twenties, and had grown bored with the more traditional ways to succeed in life. On the cusp of turning thirty Ruben planned one last commercial venture – a boutique nanotech weapons manufacturer. It outperformed all his previous endeavours, making him rich enough to retire for life. With acquiring fortunes no longer a major concern he bought the Gagarin, gutted the building, and reinvented it to become *the* place on Mars to meet truly extraordinary people. He succeeded at that with ease as well.

The Gagarin was large. Several floors, above and below ground, saw into each other, resulting in a complex layout of connected mezzanines, lifts, escalators and stairs. It looked more like an Escher drawing than Escher City did.

The decor was dedicated to a wide variety of interesting themes. To my delight I found a large sitting room dedicated to miniature space ships and naval vessels, many of which I had never seen before. The craftsmanship was magnificent.

Rosie was greeted with genuine warmth by several patrons throughout the evening. Some were gregarious and theatrical, others were quiet and sophisticated. All were exceptional in one way or another. Among them was a soft-spoken man called Isaac, who was as thin as a rake and had the most beautiful delicate features. He was also the most knowledgeable private eye on Mars, and I was paying him to locate Theo for me, and keep tabs on Clint.

I greeted him with a small but friendly nod.

'Isaac. How's business treating you?'

'It treats me as I treat it; with great mutual respect and attention to financial detail. If I may escort you to a more private environment I will regale you with tales of my capitalist adventures.' He held out his elbow in an antiquated chivalrous gesture. I accepted by putting my hand on his arm, and let him lead me away. Rosie blew me a kiss and went on to talk to yet another shining example from her coterie of extraordinary friends.

Isaac found an empty alcove, created specifically for meetings such as ours. The walls were lined with red velour and luxurious tassels. A Blue-powered chandelier provided gently sparkling illumination – an ostentatious display of wealth.

A cunningly hidden switch activated a noise dampening field. Our conversation would be as private as if we were alone.

'Oh my, Jemm, you look rather different since we last met. A new eye I see?' Isaac was showing off his own augments. My enhancements were covert and extremely hard to detect, unless one was equipped to do so with sophisticated technology. Underneath Isaac's old fashioned manners and impeccable dress sense hid an extremely sharp, capable, and dangerous man. There was more than a hint of elite force training about him. Military? Corp? The way he sat, composed himself, relaxed but always ready, always alert… It looked very familiar to me. I had seen that same aura around my father, before the sickness had stripped it all away.

'You look different yourself Isaac. It must be my new eye.' I wasn't joking; The ocular augment didn't just widen the visible spectrum; like Isaac's, it also alerted me to the presence of other people's augments, their body temperature, even involuntary physical responses indicating signs of stress, injuries, arousal and a plethora of other useful data. Whoever the eye originally belonged to had paid a lot of money for it.

'Splendid. It is gratifying to expand one's view onto the world is it not?' Isaac held out a small electronic wallet. 'Speaking of which, I would be delighted to share my findings to date with you.' I briefly touched his chip with a cred-stick, transferring a significant amount of money in the process.

'By all means,' I said 'Please report.'

'Excellent. Let me start with the good news first.' Isaac leaned back, almost arrogantly. 'Our man Theo is still on Mars.'

Relief flushed through me like a surge of adrenalin. Much of my plan was based on finding Theo.

'So ... what's the bad news?' I asked.

'My dear, there is always bad news. In this case, our friend Theo seems rather adept at hiding. I have viable reports of sightings in Colony West, and he won't have been able to get past my eyes and ears in the space port, so he must still be there. I just don't know where yet.'

'How can you be sure he hasn't already flown the coop?'

'My dear, please trust me to know my business. I can't tell you all my secrets of course, but once I have a person's DNA profile they can't travel without me knowing about it.'

I could only assume that Isaac had somehow infiltrated the screening tech on all of Mars' main transport hubs, which was an extraordinary feat if true. I decided to trust him and not belabour the point.

'So he's contained for now... That's good, but still gets me nowhere in the long run.'

Isaac pulled a slightly resentful face, as if I had spoken in bad taste. 'It is merely a matter of time, and not much time at that. I will flush him out as agreed and expect to be able to present him to you within weeks.'

'Weeks? How confident are you of that?' I already knew the answer before I asked, but it pays not to make assumptions.

'Well, as always caveats apply, but barring any "force majeure", as they say, I am very confident of success. You'll get your man soon.'

'Good. I need him soon and I need him intact. He's my best lead to get to my son.'

Another look of resentment, and this time some coldness dusted Isaac's polite words. 'You have made that very clear my dear. I do not operate like some of the spent up corporate muscle in this town. I deliver to spec and on time, and waive my final payment if the client is not satisfied.'

I nodded. 'No offence intended. I'm just restating the mission parameters.'

My thoughts wandered back to the Spectra raid, my limbs throbbing in sympathetic pain. Once more I fantasised about Theo turning to red dust, his implants falling to the floor in front of me.

I would have to be careful not to lose control when I finally got my hands on him.

Every Xeno worth their salt contemplates doing the Ceres run at some point in their career, and every Xeno with half a brain eventually rejects that option. I was no different in that regard.

Ceres used to be under Joint Government control, utilised as a testing ground for powerful artifacts. It facilitated the development of new Blue and Red prototype technology and operated as a storage and research facility for new unknown Trickari items.

The facility had been most active just at that time during the Acceleration when governments were giddy with power, playing with their new Trickari toys.

Within ten years Ceres was transformed from a cold barren rock to a massive installation, filled with countless test sites and labs and hangars and other excavations, riddling the old rock like Swiss cheese.

When things went wrong for humanity during Icarus, they went uniquely wrong on Ceres. Trick Tech escalations cascaded on an epic scale. Dimensional wormholes opened into far away stars, unleashing hell before closing forever. Previously unknown unstable particles were released – now recognised as a particularly dangerous kind of ghost-matter.

One weapons lab incident caused super-focused energy beams to slice through the guts of Ceres, crippling and killing and destroying without mercy. Nuclear reactions joined hands with catastrophic fusion events, setting off further conventional explosions. It was one hell of a shitshow.

Eventually Ceres *cracked*. A huge fissure appeared on one side of the planetoid, reaching all the way to the core. The planetoid nearly split in two, but somehow, barely, managed to hang together.

Thousands died, untold number of spaceships were destroyed. When it all calmed down and the dust finally settled it became apparent that Ceres teetered on the brink of destruction. Nobody knew for sure what would happen if the planetoid's two halves were to separate, but there were plenty of dangerous scenarios. Ceres' fragments could cause catastrophic impacts on Mars, Earth, or wreak havoc on Earth's satellites or colonies. Unstable artifacts and technology could unleash their hidden powers with unpredictable outcomes. Things could go very wrong indeed, as the Icarus years bore testimony to.

So, it was decided by Joint Governments decree that Ceres was off limits. There would be no exceptions – anybody caught trying to salvage on Ceres would be executed. Initially this didn't deter the brave and the desperate. Some extremely lucky or extremely gifted salvage crews did manage to land great scores, but Solar Command, JG's enforcement arm, soon got a grip on things and stopped most subsequent expeditions in their tracks. A spate of executions followed for those who were caught, and several deadly failed expeditions later Ceres had developed a reputation for being a place to steer well clear off.

There hasn't been a reported case of an attempted salvage mission in over twenty years, let alone a successful one. But, as is always the case, a bow kept taut for too long eventually loses its strength; Solar Command operations slowly diminished in size, and area patrol numbers came down to a trickle.

Ceres was ripe for the taking, and I was the right person to do it.

Ella had shown me several ways to decorate and personalise my own Oxy-Buddy Breather. We looked at a variety of famous themes and concepts to give me inspiration, but creating the final design was up to me. The application would be a slow and meticulous process, but that was something that I was used to, working on my miniatures back at home.

'The idea is to create something that only you could make, do you understand? Something personal, but not a bloody ego trip. It needs to say something about you, but with a bit of class.' Her own mask lay between us, a template for greatness. Ella had created an intricate design involving hundreds of metallic lines like the wiring on a circuit-board, but more organic in shape. Within the lines were hidden shapes and patterns that could only be seen by paying close attention. A skimmer, a woman's legs, a flower ... They all reflected on an aspect of her life. Some were obvious, some were not, but once you knew they were there you could find more and more. A multi-layered miniature tapestry of hidden meaning, mapping out Ella's secret desires and innermost thoughts.

Ella showed me the delicate paint brushes and tiny

chiselling tools used in the application process, her features softening as she explained how it all worked. She looked younger – more like herself than I had ever seen her. *Was this her true face?* I wondered.

'Don't stare at me.' She grunted. 'Pay attention.'

'I am. And I'm not staring, I'm thinking.' I looked at her workstation, and spotted copies of Spectra's data disks, it felt like we stole them half a lifetime ago.

'What's the progress on those?' I nodded in the direction of the disks.

'Well, that's a good question. You may not like the answers though.' She slapped my hand away when I was being too clumsy putting down a practice pattern, and showed me how to be more precise. 'Those disks are enough to get killed for, several times over.'

'Come on.' I urged. 'It's been weeks since you told me anything. What else have you learned about the Neo virus? We'll need *something* when I get him back.'

'If. *If* you get him back. And I've learned a great deal, but I'm not sure what to tell you yet. There's too much I don't know yet. I only know half the story.'

I cursed under my breath. When Ella got like this she couldn't be rushed. And truth be told, it was always worth hearing her out. I got back to my breather design, hoping to placate her.

She cleared her throat. 'That's it, keep practising that line.' I was getting the hang of it, walking a tightrope between being a good student and getting Ella to tell me more.

'The disks are more valuable than you think,' she said after a while. 'Which is both good and bad.'

'How so?'

'Well, they contain more than enough scientific data on Trickari systems and processes to be worth several fortunes. That's not to be sniffed at.' She nodded with approval at my latest pattern, and gave me a new one to practise. 'Thing is, what's really valuable, or dangerous – depending how you look at it – is the amount of data on there that would land Spectra in serious hot water, legally speaking. The stuff they did up there was highly illegal. I mean, damn … it would have massive repercussions if exposed, even now.'

'So how come we're still alive?'

'Good question.' She patted my augmented arm. 'Although easy to answer in your case; since officially you *are* dead.' Ella touched her side. The wound was still painful. 'I, on the other hand, am painfully alive, at least for now. I don't think they'll come after me though. Remember; they don't even know that I've made copies. These are insanely hard to crack data files. Even if they suspect I have access, they probably figured that I'm too scared to do anything with the data.'

Ella briefly looked me in the eyes. 'Them killing you in front of me would have a lot do with that,' she said.

'They left in a bit of a rush …' I mused. 'What if they come back to tie up loose ends?'

'They could risk another incident, but I'm betting they want to avoid that. Earth is still dealing with the fallout of their last attempt.'

'Maybe,' I said, unconvinced. 'Anyway, you said you knew half the story? What have you learned from the disks?'

'That's the best bit.' Ella grabbed my arm with excitement, her grip unexpectedly strong. 'Their bio engineering data is incredible. They messed around with gene manipulation, cellular recoding, DNA bombs, evolutionary acceleration … it's wild stuff.'

'But how does this help us. There has to be something there.'

'There might be … maybe,' said Ella. 'I think, given enough time, that we can cure Clint.' Spotting both the panic and hope in my eyes she quickly continued. 'Eventually I mean! I know we don't have much time right now, but we've already slowed down the virus. If you can get Clint to me I might be able to use what I've learned from Spectra's research to slow down the transformation even more. It might give me the time to solve this thing.'

I sighed, 'So, it's even more important that we get Clint back soon.'

'Afraid so. It's a bitch, but it is what it is.'

'What's the other half? You said that was half the story.'

Ella leaned back in her chair. Weary, but determined. 'It's figuring out what the damn Neo-virus *does*. I know it's an instruction set, but what for?'

19

Ernest was nervous. It was something I had never seen before. He was going to introduce me to somebody he knew, claiming to help me with my plan for Ceres. He hurried me along the back streets of Scar-district muttering to himself, throwing furtive glances over his shoulder as if we were being followed, which I knew we weren't. I wondered who we were meeting to have such an influence over him.

Scar-district had carried its name since the early days of Mars' terraforming project. The first workers who helped establish the early colonies suffered many accidents and injuries: people lost limbs, suffered terrible burns, got radiation poisoning … a smorgasbord of misery.

Scar District was set up by the Mars authorities to house the unfortunates. Their plan was to make them a positive example to others, despite their injuries; show that no matter what happened, the workers would be taken care of.

It worked better than anybody expected. A community arose, composed of damaged but strong-willed people who wore their injuries with pride. It was they who named the area Scar-district, not the authorities, intending the name to be a badge of honour. But, as predictable as the rising of the Sun, once these colonies were established they were soon no longer a priority to those in power. A new government was sworn in, welfare payments dwindled, urban investment dried up, and within a few years Scar district turned ugly.

The abandoned workers developed a bitter cynicism, nurtured further by the authorities' endless broken promises for aid and support. Many of them turned to crime to make ends meet, which in turn attracted further criminals from other corners of the city. Law enforcement mostly ignored Scar-district, as if embarrassed by its mere existence.

Eventually the area became too notorious for its own good, its nickname known all over Mars. Some token efforts were undertaken to restore order, with mixed results. Nonetheless, it remained a thoroughly nasty place. It wasn't an area I had expected Ernest to associate with, but he walked the streets with obvious knowledge of its people.

'What's this Ernest? Why would you bring me to this dump?' I asked, somewhat peeved.

'Yeah yeah. Wait. See.' Ernest still used few words, which I found oddly comforting.

Signs of decay and crime and despair were all around us. TJ's openly taking Mem, barely disguised prostitutes and gigolos hurrying to their next clients, run-down chop shops and augment parlours, all part of an impenetrable warren of alleys and lanes. I started to wonder how anybody could find anything in this maze of misery, when we suddenly stopped in front of a grubby little office. It was nondescript in every way except for an extraordinary little neon sign that hung over its wonky door frame. It said: "Dante's Children" in amazingly deep red neon.

'Jesus,' I muttered, to no one in particular.

Ernest squared his shoulders – another first – and rang the doorbell.

'Rang first,' he told me, in a rather abstract manner. Eventually I figured he meant to say that somebody should be home as he rang them first to make sure. But that was just a guess.

After what seemed like too long a wait a voice spoke through some hidden speaker, like a guilty conscience.

'Ernest, that you?'

'Yep,' he replied, his voice tense.

'Better come in then. It not safe there.' The voice spoke in a strange fragmented way. I had never heard anything like it. I wondered if it was Scar-district's own patois.

The door went click, and we entered.

We faced a long dark corridor, its walls interrupted every six feet or so by dirty lights that barely illuminated the ceiling, let alone the floors. Stairs were just visible at the far end, teasing us to go forward. Ernest pointed to them, 'Down.'

I suppressed the urge to giggle, and just went along with it all.

'OK, down it is,' I said, and slapped him on the shoulder.

Ernest didn't smile as we went down into the dark.

The stairs snuck down several flights like a thief in the dark. As we descended I picked up a strange musty smell, reminding me of taxidermy. A tendril of unease wormed its way into my head.

The room at the bottom was a basement office, although that wasn't its original purpose which I couldn't divine. It was cramped and small, with low ceilings for a Martian dwelling. What little light there was did a poor job illuminating the surroundings. Still, it was easy enough to locate the source of the odd smell I picked up; the walls of the room were plastered with hundreds of yellowed pages from real-books. On close inspection they appeared to contain religious texts taken from a variety of denominations. We were surrounded by snippets of Judaeo-Christianity, Buddhism, Re-Fucianism and who knows what else. It was all hokum to me.

'Ernesto, my long lost lamb. It has been too long, has it not?' said a sonorous voice, booming with purpose.

'Preacher,' was all Ernest offered in return.

Preacher was a small man, but with big presence. He was old, at least in his sixties, but broad-shouldered and strong limbed. There was intelligence in his eyes. I could feel his gaze probing. It wondered what he saw.

'And who is this poor sad creature? I can feel her sorrow, heavy like the cross on our lord's shoulder.' Preacher's voice had that sing-song quality that professional religious bullshitters use to sound righteous.

'She's not of the flock Preacher,' whispered Ernest, probably the longest sentence I had ever heard him utter. Few things wound me up as much as religion and its many self-appointed guardians of "the truth", but my respect for Ernest kept me from offering some caustic comment.

'This,' Ernest put his hand on my shoulder, 'is Jane. She's on a quest to save a soul.' He squeezed gently, again leaving me puzzled. *This is tough and rough Ernest? What the hell is going on here?*

'I see,' declared Preacher. 'And this is why have you brought her here to the sanctum?'

'She needs to reach Ceres. I will travel with her if I can, but we need help.'

'We can't help those who deny the true path brother. You know this very well.'

'I'm asking for your support Preacher, this one time. The Program services Ceres doesn't it?'

Preacher's face grew dark, a cloud's shadow settling over a landscape of stubble. He turned to face me, with pity or anger, I couldn't say.

'Has Ernesto told you about the Program?' he asked.

'Is Preacher a nickname?' I asked, ignoring his question 'Or are you really a man of the cloth? You don't seem the type …' I looked him up and down for a breath, 'in fact, you have the look of a convict more than anything.'

'It is often the sinner who understands sin most readily, miss …'

'Dyne. Call me Jane.' Neither of us moved to shake hands. 'So what's an old sinner like you doing in a dive like this? And one with such high religiosity content at that?'

'I'm here to help other sinners of course. That is my sole purpose in life. I have endeavoured to share what little I have with those who need it, ever since I've been shown how empty a life without guidance is.'

'Your "Program" I presume?'

'I do what I can to serve my flock. I provide them with guidance and they provide commitment to the Program. We offer work and camaraderie to lost souls when nobody else will. An honest paycheck for honest work in a world that would rather see them fail. This is my mission, and my flock grows ever larger.' Preacher cast a glance at the wall behind him, which was covered in mugshots. There were at least a hundred police photos of men, women, and overly augmented inbetweeners of all ages and colours.

'Are you up there too *Ernesto*?' I asked. I was genuinely curious.

Ernest grinned, then filled in the blanks; 'Preacher runs a work program for the disadvantaged. Those of us who can't get a regular work license because of past erm … *mistakes.* The Corps and local authorities get very cheap labour, the kind that nobody else wants to do. If you work hard you eventually get to rejoin humanity, on probation. It's a good system.' It was by far the longest speech I had heard Ernest make.

'And how does this help me?'

'Because the Program has a contract with J.G. and Solar Command, servicing Ceres' main defences. Those weapon systems are automated but old. Most of them started to malfunction. A lot. There's a repair crew on a little installation just off Ceres, but they've been suffering a lot of setbacks recently. Additionally, the defence grid has holes in it, and the Program has been contracted to help out with some of the repairs. Deep-space welding and upgrades and support operations … that kind of thing.'

'So the Program has clearance to operate near Ceres? They actually let you near that thing?'

'Yup,' he replied, finally reverting to his less talkative mode.

'I'm not joining a religious cult. Jesus.' I laughed out loud at the flash of irritation that thundered over Preacher's face. 'But I'm happy to pay you a good cut if you help me put together a raid on Ceres.'

'Why, Miss Dyne, do you think *you* will succeed where so many others have failed? Why should I put my trust in you?'

'Because, Mr. Preacher, I have something that gives me the edge over everybody else who has tried this in the past.' I grinned with no small amount of glibness. I hadn't even told Ernest yet. 'I have the highest level security clearance you can get. I can get into Spectra's corner of Ceres and rob them blind.'

Ernest looked puzzled. 'How? Spectra must have revoked your clearance by now?'

'On their current operations sure. But Ceres has been abandoned even longer than the Gaianista Habitats. They have no way to change their access algorithms there.'

Ernest laughed. 'Yes yes, that will work.'

'What do you say Mr Preacher? There's a lot of almost-clean money to be made here. Worth a lot more than renting out a few desperate ex-cons.'

I knew I was pushing it with the insults, but I had to show Preacher that I knew what he was, and that I wasn't afraid of him.

'You seem to have a low opinion of what I'm trying to do for these lost lambs, Sister.'

'I have no opinion on it whatsoever, *Brother*. I'm just offering a one-time deal of a lifetime here, because Ernest thinks it's a good idea. But don't think I'm gonna play along with your little humble-holy-man charade. Save it for your minions.'

Preacher finally had enough of my taunts; he swung at me, but changed his mind halfway through and just tried to grab me by my arm. A split second later I had him facedown on the floor, his right arm painfully pinned back. My new arm was performing well.

'Jane, don't.' Ernest looked embarrassed. 'It's not like that, I promise.'

'You vouch for him? And this *Program*?'

'I do. It saved my life.'

I slowly kneeled down next to Preacher and whispered in his ear, 'I don't buy your crap for a second. I've seen your type too often, but I trust Ernest, so for now I'm going to go along with this.' Mixed in with the musty old smell of real-pages was the scent of Preacher himself. He exuded a sweet-and-sour odour that conjured images of dirty old puppets, belonging to dead children. I nearly gagged.

I slowly got up, reached out a hand. Preacher slapped it away as he got to his feet. I smiled.

'No hard feelings Preacher?' I asked. 'Look, the offer stands. You know it's good. No need to tussle over it.'

He dusted himself off, trying to regain some dignity. 'My name is Pierre, and I will take half your profit so I can share it with my flock. Take it, or leave it and go your ungodly way.'

Later that evening I was at Rosie's, admiring her skill as she cooked an incredible meal, using little more than basic Martian rations and spices. Something in the way she moved around the kitchen as she cooked reminded me of an exotic dancer. She wasn't trying to titillate me, but she couldn't help but present herself in a certain way... She was just that kind of person; heart-achingly beautiful, but with no idea of her own appeal. I'm not sure what made me seek her out after they took Clint from me, but if she hadn't been there to pick what was left of me off the floor and put me back together ...

Rosie laughed heartily when I told her about my encounter with Pierre, but sobered up at the part that had him lying face down on the floor.

'That was a mistake,' she said. 'You shouldn't have humiliated this guy. I've heard of him. He's committed to this Preacher persona, and he's got a reputation to protect.'

'He seemed pretty accommodating in the end. I'm not too worried.'

'Yeah, that's what his latest victim thought. Just before he drugged him, took his eyes, and sold them on the black market.' I wondered if she was serious, but Rosie gave me a stern look. 'I'm not joking Jemm, Preacher is bad news. Watch your back.'

'OK OK. Look, it all ended up pretty amicably. Probably something to do with the massive cut he's going to take. He'll walk away with a lot of money to spend on his *flock.*'

'No don't do that. Don't dismiss him like that.' Rosie grabbed my shoulder, forcing me to look her in the eyes. 'Guys like that … he'll want to get his own back. That's just his character.'

"Right, OK, you said your piece, thanks for the warning." I lifted the lid off a battered pan, and stole a delicious spoonful. 'When do we eat?'

Later, after we had eaten and made love, I found myself in an ambivalent mood; what I had with Rosie was good, damn good, but like everything in my life it was temporary. I had to stay focused on Clint – nothing else mattered. But yet, for the first time since I lost Clint, I felt relaxed, and almost happy.

Rosie was nibbling away at her various dishes, hungry from our lovemaking. She was that kind of person who could just eat whatever she liked, when she liked it, yet remained steadily locked into the same slim body shape she had occupied all her life. She tried to feed me some morsels too but I declined with a smile.

She pouted at me. 'Haven't worked up enough of an appetite? I'm disappointed,' she said.

'That's not it.'

'There's an "*it*"?'

I rolled onto my side to better see her, touch her …

'I want you to stay on Mars. Forget about Ceres. Give me something to come back to.' It was the wrong thing to say, but I said it anyway.

Surprisingly Rosie didn't take offence.

'I'm a big girl Jemm. I'm sure you've noticed.'

'So am I. And I don't need a chaperone. Sorry, but I don't.'

'You don't, do you?' Rosie said, her calm mood in danger of evaporating in front of my eyes. 'Anyway, who says I'm going because of you. I'm not some lovesick puppy following you around. I'm going because I need a big payday. Don't want people to think I'm a kept woman.' Rosie yanked the silver necklace I had given her hard, to underline her point. For a moment I feared she would break it, but it was sturdier than it looked.

'It's too dangerous. You know this.' I lowered my voice which had started to sound slightly shrill, even to my own ears. 'This Ceres thing … It's got nothing to do with us. I'm going because I have no goddamn choice. I'm running out of time with Clint, and I need to do this to have any chance of getting to him at all.' I got up and walked to the kitchen, trying to calm myself down. Rosie followed me.

'I know that Jemm. Stop treating me like an idiot. Or a victim.'

There were words I could have said at that point that probably would have helped, but somehow they refused to be spoken out loud. I could have told her that the reason I didn't want her to go was because I needed her alive to keep me strong. That I couldn't bear the idea of losing her as well, not after Clint. That I needed to keep my head in the game, and not be distracted by worrying about her safety while on the most dangerous salvage mission of my life, with everything and more at stake for me.

I didn't say any of that. Instead I swallowed my words and agreed she would come with me. I told myself that I had accepted her for who she was – her own person with her own motivations – which was all she really wanted from me, but that was just a convenient lie. The truth was that I needed her alive on Mars to back me up on my return, rather than take chances with me on Ceres. But Rosie had never played second fiddle to me or anybody else. She would do exactly as she pleased, and that there was no point fighting it.

'If you die I will kill you,' I half joked.

She replied with a derisive snort and went to find more to eat.

We left two days later, as part of a Program workforce, made up of Ernest, Rosie, myself and two members of Preacher's Flock called "van Dijk" and "Jeremiah", no doubt carefully handpicked by the Preacher-man himself.

We were supposed to be a routine deep-space repair crew, and for security reasons were given no details about what exactly we were repairing. I was amazed they let the Program operate out here, but I guess since there hadn't been an attempted raid on Ceres for decades it was considered low risk. Hubris will always find a way.

All communications with Ceres control went via comm-link. Local forces were close by on a small Solar Command installation, but apparently didn't feel the need to be physically present.

Other than that we had no help or guidance, just schematics and a deadline. Again, I was amazed at how lax Ceres defence had become but wasn't going to complain.

Van Dijk was painfully young – I would be surprised if he was older than nineteen – whereas Jeremiah was an obvious veteran of the streets, probably in his late thirties, although it was hard to tell with these reborn "true believer" characters.

I knew the type well; a miserable lifetime of crime, vice and conflict, until they finally found religion. They then became the enforcers of the self-appointed religious "leaders", ready to commit violence at the drop of a hat, secure in the knowledge that they would be absolved of any wrongdoing as they were merely doing the lord's work.

Van Dijk, as young as he was, turned out to be an incredibly efficient pilot. Jeremiah on the other hand was a basic all-rounder, decent at most jobs he was tasked with.

Jeremiah's function on this gig was meant to be deep-space welder, which he probably was pretty good at. He certainly looked the part: he was covered in religious tattoos, taut muscles, and an air of quiet contempt. I didn't trust him at all, but there was nothing I could do about his presence. We needed Preacher's support to even get to Ceres, so I had to accept his crew. I just had to make sure that everybody knew that this was my show.

Our ride was a sleek Blue personnel carrier, designed for speed and mainly used for short hops around the general vicinity of Mars and Earth, but capable of longer trips if required. She was called "*Jezebel*" which amused and annoyed me in equal measures.

Lift-off was gruelling, despite Mars' low gravity. I tried to remain stoic while a giant hand tried to press me through the seams of my chair, as if trying to keep me in my proper place.

I felt rebellious, suddenly elated. *You can't keep me down. I'll keep getting up!* Gibson's face materialised before my mind's eye. In my vision I was laughing at him while cradling my boy, knowing that he couldn't harm us. It was a strangely joyous fantasy, something to hold onto and revisit during dark times. It put me in such an ebullient mood that I tried to laugh but the weight on my chest was too much.

After approximately two minutes of thrust we escaped the pull of Mars' gravity well. A sudden relief overcame all of us – we could literally breathe easier.

'Twelve hours to Ceres, all cooped up together,' rasped Jeremiah. His voice ravaged by years of living in the margins, or so I imagined. His gaze hungrily slid over Rosie and myself, as lecherous as a satyr.

'Lucky me,' he drawled.

Rosie and I exchanged looks. I could read her mind without difficulty. *Want me to take him out?*

I shook my head imperceptibly to anybody but the two of us. *No need for now.*

Van Dijk was oblivious to the little drama unfolding behind his pilot's seat. Or maybe he just ignored it. He reminded us of the key factors. 'When we arrive you have twenty four hours to get in and out. We've been given one day only to fix the defence node, and after that the *Jezebel* will have to get back or we'll be in big trouble.' He made it sound like we were naughty children planning a raid on the cookie jar.

'Hey kid, you sure those suits are up to it?' Rosie winked at van Dijk. He blushed with painful intensity. Even with my augmented vision dialled down he lit up like a Christmas tree.

'Yes miss. The suits have the best insulation and boosters available. The shimmer-tech should mask any emissions. I'll monitor comms and make repairs. You and Miss Dyne ghost to Ceres and get what you can. Ernest is coming as your backup, and to ermm … to report back to Preacher.'

'Strike that, boy,' Jeremiah stood up and scratched his head, then rubbed his face vigorously. 'Ernest is staying here – Preacher's orders. They'll need a *real* man to finish this job.'

Van Dijk turned red again, stammering an insulting reply, 'Instead … they have to make do with you. Just … Just their luck.' Jeremiah froze for just a moment – an instinctive rage gripped him. It was easy to miss but I caught it. For a split second I thought he might attack the boy right there in front of us, but an instant later a deep throaty laugh bubbled up in him, like noxious gas escaping from a swamp.

'Damn lucky!' He laughed, and slapped the boy on his shoulder. Van Dijk smiled gratefully, relieved by Jeremiah's response, but I could see that Jeremiah's anger was still there. The same *wrongness*, hiding behind his fake jovial smile.

'Are you fucking kidding me? This ain't the deal,' cursed Rosie.

Ernest shrugged. 'Preacher's call. Not mine.'

'Oh really …?' I walked up to Jeremiah. He didn't flinch. Instead his grin widened. 'Preacher changed the plan last minute and didn't tell us? Maybe you misunderstood?' I turned to Ernest. 'Is that typical of Preacher? Is he the type to make last minute changes like this?' Ernest shook his head.

'In that case, I'm sure it's just a misunderstanding. But since we can't check with Preacher right now, we're sticking with the original plan.'

There it was again; Jeremiah's eyes flared. That same wrongness, shining through for a split second, before he got it back under control. 'Your loss ladies,' said Jeremiah. 'Ernesto is a pretty boy, for sure, but he don't got that special juice that only Jeremiah can bring to the party.'

Ernest just shrugged, and joined Rosie and me. 'Plans?'

I nodded and pulled up several maps on my Padd, exposing Ceres' deepest secrets.

'The trick won't be finding valuable tech,' I laughed. 'but choosing what to bring home with us. It'll be like shooting fish in a barrel.'

Rosie just snorted at that, but I could tell she was up for it.

I pointed at two areas I had highlighted. 'Spectra Vision has left us some nice goodies to collect.' I pointed at a green area marked "Research & Development". 'This should be our main target. If we can get in there we're peachy. And it's not all that experimental gear they must have been working on, although some of that must be priceless, but the thousands of lovely little Blue energy cores they stored there to power that stuff. They're the Blue pearls we're diving for.'

'Sounds sexy,' said Rosie, 'but if that ain't happening?'

Good girl, I thought, *cover all bases.*

'In that case we go to their military facility over there, and stock up on weapons and fancy gear. It'll be worth more than enough.'

'That's it?' asked Ernesto.

'That's it,' I replied. 'Not saying it's going to be easy, but if we get in and out in time we've got a good chance of pulling it off.'

Ernest nodded. 'Let's go.'

'Let's go, indeed,' I said. It was going to be quite something.

20

The space suits were top notch; strong and sturdy, yet pliable and light. The inbuilt shimmer-field was a nice bonus, enveloping me completely like a protective membrane. When inside I felt like a mote of light held in the palm of a dark universe. Communication was easy; secure short range transmission, encrypted and masked by the shimmer-tech.

Ceres appeared beneath us, a looming dark behemoth gliding through space. My artificial eye scanned the terrain until I found what I was looking for; an ugly tear cutting across Ceres' surface, a monumental wound with jagged edges.

'Enhance your suit visors to pick up EM fields,' I spoke into the suit's microphone. 'Look at the South East hemisphere.'

'Big crack?' said Ernest.

'Yep. It's not the main rift, but it's nicely dark and on the shadow side of Ceres Defence Station. It'll do nicely.'

Rosie responded by firing her thrusters, launching herself at the target. She diminished in size in seconds, a tiny fish ready to be swallowed by a gaping maw.

Ernest and I followed without a word.

It didn't take long to descend. Our suits were impressively capable, and we were in a hurry to get on with things. When we got within a few hundred metres we slowed down and manoeuvred ourselves over the rift. What seemed like a small crack from a distance turned out to be an ugly gaping ravine with serrated edges, filled with floating debris, ragged tubing and tangled wires.

As we approached, it felt like we were falling an impossible distance. Now that my brain suddenly had a frame of reference vertigo kicked in with a vengeance. I actually dry-heaved several times, prompting Rosie to complain, 'Could do without that hun. You'll set me off next.'

'Thanks for the goddamn show of empathy.'

'Anything for my girl.'

'Ernest, you ok?'

'Yes yes, look. Tunnel.'

He was right, we drifted past a dark access tunnel. It was easy to miss against the visual noise of the surface damage, but the tunnel was there, providing a way in. It should lead towards a part of Ceres that was at least *somewhat* intact.

'Nice. Ernest, take point,' I said. I was impressed with his focus, relieved it was him with us, not Jeremiah. I felt a sudden stab of desire, quickly eclipsed by a longing for Rosie, as she drifted gracefully into the dark corridor. I finally joined them a few seconds later.

'Lights?' asked Ernest after a few seconds.

'Go for it,' I replied. 'We're pretty deep in, nobody can see us.'

For a moment I felt unease at my own assessment, but dismissed that feeling as irrational.

The corridor was long and spacious as it curved around the corner and out of sight. Circular supports ran across its length, reminding me of huge ribs, painted a sickly grey-red by our suit lights. Walk-jumping down its interior felt a bit too much like being inside the carcass of a giant whale.

I checked the time; we had twenty two hours left to make history.

The corridor was riddled with explosive damage. A strange copper green substance covered everything, at times appearing as a powdery residue, other times as a thick oily goo. I had no idea what it was but I couldn't imagine it being healthy to touch, despite the knowledge that our suits should protect us against any contaminants.

The decayed remnants of Ceres personnel were everywhere, the green goo encasing many of the corpses. I steered clear as much as I could. The low gravity on

Ceres was a huge boon, enabling us to make good progress despite the high level of damage in the corridor. We vaulted easily over obstacles and climbed around hotspots, like children in a slow motion monkey cage.

It didn't take us long to get our bearings. We hit a corridor junction with helpful signage: left turn would take us to some interesting sub-chambers, including weapons testing ranges and R&D facilities, but taking the right turn would lead us exactly to where I was hoping to go: Energy Supply and Maintenance Compartment, also known as "The Oyster."

I pointed at the E.S.M.C. sign; 'This is promising. If we can get there we're good.'

'And if we don't?' asked Rosie.

'If we don't then we'll just stock up on Blue guns and other toys. There are weapon caches all over this place. We may want to do that anyway after we get to the Oyster.'

'Lead the way,' said Rosie. 'I want to see them pearls you promised me.'

The shimmer-field wasn't really necessary now that we were inside. We were deep enough for our transmissions to be shielded, but somehow I didn't want to go without. Seeing things through the field gave me a sense of detachment – no bad thing on a mission like this.

Everything looked ethereal through the shimmer effect; real yet unreal, like travelling through the underworld, ghosts and apparitions fluttering at the corners of our vision. The strange effect should have made me paranoid but it just made it easier to deal with the many mutilated corpses we encountered along the way. There were plenty of those.

We made good time, soon arriving at the large entrance door to the E.S.M.C. main facility. Rosie and I both cursed under our breath; there had been a cave in. Several bulkheads had collapsed just in front of the entrance, thoroughly blocking the way. We cursed again, even Ernest. The Oyster had closed up, firmly.

'Now what? Blow it up?' asked Rosie.

'Can't risk it. Not stable enough,' said Ernest,

'And we can't risk getting noticed either,' I added.

If we had been on a regular salvage mission this would have been easy – trivial even – but we weren't, and we had to play the terrain the way it was, not the way we wanted it to be. I made the necessary mental re-adjustment and focused on plan b.

'Weapons cache it is then,' I said. 'We'll backtrack. There's enough time to still get a good haul.'

Rosie made to lead the way, but noticed Ernest staring at the door. She gently took his arm, trying to ease his mind.

'No, no. Wait,' Ernest said, unclipping his backpack. He removed several pieces of equipment and started piecing them together until a portable micro laser materialised in front of us. 'Look. I can cut through this. Easy.'

I had to smile. 'Sometimes I forget just how good you are at this.'

'Yes yes, I'm not just a pretty face.' Ernest pointed back to where we came from. 'Go check out the weapons anyway. I'll get going with this. Give me … about two hours?'

'Great. I'll get you a nice little Blue blaster.' I beckoned Rosie, conscious of time. 'We'll check in with you in two hours then.'

He didn't reply, already deep into that zone he occupied so gracefully. We set off with a small push from our legs. Little puffs of green powder stirred from the ground, reaching for us, but found no purchase on our ghostly shimmering bodies.

We returned to the previous junction with speed and this time continued down the left path leading to the weapons testing facility. Something inside urged me to check out Research & Development first but I decided against it. Its contents would be too difficult to assess quickly, although potentially incredibly valuable. I figured it would be best kept as our fall-back plan.

The corridor leading to Armaments and Munitions was in much worse shape than the one we emerged from. The odd green goo and dust was even more prevalent, but the biggest problem was the sheer amount of jagged metal and plastics sticking into the corridor, blown out from the walls and pipes which normally hid under the surface like veins under the skin.

I thought back to my time with Ballard and his crew, and my terrible decision to take Clint with me on the Gaianista mission, and just like that I was overcome by a wave of fear and pain and anger, all wrapped up tightly into a ball of vicious acid, burning in my stomach.

'Rosie? I need to ask you something, I need your promise.'

'What's the deal hun? What can I do?' Rosie replied gently, she could tell that I was gripped by something.

'If it doesn't work out … If I'm too late …'

'I'll help you,' Rosie said. 'You can count on me.'

'Listen … I'm trying to say this, but it's hard … If it's too late to help Clint I'll need you.'

'We'll get through it. You're a tough cookie.'

Although I loved her for it, she didn't understand what I was saying.

'No, listen. I'm trying to say that I'll need you to keep my head straight so I can kill Gibson. I will have to hunt him down and make him pay. I promised this to myself, and to Clint.'

Rosie was silent after that, disappointed I presumed. I gave her some time, but I needed an answer.

'That won't solve anything babe, it'll just get you killed.'

'Promise me.'

Another period of silence. Seconds … minutes …

'Rosie I need to–'

'Ok babe, time to play all our cards,' said Rosie, and stopped to grab my arm, turning me around to face her. 'Do you love me? Tell me the truth, or I'm gone right now. Tell me.'

I thought that if Caravaggio was alive that day even he would not have been able to capture Rosie's beauty at that moment.

I slowly nodded, aware that she couldn't see my face through the shimmer-field. 'Yes, I love you. More than I've ever loved anybody before. I tried to lie to myself about it, and to you… and I'm really fucking good at lying to myself, but this is the truth.' I let out a long breath.

'OK hun, that's all I needed. If we need to we'll hunt that bastard down together and feed him to the-.'

Just then a tremor shook the corridor. It wasn't strong, but it was clear. Moments later, a second tremor shook the corridor, more forceful that time. Green dust filled the air, debris floated away …

'We'd better get going. This place gives me the creeps'. Something felt wrong to me, as if the air was supercharged, but I couldn't explain why.

We had about eighteen hours left.

We rushed down the corridors, trying to reach the weapons facility, hoping the tremors were explained by legacy stresses and tectonic movements still reverberating from the catastrophe that had hit Ceres years ago. Several more tremors occurred, no worse than the first one, so we carried on.

It took an hour to make it to Armaments and Munitions. By the time we found a working entrance I was on edge. The heavy door was already wedged half open, bent and cracked a long time ago by some extreme force. The door-frame had exploded outwards like a grisly exit wound. The darkness in the facility beyond was occasionally dispersed by strong Blue lights, still active after all these years.

The dead were everywhere, this time mostly wearing military green. It was the same awful scene I had witnessed on countless missions before. The same horrors dressed in different clothes, as if that mattered to the dead.

The facility was in ruins as expected. Everywhere we looked we saw heaps of rubble and debris; but equally, there were weapons everywhere. Boxes and crates, shelves and stacks, hundreds and hundreds of pieces of weaponry and armour. The space we stood in was large, cathedral sized, which hinted at a lot of potential.

Rosie whistled in appreciation. 'Right hun, let's get to work. This should be easy.'

'That right there's what gets you killed,' I said. 'It's *never* easy, and it's never *safe*, even if you think it is.'

Rosie snorted again, putting her hands on her hips. 'Are you gonna treat me like a little girl all day or are you gonna help us get rich, sweetcakes?'

'OK OK... Let's see.' I cast my eye around, looking at what was on offer. 'Forget about the really big stuff,' I said. 'We've got no space on our shitty little transport. We want *small* and *rare*.'

I kept carefully scanning the environment until I spotted something intriguing; a corner of the facility which had been stripped of all content in a radius of approximately fifteen metres. A perfect circular area completely devoid of debris.

'There,' I said, pointing at the area. 'I know what that is. Something very nasty and very valuable.'

We walked over together. Rosie seemed puzzled.

'There's nothing here. I don't get it.'

I pointed at a small blue cube on the floor. 'Look, there's one.'

'What is it?'

'Reverse Pandora. Activate it, throw it in a room, it opens up, and it sucks up everything within its radius. Nobody knows where it ends up.'

'Into the box? You're kidding me?'

'Nope. Everything. I don't think anybody ever figured out how it does it. Best guess amounts to just more speculation about Trickster intra or interdimensional hoodoo or vortexes.'

'I see …' Noting the strain in her voice I found Rosie standing over a corpse. Or rather, half a corpse. There were two legs and a midsection. The rest of the torso must have been inside the Pandora radius when it went off.

'They're also used in garbage disposable facilities. That's where the real value lies.'

'You take it, I don't want it,' said Rosie.

I did, tucking it into my backpack. It was a vicious piece of gear, but worth a small fortune.

'Come on,' I said. 'We're on the clock. I don't want to stick around here any longer than I have to.'

As if to underwrite my unease another tremor hit. That these tremors were happening just after we arrived on Ceres seemed too much of a coincidence to me, but I couldn't see how we could have caused a deterioration in the planetoid's stability.

'I don't like it here so much anymore babe,' said Rosie. 'I'm gonna try and find something that's a bit more *me*. A nice little gun for personal defence or maybe a groovy portable shield… Something not so extreme.'

'Just remember what this place is and why we're here.'

'How could I forget?' Rosie walked off, clearly annoyed. It was a good idea to split up though. As much as she liked to underplay her smarts, Rosie had a keen eye and a sharp mind. She was likely to find some good valuable gear.

I checked the time. Ernest should be about half way through the bulkhead now. I gave myself an hour to explore here before I would try to contact him again.

It was hard not to indulge in sightseeing. There was a lot of interesting equipment, much of it hooked up to Blue. Most of the gear I saw was new to me.

The facility had suffered a lot of damage, some of it severe. Presumably some of the weaponry was originally coupled with Red power, and had escalated in some typically destructive manner.

One corner of the facility had been reduced to nothing but molten slag, interspersed with veins of metal that looked suspiciously like gold. For all I knew it *was* gold, which was interesting, but we didn't really have the time or means to extract it. Besides, the right artifacts or devices would be worth a lot more than gold.

I spotted another oddity – a white-tinted area producing feint sparkling lights. At a hunch I switched my artificial eye to infrared, revealing an area much colder than its surroundings. On approach it became clear that the area was covered in rime, blanketing everything inside it. Ice crystals sparkled gently in the light of my torch. A little burst of excitement went off in my head, immediately tempered by caution. *Stay calm, look first, celebrate later.*

At the edge of the area stood a large piece of weaponry on a massive tripod. It seemed to be a super-focused laser attached to a feedback loop device. A corpse lay nearby – a man in a green lab coat – frozen solid. It wasn't clear what had killed him. Maybe it was the cold, maybe a radiation accident, maybe something else. I would never know.

The laser was pointed at a large metal table in the centre of the frozen area. A metal statue of Prometheus stood exactly in the middle on the table surface. It was rather beautiful. Next to the statue stood an artifact: a tiny array of flat rectangles, wafer thin, with slivers of Blue layered in between. It was a Kelvin Box.

I always had an eye out for one of these, but they were so rare that I never really expected to find one. A Kelvin box could project an extremely precise volumetric field, easily shaped to the precise dimensions required by the user. Anything inside the field was held at absolute zero for as long as the field was active. It was unbelievably valuable.

The table was surrounded by shielded workstations and partitions, desks and pods and all kinds of additional equipment. At some point during or before the Ceres disaster the Box had been turned on and the resulting field had kept its shape for decades. Trickari tech never ceased to amaze me. It was useless to me however, unless I figured out a way to shut it off.

A quick infrared scan of the support equipment revealed nothing of use. All that stood out was the afterglow of my own footsteps on the cold metal floor. I studied them for a moment; there was something odd about them … I felt the tiniest shiver of unease come over me. I traced the path of footsteps, realising they followed a different route to the one I took.

I checked to see if Rosie has somehow caught up with me when a humanoid shape appeared in the periphery of my vision, carrying a long object in its hand. It lunged at me. A loud sharp noise hurt my ears as I fell to the ground. I desperately tried to get back up on my feet, but it was strangely difficult to coordinate my movements. My concentration dissolved, I was overcome with confusion. My enemy had done something to me.

Another sharp sound, and after that all I knew was pain, lasting long seconds that felt like long hours. I tried to look up to see the face of my attacker but before I could focus I slid into deep unconsciousness, like a child slipping under a sheet of ice, realising they're about to drown but unable to do anything about it.

A thousand migraines rampaged inside my skull. The pain was sickening. A deep, unsettling nausea grabbed my stomach and *squeezed*. I heaved but nothing came up but saliva, speckled with small drops of blood. Everything was hazy, even my hearing was muffled. I could just about hear a voice dancing at the edge of my understanding. Insistent. Urgent …

I tried to turn off my shimmer-suit only to find it was already switched off. Slowly, the scene in front of me came into focus, both visually and aurally. A face appeared close to mine … a mouth, whispering in my ear. It was Rosie, kneeling over me. I was lying down.

We were still in the weapons testing facility, but now somewhere in the far north side. There was some illumination, coming from a small construction light which threw long, orange-edged shadows. About ten metres to our left stood a strange rectangular array of metal pipes, holding a round Trickari artifact in its centre.

It shone with a deep red light – the eye of a demon, ready to destroy all it could behold. The artifact looked familiar to me, but trying to remember what it was caused another wave of pain and nausea. I sat up, and moaned as the pain in my head intensified.

'– should have known the creep was gonna come for us… Wake up hun, I need you alert now…'

'Wait,' I groaned. 'I can't think… pain…' I tried to touch my head but somehow failed to do so. I was tied up. 'Who did this?'

'Our friend Jeremiah. Should have decked him back on the ship.'

'It makes no sense… We hardly salvaged anything yet. If he wanted to rob us he would have done it after we got back on the ship.' I started to get my head together now. 'Damnit, I'm going to kill Preacher. He must be behind this.'

'No time for that now babe. Can you get out of these?' Rosie showed me her bonds. She was tied at the ankles and wrists. Both sets of knots were tied together, forcing her to sit on her knees, arms tied behind her.

I flexed my muscles testing the rope for any give. I was tied up in the same manner as Rosie, but Jeremiah didn't know about my augmented left arm.

'I reckon I can,' I whispered, 'but it'll take a while. If I'm not careful I'll pull too hard and crush my real arm.'

Although I couldn't see, I thought I could pull the cords against my augmented leg, which could easily take the stress. With some luck, between my augmented left arm and right leg, I could stretch the bonds enough to free my right arm. I should be easy from then on.

I started to turn to get the right leverage when a shadow fell over me.

'Ladies, you're awake. Good,' said Jeremiah. He

looked different. Elated. In control. His smirk was absent, replaced by an expression I couldn't fathom.

'What the hell did you hit me with?' I asked, vying for time. I was still trying to recall what the artifact was for. Something told me it was important to know.

'Synaptic prod. Simple, but does the job. Hurts like a mother but I knew you two could take it.' Jeremiah put his hand on my hair, slowly stroking it. 'Soon you'll meet *her*. It's going to be wonderful.' I would have bitten his fingers off if the face mask hadn't been in the way.

'Meet who, creep? And what the hell does Preacher want from us?'

'Trying to get under Jeremiah's skin with a bit of cursing eh? It don't work. Heard it all before.' He walked up to the array, and hooked up a wire that led to a small computer. He talked as he worked.

'Wasn't Preacher that did this. Oh, He wanted me to rough you up a bit, take all the loot, you know? If I could. But that's just a waste. A bit of fun sure, but I've got better use for you.'

While he was talking I managed to rotate my wrist just enough to get some leverage. I slowly pulled the cords between my augmented arm and leg, and although it hurt like hell on my other limbs I started to slowly create some wriggle room.

'Can't get it up when we're not trussed up like pigs? That what turns you on?' said Rosie.

Jeremiah froze for a moment. A cold look flashed in his eyes, to be replaced by a smile. He got back to work but kept talking. He seemed eager to tell us his story.

'When I was a young boy, before all this shit. Yeah there was a time I was young and innocent too... Anyway, it was Saturday... so my dad tried to beat the crap out of me like he always did on Saturday. He used a big rod he did. Padded with lots of tape and stuff so no bones would break. Anyway, that day he was all messed up on some cheap new drug, so it was easy to get away from him. Which I did, I ran to the beach.'

Jeremiah's entire expression changed. The lined and

weathered features, shaped by forces of hatred and suffering, gave way to genuine wonder, innocence and softness.

'That beach wasn't nuttin' special. Full of garbage and the crap that people throw away. Water wasn't too clean either, but it was still the beach and the ocean and all that stuff calms a boy down, right? That's what I was doing, calming down my mind, looking at the sunshine dancing on the water. Wasn't much wind that day, just little waves, coming to say hi to me.'

Jeremiah looked like a child again. His face had taken on the calm mood of the boy he was back then.

Rosie and I exchanged glances. *Where was this going?*

'And then I saw her,' he continued, 'and she saw me. Right there, in front of me, I saw my angel. She was made of the light that danced just behind the waves. Just behind this world. I reached out to her, and she *needed* me, you see … She needed me so she could come into my world. I think she got lost and got stuck in between things. And we could help each other.'

Tears were running down Jeremiah's face. Pure bliss radiated from him.

'I could feel her touch, and she could feel mine. She was coming into my world, because of me! I knew everything would be better once she was here. But then, when she was nearly through, I was hit on the arm, hard enough to break it.' Jeremiah rubbed his right forearm, as if it still hurt. Maybe it did, there was an obvious bump there. The bone probably never mended correctly.

'It was my old dad. I reckon he took some of them uppers, getting himself all awake again, and this time he came to finish the job. Every time he hit me my angel was pushed back a bit, back into the place she was tryin' to escape from. It was all wrong. I tried to tell my dad but he just hit me harder.' Jeremiah's eyes were filled with hurt and regret. He had to swallow several times before he could carry on. 'It was the dumbest thing you see? The angel was going to help all of us, even my dad … But he fucked it up. Like he always did.'

'What happened to you?' I asked, feeling a sliver of empathy despite my situation.

'To me? Hah! Nuttin' much. I licked my wounds for a few days, and then, one night, I prepared to do something. I prepared …' Jeremiah's face had regained the hard edged quality that had seemed his true face only hours before. 'I waited till my dad slept, took a hammer and a large spike. I put the spike in his earhole and I rammed it into his brain. It was beautiful. There was no pain or nuttin'… Just like that.'

'Look Jeremiah,' I said. 'I'm sorry that–'

'I see her all the time, she's still trying to get to me. Sometimes in a mirror, or in somebody's tears. She's always there but I never did know how to help her get here. Not like that day on the beach.'

'Why are we here, creep?' said Rosie. 'What do you want from us?'

But Jeremiah was lost in reverie again.

'But I've figured it out now. I know what it is that can free my angel. I know how she can be reborn.' Jeremiah motioned to the array and the artifact. 'I love her you know?'

Finally, recognition came to me, hitting me with force. I felt myself go cold inside with fear. 'Jeremiah… do you know what that is?'

'Of course, I did my research. It's a crucible. It'll be the cradle for my angel reborn. Finally, we'll be together and she will tell me her true name while she brings hope and justice to everybody.' He spoke with the fervour and precision of somebody who had perfectly memorised scripture, after reciting the lines over and over again.

'It's not a cradle,' I said. 'It's a Trickari core-field generator. They tap into the core of some faraway star, generate a field around it, and syphon off massive amounts of energy.'

'Yes. A perfect crucible for my love reborn,' said Jeremiah. There was no real understanding in his eyes.

'You don't understand. This thing is *Red*-powered. It's not stable. And it's larger than any I have ever seen before.

Imagine what would happen if the core of a star manifests inside Ceres, and this thing loses containment. Think!'

'A new star will be born. It will be glorious.'

'It will eat this whole facility, sucking it all inside its gravity well. Then it will devour Ceres, and if it gains enough energy from that – which it might do considering all the shit that's stored here – it could grow large enough to eat half the solar system! Or maybe it will escalate, releasing enough radiation to kill everything in the goddamn solar neighbourhood.'

I had nearly wiggled my augmented arm out of its bonds. I had a plan if I could only get my hand free…

'Oh girl… I'm grateful, really.' Jeremiah's fingers raked through my hair again. 'If it weren't for you I'd never been able to get in here and find the cradle. I'll make sure you'll be remembered.'

Jeremiah's demeanour hardened. He walked up to the array and started punching in settings. He was coming to the end of the sequence. We were nearly out of time.

With a sudden jolt my hand pulled free from the bonds. For a moment I worried that Jeremiah had noticed, but he continued prepping the device.

Rosie spotted my progress and tried to stall for time. 'Hey Jeremiah! What if you're wrong feller? What if this ain't the Angel reborn but the Devil himself? Look at it, you can see his red eye staring right at us.' *That got his attention.*

'No … Don't say that. I know the devil. I'd know if it was him.'

'Would you now?' sneered Rosie. 'Like those other times you let him get to you? You said it yourself; you're a sinner – through and through. The devil *knows* you Jeremiah. And you know that to be true.'

Jeremiah paused. A look of panic came over him. The look of a little boy, scared to do the wrong thing. 'No… it's my angel. I can tell!'

'Ain't that what happens every time?' said Rosie. 'You think you got it made, and then that old devil gets in your head and starts whispering. Soon enough you're in the shit again. That thing over there, is no Angel.'

'Shut your filthy mouth you godless whore!' roared Jeremiah. He lifted the synaptic prod and approached Rosie. 'Or I'll do it for you!'

'Back to that again?' she spat. '"The devil made me do it" "An angel made me do it". Seems to me there's always a reason for you to hurt innocent women.'

'Innocent? Innocent? You… you lie together, in sin, worse than beasts. You make me sick!'

Jeremiah turned, his eyes bloodshot, his hands trembling. He strode towards us, a vengeful man, ready to turn his wrath on us. He didn't know that my augmented arm was now free. He just needed to get in my reach … I prodded Rosie, letting her know I was ready.

'What's the matter little boy? Girls don't do it for you unless you hurt them a bit? You really want boys don't you? I seen you look at Ernest. He's fine, I'll give you that.'

What happened next was fast, violent, and will haunt me for the rest of my life.

Jeremiah swung the prod at Rosie's head. I caught his wrist just before it connected. A look of surprise appeared on his face, turning to worry as I started to squeeze, then horror as I snapped his wrist with a sickening crunch. He fell to the floor screaming, crawling away, holding his wrist. I frantically tried to extricate Rosie and myself from the remaining bonds.

Jeremiah's screams turned into the whimpers of a wounded animal, eventually dying down, but he hadn't given up. Something inside him had pushed him on until he had nearly reached the control panel wired into the core-field generator.

With a final struggle I broke free. I jumped up and frantically raced to stop him. Maybe I could reach him in time to prevent the activation of the artifact …

I was too late. Arm hanging limp by his side, emitting a low moan, Jeremiah activated the core-field generator.

A loud hum instantly shook the air. The artifact's red eye started to glow, slowly increasing in intensity as Jeremiah flipped switch after switch, increasing the power levels of the gestating core.

Jeremiah cried, huge tears of ecstasy and fervour, running freely down his face like rain down a windowpane.

'She's here! Finally, she's here!'

Something *rippled* around the artifact, like a Fata Morgana. A shimmering shape moved towards Jeremiah, who opened his arms wide despite his hand dangling at a sickening angle off his broken wrist. Pure bliss had made him forget any pain.

The shimmering shape reached Jeremiah, picked him up and threw him against the controls. I stared in shock, unable to move, until I felt a hand shaking me; it was Rosie, who had escaped her bonds as well.

The artifact's hum was rapidly turning into a roar, its red eye bathed the surroundings in a crimson glow.

Jeremiah kneeled in front of the shimmering shape, his head bowed, tears still flowing freely. Electricity arced, jumping onto Jeremiah who screamed once more, then fell over. Angelfire engulfed him from top to bottom until his body was completely consumed and all that remained was the ominous roar of the artifact.

The shimmering effect intensified briefly before materialising into a familiar shape. It was Ernest, holding some kind of experimental weapon.

'Rosie, Jemm. Let's go,' he said. Deadpan as always.

'Ernest, what the flying … ' Rosie was lost for words.

'No time. We need to turn that off.' Ernest pointed at the artifact. 'Jemm?'

I was ahead of both of them, inspecting the control panel, trying to turn off the power feed without success. My worst fears had manifested.

'It's too late,' I shouted. 'It's escalating, it will just keep drawing more and more power now. We need to get the hell out of here'

'But you said …' Rosie looked stricken.

'I know what I said, but I don't know how to stop it …' The moment I spoke those words a defiant idea formed in my mind. I removed the Pandora from my backpack. 'This won't stop it, but might limit the impact. Help me hook this thing up.'

We worked together with feverish speed, born from fear and necessity. There was no need for words, we knew almost instinctively how to help each other after the many missions we had undertaken together.

It took less than ten minutes, but by the time we were done the escalation was overwhelming; the noise had become a battering ram, the temperature was skyrocketing. I wasn't sure if we could get out in time.

We fled with all the speed we could muster, which in the low gravity was agonisingly slow.

Ceres groaned and trembled. Bulkheads screamed under the abuse, metal beams bent violently in front of our eyes. Pipes broke, dust filled the air, explosions could be felt and heard. Our shimmer-suits were useless now; there was no hiding from this.

'Babe, next time talk me out of joining you on your little adventures ok?' Rosie gasped.

'I tried damnit. You're as stubborn as a goddamn mule.'

'I'd feel better if we got them energy pearls at least. Guess we ran out of luck.'

Ernesto grunted, 'Got the pearls. Backpack full. We're rich.'

We all laughed in disbelief until another tremor prompted us to press on. Things were looking promising when we entered the final corridor, until, with a sickening breaking sound, an exploding conduit picked us up and slammed us into the opposite wall. We were completely enveloped by debris, smoke and pain.

A loud ringing filled my ear, making me think I had burst an eardrum, until it became clear that it was my suit alarm, warning me about punctures. I feared it would stop me reaching our ship, but a quick system check showed that the shimmer-field would probably offer enough protection.

'System check, both of you. Are you good to keep going?'

'Yes. Fine here,' said Ernest.

'Just … Just about.' I didn't like the note of pain in Rosie's reply, but there was no time to worry.

'OK, me too. Let's go.'

My memory of the final journey through Ceres, and the ascent to the *Jezebel*, is painfully vivid to this day. Minute details and key moments are etched into my soul; Rosie's rasping breath growing more and more ragged, the ominous sounds and vibrations increasing in strength and frequency, the naked unprotected feeling of ascending to the *Jezebel* in a riddled suit that could give out any moment… But somehow we made it and were greeted by an anxious van Dijk.

'What happened?' asked van Dijk. 'Solar Command has been going nuts. They're ordering me to rendezvous but I told them we had technical problems, which I guess is spectacularly true.'

'No time to explain. We need to get as far away from here as we can. Right now.' I tried to sound authoritative but everybody could hear the fear in my voice. Yet that fear was a better incentive than any air of command I could muster.

The *Jezebel* picked up speed gradually; Ceres slowly receded behind us. Twenty seconds … thirty… sixty … There was no explosion.

Ernest clapped me on the shoulder. 'Not bad Jemm. Plan worked.'

I nearly burst into tears, but instead said, 'Show me the damn pearls Ernest. We deserve it.'

We all gathered round him as Ernest opened his backpack. Inside were dozens of tube-shaped containers, each containing ten brilliant blue spheres, all about the size of a marble. They swirled and pulsed with Blue energy. Trickari tech at its most basic and raw, easy to hook up to depleted artifacts or to adapted Earth-tech. Together they were worth many fortunes.

Rosie whistled. 'Will you look at–'

'We've got trouble!' exclaimed van Dijk. 'Look!'

Ceres, smaller but still clearly visible on the main

screen was changing. Plumes of gas and debris erupted from cracks on its surface. For the plumes to be visible at this distance they had to be huge. The eruptions increased rapidly, it looked like the whole planetoid would explode, but suddenly it stopped.

'*Jezebel* what the hell is going on with Ceres? What did you do?' A Solar Command officer all but screamed over the radio.

'Not us sir, we're as puzzled as you,' replied van Dijk.

'Then why are you hauling tail like that?'

'Environmental systems compromised sir, got to take her back pronto.'

'Bullshit, too much of a coincidence. I don't buy it *Jezebel*, prepare for rendezvous and interroga–'

The voice cut off abruptly as Ceres *convulsed.*

'What the …,' said the officer. Fear injected a wobble into his voice. '*Jezebel* are you seeing th–'

Ceres collapsed in on itself. One moment it was there, the next it was only half the size it was before.

'I think the Pandora Box stopped working…' I said, as the enormity of what we were witnessing set in. 'Everybody strap in now.'

Ceres kept shrinking and started to emit light. For a moment the process reached an equilibrium, but then turmoil inside the planetoid could no longer be contained. White patches of light appeared on the surface, increasing in intensity as more patches appeared. There was a flash, momentarily overloading the *Jezebel*'s cameras, before the planetoid came back into focus.

'Is it growing? It is isn't it?' van Dijk sounded near hysteria, but he had every right to be.

Ceres rapidly grew to twice the size it was before. It shone brighter still. Three times in size, four times… The ship shook and vibrated, groaning and complaining at the sudden stress of extreme acceleration. The *Jezebel* was pushed far past accepted safety tolerances.

'Hold on!' screamed van Dijk.

Another flash, much brighter than the previous one. Ceres leapt in size again, only to revert and collapse in on itself, emitting waves of light and debris, until finally it was no more than a pinprick of pure white; a tiny hole in the black cloth of deep space, offering a glimpse at the hidden light behind the universe. Maybe this really was where angels lived.

The light flickered once, twice, and then it was gone.

Debris caught up with us, some even bouncing off the *Jezebel*'s thick plating, but the ship suffered no serious damage. Ceres Station on the other hand, together with Ceres, was gone.

Nobody dared speak. We all just sat there and contemplated what had just happened, wondering how many had died on Ceres Station. What other repercussions were as of yet unknown? I was so tired that it was tempting to just lie down and sleep, but I knew we weren't out of the woods just yet.

'van Dijk ... do we have to worry about radiation?' I asked.

'Jan ...'

'Excuse me?'

'My name is Jan. I mean, after all this ...'

'OK Jan,' I said gently. 'Did you pick up any radiation events? Anything else we should worry about?'

Jan stared straight ahead into nothing, but just as I was going to repeat my question he seemed to find his focus again.

'No ... Radiation levels have been within acceptable parameters. Surprisingly really, considering ...'

'I trapped most of it in the Reverse Pandora, *I think*. That was the plan anyway. Anything else?'

He scratched his nose for a moment, thinking things over ... 'Gravity is a concern.'

'How so?'

'Well, Ceres is ... *was* right on the edge of the asteroid belt. And now it's gone so...'

'OK that's pretty scary.' I still wanted to lie down.

'Any way to find out if any major asteroids have left their orbit?'

'Not yet. It's just too chaotic. Too many factors. Like life.' I smiled at the weird little nugget of philosophy.

'Then for now we're OK?' I asked to make sure.

'Probably, yes.' Jan shrugged. It would have to do.

The *Jezebel* suddenly struck me as an awful ship. Confined, cramped and racing away from a terrible legacy. She was cursed, and I had been a fool to travel on this path. *But I have the pearls. The money I need to get my boy.* I hugged myself and sat down with Rosie, putting my arm around her.

'Hey babe, I missed you,' said Rosie. Her words slurred with fatigue.

'Me too.'

'You got me them pearls, didn't you, just like you said.'

'I did.'

I squeezed her gently, but she was too weak to react. She slid away from me with a low moan. That's when I noticed the pool of blood that had gathered underneath her. A terrible feeling of dread grabbed my throat. There was another moan, slowly rising to become a high pitched keening sound. It was my own voice.

'Rosie …'

I tried to get her out of her space suit as fast as I could, but it was infuriatingly slow without her help. She had lost consciousness.

Another pair of hands appeared and helped me strip off her suit. Ernest had spotted the situation. Rosie's clothes were soaked through with blood, especially around her midsection. We gently undressed her further.

'She's not right,' I muttered uselessly.

When her jumpsuit had finally come off it revealed a dozen small punctures around her hips and abdomen. The explosion in the corridor had hurt her badly. The wounds were small, but clearly something terrible had happened to her insides.

Jan appeared with a first aid kit. He jammed a

morphine ampule into her skin, and checked Rosie with a basic medical scanner.

'She's bleeding inside. She needs a hospital right now.'

'We're in space …' I mumbled.

'I know,' said Jan. 'Back on Mars I mean. We need to get her there as fast as we can. Try to stabilise her for now.'

We did what we could, but the on-board medical equipment wasn't meant to deal with situations like this. Her vital signs were all over the place, getting worse rapidly. Taking her back to Mars turned into the longest flight of my life.

Hours passed. Rosie never regained consciousness. She died in my arms, moments before we arrived back on Mars. I kissed her lips one last time while they were still warm, removed the silver necklace, and hung it around my own neck. A reminder of my hubris.

For Rosie, Jeremiah's angel was the angel of death.

21

The spaceport was a scene of pure turmoil – a giant ant nest kicked by a Leviathan. I expected interrogation and detention, but nobody even spoke to us. The destruction of Ceres had scrambled any sense of protocol.

We smuggled Rosie's corpse out of the port and through customs. We had all the correct paperwork expected from a repair crew, so there was no reason to inspect our cargo. The customs officer didn't even spot that we came from a job near Ceres, or that we were two people short.

We took Rosie to an industrial incinerator on an old but not quite disbanded mining site outside the main dome. The incinerator maw gaped like the mouth of a demon bird, demanding to be fed souls. Rosie's body disappeared in the furnace blaze as if she had never been there to begin with.

How somebody so full of life and radiance could so easily be transformed into nothing but ashes, to be disposed of with the press of a button, was beyond my understanding.

There were no wise words. There was no wake. There was no funeral. There was just another gaping hole in the fabric of my existence.

I had to find a way to fill that hole with something, or it would swallow me whole.

The next day we went to see Preacher.

Ernest set up a meeting and insisted on coming with me, I think he knew that I would likely kill Preacher within minutes if left to my own devices.

We were to meet him in one of the basement tunnels under an old refinery. He was now a fugitive; the Mars authorities had finally realised that the *Jezebel* – registered in his name – was the last ship to go near Ceres.

The refinery was in an old part of town that was barely visited these days. One too many radiation leaks and chemical spills had left the neighbourhood less than desirable, and these days Martians wanted to look forward to a new life, not be reminded of the grubby early days of colonial existence.

Personally I quite liked the sense of history and the weight and solidity of old terraforming equipment. I always found it rather inspiring, although that day I had something less noble on my mind.

'You OK?' asked Ernest, as we walked down the old alleyways, looking for a way into the underground tunnels.

'I will be, once I get to Preacher.'

'No, no, that's not what we agreed.' He put his arm on my shoulder, and I flinched despite the gentleness of his touch. 'Preacher didn't know what Jeremiah would do.'

I made a noncommittal sound, not at all willing to let go of my anger.

'There,' said Ernest. 'Tunnel entrance.' He pointed at a shabby little building, featureless except for a sign showing an image of descending stairs. The image was almost funny in its minimalism. Very Martian.

'Let's do it.'

Ernest gently halted me as I was about to enter.

'No killing,' he said. 'I know the kind of man he is Jemm, but he is not Jeremiah.'

I slowly but firmly pushed Ernest out of the way. He was a powerful man but it was easy with my augmented strength.

'No promises,' I said.

The tunnels were small and oppressive, and smelled of sulphur and tar. Ancient lights cast a sickly green glow on ugly grey walls. Our shadows resembled sinister characters from an old German expressionist movie. I smiled at their grotesque shapes.

Ernest noticed my expression, slight as it was, and picked up on my mood.

'Atmospheric here.'

'Damn right,' I laughed, but there was little real humour behind it.

We walked in silence for a long time. The tunnels were extensive. Ernest led the way, guiding us past old junctions with crusty signs, barely legible. He clearly knew his way around here. Ernest, as always, was full of surprises.

We passed countless featureless doors, leading to storage rooms, offices and other tunnels. Eventually Ernest stopped in front of a door that looked no different from any of the others. He knocked a little paradiddle. After a few seconds a slightly different paradiddle formed the reply. We entered.

Preacher was almost unrecognisable. He had shaved off his scraggly beard, cut his hair, and dressed in expensive but neutral clothes. I was shocked to find that he was a handsome man, younger than he appeared before.

'Well look at you,' I said. I whistled in appreciation. 'Not bad at all.'

'Do you have any idea what you've done?' hissed Preacher. 'The trouble you have caused? The repercussions?'

Ernest froze – he knew how close I was to violence. I did briefly contemplate what it would be like to smash Preacher through a solid wall, but decided against it.

'The question is, Byron, do you?' *That got his attention.*

Preacher and Ernest both looked like startled deer. I wondered if Ernest had known Preacher's real name.

'That's right *Byron*,' I said. 'I know your name isn't *Pierre* or *Preacher*. In fact I know a great deal more about you than just your god-damned name.'

'Fuck you, bitch. I want my cut.'

'Preacher no …' pleaded Ernest. I felt sorry for him.

'And what money is that?' I whispered. 'Rosie's cut? Jeremiah's? They don't need it anymore I guess. What about the people on Ceres Defence Station?'

'We had a deal,' said Preacher. 'A deal is a deal. None of that other stuff is my problem.' He huffed himself up. It almost looked impressive, but I could smell the fear oozing out of him. 'I'm entitled to compensation. My ship has been confiscated. My program has been shut down, I had to change identity… All because of you.'

'Ah that's cute. You think that I don't know that you gave Jeremiah orders to rob us. How about that?'

'What… what do you mean?'

'He admitted it to us, just before he turned Ceres into an imploding star.' I let that sink in for a moment. 'What did he say again? Ah yes, he said that you wanted him to "rough us up a bit," "Take all the salvage." Yeah those were the words, weren't they?'

There was no reply. For a moment we all stood there, silently contemplating our situation, each of us with a very different point of view, when all of a sudden Preacher reached inside his pocket. I was grateful for his stupidity, giving me cause to act. As tired as I was, he was still no match for me. I lashed out fast as a cobra, punched his spleen. Hard. He crumpled without a sound. A small fat gun fell out of his powerless hand.

'Get up.' I spat at him. 'Before I lose my temper.'

Preacher rose, wobbly but – I had to grudgingly admit – with some fire still left in him.

'What do you want?' he groaned between clenched teeth.

'That depends …' I picked up his gun, weighed it in my hand, and aimed it at his head. 'First, I need you to tell me the truth about Jeremiah. And if you survive that story you *might* still be useful to me. So, I'm going to ask you this one time only.' I tapped the side of my head. 'And don't even try to lie. I can literally tell if you do.'

'OK. Ask,' said Preacher, trying to stand up straight.

'Did you order Jeremiah to steal from us?'

'I did.' No hesitation. Again, I had to admit to a measure of respect for the man.

'Did you tell him to kill us.'

'I did not. I'm as pissed off about it as you.'

I slowly let out a breath that I didn't know I was holding in. I suspected Jeremiah went way past his remit, but I had to be sure.

'Oh believe me,' I said. 'You have no clue just how pissed off I am. None.'

'What do you want? You'd better tell me now, because I think I'll need a doctor very soon.'

'Well, Byron, here's the deal. I am going to let you live, but you'll have to work for me for a while. I'll even pay you a wage, which is rather generous of me, all things considered.'

'Get to the fucking point.'

I laughed. 'I need you to help flush out a scared little rabbit named Theo. You still have contacts in your Program right?'

'I do.'

'Ok then. Ernest is hereby promoted to the caretaker of your precious Program. He had to step in after the sad news of your "death" reached him. Through him, you will direct your flock to assist my operative Isaac in finding my guy.'

'Isaac?'

'Yeah, he's a very talented person. Took him no time at all to uncover your old identity, and your hilariously long list of fraud convictions and warrants. Facts that will be shared with the local constabulary if you were to decide that this assignment is not for you.'

'OK OK, no need to rub it in. Now take me to a goddamn hospital before I die in this shithole.'

'Preacher! These are not the words of a man of god.'

'Just do it. I'm no use to you dead.'

'Don't tempt me, Byron.'

Ernest stepped in and helped him up. There was still a tenderness in Ernest that I found surprising. He was as much a victim as any of Byron's flock, but I respected him too much to question his reluctance to get revenge. I guess that despite Preacher creaming off the top and undoubtedly taking numerous kickbacks, his Program still legitimately helped hundreds of people.

We delivered Preacher to a freelance medical student in Scar District, who managed to patch him up without too much fuss. Two days later he was on the case.

I was finally closing in on my prey.

During the following days, while Preacher and Isaac did their thing to find Theo, I was finally able to finish my physical transformation. With the fortune I acquired at Ceres I could have walked away from everything and started over. I could have bought a sleek vessel for high-end salvage, hired myself a crew, and spent the foreseeable future building a new life, doing what I love. Instead, I spent three weeks under Ella's knife.

There were at least seven procedures covering a wide assortments of augments and enhancements. Slowly, painfully, but irrefutably, I was finally becoming the true monster I had to be to take on Gibson.

My newfound riches allowed me to pay for the best gear on the market – both legal and clandestine. I received military grade combat conditioning, allowing me to learn and employ various fighting techniques with only a few weeks of practise. Subdermal shielding was implanted to protect key parts of my anatomy. There were sensory augments, including enhanced hearing and touch to become more aware of my surroundings. Brutally efficient strength mods would allow me to dominate almost any opponent in terms of sheer power. I even opted for a highly experimental neural accelerator, to give me enhanced reflexes and reaction speed, especially in high-stress situations.

Although Ella was there for everything she became more and more despondent as we went through the process. As she was wrapping up her work on my hands her shoulders shook for a moment. She sniffed, coughed, and rubbed her eye with the back of her hand. I wasn't sure what was troubling her.

'What's the matter? Is there an issue with the mesh?' I asked.'

'The mesh is fine,' said Ella, but her body language signalled something different.

'Then what? If there's an issue I need to know ...'

'The frigging mesh is fine, I already told you.'

'So what th–'

'For fucks sake Jemm, look at yourself ... What have we done to you? What have *I* done?'

I sighed. 'It doesn't matter. I don't care about my body. All this isn't for me, it's for Clint.'

'It matters to me.'

'After this we are done with this stuff,' I said. 'And if I succeed, if I get Clint back, it will have been worth it,' I spoke softly, compassionately. 'You know it's the only way.'

'Do I?' An edge of desperation touched her voice. 'How do you know? How will you get to Gibson? How will you get to Clint? You act like you know it all but you don't. You're human Jemm, no better than the rest of us. Despite all this crap we're putting inside you.'

'Ella... Calm down, this isn't helping.' I sat up, flexing my slightly swollen hands. I suddenly felt great. Ready to take on any challenge.

'It's all going to be OK,' I said. I was convinced it was true.

I went to The God Axe one last time. As before, the ridge provided an awe inspiring view. The long shadows and dawn's light competed to present a tableaux to rival any painting in human history. I had made the ascent many times before but this time it felt different. *I* felt different.

When I arrived at the summit I felt a nervous energy flow through my entire being, crackling and distinct, like ozone, moments before a thunderstorm. It reminded me of the sexual energy that existed so potently at that auction house back on Earth.

I stepped out of the skimmer and prepared myself for my ritual, once more running through the litany of crimes committed by my enemies, honing my anger into a sharp edge, ready to strike out in revenge. Rosie's death had shaken me, but ultimately it had added more heat to the fire of my resolve.

As I took off my breather, the fields of lichen glittered in the early sunlight, daring me to join them. I smiled and took a deep breath, re-affirming my singular goals – *Free Clint. Destroy my enemies*. It sounded so simple.

A calmness came over me. At first I thought it was just a weakening of my muscles because of the reduced flow of oxygen, but gradually, as I took in cold breath after cold breath, it became clear to me that I was not going to lose consciousness. My augmented physique – the improvements to my heart and lungs – allowed me to survive on the surface of the planet without protection.

I had finally become a true Martian, and I was a terrible thing to behold.

Isaac contacted me a few days later. He wanted to meet in the Gagarin. It was obvious he had news, but he was ambiguous as to the nature of it. I didn't want to risk sharing sensitive data via Padd so I agreed to meet with him that evening.

The Gagarin enforced a strict dress code, so I went through my humble wardrobe trying to find something that would make me blend in with the glitzy regulars that visited the club. I'm not one for dresses, but I had a few trendy street outfits that would do the Gagarin justice.

While I was browsing my clothes collection I came across a slick mono-suit that I didn't immediately recognise. It wasn't really my style – too overtly sexual.

I had no memory of buying it, yet it was exactly my

size. I pondered this for a minute when it hit me: *It was a gift from Rosie.* I could smell her perfume on the dress.

There was a note, but I had trouble reading it through my tears. I had to sit down, images of a life that could have been swirled around my mind, raging, demanding to be heard.

At that moment, nothing I had been doing made sense to me; Clint was gone, probably forever. Rosie was killed, trying to help me. I had betrayed the sanctity of my own body in ways that I hadn't even known I was capable of. Like my father, I was now exposed to insanely dangerous augments. I feared for my own sanity.

I dragged myself to my bathroom and splashed water on my face, but to no avail. The face looking back at me from the mirror was the face of my father – mad, unhinged, and frighteningly similar to my own. I sank down onto the bathroom floor, hyperventilating, trying to make sense of the breakdown I was experiencing. My gasps for air echoed with tinny reverberations off the bathroom walls.

Eventually the episode ran out of steam. Not because of any mental strength on my part, but because my perverted body's augments activated a regulation protocol, releasing a cocktail of serotonin and dopamine, steering me into happier waters. I knew as it was happening that it was an entirely artificial sensation, but nonetheless it did what it had to do and I calmed down.

I regained my composure, picked myself up and mentally dusted myself off. The person in the mirror now resembled somebody else. Not my father, nor my old self, but somebody *new*. I felt strangely powerful. I had shed my old skin, no longer fit for purpose. Whoever this new person was, she was ready.

I briefly held Rosie's necklace – *If she could see me now* – and dressed to go see Isaac.

The Gagarin was heaving by the time I got there. A sense

of déjà vu fell over me, hints of my old doubts and fears tried to reassert themselves, but I discarded them with an easy anger. *Enough of that shit.*

I cut through the crowd like a lion on a hunt. People recoiled when they saw the look in my eyes. I didn't care.

Isaac had reserved the same alcove we used last time. He was dressed the same, and had even ordered the same drink as last time. Sitting in the alcove he was framed by red tassels and velour. It felt like I had returned to see a play that I had seen many times before; funny little puppets performing on a mad little stage.

'"Jane Dyne" I presume?' Isaac performed his role to perfection.

I sat down without a word, and waited for him to activate the privacy field.

'You look well Isaac, as always,' I said after we were shielded from eavesdropping.

'Thank you my dear. You look rather… powerful yourself. I take it you have embarked on a course of self-improvement?'

'How have you found working with *Pierre* or whatever he wants to be called these days?'

'Ah yes, Pierre …' Isaac folded his hands together, fingers intertwined. 'He is certainly a resourceful man, and still has extensive connections through his old network.'

'That's what I was hoping for,' I said.

'He is of course not to be trusted, but I made it clear early on that I'm not a man to be trifled with.' Isaac's mouth twitched into a thin smile, which left an instant later.

'Good,' I said. 'I don't give a damn what he does after this is over, but for now he needs to do his job.'

'That is clearly understood my dear.'

'So, apologies for rushing things, but what's the news?'

'We found young master Theo, keeping a low profile, but apparently running some mid-level Mem schemes, as people of his calibre are wont to do.' Isaac hesitated briefly before continuing. 'But there is a problem of sorts.'

'A problem?' I tried to keep my voice measured. 'Isn't that what I pay you for? To solve problems?'

'Please Jemm, there is no need to be vulgar.' Isaac untangled his hands, reached into a pocket, and pulled out some photos. They showed Theo, arrogant smirk and all, and another character, who seemed vaguely familiar to me...

'Who's the other guy?'

'He's the problem I mentioned.'

'What makes him special?'

'He's a high level Spectra enforcer. We will have to take extreme care if we are going to extract Theo successfully.'

'If it's a matter of funds ...'

'Please, Jemm. What do you take me for? I'm not looking to change my contractual fees, but I am concerned with the success of this mission. There are some additional operational costs yes, but they are justified.'

'What do you need?'

Isaac showed a list on his Padd. I tapped it with mine, downloading the data, then paid his costs with a quick transfer.

'Now then, what's the plan?' I asked.

'Diversion, then extraction. Pierre will handle the former, my personal team the latter. With somebody like this enforcer involved things could get messy, and will certainly attract serious Spectra attention.'

'I consider that a positive.'

'In that case I'd like to proceed?' I nodded my approval. 'I will keep you posted on progress,' said Isaac. 'Be prepared for events to move fast once we have secured Master Theo.'

'Good. I'm tired of sitting on my arse. I want to be part of the extraction team.'

Isaac looked like he wanted to say something, but hesitated.

'What's bothering you Isaac?'

'I'm under no illusion regarding the nature of our contract, and naturally I respect the boundaries of a professional relationship like ours...'

'Come on, out with it.'

'Sometimes people who have suffered a personal loss become… let's say *enamoured* with the idea of conflict. In your case, having lost two loved ones, I would be remiss not to warn you of the inherent dangers in your personal involvement in this operation. There is potential for a… a *blurring* of lines between professional and personal desires.'

I was taken aback for a moment, feeling embarrassed and angry, but, I had to admit he was right to warn me.

'I will take your advice to heart Isaac. Thank you.' Isaac nodded slightly, probably relieved. 'But,' I continued, 'I will be part of the extraction team.'

'If you must… But only under a number of preconditions.'

'Go on…'

'You will be under my operational command. There is no time or space for leadership confusion.'

'Of course.'

'You will have to temper your desire for vengeance. No excessive violence. The goal of the mission is extraction only. Once master Theo is safely under our control you may do what you please with him, but only then.'

I admired Isaac's professionalism. It took guts to stand up to a client like me, but he never got flustered or defensive.

I considered my words carefully, and said, 'Isaac… please listen carefully…' I leaned in to make sure he could see and hear me clearly; 'I will perform like any other member of your crew. I would *never* jeopardise a mission that's designed to get me closer to my son.' I waited for Isaac to acknowledge my words with another small nod, then continued, 'But know this: if there is any chance of Theo getting away, or if anybody gets in our way… I will do whatever it takes. *Nothing* is off the table.'

Isaac tapped the table, considering my words, then nodded. The matter was settled, I was part of the extraction team.

Next, we went over some of the detail in Isaac's plan. I was excited. Finally I was getting somewhere.

22

Mars Colony West, or rather "Red Colony" (sometimes just "Red") as the locals called it, was everything that Escher wasn't. It was exuberant, colourful and beautiful. Architecture was less restrictive, joyful even. And, although the streets were equally maze-like, it was much less confusing to navigate because there were so many distinct neighbourhoods and landmarks.

Red Colony was the last colony to be established before Icarus, and was attractive to a different breed of colonist. Yes, there were still the same hardworking builders and engineers and botanists and the whole lot – the bedrock of Martian society – but they were younger on average, and they were more diverse. These factors had combined to form a cultural cocktail that felt very different from Escher's more austere vibe.

Like-minded souls from other colonies flocked to Red, generating a positive feedback loop: the more people it attracted, the stronger the pull for others to follow.

Red Colony also held the dubious honour of being Mars' drug capital. Somehow, despite being 55 million kilometres away from Earth, there was a steady supply of classic drugs from the home planet. Local bohemians and other recreational users indulged frequently in anything from marijuana to potent designer drugs tailored to the specific individual.

Worryingly, Red was home to a very large concentration of Trick-Junkies of all ages and circumstances; Mem was one of those drugs that appealed to people from all walks of life, and the local scene was awash with many strains of the drug. Because TJs were typically able to maintain professional duties and generally took decent care of themselves, they didn't burn out like more traditional junkies until very late in their addiction cycle, so their numbers stayed high.

This diverse pool of Trick-junkies attracted certain creative types desperate to incorporate the startling visions and memories experienced by TJs into their art. Mem-inspired poetry, sims, fine art and books were part of a successful niche in the local Martian scene, with Red Colony as the nexus.

I was overcome by the sheer craziness of it all. Red was an intense town, and I said as much to Isaac.

'I find it rather fetching, I must say,' replied Isaac, as we walked down one of the main thoroughfares.

'It's certainly colourful,' I offered. 'I guess this is how Theo stayed hidden this long. He fits right in.'

'Indeed, but as expected; his luck has finally run out.'

'How did that happen exactly?' I asked. Isaac hadn't filled me in on the precise detail of Theo's discovery, which to be fair didn't interest me much anyway. But since I was part of the extraction team it seemed prudent to ask.

'Master Theo has been a very naughty boy it seems. He has been offering his wares to the local junkies, which shouldn't have been a surprise to us. Where things seemed to have taken a more sinister turn is that he has been targeting random Trick-Junkies for some sort of covert Spectra Vision project.'

'Oh?' That sounded more relevant than I expected. 'How so?'

'Well, my dear, it seems that Theo and his Spectra enforcer have been taking home Trick-Junkies, only for them to re-appear a few days later with little left of their… let's say *cognitive* faculties. The term "lobotomised" comes to mind.'

'Well, that sounds creepy. Why?'

'Nobody knows, but the pair have been active enough for word to spread through the junkie community. This is where Pierre's assistance has been instrumental. Many of his err… *associates* have connections in these… *communities*, shall we say? When I provided Pierre with a detailed profile of our friend Theo it didn't take long for one of his little birds to sing.'

'So what do we know?' I asked. Impatience getting the best of me.

'We know where he lives, and we know where he works. The former is a well-defended location while the latter is very public; he tends to do his business in local marketplaces and other busy locales. No shortage of clients there.'

'So what's the play?' While I asked the question I suddenly felt odd. A certain tugging sensation manifested inside my mind. I felt disoriented. My mouth developed a strange yet familiar taste, like candy from my childhood.

'That, my dear, is the questions is it not?' I didn't reply, distracted by the strange sensations I was experiencing. 'Both scenarios offer serious disadvantages,' continued Isaac. 'But on balance we think it is best to confront Theo out in the open.'

The streets felt too busy. Claustrophobia smothered me. I saw people everywhere. Some of them seemed to be looking at me with strange knowing expressions.

'Is something the matter dear? You don't look quite–'

A man came up to us and matched our pace and direction, all the while looking at me. My mouth watered, the taste of metal abruptly overwhelming me.

'I've dreamt you,' he said, his voice strangely unemotional. He was a Trick-Junkie. By the looks of it recently converted.

Isaac looked on with interest, but didn't interfere.

'Go away creep,' I spat.

'Mother, hear my dreams…'

'I said go away!' I pushed him. Not hard, but he fell, only to be caught by Isaac.

'My dear man, you must pay more attention to where you walk,' grinned Isaac.

'My… my apologies,' mumbled the man, and slunk away back into the background masses – a human pebble, causing small ripples in a pond before the water smoothed out again.

'That was decidedly odd don't you think?' I nodded and shrugged, not sure what to say. Something about the

TJ's odd behaviour had disturbed me.

'Tell me about the enforcer,' I asked, trying to change the subject.

Isaac shrugged, playing along.

'Bryant. His name is Bryant.'

The extraction team consisted of four people; Isaac – which surprised me, as I thought he would take a more distant, guiding role – two stocky operatives called Jin and Kelly, obviously very experienced and very capable, and myself.

My augments made me a useful addition to the team, and I was absolutely determined to make sure Theo fell into our hands.

The bazaar was huge. Hundreds of stalls, tents, containers and warehouses all competing for attention and customers. As different as the local Martians seemed compared to those in Colony East, they still sported their intricately decorated breathers and carried themselves with the same tough and hardened attitude that all Martians seemed to develop over time.

Between Isaac and Preacher's efforts it had become clear that Theo used alternating routes to cover his rounds, but he would always pass certain markers. This was his weakness.

Theo's path took him past an old abandoned warehouse, which had been locked up and plastered over for such a long time that the locals no longer even thought of it as an actual building. We managed to gain entry the previous night, scoped the place out, and concluded that it was a perfect place to disappear Theo to.

All it would take was a distraction to get rid of Bryant, and a moment or two to snatch Theo and take him to our new lair. It all sounded feasible on paper, but everybody knew it was risky because of the public environment. Still, we had the element of surprise and some very capable people.

By the time we were all in position the Martian sunset was beaming its magic through the colony dome, bathing everything in a stunning faint purple light. If this mission wasn't so crucial and dangerous I would have stopped and basked in the glory of that light, savouring the most beautiful sunset in all the colonies.

The next day was a difficult one for me; I had slept badly owing to a combination of augment pain and nerves. Various disaster scenarios kept messing with my head, lighting little fires of doubt and uncertainty. Physically I was fine – my enhanced physique took care of that – but mentally I was tired and on edge. The encounter with the Trick-Junkie was bothering me on some unconscious level, but I couldn't put my finger on the *why* of it. Which caused even more concern.

Frankly, I was cranky. Short-tempered even. My team-mates gave me space to collect myself, for which I was grateful. I rewarded them with strong, hot coffee, handing it out silently, indicating that I wasn't ready to talk yet but that I would be OK soon. They understood this immediately, and let me be.

After a while Isaac came over. He looked very different from the effete gentleman who I occasionally met with at the Gagarin. This Isaac was hard edged, athletic, armed to the teeth. Again, I wondered if he was ex-Corp, Samurai class perhaps. Impressive if true. It's dangerous to leave a position like that and set up as an independent.

'Nerves?' he asked.

'No. I'm not a rookie.'

He took my truculence in his stride, and sat down next to me. 'I have more news.'

'Good news?' I asked, attempting a smile.

'I'd rather think so. But it's curious as well.' Isaac considered his next words for a moment. 'My sources confirm that Clint is alive and well, which you already know.'

I sat up. What's this?

'But there is more going on. Spectra are treating him as a very valuable commodity indeed.'

'Of course they are. His crystals…'

'No, that's not it. There are no reports of new Mem hitting the streets, and my sources tell me they aren't harvesting or synthesising anything new.'

'Your sources could be wrong.'

'They could be, but if Clint is simply there as a Neo, kept alive to get a new supply line of TrickMem, then surely they would have released the stuff by now.'

'Maybe…' I said. 'Does it matter?'

'It most certainly does my dear. For now, it seems your son is worth a lot to them for some reason that goes beyond the merely financial. He is being held at Spectra's most discreet research facility in London, and interestingly, your friend Gibson has been visiting nearly every day.'

A cold hand twisted my innards. 'Gibson… I'll get to him soon enough if we pull this off.'

'Jemm, my dear. Please understand what I'm saying. Something serious and important is happening at Spectra, and your son is central to it all.'

'More reason to get this mission over with.'

'I don't dispute that.' Isaac was going to say more, but thought better of it. 'I'll let you process this on your own,' he said, leaving me both elated and troubled. If Clint was this important to Spectra he would be kept safe, but it would be very hard to free him. But then again, it was always going to be hard.

For a while I observed my team-mates. I cycled through the various enhanced vision modes my augmented eye offered me, eventually settling on an infrared surveillance preset, overlaid with heart-rate and perspiration data. It painted an intimate picture of a diverse group of individuals:

Jin and Kelly were fascinating to watch. They moved with incredible grace and fluidity –tigers, secure and superior, patrolling their territory. They didn't seem especially enhanced, other than what I guessed were some metabolic reinforcements and shielding, but they exuded an air of power and confidence that was hard to miss.

They moved around each other with an ease that few people displayed. Rosie and I used to move around each other like that. Then it dawned on me that Jin and Kelly were lovers. I wondered at their decision to work together despite the obvious dangers, but then again, maybe it was danger that fuelled their relationship. Something did anyway, as I could literally see their bodies heat up when they got close to each other.

I felt too much like a voyeur to keep on watching them, so I switched my attention to Isaac. He was cool and enigmatic where Jin and Kelly were passionate and transparent. It wasn't just because of his augments, although I'm sure they played a part, it was also apparent to me that Isaac was very much in control of his emotions. He held them under tight reign, never showing a glimpse of weakness.

I wondered what it would take to shake him into revealing his true self, without filters or discipline. Everybody has their buttons, no matter how well they try to hide them.

I chewed on that thought for the rest of the morning, until it was time to prep for the mission. Theo would be mine by the end of the afternoon.

Isaac had us dress like locals, shopping for wares in the great bazaar. Our job was to mingle and blend in with the crowds. By the time Theo's round would take him close to our ambush site nobody would look at us twice – until it was too late to stop us.

We had several hours to browse the stalls, haggle over purchases and to scope the lay of the land. The market was a huge affair, sprawling for hundreds of metres beneath the golden translucent skin of an ancient Martian dome.

It was relatively easy to get lost in the hustle and bustle and show genuine interest in the items we perused. I haggled properly, extolling genuine fake outrage at some of the opening offers made. I loved the distinct smell of these kinds of markets: a heady mix of spices, antiques, fresh food and people, who themselves smelled of hard work and graft.

We went in equipped with earpieces and transmitters, allowing us to receive updates on Theo's position and call in our own movements. Isaac directed us as a conductor, and we played our parts to perfection.

To my astonishment and delight I discovered a stall selling miniature models of ships. It sported a wide range of wonderful samples – many of which I already owned – but carrying many more I did not. A gaudy sign announced the content on display:

> Aramici's Ships of the Universe
> ~ Best Collection on Mars

I couldn't help myself and stopped, deciding to make a purchase almost immediately. My eyes roamed over the ships on offer, while I tried to hide my excitement.

'An experienced collector I see? You will find that my collection of ships is unrivalled on all of Mars.' The man's voice was dripping with an abundance of pride, or disdain. I couldn't tell. Maybe it was both.

'You have some decent pieces…' I said, noncommittal.

'Oh please, young lady, you may drop the charade, it ill suits you.'

'Charade? How so?'

'Your eyes my dear, they tell the full story, clear as day. First you inspected my replica of the *Beagle*. You noticed the exquisite workmanship, but moved on. I assume you already own this piece, but in a less pristine condition.' I didn't contradict him and he continued. 'Then your eyes feasted on that magnificent reconstruction of the *Nautilus*. Slightly out of your price league I presume, as you then spotted the price on my classic little model of the *Galactica*. More affordable for sure, but not as nice as the aforementioned pieces. You see young lady; Aramici sees all!'

'Not bad, not bad... So where are we now?' I asked, impressed despite myself.

'Now we are waiting for me to point out an item that would surely be the crown jewel of your collection. All we have to do is be honest with each other.'

'And what would this impressive piece be?'

Aramici produced a bottle. Inside, an incredibly intricate model, perfectly constructed, painted, and weathered. The bottle carried an inscription, showing the name of the ship. It was the *Pequod,* Captain Ahab's ship.

'It seems I have hit the bullseye, as it were?'

I took a moment to compose myself before I answered, 'I'm not sure I want that ship. It carries... connotations.'

Aramici looked sharply at me. I think he could tell I was impressed with the model, but he could also hear the sincerity in my voice.

'Let me think about that particular piece for a moment. Do you have any classic Moebius vessels?'

'Of course I do. Just as you suspected.'

'Excellent, may I see th–'

'Enjoying yourself?' Isaac's voice startled me, pulling me back into the here and now. I was suddenly aware just how much I let myself get distracted.

'Please conclude your purchase within the next few minutes and get ready. Our target is approaching, and he is accompanied by Bryant, as we expected. I need you ready for anything.'

I turned to Aramici, and said, 'I'll take the Pequod and the Galactica both, at seventy percent off your listed price. I have no time to haggle, it's a take it or leave it kind of deal. If I'm still happy one month after the purchase I will come back for more. Decide now please.'

Aramici thought it over, a somewhat bemused

expression breaking through his composure. He wasn't used to such forthright dealings.

'My my, aren't we confident.'

'Time to wrap up Jemm,' hissed Isaac. 'Two minutes.'

I showed Aramici my cred stick, and waited for his response.

'Yes, well … A man has to make a living,' he started. I gave him a humourless smile.

'A girl has better things to do than stand here and haggle all day.'

Aramici adopted an air of distaste and disdain. 'There is no need to be vulgar madam. We are not slapping palms at the butcher's.'

'One minute. Are you ready?' Isaac's voice was calm, but there was no mistaking the urgency. I sighed and made to leave, resigned to lose this opportunity, when Aramici finally saw the light.

'Oh, why not eh? I am not averse to sacrificing a bit of profit in order to welcome a new member to my family of enthusiasts.'

He held out a Padd, which I touched with my cred stick. 'Good. My address is on the payment confirmation. Please mail me the ships within seven days.'

'He's here. Get ready,' Isaac hissed.

I spotted Theo only a moment later. I recognised his arrogant swagger from a mile away. A shiver of disgust raced up my spine and turned into a dull rage – like an ember, kicked hard enough to reveal its smouldering hot core.

This is the man who sold me out. I thought.

Theo looked every inch the part of a small-time crook who had lucked into the big time. Next to him, muscular and supple like a panther, walked his corporate chaperone.

I moved away from the stall, Aramici still muttering his inanities, and pretended to browse a stall closer to the target.

'Everybody assume your positions,' whispered Isaac. I wondered where he was.

Theo was talking to a Junkie, all attitude and self-important posturing, whereas Bryant was quietly scoping out the market. Compared to Theo he was impressively alert. A pro.

There were three lanes in this section of the market. Theo and Bryant were in the middle lane. Jin was leaning against a wall in the first, while Kelly was arguing with a cloth merchant in the third. I was in the central lane, and therefore closest to Theo.

Theo was getting rough with his client, pushing him around, being an overbearing arsehole – bullying 101. The TJ was a sad and frightened creature, frantically looking for a way out of the encounter. Just when he managed to pull away Theo produced a small vial and waved it in front of his face. Trick Mem. He didn't even try to hide it. The junkie was a mess, trying pitifully to reach out and grab it. Theo laughed and pulled it out of reach.

'Now people,' said Isaac. 'All operatives engage when ready. Wait for the signal ...'

I started a mental countdown from sixty. At the count of twelve there was a low rumble and a shudder, followed by a clearly audible explosion. A voice spoke over the bazaar's intercom system.

"WARNING – DOME INTEGRITY COMPROMISED"

The crowd fell silent as the message looped. A thousand worried glances shot at the dome above our head. The lights flickered – once, twice – as if uncomfortable with all the attention. A murmur rose up from the people, swelling into a roar of panic in minutes. Some people started to push for the exits. Emergency lights turned on, their red glow only succeeding in making everybody look crazed.

The crowd now moved en masse to the exits. I went with the flow, slowly drifting towards Theo, a pebble on a river of lava. Those carrying breathers quickly put them on. I could actually smell the fear in the air.

'Kelly, Jin, move in.' Isaac's voice was calmness

personified. 'Jemm, back them up. We have about ten minutes before the system's countermeasures take down my crashware.'

I saw Jin and Kelly close in on Theo and Bryant, moving as if they were simply borne along by the crowd, but to me they moved with the same sense of purpose a lion shows when choosing a target in a herd of impala.

'Very good,' said Isaac. 'Extraction point nearly upon us…'

Then, as Jin and Kelly reached Theo, the lights went out completely. My ocular augment kicked in immediately, and I saw a ghostly tableaux of people reacting with a mixture of fear, panic, or just plain anger. Their mouths forming "O's" and "A's", circles and arches of dismay.

My augmented vision revealed Kelly's shape to me, as clear as day. She honed in on her prey and took him down with ruthless efficiency. One moment Theo was standing, the next moment he crumpled to the floor. Kelly caught him as he went down and dragged him away.

Jin meanwhile worked his way in between Kelly and Bryant, who was looking around him with suspicion. I was impressed with his instincts. I inched closer until I was only a few metres away, and held my position.

Kelly dragged Theo away from the main throng of people. She was mostly shielded by the dark but nobody cared anyway. Those who noticed assumed somebody had fainted in the panic and had to be removed.

She was half way to the door when the lights started to flicker; oscillating between regular lighting and the emergency lights. The strobing effect was disconcerting, but a small adjustment to my ocular augment filtered out the worst of it.

Bryant was agitated. He noticed Theo was missing, but hadn't spotted Kelly dragging him away yet. It would only be seconds before he did.

Isaac was in full control; 'Jin, interference, now,' he said. His normal flowery and formal way of speaking replaced by clipped commands; to the point. Professional.

Jin stepped out in front of Bryant, bumping into the Spectra enforcer with force. Both stumbled. Jin reacted with feigned fury, pushing Bryant away from him. 'Watch it fucker!' he shouted, acting drunk.

Bryant tried to push past him, slightly annoyed but more interested in locating Theo, who was being dragged ever closer to the warehouse door by Kelly.

Jin didn't budge. He pushed Bryant again.

'I said, watch it fucker!' he said, slightly wobbly on his legs. It was quite a performance. Jin shouted again, 'Hey buddy! I'm talking to you!'

At that moment, Bryant finally spotted Kelly, and it dawned on him that there was something very wrong.

'What *is* this?' said Bryant. I felt a shiver of unease on hearing him speak. *I know that voice* ...

'Hey, you!' he shouted at Kelly, but it was obviously too noisy for his voice to carry that far. 'Oh for fuck's sake,' cursed Bryant. The sound was enough for my memory to finally latch on and do its job; the voice belonged to one of the operatives who had taken Clint and left me for dead. My unease turned to pure hatred.

Bryant finally took a moment to consider Jin properly, who stood swaying but proud, fists raised. Every inch the angry drunk.

'Best move out of my way little man,' said Bryant – softly, but clear in intent.

The lights stopped flashing. The looping message faltered mid-sentence. I could now clearly hear Bryant's voice.

'Make me, arsehole,' said Jin, still playing his part.

'Oh believe me, I will.'

Bryant wasted little time. He moved in with a series of jabs, fully expecting to go straight through Jin, but was parried easily. Even now Jin didn't drop the angry drunk act. He almost accidentally blocked all the punches, and concentrated on countering with messy jabs of his own. They never landed anywhere they could do damage, but stopped Bryant in his tracks.

'Didn't expect that did ya?' slurred Jin. 'Shouldn't have picked on a veteran.'

Bryant took the bait, coming in with kicks and jabs. Jin blocked most of them, but now that Bryant was getting serious some connected and did damage. Bryant was obviously well trained, and probably powerfully enhanced. Jin wasn't going to last long like this.

Then, Jin unexpectedly stepped in under Bryant's guard and threw an elbow aimed at his larynx. It was meant to take him out with a surprise move, but Bryant was too fast and the attack merely grazed his nose; it broke with an audible crack.

Bryant stood stunned for a moment, inviting Jin to come in with a hard right, hoping to finish him off, but Bryant was through playing Jin's game. A glass dagger appeared in his hand, almost impossible to see. Bryant grabbed Jin's incoming fist, twisted, and was about to plunge the dagger into Jin's armpit. The attack would have been lethal if I hadn't stepped in.

I took one swift stride and punched his bicep hard. The knife fell to the floor; Bryant's eyes clouded momentarily in pain as he instinctively retreated.

'I see,' he rasped. 'Not quite as stupid as you look then.'

I stepped in, 'Who's the civilian, Bobby?'

It was a gamble; our previous encounter was at night, and Bryant had worn a shimmer-suit. My hair was completely different now, as was my physique. But Bryant was a pro …

'Clear it, mister,' I continued. 'Never no mind Bobby here, he ain't nuttin' but an angry drunk, but he my partner. No need to stick him, eh?'

Bryant looked at me suspiciously. 'Are you for real?'

'Try me fucker,' I laughed, copying Jin's turn of phrase, and settled into a military-style fighting stance.

Bryant scanned the surroundings. No sign of Theo. Again, he looked at me suspiciously. I grinned, ready to dance.

'I don't have time for this shit,' said Bryant, incredulity

in his voice, before backing off and making his way out of the market.

Jin and I looked at each other and burst out laughing.

We'd done it. Theo was mine.

When we returned to the warehouse Jin spotted Kelly, and a smile dawned on his face as wide the Martian sky. They kissed passionately, momentarily oblivious to my presence. I felt a twitch of envy.

'And the award for best actor goes to...' laughed Kelly. 'Man... I could hear your performance over my ear piece. Very impressive, *fucker*.'

'Where's Theo,' I said impatiently.

Kelly pointed at an old pallet, stacked with bags of industrial compound. Theo lay on top, on his back, eyes closed. The shark on Theo's throat slowly bobbed up and down, lazily swimming to the rhythm of his respiration.

Isaac stood by his side. I walked up, relieved but still jittery.

'Your luck ran out, didn't it?' snapped Isaac, for once showing real emotion. I turned on my surveillance preset. He was lit up like a Christmas tree.

'What are you talking about?'

'Bryant. You know him, don't you? I saw your reaction, you recognised him.'

I didn't see any point in lying. 'Yes, he was on the team that took Clint. I recognised his voice.'

'Damn it to hell. Of all the stupid things...' Isaac had trouble controlling his anger. 'Did he recognise you?'

'Nope. I'm pretty sure I would have known.'

'Pretty sure? Listen to me my dear, this is–'

'No you listen to me.' I stepped closer until we were just centimetres apart. 'I performed perfectly, despite standing face to face with one of the monsters I swore to take down. I did not lose my cool. I did not lose sight of the mission. I did not let him know who I was.' Isaac tried to speak but I interrupted him. 'Not only that, I saved your guy's arse out there, and yours for that matter. If I hadn't stepped in Bryant would have killed Jin, caught up with Kelly and we all would have been in a world of shit.'

Apart from the sound of our breathing there was silence. Jin and Kelly studiously avoided looking at us.

'Well, you did at that,' said Isaac as he regained his composure. 'I do apologise, I was disturbed at the... *unlucky* sequence of events. I'm not used to the client also being part of the team in the field. You did well indeed.'

'Damn right I did.' I smiled at him then, and he returned the smile with one of his own. 'We've got the bastard,' I laughed.

'We do indeed.'

Theo was laid out in front of me, quiet, still and as vulnerable as an offering to a jealous god. His breathing shallow but consistent. His pallor healthy. Rosy even.

I'd been waiting for this moment for a long time and had anticipated an insatiable need for revenge, but in practice, now that the moment had arrived, I felt almost nothing. All I wanted to do was secure the mission.

We would have to move him soon. Jin came out of his tussle with Bryant with two broken ribs, a fractured arm, and several nasty bruises. There was probably some internal bleeding as well. We patched him up as well as we could, but he would need professional attention. Both he and Kelly were putting a brave face on it but it was obvious that we needed to act swiftly or risk complications.

While prepping Theo to take him to a more secure facility we searched his belongings. This yielded some intriguing results; Theo's Padd had been paired with a strange pronged device – not unlike a tiara, but decorated with electrical wires and skin-contact patches. It was almost comically reminiscent of something out of an old horror sim, something an evil genius would construct. It was no joke however; the device was real, exquisitely made, and although it sported no identifying logos or writing I was pretty sure it came from a Spectra R&D lab.

Theo's Padd yielded another surprise; the last accessed file was a large database containing in-depth info on dozens of different types of TrickMem. It was an odd thing to be carrying around with him.

'What do you make of this Isaac?' I asked, showing him the data and the device.

'It looks rather menacing, doesn't it?'

'It seems to tie in to some Trickari related Spectra project.'

'It might well be. And as intriguing as it looks, we can't indulge in scratching that itch right now. We have a lot more to do to get your son back in your hands.'

I looked at Theo, then at Jin. Isaac was right. Hanging around here was just inviting trouble.

'OK, let's wrap him up,' I said. 'Time to take this to the next stage.'

23

Isaac put Theo up in one of his safe houses, which had been prepared to keep Theo sedated well before the mission. We agreed that we needed time to try and figure out what Theo had been up to before proceeding to interrogation.

Once again I turned to Ella to help me make sense of things. When I returned to Escher I made sure that she immediately got access to Theo's Padd and his strange device. I told her what was at stake. It didn't take her long to get stuck in.

I wondered what kind of life she could have had if it weren't for her particular circumstances. She was smart enough to have had a meteoric career at any Corp, but I guess that was never her style.

Two days after my return she rang me on my Padd. There was no exchange of meaningless pleasantries;

'Come on over. This is interesting stuff,' she said. I didn't hesitate, and a cab got me to her lab within minutes. She let me in, looking excited, and a little bit on edge.

'You won't believe this freaky shit,' she said, out of breath.

'Try me.'

Ella practically dragged me into her lab. The device and Theo's Padd were hooked up to a computer. Several screens lit up the room. Readouts and graphics rapidly scrolled down the screens, animating them with data, dancing to the rhythm of Ella's research.

'OK get this,' she said, recovering her breath. 'This thing … this device, takes snapshots of brains. And not like a nice little portable EEG device or something like that. No ma'am …'

'What does it do exactly? Do you know?'

'Yes, of course, that's why I called you here.' Ella took

a deep breath, trying to calm down. 'This... It's a hyper aggressive *synaptic copier*.'

'OK... which means?'

'This device was designed to somehow freeze or *halt* a person's synaptic activity – long enough to take an imprint from the subject's brain – which is then added to a database on that Padd.'

I felt my skin crawl, but I wasn't sure why. 'That sounds unhealthy,' I offered speculatively.

'Damn right it is. The process takes long enough to cause permanent synaptic damage. Anybody subjected to that thing is going to suffer serious cognitive impairments. No way is this legal, but I guess that's no surprise.'

'Well, that would explain the lobotomised junkies that had been popping up in Red Colony,' I mused out loud. 'But what does Spectra want with this?'

Ella just shrugged. 'That's your job, Jemm.'

Isaac's safe-house was on the outskirts of Scar district. It was an old robust building, standing alone, surrounded by condemned structures. It was completely cut off from the main facilities. Nobody was going to disturb us there.

I arrived in the area after dark, but the streets – badly lit, badly repaired – were far from empty. There was always nighttime activity in Scar district. Contrary to the scare stories people like to tell each other the neighbourhood was pretty safe at night. Maybe more so than some other, nicer looking neighbourhoods. Scar's inhabitants didn't want attention from law enforcement, so the locals generally policed themselves quite well.

Isaac let me in after I messaged my arrival via my Padd. He opened the door wearing an impeccable suit. He smiled his polite smile, showing off perfect teeth. Ernest and Kelly were playing cards at a table near a grubby wall.

'Work clothes?' I asked, nodding at his attire.

'One must always observe the standards of civilised

society, even when dealing with the likes of Master Theo over there.' He pointed at an old chair at the far wall, in which Theo sat, slumped and dejected like a spoilt princeling. Theo's demeanour was unrecognisable from his regular cockiness. He knew he was in serious trouble, yet couldn't quite let go of his intransigence. I intended to help him with that.

I slowly walked up to him, eyeing him all the way.

'Hello Theo,' I said pleasantly smiling. 'Are you comfortable?' I received no reply, other than a rude gaze gliding up and down my body. 'Do you know who I am?' I asked.

'Don't give a toss, luv.'

'We met a few times, last was at Rosie's bar.' I gave Theo some time to think, watching signs of recognition slowly materialise on his face, like night-frost on a window.

'You're Jemm. You're … You're supposed to be dead.'

'That's right. And thanks for not denying your part in that.'

'Wasn't me that attacked you.' Theo's eyes were darting around the room, as the gravity of his situation was starting to sink in.

'No, that wasn't you. That was Bryant, and some other goons.' I stepped in close enough to smell his breath. Theo started rubbing the shark-shaped birthmark on his neck. Tiny pearls of sweat popped into being on his face. 'All *you* did was sell me out to Spectra in the first place. Isn't that right?'

'I didn't know they would–'

'Would what? Take my son away from me? Try and murder me and my friend?

'What do you want from me? Are you going to kill me?' A whining quality had entered his voice. It was an awful sound.

'How's your neck?'

'My neck?'

'Yes, your neck. The operation seemed to go well enough but you know, we had to rush it a bit.'

Theo touched his shark again, then groped around his throat and neck until he felt the Stim-Jack we implanted.

'What … what the fuck have you done?'

'Hold him,' I said, not taking my eyes off Theo. Ernest and Kelly dropped their cards on the table and got up.

'Stop it, what are you doing?' he whimpered. Kelly suddenly lunged, grabbed an arm, tossed and pushed, and had him on the floor with his arm pushed up high behind his back.

'Don't move,' she said matter-of-factly.

Ernest proceeded to hold Theo's head in a vice-like grip.

'Definitely don't move,' I reiterated.

I knelt down in front of Theo so he could see what I was doing, and opened the box of TrickMem samples he had with him at the market in Red Colony. This prompted frantic struggles and wordless shrieking, soon quelled by Kelly, who put her knee on the small of his back. Theo went very still. His eyes grew wide, darting around, looking for an escape or help or *something*.

I slowly dragged my finger over the many-coloured ampules, reading out the labels; 'Red Beach, Night Flower, Starshine, Moon Break … ' There were dozens more. 'That's quite a collection you have here Theo.'

'You don't wanna do this. I'm working for Spectra do you understand? If they find out what you're doing …'

'If they *find out*? Don't worry, I'm going to tell them exactly what I've been doing. That's not really the issue here. I've got something they really want, and it isn't you I'm afraid.'

'What do you mean?'

'Never mind that, *luv*. You have other things to consider.' I made a choice from the stash of drug samples and showed it to Theo. '"Trickari Sunset" … I like the ring of that.' Theo vainly tried to break free, but it was no use. I pushed the ampule into the jack at the back of the neck. It automatically deployed its content straight into his brain. A data storm of alien memories, senses and emotions invaded his neo-cortex, temporarily re-writing his human operating system with alien malware.

Theo's eyes instantly stopped their frantic movement, focusing instead on some interior vista, only known to himself and the Trickari being from whom the sensations originated. He stopped struggling, stood up slowly, walked to the chair he had occupied before, and slowly sat down. He would stay in this state for at least an hour.

'Make sure you tie him up before it fades away,' I said to nobody in particular.

'OK. What next?' asked Ernest. Unfazed as always.

'Depends on him really. By tomorrow there are two options: he will either try and fight the addiction, and beg us not to give him anymore, or he will break, and beg us for another dose. Either way he'll tell us all we need to know.'

'I'm not sure I approve of your approach Jemm,' said Isaac. 'But I must admit there is a pleasing sense of symmetry here.'

'Fuck him. I'm giving him a lot more choice than he gave his victims in Red Colony.'

Both Isaac and Ernest gave me a worried look. As if I would hold back now, when I was so close to succeeding with this part of the plan.

They didn't know there was much worse to come.

That same evening I received a message from Ella, telling me to come and talk to her without delay. I rushed over, hoping for a breakthrough with her research.

It was late by the time I arrived. The night lights cast a sickly orange glow on her building, throwing deep red shadows onto the walls, like blood stained fingers.

Ella let me in, wearing a serious, almost frightened expression on her face.

'What's the story?' I asked, forced cheerfulness awkwardly spilling out.

'Just come with me, I'll show you.'

I followed without further questions.

Ella's lab was getting messy. Or rather, getting even messier than normal. She never was the tidiest person, but there was a certain consistency to her disorganisation. That seemed to be less true every day; there were papers everywhere, data prints, real-books, food remnants, and a wide spectrum of scientific instruments, wiring, and computers.

Similarly, Ella herself was looking chaotic, dishevelled. She had obviously worn the same clothes for a long time, her nails were ragged and long. There was even a whiff of body odour around the place, which was unheard of for a Martian dwelling. Something was clearly distracting her, but when I tried to think of what it could be the list of factors was so long I ended up laughing at myself for not giving her more slack. It was amazing just *how well* she was doing.

My subconscious tried to steer that same scrutiny onto my own mental wellbeing, but I angrily rejected that line of thinking; I didn't have time for self-analysis.

'This place is disgusting. Even more so than usual,' I half-joked. 'Good thing you don't have a boyfriend.'

'Don't be stupid. Come over here.' Ella showed me the comparative footage of cellular growth and transformation we had studied before. 'Recognise this?' I nodded. 'Well, that was then. This is now…' The footage looked nearly identical.

'Am I looking at what I think I'm looking at?'

'Almost. Yes. Maybe.' I shot her a sharp look. 'I have come up with a treatment yes, but this is it applied to a tissue sample taken several months ago. It might not work with his current cellular make-up.'

'Still…'

'Don't get too excited. I have too many questions still to answer, and this was my last damn tissue sample. From here on all I can do is use computer models and extrapolations. But… yeah, it's pretty damn promising.'

'But, just so we're clear… you made a potential cure?'

'I did.'

Can it be true? The thought flashed through me like a fever. 'So what's the glumness?' I asked, with a sense of trepidation.

Ella was lost for words for a moment. She got up, paced for a small eternity, sat down again. 'I'm not glum.'

'What is it Ella?'

'I'm *scared* goddammit!' she shouted, and kicked an empty can. It bounced off the wall with a wet clang. 'Jesus Christ do you have any idea what we're dealing with?'

'What *is* it,' I repeated softly.

'I checked out Theo's Padd. There's a lot more data on there than I thought.' She pointed at one of her many screens. 'There, that's my attempt to visualise parts of the Neo-Virus, to map out its components. Remember that Clint thinks it's a set of computational instructions?'

'I remember, yeah.'

'Well, I agree. And so does Spectra, it seems. They've been chasing the same rabbit, mining those junkie brain scans for data. Trying to find Trickari instructions. They've collected a lot of data.'

'Do you think they're close to cracking it?'

'No … Maybe. But definitely if they get hold of my research. Imagine what would happen if Spectra unlock the key to Trickari science. Trick-tech on demand, in the hands of one of the biggest and most ruthless Corps in the world.'

'We won't let that happen. We–'

'Just… Just listen OK?' I held up my hands, letting her continue. 'This whole thing is too big. It's too much power to give to anybody.' She looked at me as if daring me to disagree with her. 'It could be even worse. What if this stuff is booby-trapped? Like Trick-Red? What if, by going down this route, we trigger the final Trickari trap?' I didn't have an answer for her, but she continued anyway. 'What if all we're doing is following the breadcrumbs left by a perverse alien species, meekly doing exactly what they want. Like a bunch of Turkeys clucking all the way to the butcher's block.'

A deep silence followed her words. She was right of course, but the awful truth was that I didn't care. I didn't care about the dangers or the consequences. I needed her to lure Spectra in my trap, to get Clint back, and to cure him from this virus. I wasn't going to give up on that, and I needed her on board, working with me.

'We can't stop now, you know that,' I said, my voice steady, despite my fears. 'What if it's the other way around?'

'What do you mean?' she asked, suspiciously.

'What if our only way to stop Spectra from getting what they want is for us to get there first?' Ella looked dubious, but she let me continue. 'What if you're right about the Trickari plan – whatever it is – but the only way to stop it is to continue your research?'

Ella was torn. It was an impossible choice and we shouldn't be the ones to make it. She took a breath, calming herself, before continuing. 'I told you I want out. Out of all this *shit*. I want to walk again,' she said, softly.

'Help me get Clint back, and help me get him cured. After that we hand everything we have over to the authorities. Let them deal with it. You'll be free. You'll have another chance at life.'

'Promise me,' she said. 'Promise me or I walk away now.'

'I promise. All I want is my boy. That is all I ever wanted.'

Ella looked uncertain for a moment. There was an odd sound I couldn't place, until I realised she had burst into tears. I came over and hugged her hard, but I couldn't stop myself from wondering if I was still capable of crying.

Over the weeks I had kept working in private on decorating my personal breather. When I finally finished I was taken aback by the intensity of what I had crafted: the final layer of detailing and polish revealed an intensely complicated latticework of illustrated connections made up of organic and mechanical components. Physical metallic gears and cogs linked to painted bones and cartilage, powered by electrical wiring and musculature. The mask presented the facade of a bio-mechanoid demon, looking both human and monstrous at the same time.

I had worn it once, on the streets of Scar-district, and although nobody said anything out loud I received many disturbed glances and furtive second looks. It was a successful design in an artistic sense, but not the most anonymous.

I hadn't shown it to any of my friends, even though I felt it suited me and I carried it with me everywhere. I had it with me when I returned to Isaac's safe-house the next day, ready to break Theo.

Isaac let me in, once again, still dressed impeccably but incongruously in need of a shave.

'All set?' he asked, seeing the resolve in my eyes plain and clear.

'All set.' I looked around the flat until I spotted Theo. He had regained a little bit of his composure, but it was paper thin. I wondered which way he would bend. 'How's our guest?'

'Nicely stewed, I gather. Come and see for yourself.'

'Oh, I'm dying to. Believe me.'

I approached Theo slowly, so he could see me and have time to wonder about what I would do to him. Just before I reached him I took out my breather and put it over my mouth. The impact was immediate – not just on Theo but on everybody in the room, just as I intended.

'Jesus… Jemm…' said Kelly. 'What are you doing?' Ernest and Isaac were more discreet, but both looked uncomfortable. Their reaction had as much impact on Theo as the mask itself. He started to fidget with his fingers, rubbing his tattoos, looking around the room, desperate for somebody to intervene.

'What do you want? What is that thing?'

I walked up too close to him, well into his personal space, until my breather nearly touched his face.

'No, Theo, what do *you* want?' My voice sounded odd

through the mask, like it didn't belong to me. 'Do you want another hit? Or do you want me to get that Jack removed? What's it going to be?'

Theo's face slowly turned red. 'Don't threaten me you slag. Do you have any idea what Spectra will let me do to you when they get their hands on you?'

I had turned on the surveillance preset on my ocular augment. It showed up Theo's bravado as a sham; his heart-rate was up, as was adrenaline, body temperature and respiration. I could literally smell his fear. 'Oh yeah luv, I'm going to–'

My left handed slap struck him across the face *hard,* with augmented strength. He stumbled, trying to step backwards, but I grabbed him by his throat. I hit him again, a backhanded slap. A bit of blood trickled out of his ear, down his neck, crossing out his stupid tattoos.

'What's it going to be,' I repeated.

'Jemm…' Kelly tried again. I ignored her.

Theo's hand returned to manic fidgeting. Sweat dripped down his face, his cheek burned a bright red. He touched the back of his neck. 'I don't want you to put this alien shit in my head. I'll tell you what I know, just get this thing out of me.'

'Good. This won't take long. Sit down.' I pointed at a chair. He complied without comment. 'First, you will answer some questions. Don't lie. I can tell when you do. If you do lie, I'll give you a few more shots from your own stash, until you're as hooked as the poor souls you take advantage of for a living. And then, I'll just withhold Mem until you dance just the way I like it. It takes longer that way, but I'll still get what I want.' I pushed my face right up to his. 'Do you understand?'

'Yes lu–' He caught himself just in time. 'Yes, I understand.'

'Good. Let's start.' I showed him his own Padd, and the synaptic scanner. 'What is it that you are doing with this stuff?'

'Spectra are paying me to get synaptic scans, clean ones, of TJs who have used different types of Mem. I'm supposed to get scans that cover every type of Mem there's ever been.'

'Why?'

'Don't know luv,' he stammered, not even realising what he called me again. 'All I know is that the software they put on my Padd filters out traces of TrickMem that it already has data on. I'm supposed to make sure it ends up with data on all the different types of Mem, and how it affected people's brains. Right?'

'So, Spectra is building a historical database of TrickMem data, based on the synaptic scans you provide?'

'Yeah, not just me, they got people that do this on Earth too. It's just that here on Mars, there are a lot of people who have dabbled with the really old stuff, the earliest Mem, right? There's even some who still have some old stash. They hung on to it after they moved on to newer stuff.'

'OK, that fits with what I know, that's good. Keep telling me the truth and you'll get out of this in one piece.' Relief washed over Theo. He was eager to talk now.

'What do you know about my son,' I asked, tentatively.

'Not much. He's errr... He's slowly changing, but healthy, right?'

They don't know we slowed down the transformation process. I thought. 'What else?'

'Your son, he's a big deal it seems. Everybody at Spectra is pretty excited. Not only for the new Mem...' I stiffened and Theo noticed. 'Sorry... I didn't mean to... Well, anyway, he's always protected, innit? Gibson's spending a lot of time with him. He's running this operation you see?'

'You don't say?'

'Yeah. He was pissed off though when them drives turned out to be useless.'

Theo was starting to sweat, his movements jerky. His faltering grammar betrayed the nerves hiding behind his street persona. I was getting to him.

'Why hasn't he come after me or Ella?'

'We thought you was dead, not sure how you survived from what I heard they done to you… And Ella… what use is she to them?

They don't realise we have the original data. 'How do you report to Gibson?'

'Encrypted data link. That Padd is pretty powerful. And they got their own satellites innit?'

'When is your next report due?'

Theo looked uncomfortable, shifting around in his seat. 'Today. It's today.'

'I see. And you were hoping to keep that quiet? Why bother? Bryant already knows you were taken.'

'I was gonna tell you, I swear. Just didn't get round to it yet, right?'

'Tell me what?' I whispered, my demon mask next to his grimacing face.

'I … If I don't call in at the right time the Padd locks down and starts sending out a homing signal.' Theo looked close to tears, touching his throat, fidgeting his fingers. 'I'm sorry, I should have said earlier.'

'I'll let you make up for it, don't worry,' I said. 'All you have to do is show me how to reach Gibson on this.'

'Contact Gibson?'

'Is that a problem?' I opened the TrickMem sample case, inspecting the various ampules inside.

All colour left Theo's face; his eyes widened.

'No… not a problem. Not a problem at all.'

I sent Gibson a recorded message announcing my continued existence and explaining how I was still in possession of the original Spectra data drives. I included a data dump containing *just* enough genuine files for him to know that it was the real deal.

My demands amounted to a simple exchange: the drives for my son. If he did not agree to this, or if he dared to hurt my son, I would hand them over to the authorities. There was more than enough incriminating material there to hammer Spectra for years, the legal jeopardy and cost likely to push them down to the level of smaller Corps.

Gibson himself had to make the exchange here on Mars, as an insurance policy against foul play. The drives were protected by an aggressive worm virus, which needed to be fed a rotating password or they would be turned to the digital equivalence of smoking slag.

It was a compelling pitch, and it took Gibson less than a day to agree. He would come to Mars five days later, awaiting further instructions. Clint would be by his side, unharmed, and ready to be returned to his mother.

That, at least, was the plan. Reality was another matter entirely.

24

My ship models arrived the next day; The *Pequod* and the *Galactica*, both impeccably wrapped in Aramici's branded wrapping paper. A little note accompanied the ships:

> *May galactic winds steer you into gentle waters.*

I was surprised by the poetic quality of Aramici's note. It put me into a pensive state of mind, contemplating the journeys both of these ships had embarked upon. The *Pequod* was an instrument, in the service of an obsessive monomaniac; the *Galactica* was meant to take a lost strand of humanity home. Both ships were meant to bring salvation, of sorts, against impossible odds. Maybe that was what attracted me to them in the first place.

The wrapping paper smelled pleasantly of wax and oil, the creases were folded meticulously to create a neat, perfect parcel. Even the tape was of the best quality. I could see myself doing more business with Aramici.

For a while I lay back in bed, simply enjoying the models now in my possession, but I grew restless – I still wasn't used to lying in bed alone. A feeling made worse by still living in Rosie's old house, surrounded by all the little things a person accrues over time, reminding me of who I lost.

There was no need for me to stay there – the Ceres mission had given me the funds to buy half the housing stock in Escher – but for some reason I found it impossible to leave. I often found myself walking through the rooms, touching random objects, smelling Rosie's scent, lingering like a ghost with unfinished business.

I wondered what Clint would look like now. How much was there left of his mind … his own thoughts … It was hard not to feed the despair that was simmering just beneath the surface of my life. *His mind must be destroyed by now. Spectra will never let him go. He won't even know who I am anymore…* It was the last thought that hurt the most. I decided to go for a walk to clear my mind.

I donned my breather, knowing fully well that the extreme decorations would make it harder for me to stay anonymous, but I needed these little acts of rebellion to maintain a sense of control over my life, even if that control was no more than a fanciful illusion. It hit me then that I didn't even need the breather to survive on Mars, but I was desperate to feel some kind of connection to my former self; a tether that kept me from drifting away from my own sense of humanity.

Outside on the streets my spirit lifted. Maybe it was the warm light falling through the great dome, or maybe it was the sense of industry and purpose Martians always seemed to exude. I did notice it was even busier than normal; lots of people on scaffolding, rooftops, and elevated platforms, tinkering with lighting rigs.

Curious as to what it was all about I stopped a young man on the street. He was carrying a bundle of cables and various multi-coloured lights thrown over his shoulder.

'Hey, what's all that for?' I asked.

'Light show!' he said loudly, although there was no need to shout.

'What's the occasion?'

'New Year!'

'What do you mean?' I asked, confused.

'Martian New year!' he shouted. 'Gotta get ready for it!'

'When is it happening?'

'Ten days?'

'Really?'

'Really!'

I wondered why he kept shouting even though we were right next to each other, before I remembered that there were a lot of Martians with ruptured eardrums or otherwise damaged hearing. A side effect of the Martian way of life, constantly dealing with differing pressure levels between home and work and the surface. Ears often got inflamed or infected.

But – as with most of the challenges in their lives – people took these things in their stride and just got on with their lives as best they could.

It was the Martian way.

Isaac kept tabs on Gibson with impressive diligence and efficiency. He received daily reports from his associates on Earth, and knew exactly when Gibson would arrive on Mars. The reports indicated that Gibson was travelling with a skeleton crew, and one single guest. The latter was likely Clint, which if true meant that it was still possible to disguise his transformation to the public. Technically it wasn't illegal to travel with an established Neo, but there hadn't been a new transformation in a long time which would make it impossible for Clint to travel undisguised and clandestine.

I spent the days leading up to the arrival in a haze of preparation and anticipation. I went over the plan time after time, checking every detail, making sure there was a fall-back position or backup plan at every possible junction along the way. This was my one and only chance to pull off the unimaginable. I had to get every facet of my plan right. Even if I did, I still faced a monumental task, against sobering odds.

Gibson finally arrived on Thursday morning, 08:00 hours Martian time. We had agreed that he would contact me within two hours of arriving, after passing all the customs and safety checks. My Padd chimed exactly ninety minutes later. I composed myself as well as I could before answering. It was a vid-feed, but I did not reciprocate. There was nothing to be gained by sharing my likeness with the man who would probably try to kill me the first chance he got.

Gibson's face appeared on the small Padd screen, well groomed, relaxed, and just as composed as the last time I saw him. I'm not sure what else I was expecting, but I was taken aback at how little he had changed. Perhaps because in my life, nothing had remained the same.

'Good morning Miss Delaney, I trust you are well?'

'Hello Jeremy, I'm fine thank you. Currently I'm known as Jane Dyne, but as we *are* old acquaintances you may stick with Miss Delaney.'

'Ah yes. I must admit we were surprised you survived the… *unfortunately* harsh measures we had to undertake to retrieve our property.'

'I bet you were surprised when those drives turned round and bit you in the arse, weren't you?' My attempt to rattle him had little effect.

'Surprised? Yes. But we managed to get over it, especially as your son has given us so much of value since then.'

His words hit me with the force of a perfect body blow. 'He's with you, as we agreed?' I asked, steadying myself. 'I need to see him or we don't deal.'

The Padd's vid-stream lurched as Gibson stood up and walked a short distance, eventually pointing it at the shape of a hooded man.

'Clint?' said Gibson. 'Can you look at my Padd for a moment?'

It was as if time itself was reluctant to proceed, forcing the next few seconds to slow down to a crawl, gradually revealing the face underneath the hood. It was Clint, yet in some way it wasn't. His actual facial features had barely changed, but there was an expression there that I had never seen before and didn't belong there. A certain *distance* maybe, a feeling that he was somewhere else entirely, seeing a different world from ours.

'Mum?' he croaked, his voice familiar and alien at the same time. 'I… wondered where you'd been. I would like to see you I think. I have some new ideas to discuss with you.'

Only when I felt a wetness on the back of my hands did I realise I was clutching my face, tears rolling down. 'Yes sweetheart, I want to see you too,' I managed to reply. 'It shouldn't be long now.'

The vid-feed swung back to Gibson.

'Indeed. If we don't lose our heads this could work out nicely for both of us.'

'Listen carefully Gibson. I'm willing to do a straight swap with you. The data drives for my son. But if you try anything that might jeopardise him or me, in any way, I *will* come for you personally. Do you understand?'

'My dear Miss Delaney. So far, I have been willing to indulge you, because I would like to keep my backyard clean, as it were, and I think we can do business. You understand the Corp way better than most, after all.' Gibson's face briefly took on a menacing sneer, but he managed to get it under control before continuing. 'But be clear on this. If this equation becomes unbalanced, if you become too much of a burden on our resources, we will squash you like the diseased little fly that you are. After that we will send in a cleanup crew, torture your friends and associates, and if anybody does divulge any of *our* private data to other parties, we will simply deny it all and bribe our way out of it. Tread carefully please.'

I expected these kinds of threats, so I wasn't completely intimidated. Still, it was hard not to feel small against the might of a Corp the size of Spectra Vision. But there was only one way out of this, and it was straight through the middle; through the fire.

'Don't kid yourself, Gibson. You won't just be dealing with a few Mars cops and politicians. If you go after me, the drives will also be shared with your biggest rival Corp. And if that happens it will be on you, nobody else. A lost chance to regain your honour, after losing the drives in the first place. Imagine your superiors finding out about that. Can you picture it? I can.'

The vid-feed wobbled momentarily, and I imagined Gibson struggling not to smash the device and order me killed right then, but eventually his face appeared again.

'Send me the details of our meeting and we will get this over with,' he said. 'I would like to be done with this little charade as soon as possible.'

'Just remember to follow my lead Gibson, or this won't end well.'

It seemed we both agreed on that, with good reason.

Ella looked ashen. Her appearance had become even more unkempt and haggard. Her lab wasn't looking great either; ceiling lights had started to fail, the furniture was dirty … it was getting out of hand. Yet despite the superficial disarray, her mind was sharper than it had been in ages. Her current state reminded me a bit of what most Trick-Junkies went through – the more they let the small stuff go, the more they were able to focus when doing Mem.

'Are you sure it's him?' she asked.

'Of course I am. He's my son.'

'OK, OK, of course. Well, everything is in place.'

'The drives?'

'Drives are ready. I left the data structure intact. Most directories, most areas of research are there, but I scrubbed any useful Trickari data and replaced it with obscure biological research mixed with data that's out there in public domain. I left enough original data in there to make it all appear authentic and juicy. To some degree it is, but not to a dangerous degree.'

'OK, and you made copies?'

'Of course I made fucking copies. Jesus.'

'Where are they?'

'Best you don't know. They might torture you.' She looked up at me, a guilty gleam in her eyes. 'Sorry to be blunt, but we need to be smart about this.'

'Fine, as long as they're safe.'

I winced, but not because of the torture prospect; I was still suffering the occasional bout of augment pain, and that day was particularly bad. It was distracting but I wasn't going to let it push me off course. Tomorrow was the day I would get my son back.

'Are you packed then?' I asked, knowing that she was. 'Ernest will be here any moment to take you to Red Colony. I bought a great place there. It's stacked with geeky equipment and instruments. A total mess, you'll love it.'

'Good, I need to get to work prepping Clint's treatment,' she said, not even realising I was teasing her.

I nodded, not sure what to say. It struck me that Ella was an enigma. She had everything in her life going against her, yet the harder things got the more she fought back. To me she personified human grit and inventiveness, something that had been lacking in large parts of the population on Earth. A malaise had set in ever since the horrors of Icarus had laid waste to what should have been humanity's new golden era. So many people had given up, one way or another, but people like Ella kept us all going.

I was on the cusp of telling her these things but imagined her disdain, sure to follow, so I just smiled, tried to hug her, and quickly stepped away as she countered with a sharp jab.

'Don't fuck up,' she said.

'No more than usual,' I replied laughing. Then, more seriously, 'I can't. This is the real deal, this is my son.'

'See you in Red,' she said, the beginnings of a tear in the corner of her eye, but quickly wiped away. 'Now fuck off, I need to get ready.'

I arrived at the God Axe well before dawn. I thought I was done with this place, but I had one final use for it.

It was still dark but for a purple glow teasing the horizon. My heart skipped a beat, anticipating the splendour that was to come with the sunrise. It was an appropriate setting for what I was there to do. A new dawn was close.

I didn't perform my breathing ritual. I was beyond that now. The ritual had sustained me to reach this exact point in my life, and if I wasn't ready and motivated now I would never be.

I wore my breather with pride, and when I caught a glimpse of myself in the mirrored surface of the skimmer I smiled in appreciation. It was going to happen, today. *Dad would have been proud.*

I picked up a rock with my augmented arm. It was like any other rock on Mars. Red, dry, but this one showed some small patches of green as well. Lichen and moss, slowly infiltrating the arid wasteland, turning it into something else. The first real change on the planet for billions of years since Mars had lost its magnetic field.

I looked out over the landscape and threw the rock with all my might. A shuddering groan forced itself out of my mouth as my arm flexed and exploded in a short sharp move, propelling the rock through the air for a surprisingly long time. It arced beautifully, reaching further than I imagined possible. When it finally hit the ground deep below it was too small to see if not for the plume of dust thrown up by impact.

As the dust rose in the air, higher and higher, I saw movement a few miles ahead of the plume. A reflective glimmer, a small dust trail … I zoomed in with my augmented eye, and saw a rugged little vehicle working its way across the hostile landscape like an angry, exotic beetle, slowly approaching my position. Gibson. It looked like he was about forty-five minutes away.

I watched that plume slowly grow bigger, silhouetted against the Martian skyline, and I felt something stir inside of me. A sense of anticipation so strong that it threatened to overwhelm all my other emotions. I used to feel similarly when I was a little girl – before my father lost his mind – waiting for him to come home after spending days, sometimes weeks, away from us on some Corp assignment. I wondered if Clint was still capable of feeling that kind of excitement: a need for contact, warmth, finally being fulfilled after a long absence. I cursed Gibson for denying us this feeling for so long.

Finally, the little Mars buggy made it to the top of the ridge. It was much bigger than it had initially appeared when creeping its way up. There was a small pause after the engine turned off and the dust cleared, when nothing seemed to happen. Then, two side doors hinged upwards, opening like the wings of a fat insect basking in the sun. I caught myself holding my breath as somebody emerged from the car, impossibly slow. He was wearing a breather and a white environment suit, and I could tell he was padded out with body armour. It was Gibson, not Clint.

Gibson leaned inside and gave a few short commands in Corp-Speak, but I was too far away to hear what he said. A figure inside nodded, staying within the car. I turned on my surveillance vision, hoping it would give me an edge.

Gibson looked at me as if seeing me for the first time. He dusted himself off theatrically, and walked up to me. We were exactly the same height.

'Half my colleagues voted to kill you, regardless of the consequences. *Remove the person, remove the problem*, as a great man once said.'

'And the other half?'

'Kidnap and torture, maybe some aggressive reconditioning. Make you reveal any contingency plans you may have concocted.'

'I see,' I said, and adjusted my breather. He didn't flinch at the mask's disturbing imagery.

'And what did you decide?'

'I decided to go ahead with the swap. It's the only sensible path forward. If you betray our agreement you will die, that's a given, and torturing you is useless if you have instructed others to hand our data over to third parties.'

'I have. I'm not stupid.'

'That is what I expected. So, here we are.'

'Show me my son,' I rasped; the need to touch Clint clawed at my sanity.

Gibson barked at the figure in the car. There was movement; Lawrence stepped out, gently leading a hooded figure out of the vehicle. At first he appeared too tall to be my son, and I nearly killed Gibson right there and then, but as Lawrence brought the hooded figure closer I realised that the hood itself distorted the real height of the wearer.

'Show her,' said Gibson. 'She has waited long enough.'

Lawrence looked like he wanted to tell me something but thought the better of it. He pulled down the hood to reveal a cacophony of colour. Impossibly beautiful strands of alien hair, chiming softly, bright as crystal. A face emerged from the hood like a diver rising from the depths, a look of curiosity and wonder on his face.

'Mother?' asked Clint, a strange musical quality to his inflection, audible even through the breather.

I couldn't speak, so I nodded.

There were sharp angles to him now. His nails had turned into crystal claws, his cheekbones jutted out, but he was still able to smile with the love and warmth that he had always shown me.

'Very touching,' sneered Gibson. 'Now show me the drives. I need to verify them.'

This is it. I thought. If Ella had made even the smallest mistake Gibson would know they were rigged. Gibson connected the drives to his Padd, and run some kind of corporate sniffer program to see if the data was authentic. It took time. I thought I could see the shadows across the landscape grow shorter as the check took place. Finally, a soft chime indicated that the scan was complete.

Gibson looked me up and down. I gave him a smile.

'Very good,' he said. 'I thank you for holding up your part of the bargain.'

The next sequence of events happened quickly, like clockwork unwinding with terrible mechanical inevitability.

Gibson, nodded at Lawrence, 'Kill her,' he said, his voice flat, lacking any emotion.

Lawrence reached into his coat. His hand emerged holding a gun.

I had already anticipated such a move, and was ready for it, drawing my own gun – the little flechette shooter – set to dispersed targeting. I aimed it at Gibson's head.

'Don't you fucking dare you piece of garbage.'

Lawrence continued to raise his hand, appearing to my augmented senses to move as slow as if he was made of clay.

Clint moved towards Lawrence with such speed that nobody had time to react and slashed with his crystal-clawed hand. Four pink stripes materialised across Lawrence's throat, turned red, then spurted dark blood all over him and Gibson's white suit.

I didn't dare squeeze the trigger while the flechette gun was still set to wide dispersal with Clint standing so close to Gibson.

'Clint! Into my skimmer, now!' I shouted. He hesitated, not clear on what to do, so I pointed to my skimmer further down the path. 'Go! In there!'

Gibson took the opportunity to scramble for cover behind his vehicle. Finally Clint moved. He was impossibly fast – his legs no longer working the way human legs worked. His joints seemed all angular and wrong as he sped away. For a moment I was too distracted to notice Lawrence slowly crawling towards his gun. I was about to stop him when he shuddered once … twice … and stopped moving. I assumed he was dead.

A sudden sound made me turn and shoot at the bug-like vehicle. Holes rapidly opening up all over its side and its engine block.

'You don't want to do this Jemm,' shouted Gibson from behind his cover. 'You'll condemn him to a life on the run while he slowly loses his mind. You can't protect him!'

I hastily shuffled Clint into my skimmer, keeping an eye on Gibson. My enhanced vision picked him out with ease, huddling behind his car. I shot again, and one of the flechette darts must have found the target as I heard a sharp intake of breath and a grunt.

'You've got the drives, let it be!' I shouted.

There was no reply as I frantically strapped Clint in, trying not to flinch as I touched his skin, now no longer soft, but leathery and cool. I shot Gibson's car again, hoping to disable it, and saw a satisfying plume of smoke rise from the engine.

We sped away, fast and silent, the skimmer rapidly gaining speed – a barracuda scything through water.

25

Isaac met me later that evening by a dome exit at the outskirts of Escher. The sun had sunk beneath the ridges surrounding the settlement, a pinkish indirect light its final attempt to warm the surface. Soon it would get very cold.

I parked the skimmer a few metres away and quickly briefed him on the events of earlier that day. Adrenaline still flooded my systems, making me stumble over my words.

'Have you made all the preparations?' I asked, my head spinning with too many possibilities and eventualities. 'I wonder if he's dead. That bastard. Lawrence is gone, his throat … I need to get out of here.' I all but shouted the last sentence. 'I'll ditch the skimmer,' I added, uselessly.

'Jemm, you must calm down, take a moment. You have done the impossible, somehow, but you aren't there yet. This is the time to compose yourself and make sure you don't make rash mistakes.' He was right of course.

'OK. We prepared for this, we can do it.' I took a deep breath. 'How's the transport?'

'It's exactly what you need right now: multi-terrain capability, sleeping accommodation, perfectly insulated and secure.'

'Fuel?'

'Electrical with solar recharge capability. It's perfect for your situation.'

'Expenses?'

'The expense account you provided is more than adequate. As much as Ceres was a tragedy, at least it has taken care of that.'

I wasn't ready to discuss Ceres yet, having locked it away in a particularly dark corner of my mind. But Isaac was right, the money was important right now.

'I should go, Clint is alone,' I said, pointing at the

skimmer behind me, but strangely unwilling to go just yet.

After enduring a few seconds of my dithering Isaac tutted, and – against all I had come to expect from him – suddenly hugged me, long, hard, and earnest. 'Go now, we can rendezvous when things have settled down. Contact me by Padd when you need me.'

'When, not if?'

'Either. Now go please, before I'm tempted into further emotional displays.'

'Thanks Isaac,' I said lamely. He nodded once, and left without further ado.

I stood alone for a moment before returning to Clint in the skimmer. We were back together again.

We drove throughout the night, our headlights chasing ragged shadows.

Clint barely spoke. He was clearly pleased to be with me, but struggled to articulate himself beyond expressing his most basic needs; hunger … cold … thirst. Had his transformation pushed him beyond the ability to communicate? There was no sense of warmth, no sense of *familiarity*. But then his slumped posture made clear that he was utterly exhausted, and I felt guilty for my thoughts.

I put my arm around him. He gently laid his head on my lap like he used to do when he was young. I switched the transport to auto-pilot, adjusted the interior lights, and within a few minutes he fell asleep, his crystal-clawed hand holding mine. It was a moment of such pure joy, mixed with bittersweet memories, that I stayed seated that way for the next two hours, enjoying the sensation of being near my son again, while marvelling at his radically changed appearance.

I tried stroking his hair, but the sensation was simply too strange. I stroked his face instead, until I became too tired to drive. I parked the transport under a few overhanging rocks, jutting out of the side of a ridge and went to sleep.

A falling sensation grabbed hold of me just as I drifted away from the conscious world. Falling … falling … touching water, and drifting down to dark depths, into a world of ancient ghosts. My old recurring dream had come back to me after many weeks of absence, and with it came sensations – a taste of colour, voices tugging at my mind, and something new; a feeling of immense responsibility, although I did not understand who or what for. And then the voices came again:

... come down here to us we are here come please we want you to come you have to find us you are coming to find us we are here please come to us...

In the dream-water Clint drifted deep beneath me, beckoning me to follow. This time he was smiling, and this time there was no monstrous creature. I followed him down, kicking my legs hard to catch up, and when I did we both smiled.

I woke up, completely disoriented at first. I couldn't figure out where I was or what I was doing. It was still dark outside. The lights inside the Transport were still set to sleep mode. I was alone.

Icy panic stabbed me, deep, hard.

He's been taken, again.

I jumped out of the bunk bed, searching for any sign to explain what had happened, when the Transport's back door opened and Clint climbed on-board.

'That's odd. I don't feel the cold anymore,' he said. 'In fact, I quite like it.'

He sounded so much more like himself that I finally accepted that we were together again, despite everything. A sudden urge to know all that had happened to him since that night overwhelmed me. I fired question after question at him:

'How did they treat you? Have they hurt you? How do you feel? The infection...' I couldn't contain the many questions, having been denied answers for so long. 'Sorry, just… tell me how you are… how you've been.'

Clint tilted his head in a strange bird-like move, as if listening to a voice only he could hear, then sat down and began to talk.

'It was… very confusing at first. They drugged me, and kept me drugged for long periods of time. It's hard to remember the early days.' I nodded encouragement. 'They… they said you were gone, and that they would take care of me from then on.' Clint's speech was strangely formal at first, but slowly regained the quality and nuances of a teenage boy. 'I suspected they had killed you, but there was no way to be sure. They never told me outright, but I'm not stupid.'

'I know you're not, sweetheart.' I grabbed his hand, squeezing it gently. 'What did they want with you? I mean, what did they do with you all that time?' I asked, fearful of the answers, but given a smile in return.

'Tests. Hundreds of them. Every day. I was hooked up to all kinds of computers and Padds, and medical devices. I think they kept feeding me some kind of feel-good drug because I mostly accepted it all. I mean, what else was I supposed to do?' He tilted his head again, listening. 'Nights were bad… Mum, I thought you were dead. And my brain… my *mind* was slipping away from me.' Clint raised his crystal clawed hands, touched his hair. 'My body… Look at me. I don't know what I am anymore.'

'Clint, listen to me. I have a plan. We are working on a cure …'

'I tried to cry, mum. Every night at first, but this body… I don't even think I have tear-ducts anymore.'

'You've changed so much Clint. I'm so sorry…' I said.

'At first I felt like I was splintering. My mind I mean. It was getting harder and harder to finish my thoughts, to be *coherent*. But slowly the feeling settled into something different. It's like another mind has *moved in*. Like we're sharing the same head, but we have our own rooms, if that makes sense. Sometimes it's me in control, sometimes it's like I'm locked out.'

I nodded slightly, but I was puzzled. 'That sounds different from other Neo cases.'

'I think so. The people that took care of me, who tested me... I could tell that they thought I should have lost my mind by now. I shouldn't be able to have conversations like this. They got very excited about it. Somehow, my case is different.'

'I know why,' I whispered. 'Ella augmented you. We did it to slow progression of the virus. To slow down your transformation to give me time to get you back. It's what made all this possible.'

Clint looked confused as he said, 'That can't be why. Gibson told his doctors to look for augments. They removed them all in the first month. Something else is going on.'

We both fell silent, trying to process the strange situation we found ourselves in, to understand the events that had shaped our lives in such extreme ways.

Outside the Transport's windows the night-sky was as dark as sin, barely punctuated by lonely pinpricks of light – the stars couldn't help us either. Clint followed my gaze, curious as to what I was looking at. Then, a flash! Followed by an eruption of concentric circles made of bright sparkling shapes. Another flash, this time followed by a series of staggered explosions. We were looking at fireworks, erupting high over Escher. Probably set off by enthusiasts who couldn't wait for the Martian New Year.

The exploding lights were reflected by the facets in Clint's extraordinary hair, creating a second, altogether more curious light show. At that moment he was the most beautiful creature in the universe.

'Mum... I killed that man.'

'You had no choice. He was going to kill me.'

'But I don't feel it was me. I remember a sudden need to act, and then it just happened. I knew exactly what to do and I did it. I killed him, but it wasn't me. Does that make any sense to you?'

'We should get some sleep,' I said, but we kept talking for the rest of the night, telling our stories, sharing our pain. Finally, when the sun came up, we both felt better. Cleansed. We were finally ready to continue our journey to Red Colony.

The sun, although tempered by Mars's fledgling atmosphere, still had the power to burn. The landscape lit up as if on fire, bright and harshly red in some places, green and lush in others. The lichen and moss, so crucial to the terraforming process, took to Mars with enthusiasm.

As the morning shadows gave way so did Clint's sense of self. His entire demeanour changed. His movements took on a strange animalistic quality, his language degraded into bizarre fractured utterings. Despite Clint telling me that this could happen it felt like I was losing him all over again. I tried to use the situation to my advantage, and learn what I could about the Trickari psyche that tried to dominate my son.

'You are the mother,' said Clint out of nowhere. Our conversation had stalled a little while ago, precisely because of these strange, cryptic remarks.

'I am *your* mother,' I replied.

'You are our mother.'

'Our? Are you not alone?' I asked.

'We are alone.'

It was frustrating. I needed a way in. A way to understand the context.

'Where are you?' I tried.

'We are down here.'

'Where is that? What do you want?'

'We want to live, mother.'

'Everybody wants to live. Are you in danger?

I felt ridiculous, like arguing with a toddler, or a drunk. Nothing made sense, but I tried again. 'What are you doing here, in our solar system. In my son's head?' I almost shouted the last words. This wasn't going well.

Clint looked at me, piercing eyes boring into my soul.

'We need you to understand.'

'I want to understand but how–' A horrific sense of vertigo took over. The metallic taste in my mouth returned but this time accompanied by an impossible sound. I could *hear* pain. Not screams or moans, but the actual sensation. Words/thoughts/images/feelings rushed me like a tide:

... yes you are the mother the son the mother we are alone together down here waiting for you to come the son the mother the program has to run to complete the program come to us to here down find us under the water we are alone together ...

I could barely take the onslaught for its ferocity. A psychic battering ram made of pure need crashed into my mental defences, nearly tearing them down, but I started to understand, or at least to *suspect*, aspects of what was happening.

Clint *was* different from the other Neos. He had a purpose. He was a key, capable of unlocking this mystery, if only we could find the door. And somehow I was mixed up in this by virtue of being his mother.

The voices I heard in my mind were Trickari voices, and their message was slowly becoming louder and clearer. Once their message was complete we would know what the Trickari intended when they seeded our solar system with their artifacts. We could learn the reason why they had left us their rigged technology.

Another revelation dawned on me: the strange TJs who had spoken to me over the last few months knew I was involved. Their exposure to Mem had something to do with all of this. There was data in Mem, computational instructions of sorts, just as Ella and Clint suspected, and it was seeping into the consciousness of those that got addicted. People dismissed them as pathetic junkies but they were all involved. Millions of people, carrying pieces of the larger puzzle in their broken minds.

... yes the mother the son to come to us down here to us to bring us the new us the new life the new son the new mother down here where we are alone together to ...

The voices tailed off then, receding gradually until there was nothing left but a psychic afterimage on my mind. A sense of being buried, a need to be free... The taste of metal in my mouth lingered uncomfortably long. It hurt badly, my mouth pulsing with pain. I had bitten my tongue during the psychic onslaught.

'What have they done to us?' I asked out loud.

This much I knew: I still had to try Ella's cure to save my son, and I had to do it fast. Spectra was trying to solve the Trickari puzzle, to unlock the door to untold technological power. Once they discovered that the drives I had given Gibson were useless, they would stop at nothing to get him back and get me killed. This time for good.

Afterwards, Clint became still, almost listless, his energy expended. At first I thought he had gone to sleep, but he was still alert. His eyes, somehow still gentle and young, fixed on the scenery outside. The rocks, the valleys, the fields of lichen and moss. He seemed more at home on this alien world than the Martians did. I wondered what the Trickari home world looked like.

'I can feel your thoughts mum,' Clint said, making me jump.

'Oh? Do I need to be careful what I think?' *He sounds human again.* I thought.

An incongruous chuckle escaped his mouth. 'Not like that, it's not telepathy. It's more a... a *mood* thing. Like I can tell that you're there and that you're thinking about something. Maybe even a general idea of your state of mind.' He looked at me, suddenly shy. 'It's hard to explain.'

'We'll figure it out,' I said soothingly. 'I've got a plan.'

'Uh oh. Here comes trouble.'

I was about to berate him for rudeness when, suddenly, the whole situation seemed so absurd that I started laughing uncontrollably. This set Clint off in return, leaving both of us erupting in fits of laughter for minutes. An alien-human hybrid and a cyborg, slapping thighs and guffawing away like a bunch of old friends.

Later, when the sun started to set, a more serious mood took over. As joyous as our reunion was, we couldn't escape the harsh realities of our situation, or the many mysteries that surrounded us.

'So what have you learned?' I asked.

'About what?'

'About Trickari secrets, about Mem, about what Spectra knows… About all of it.' I put my hand on his, almost without thinking. 'We don't have much time Clint. We need to pool our knowledge. We need to give Ella the best chance we can to help you get free of this shit.'

Clint didn't respond. He looked out the window, his head tilted again to listen to unheard voices, secrets hiding in their unspoken words.

'I'm not sure about anything, but I have some ideas,' said Clint. 'I heard the Spectra scientists discuss stuff similar to what we were looking at.'

'So, what did they say?'

'Well, I think it's all about the Junkies. The Trickari data they carry… It's complex stuff. Much more sophisticated than I thought at first… Mem is like a virus, infecting brains – human processing units – with self-replicating code snippets.

'It writes itself? Like a virus?' I asked. The thought made me ill.

'Yeah I think so, but it's not too destructive, Trick-junkies are still capable of taking care of themselves. But I think it's all part of a much larger, slowly expanding program. The software is dormant for now, but I think the junkies are like distributed nodes in a computer network.

The main program is simply not live yet.'

'Like malware infecting their brains?' I wondered.

'Yes, sort of. Neos produce vast amounts of condensed code in their crystals, some of it procedural I suspect, and it gets deployed via Mem.' Clint's voice trembled. He kept touching his hair while talking to me, fully aware that he was speaking about himself as much as anybody. 'And at some point I reckon it will hit critical mass, and execute.'

'And do what?'

'That's what Spectra wants to know. And that's why we need to crack the rest of what's on those data drives. I think I can figure out the Trickari code. My brain is...' He didn't finish his sentence, but I knew what he meant; he was more and more able to think like a Trickari.

'We just need to get you to Ella,' I said, and I almost believed it.

Just as I was ready to set off the sky exploded. A blinding flash followed by multiple pinpricks of pure white fire, racing across the landscape. These were no fireworks. The scale was humongous. More flashes appeared, and I saw a huge plume of smoke and ash rise from the horizon. I learned later that after Ceres, several asteroids had entered a decaying orbit around Mars and had begun smashing into the planet surface.

Everywhere I went, destruction followed, like a jealous lover lashing out.

We finally arrived at Red Colony around midnight. Its many domes emitted a faint blue light, giving the settlement the appearance of a strange deep-sea creature – bio-luminescent and gargantuan, looming over us, too big to consider us prey.

I had messaged Ella via Padd ahead of our arrival to warn her of our direction of approach. She came to pick us up outside the city in a beaten up all-terrain crawler, once used to haul cargo and equipment. Ella hadn't brought her skimmer. When I asked her how she managed to move so well, she showed me an expensive-looking exoskeleton.

'Does the trick. Makes me feel like I could be a crime fighter,' she joked.

She had brought old dirty clothes for Clint and myself, to disguise us as veteran miners. Clint's hood didn't appear out of place – there were always plenty of accidents in the mines, and lots of disfigured workers.

'Is this really going to be good enough?' I asked, not trusting the disguise, but I shouldn't have worried. Even at midnight the streets of Red Colony were brimming with life in all its forms, shapes and sizes. I counted ten other hooded people within a few minutes. We blended in perfectly, strange fish in a shoal of other strange fish.

Trick-Junkies were everywhere. Walking around with various degrees of stagger, sitting down in doorways, alleys and cafes, their heads adorned with dull crystal carbuncles, not shiny like Neo hair, nor as graceful. I shuddered, wondering with renewed curiosity if the crystal growths performed some hidden function, playing a secret part in the Trickari master-plan. I tuned in to my visual surveillance mode on a whim. The carbuncles were slightly warmer than skin temperature, as if they were organic growths.

A nauseating feeling of dread crept up on me. I wanted to run, to get away from these creatures. A taste of metal threatened to manifest in my mouth on several occasions only to recede again, but I could sense something was wrong. Dread turned into paranoia. I *knew* we were being followed but every time I made us duck into an alley or doorway to check, it turned out to be a false alarm. Clint was getting the jitters too, but I didn't know if it was because he tuned into my anxiety or if he also felt that something was wrong.

Ella threw me evermore exasperated looks until eventually she had had enough. 'What's wrong with you?' she hissed. 'All you need to do is follow me, keep your nose down and keep Clint from doing something weird. Why is that so damn hard?'

'Something is wrong,' I stammered. 'I can't explain it.'

'Fine, that sounds perfectly awful, but there's nobody following us.' Ella took a breath and forced herself to calm down. 'Look, just keep a lid on it till we're at the house, OK?'

I nodded, drawing Clint closer to me. But no matter how hard I tried I couldn't shake it. I felt in the core of my being that something terrible was about to happen, and that there was nothing I could do about it.

26

The property I had bought for Ella was incredible. On the outside it appeared to be no more than a large and chunky piece of typical Martian real estate. Functional, sturdy, *utilitarian*. Maybe an old converted government office, or a corporate workhouse. Nothing too remarkable. But on the inside an entirely different reality unfolded. Every room, every corridor, every corner, every square centimetre of the house was dedicated to different architectural styles. I counted at least a dozen distinct architectural schools just on the first walk-through.

The previous owner must have been rich, both in funds and time, and had treated the house as a shrine to humanity's ability to keep reinventing the ways in which it houses itself. The results were impressive and completely mad.

There were two kitchens. One was strikingly modernist, the other was ruggedly Victorian. There were Brutalist offices, Goya inspired bedrooms, Gothic toilets. Arabesque corridors led to Roman rooms, Edwardian reading rooms competed with wonderful indoor follies. It was the most amazing interior I had ever seen in my life.

Ella had cleared one especially large dining hall, and filled it to the brim with her equipment. It was to be the nexus of our attempt to cure Clint and to rid the world of the Trickari disease.

Something was tugging at the corner of my mind, but I couldn't put my finger on it. I let it go for the time being and wondered where to put up Clint.

As if reading my mind Ella said, 'I've got a big shared room for both of you, so you can stay together. The beds are incredible.' The mere mention of beds made me realise how desperately tired I was. I could barely thank her, as she led us up a flight of stairs, and showed us a beautiful art deco styled room, with two beds, two sofas, several wardrobes and tables, and a disturbing collection of taxidermy samples: foxes, snakes, rabbits, pheasants, even a dodo – which had to be a fake but looked disturbingly real. It must have cost a fortune to get all this shipped to Mars. I was amazed the previous owner had left it all behind.

'Not bad huh?' Ella sad, rubbing her eyes. She looked like she had been crying but she didn't look upset. I felt it wasn't my business but I couldn't help wonder why. Then, I honed in on what was bothering me before; Ella no longer looked so scruffy and dishevelled. Whatever it was that had been tormenting her had been dealt with. She had found some kind of resolution.

'Not bad,' I agreed.

'We start tomorrow?' Ella said, somewhere between a question and a plea.

'We start tomorrow,' I replied, still not quite believing it. *We had made it*.

I woke up before everybody else, about an hour before sunrise. There had been no dreams.

I gave myself a private tour of the property and was struck again by the incredible architectural wealth on display. Not too long ago I couldn't even have dreamed of owning a place like this.

I settled myself in the modernist kitchen. It was fully stocked, including a rich choice of coffee blends. The larder was a culinary treasure and there was even a choice of relatively fresh bread. Ella hadn't been shy about using my money to set up this place for human comfort; which was exactly what I wanted, as we would likely spend most of our time in Red Colony indoors.

I made myself a breakfast of eggs, rustic bread and cheese, and prepared a pot of Italian coffee. I savoured every bite and every sip, glorifying in the simplicity of a good breakfast. I needed to feel like I could still enjoy things like that.

The walls were adorned with modernist paintings and poster art. I smiled when I spotted a poster announcing the maiden voyage of the Titanic – probably the most famous ship in history. I missed my collection of miniature ships.

'Wow. I don't think I've ever wanted a coffee more than that one,' said Clint as he walked into the kitchen.

'Grab a mug,' I said. 'Have some bread and cheese too.'

Clint sat down next to me, poured a coffee and prepared bread. He presented a strange duality – crystal hair and nails, odd gait, otherworldly skin, but also a teenager's cockiness, naivety, and insecurity. Soon I would learn which side of him would survive – Trickari or human – if he would survive at all.

We ate in silence, content in the moment. It was as happy an occasion as I could remember experiencing in the last few months. I didn't want it to end. I just sat there, drinking my coffee, trying to stretch time, hoping this moment would last forever.

Ella walked into the kitchen, bags under her eyes, looking tired. She joined us without speaking a word, and made a large breakfast for herself. Eventually the silence shattered for the most mundane reason:

'Pass the salt?' asked Clint.

We all looked up from our coffees at the same time. A split second later we erupted in loud laughter, lasting several minutes. It felt like somebody opened all the windows in an old musty house, the draft pushing all the bad air out of the room. A big cleanup, venting old mojo and bad thoughts.

'I need to get some supplies,' said Ella, after the laughter died away. 'When I get back we need to map out Clint's physiology, see where it is right now with the transformation. We can then compare with my last data set.'

'And compensate your treatment accordingly?' I asked.

'That's the plan.'

'How long do you need?'

'A few hours. Maybe the rest of the morning.'

'OK, go for it.'

Ella left soon after. I was struck by how much more *together* she seemed, compared to only a few short days ago. A welcome sight – I needed her at the top of her game.

'Mum, this cure…'

'It may not work Clint. There are no guarantees.'

'Yeah I know. But it could, right?'

'That's why I…' I couldn't finish the sentence. How could I explain what I had gone through to be reunited with him? The sacrifices I made. The sacrifices others made on my behalf… The things I had done to myself, and to others. 'Yes, it could, sweetheart,' I said, instead.

'What if it goes wrong? I could be killed. Or it could accelerate the transformation.'

'Sweetheart, please–'

'No listen. I know there are risks, and I know the outcome isn't clear.' Clint fidgeted a bit before continuing. 'This could be our last day together. Do you understand?'

'I do,' I said, not knowing what else to say.

'So… we should spend it differently. I mean, I don't want to sit here feeling scared. I want to go outside. See the town. Eat things I never had before.'

'It's not safe,' I sighed.

'Fuck safe! None of this is safe!' Clint's outburst silenced me. 'It's *my* life we're talking about.' He glowered at me with the intensity of desperation. 'It's not all about you, don't you understand that? *I* have a say in all this. This might be my last day with you. If I'm going to do this treatment then I need to find the courage somehow. I need one normal day or I don't think I can go through with it.'

He had a point.

What if something did go wrong, and his last moments with me were marred by resentment? After everything I'd been through I couldn't face that possibility. Despite the obvious risks, the sheer stupidity of courting disaster, I understood his need. More than that, I agreed with him. A life was not a life unless it was lived to its fullest potential.

'We'll need to disguise you,' I said, and hugged him close and tight. Despite his advanced transformation he still *smelled* like Clint. It's a strange thing, but that comforting biological familiarity, that deeply physical connection, was as fundamental to our relationship as anything. To find that connection still present was a moment of sheer, pure joy.

For Clint's disguise I opted for a swaddled and hooded approach, hinting at some kind of terrible disease, to make sure that people wouldn't approach us too closely. Clint's weird gait sold it completely.

To balance things out I added various belts, spiky fashion items and paraphernalia associated with underworld types, to show that he wasn't an easy target. People in the street afforded us a respectful distance, which was exactly what we needed.

I dressed in generic work clothes, worn by most people on Mars, and fitted a standard issue breather. We made a strange pair, but not so strange as to attract unwanted attention.

Initially we just walked, allowing Clint to submerge his senses into Red Colony crowds. This place was the closest Mars had to offer to compete with Diamond-Town. I could tell Clint felt at home.

After an hour's walk we stopped for refreshments at one of the hundreds of random little food stalls that littered the alleyways. We bought some food and found a dark little corner under a red awning to eat. Clint savoured a deeply marinated tofu kebab, no easy task with his disguise, while I indulged in a bento box overflowing with sugar-coated soft candy cubes and other treats. Both our meals were delicious.

Halfway through his dish he looked at me askance, and

said, 'I know you want to ask me, mum. Go on, let's get it out of the way.'

'Ask you what?' I said, bemused.

'Why I did it.'

'Why you did what?'

'Come on, you know what I mean.'

'I really don't,' I said, slightly irritated.

'Why I went off on my own, back on Habitat 6,' he said, a note of defiance in his voice. 'I didn't go to prove myself or anything that stupid.'

'I thought…' I considered my reply for a moment. 'I thought you were pissed off with me, and you wanted to show me you could pull your weight, after things went wrong with the seed-bank.'

Clint put down his food, and looked into the distance, remembering that day. 'Yeah well… That's what I figured you'd think.'

'What do you mean?' I said. Something in his voice made me sit up.

'It was the letter. From the Residency Board. I knew what was happening. You needed money as soon as possible so I could stay with you and so you could buy a ship.'

'You knew all along?'

'Yes, I knew all along. I kept close tabs on any changes in residency legislation. I figured it was important, and I was right.' Clint looked down at his feet, a boy confessing to his mother. 'I didn't want to be treated like a child. I figured if I completed the Spectra mission myself I would feel better about myself. Dunno… sounds stupid when I say it out loud.'

'Not at all. I completely understand. I was the stupid one. I should have told you from the start.'

'It's fine, we can both be stupid.'

We sat quietly for a bit, enjoying each other's company, but I felt nervous staying out too long.

I said, 'We should get going,' and I made to stand up.

Clint put his hand on my arm to stop me.

'What is it? We need to g–' I started to ask

'I'm not finished…'

'We don't have time…' I said, gently removing his hand. 'This is crazy, we should go back. You can tell me back at the house.'

Clint stared into nothing, ignoring my request.

'Come on…' I held out my hand.

'I need to know if you can feel it too mum.'

'I don't know what you mean. Can I feel what?'

'Ever since I got infected I've been hearing things… in my mind.'

'Aren't they the Trickari memories?'

'No. Well, yes that too, but I can separate it.'

'What is it then?'

'I can feel something … some organising force. I'm getting information, concepts, ideas … plans… I thought at first it was the Trickari master-program, the code hidden in Mem, somehow running its course, and that is probably true, but …' Clint suddenly looked scared, his gaze firmly fixed on something terrible, something I couldn't see.'

'Tell me,' I urged.

'I think there is an intelligence as well, like a caretaker, and it knows about us.'

'Spectra you mean?' I stammered. 'I knew something was going on…'

'Maybe. I don't know. I can barely keep myself together, let alone figure this out, but I know what I'm feeling is true. There's a lot more going on than we think. We've been involved in this thing much longer than we realised. You too mum, look what's been happening to you. The junkies, the dreams, the voices… it's all connected.'

My head was spinning. I was starting to feel nauseous. I could feel my mind rebelling against this idea, but it made too much sense to dismiss. I tried to tell Clint but the spinning sensation in my head got worse. A taste of metal seeped into my mouth, my teeth, my gums… A sensation of *seeing sounds* bubbled over inside my brain. *No! Please, not now!*

I looked up with great difficulty, trying to find the source, and spotted two TJ's approaching us.

'Clint, we have to go, *now.*'

The first TJ arrived at our stall. She was in her thirties, almost pretty despite the crystal carbuncles caking her skull. She walked with the uncaring directness associated with her condition, making no efforts to fit in with other people around her. An older man carrying a basket of fruit stepped in her path. There was a collision … Fruit rolled over the dirty floor.

'Careful!' He shouted, before realising what she was. Then muttering, 'Fuck-damn Carbuncle heads. Too many of em these days.' He stopped to collect his fruit while the girl reached out to us. I could see the veins in her eyes as she spoke.

'Mother Son. We need you. We can see you. We can hear you,' she droned. She sounded barely human.

I recoiled, spitting to get the impossible taste out of my mouth. 'Get away from us. We can't help you.'

The other TJ also arrived by now. An old man, his frame bent over, warped by a deformed spine.

'Can you take us dear?' he croaked at us, like some ancient cult member. 'Yes, take us. We need to go soon.'

I didn't understand why they behaved like this. It was all wrong, and it scared me. I grabbed Clint's hand, dragging him backwards into the alley, away from them. The commotion hadn't gone unnoticed however. Two local thugs, crudely augmented, were moving down the alley towards us, chest puffed out, faces set to dumb.

They looked roughly similar; red beards and matching cheap tattoos and probably the same steroid treatments. The left thug's face was a mass of scars. A badly healed gash stood out, slicing across his forehead. It didn't make much of a difference to his looks.

Both of them wore that vacant slack-jawed expression, typical of the truly dim. Textbook neighbourhood bullies, looking for a chance to show off how tough they were.

'Hey! What you doing in our street.' Roared the scarred one.

'Piss off,' I snapped. 'We don't have time for this.'

They both grinned at that, predictably.

The scar-less brother tried to grab me, but Clint intercepted him and *slashed*. The thug turned to him, only to recoil in shock at the sight of his right arm, now a blood-spurting mess, ribbons of flesh hanging off the bone. Clint moved in for another attack, a hooded apparition, dealing death and chaos.

The scarred brother tried to hit me with a slow and clumsy haymaker. I stepped sideways and in, avoiding his big meaty fist as it uselessly swung past my head. It was easy to grab his outstretched arm, kick the back of his knees to force him to the ground, and wrench *up*. His arm dislocated with a surprisingly loud pop.

Both men whimpered, disbelief and horror strangling their voices. A crowd of people had formed, several of them talking into their Padd, others looking on with undisguised curiosity. This was not a tenable situation.

Clint stood over our attackers, blood and tissue dripping off his crystal claws, a crazed look in his eyes. I feared he was about to suffer another fit. Thankfully his hood was still in place, protecting his identity from the crowd, which was more than I could say for myself. I was completely exposed.

Clint moaned and clutched his head, pointing behind me. The Trick-Junkies that caused all this in the first place had re-appeared, now joined by two more. Together they produced a chorus of gibberish. Pleas for help that made no sense. Clint moaned again, a raw edge of despair. His distress infected my thoughts. Another fit was imminent.

'Snap out of it. We have to go!' I shouted – refitting my breather. My heart tried to escape via my throat, my tongue pulsed with pain where I had bitten it earlier. I couldn't swallow.

We pushed through the crowd which parted around us as if our merest touch had the power to kill – which wasn't far from the truth.

We had to get away.

We rushed down countless alleys, streets, and lanes to get away. We took sudden shortcuts, lost ourselves in bustling markets, and did everything else we could think of to make sure nobody followed us, until Clint desperately urged me to stop.

'They…' he gasped, 'They're gone… I can't sense them anymore'

We both leaned with our back against the wall of an old hardware store, trying to catch our breath. I let myself slide down to the ground, taking deep breaths, quickly recovering. My augments did their work perfectly.

'Ready to take the treatment now?' I half laughed, half gasped. 'Because I can't take much more of this.' Clint just nodded, a half-smile on his face.

'Good, let's go.'

We got back to the mansion one hour before Ella did. She looked suspiciously at our sweat-streaked faces but refrained from asking any embarrassing questions.

'Clint are you OK?' she asked with real concern. 'Why don't you take a shower and get dressed in this?' She handed him an orange hospital gown.

Clint nodded gratefully and left the room.

'What the hell Jemm?'

I just shrugged, which didn't satisfy Ella but she asked no further questions about what had happened.

'Help me prep the treatment room,' commanded Ella as she left the room. I followed her, picking up supplies and equipment as directed. 'This is it,' she said. 'The big show. I'm nowhere near properly prepared for this, do you understand?'

'I know, but we have to try.' I put my hand on her shoulder, trying to ease her nerves. 'You are the smartest person I have ever met. If anybody can do this it's you. I trust you.'

That earned me a look of withering annoyance. 'Don't be stupid. I'm one woman with some fancy gear. If I pull this off it's a miracle.'

'You've had a lot of time with Clint, and you have the

data on the Spectra drives, as well as the files on Theo's Padd. That's more than anybody else had.'

We finished the final preparations in silence. Ella checked her equipment, consulted her Padd, and made some final adjustments. Clint walked into the room as Ella finished up. He was wearing the hospital gown, looking completely out of place. Clint, fully aware of this, tried to change the focus.

'Talk me through the plan please, maybe I can help,' he said, quietly, but with surprising confidence. 'I know a bit about Trickari physiology these days.'

Ella, took a deep breath before she explained her approach.

'OK. It's a bit experimental, you understand that right? I mean, everything we're doing here has never been done before.' Clint nodded. 'Well, my original approach was to just slow it all down. Use what is basically an aggressive medicinal treatment to discourage cells from changing, administered and managed by bespoke augments. This seems to have worked up to a point, until Spectra removed the regulators anyway.'

'Weren't those augments supposed to prevent me from dying?' asked Clint. 'I mean, I feel pretty healthy despite all this.' He couldn't suppress a nervy little laugh as he indicated his new body.

'Yeah that's been bothering me too,' said Ella. 'I mean, it's good that you're not negatively affected, but it's weird... I think the transformation, the infection, has some agency of its own. The virus, the code, whatever it is inside you, might be able to react to different circumstances to make sure the process continues without killing the host.' Everybody fell silent, and Ella looked uncomfortable. 'Sorry,' she whispered. 'I know you're not a host. It's just, I have to talk in these medical terms or I'm going to lose my nerves. They're shredded as it is.'

'We know Ella, it's fine,' I said 'Just keep going.'

'OK, sure. So, the problem is ... well time is running out. My original treatment seems to have run into a wall.

Or defences or whatever. So I have a different idea now.'

'Because of all the new data on Theo's Padd?' asked Clint.

Ella nodded, 'Yeah, and more time with the data on the cracked Spectra drives, cross referencing the two… and frankly the extra cash that pays for all this gear.' Ella seemed momentarily distracted, before continuing. 'It helps that this kind of work has been my specialism for years, trying to come up with some treatment for my own condition you know?' Once again she looked lost. Something was obviously bothering her on a fundamental level. 'Anyway,' she continued. 'My new plan is to go for a more decentralised approach. I still want to work at this on a cellular level, but with a supercharged agent: part nanite, part chemical compound. I want to attack each individual cell with this agent. Cells that still contain enough original DNA will be fortified. Those that are too far gone will be replaced with new healthy cell growth.'

'That sounds incredibly aggressive and dangerous.'

Ella nodded, not realising she still needed to convince me to go through with this. 'It is,' she said. 'Something similar seemed to have worked on the subjects in the Spectra lab in the habitat.'

'Subjects? You mean those abominations we found up there?' I said, almost too softly to hear.

'Yes. But it won't be like that. That was meant to create some non-baseline human being. I … I wouldn't …' Ella stammered, nearly too flustered to continue, until she found new resolve. 'There isn't time for anything else Jemm. He's nearly gone. If we wait too long he'll be stuck in this Trickari prison forever. His mind… his body… We might be too late already.'

I was about to protest when Clint intervened.

'Mum, look at me …' He had lifted his hospital gown and removed his slippers. His feet no longer looked human, the toes had nearly merged together into two appendages. Claws were forming where there used to be nails. A strange bony spur had grown just behind his heel. Clint was being eaten up from the inside.

'We need to do this,' he said, looking to me for help. The pleading in his eyes was too much. I gave him a quick nod, and left the room.

The initial tests and the subsequent procedure took only a few hours. Ella had prepped well for the moment, wasting no time. I had been waiting in a remarkably well stocked library – beautifully decorated in a 1950s Frank Lloyd Wright style – when she entered, looking tired but calm.

The library held several books on classic ships which I was quietly impressed with. I showed them to her.

'These are nice.'

'This house is ridiculous,' she replied. 'I can't believe you could just pay for it. Just like that.'

I thought of Rosie, lying dead in my arms. I wondered what she would have thought of the place. 'Not *just* like that.'

'Yeah… I know. I'm sorry.'

'How's Clint. Did it work?'

'It's too early to tell, but so far so good. His cells are responding the way I hoped. But who knows, this is uncharted territory.'

'I want to see him.'

Ella led me back into the makeshift lab. The lights had been dimmed, I assume to provide a soothing atmosphere but it felt sinister to me. Clint was lying quietly on a bunk bed, studying his own vital signs on a wrist monitor and checking a rapidly updating data stream on a computer screen. He looked both human and utterly alien. Just then I noticed he still had the matching tattoos we got a lifetime ago. I took comfort in that; despite his transformation there was still a link to his old self.

'How do you feel?' I asked, feeling useless.

'It… tingles.' We both laughed halfheartedly.

'It's going to be a while before we know anything useful,' offered Ella. 'Probably nothing will change until tomorrow, so why don't you go get some rest?'

I sat down next to Clint, holding his hand, rubbing it. 'I don't think so. I wouldn't be able to sleep.'

'Mum, go to sleep. We need you alert and ready tomorrow, when it's time to get out of here.'

Ella shrugged, and pointed at another bunk-bed. 'You can sleep right here. It's fine, I'll be up all night monitoring him so if anything happens I'll wake you up immediately.'

'OK, OK,' I sighed. 'I know when I'm beaten.' I dramatically threw myself on the bed, making a show out of going to sleep. The reality was that I was bone tired, and that they were making perfect sense. I was asleep in seconds. My last thoughts were of my father, filled with sadness that I had not been able to save him.

I woke up to blood-curdling screams – high pitched, desperate. The sounds savagely drilled into my head. It was almost impossible to think clear thoughts. Somebody was being tortured, or murdered.

I scanned my surroundings, only to discover that the screams were coming from Clint. It sounded nothing like him. Ella was nearby lying on the floor, her clothes ripped. Long gashes across her stomach welled up with deep red blood. She tried to stand but her body was clearly in shock.

Clint stood hunched over her, taking deep halting breaths between horrifying shrieks. At that moment there was nothing remotely human about him.

'Clint …,' I tried. 'Calm down … please. Look at me.'

His eyes made contact with mine, but there was no sign of recognition – Just a crazed, otherworldly expression. I switched my augments to full-on combat mode. Adrenaline and other useful chemicals entered my system. Time seemed to slow down, but I knew it was just a side effect of my increased responses and heightened senses. Yet, even with my enhanced reflexes, I was too slow to fully avoid Clint's sudden and vicious attack. He slashed at my throat, his arm shooting out like a cobra. His claws glittered and sparkled, even in the little light available. My augmented reflexes saved me as I blocked his claw from reaching my throat, but it still slashed across my left arm. If it weren't for the subdermal shielding he would have cut the arteries in my wrist.

I had to calm him down somehow, but first I needed to get some distance between us. Clint came at me again but this time I countered with a brutal but effective forward kick, stomping down diagonally with my heel, straight into his stomach. He went gliding across the floor until he smashed into the far wall. The impact dazed him.

Ella managed to raise herself, but it was doubtful she would stay up if she didn't address her bleeding wounds – fast. I spotted a first aid kit on the wall and threw it to her. 'What the hell is happening, Ella!' I cried, already knowing in my heart what the answer would be. 'It's the treatment isn't it?'

'The virus is fighting back,' she replied, barely able to make herself audible, weakened by the pain she was in. 'I've never seen anything like it.' Ella applied bandages and stabbed herself with a syringe – pain relief flooded her veins. 'My treatment was working perfectly, but his infected cells started attacking the nanites. It must be an in-built defence mechanism.'

'Now what?' I asked desperately.

'Now nothing. I can't beat this thing. And we need to get out of here soon before anybody finds us.'

Something snapped into focus in my mind. Something that should have been clear a long time ago. 'What do you mean? Nobody knows we're here.'

'I'm telling you, we have to go. Just believe me please.'

A truth crystalised in my mind, icy cold. 'What have you done?'

Ella held out her hand, a syringe inside. 'Give this to Clint, we need to calm him down before we move him.'

'Tell me what you've done Ella. Now.'

Seeing a glint of danger in my eyes Ella slowly stood up straight. 'I made a deal.'

'With who? What are you talking about?'

'With Spectra. I promised them my research data. Everything I have learned so far. I'm cooperating with them to get all this resolved.'

'What?' I stammered. 'What else. Tell me!'

'Why, what does it matter?' said Ella, her face ashen with tiredness.

'I need to know,' I said, close to shouting. 'Why would you do that!?'

'Don't you get it? Isn't it obvious? They will help me *walk* Jemm. In exchange for keeping the Gaianista drives out of the hands of competitors they're offering me the full range of cellular reset therapy to cure my illness. With the help of my own recent research it should be possible.' I had no reply. Ella's words dragged me into a vortex of anger and frustration.

Ella sighed, 'I don't expect you to understand.'

'You betrayed us?'

'I only agreed to it if I could destroy the original drives, which I would do the moment after finishing Clint's treatment.'

'What about Clint? What do I do now?'

'We just had this one shot. This was it. There were only two possible outcomes. If successful you would be gone by now. Free. Failure meant we would be out of time anyway. Which we are.'

'What the hell does that mean,' I asked, close to whispering to prevent myself from screaming.

'They'll come in a few hours.' She held out her hand with the syringe. 'Do it, then get out. Save yourself.' I just stared at her, at her hand, her face, betrayal burning hot inside me. I reached out to grab the syringe, but halted at the last moment.

Her arm started to glow, as if lit from the inside. The skin bubbled, like fat in a pan. Little rivulets of smoke appeared as her arm melted, right in front of my eyes. Ella's face contorted, she made a sound that was unlike any I have ever heard before; a low guttural harsh moan, increasing in intensity and volume until it turned into a ragged scream, equally inhuman as Clint's agonised wailing.

A voice cut through the smoke, 'That wasn't the deal Ella. You promised us the boy.' It was Bryant. I adjusted my ocular augment, and there he was, clear as blood. I was too caught up in Ella's betrayal to notice the telltale shimmer sparkle. I cursed under my breath.

Another shimmering shape entered the room, carrying a bulky gun of a type I had seen only once before; a vicious weapon, designed to focus microwaves. It had literally boiled the blood in Ella's arm. Bryant gave a curt order, and the second intruder slapped a small device on the back of Clint's neck, who instantly crumpled like a puppet whose strings were cut. A neural inhibitor by the looks of it.

I was on the second shimmer-man fast as a shadow. My right foot shot out and kicked his head against the far wall with a dull crunching sound. He was dead before he hit the ground. I kept up my momentum, not stopping to see where Bryant was. Part of the wall behind me exploded, raining sharp debris everywhere. Bryant was using some kind of weapon with explosive ammo. It didn't matter; this time I would make him pay.

I ran across the room, looking for cover. Another explosive impact, this time just behind my running feet, gave away Bryant's position. I produced my flechette gun and set it to burst mode, spraying the area where I hoped he would go next, while diving behind a steel desk for cover. A low grunt indicated that at least one of my darts had hid the target.

Return-fire peppered the steel desk, dents appearing in rapid succession. I swept the room with my augmented vision – *where was he?* – before spotting a vague human shape in front of a hot blur; Bryant was smart, hiding near a heat source. I kicked a chair to my right trying to draw his fire, and came for him when he aimed a shot at the sudden movement. I was on him – faster than he could adjust his aim. He managed to squeeze off one shot which only just went wide before I reached him and slapped the gun out of his hand.

There was a collision of bodies, a flurry of hard

punches and kicks, and then I had hold of his right arm. I squeezed *hard* in triumph, sure to break it, but received a vicious backhand to my nose instead. I didn't let go, squeezing harder, but his arm wouldn't buckle. It must have been enhanced.

I felt like I was wrestling a ghost; I should have known a high level corporate enforcer like Bryant wasn't that easy to kill.

He backhanded me again, this time breaking several of my teeth, making me drop my gun. I was in danger of losing control of this fight.

I changed tactics and suddenly let go of his arm, causing him to lose balance and stagger backwards. This gave me the opening I needed; I stepped forward and punched his ribs as hard as I could – once, twice. I could feel the bone crack on both hits. Bryant was forced down to his knees. He actually laughed.

'Not bad girl. That's gonna hurt in the morning.'

'Oh I'm not done yet,' I replied, reaching for the gun he had dropped. I laughed in triumph as my fingers wrapped around the sturdy grip. The fat little gun felt perfectly balanced in my hand as I raised it to aim at his head, slow and deliberate.

'You don't want to do that,' he grunted, some of the pain from his shattered ribs breaking through his augmented defences.

'This is *exactly* what I want to do,' I said, and squeezed the trigger.

The explosion that followed threw me spinning through the air, knocking the air from my lungs when I landed. My head was ringing. I had trouble figuring out where I was …

The gun was in pieces. Booby-trapped, rigged to explode in the hands of whoever took it from its approved Spectra owner. I should have gone for my flechette gun, but I let my ego get in the way, going for the big dramatic gesture.

I saw Bryant slowly stand up, unsteady, groggy from the blow and the damage to his ribs. He started to walk towards me – no doubt to finish the job for good – then hesitated. I could understand why; he had no gun, and considering the damage he had already suffered, there was no guarantee he would come out on top. A moan from Clint refocused him on his main objective. Bryant helped Clint up – compliant and docile due to the neural inhibitor – and escorted him out of the room, like a gentle older brother.

I tried to get up and follow, but somehow my legs kept folding up under me. My vision blurred and everything started to phase in and out of focus, even while my inner voice shouted at me to *wake up!*

When I did finally manage to get back up I felt like I was outside my own body. I watched myself take one step, two… but then the world fell up and smashed into my head.

Darkness drew me into its embrace with greedy fingers. I gratefully let myself be taken, tired of fighting the world.

I was a little girl again, riding a golden horse on an antique merry-go-round. My father had taken me to a funfair on my 5th birthday. It was one of the happiest days of my life, and even at that tender age I knew I would always remember it as such.

My father's smile was warm and proud, full of the knowledge that he had created a perfect day for me. A day I would always cherish.

I went round and round and round, who knows how many times, watching the world blur from the speed of the ride through tears of happiness.

Oddly, there were no other children, and my father was no longer smiling. He was saying something but I couldn't understand him. I lifted my arms up at him, desperate for him to pick me up and hug me, tears ran down my face as I cried for him to take me home.

'Here take this,' a sudden sharp pain in my left arm … 'Hang in there, this will kick in in a minute.'

The spinning of the merry-go-round slowed down, the world forced itself on me. Dad was gone, Ella stood in his place, pale as a sheet, blood dripping from a crudely bandaged stump. My head cleared rapidly, understanding and anger filling me up.

'How could you,' I spat at Ella. 'We trusted you … How could you be so–'

'Shut up. If the treatment had worked you two would have been out of here. I did what I could, for months. I never wanted any of this shit. All I ever wanted was to be healthy again.'

'I would have paid for your treatment,' I shouted, my voice cracking on the last word. I was going to say more but a deep pulsing pain in my hand made me check myself for injuries. Miraculously it was mostly scrapes and bruises.

'I said shut up. There's no time for this shit.' I felt a cold rush as Ella's injection kicked in, and I relaxed a bit.

She smiled quietly, 'That's better isn't it? Now listen carefully. You've only been out for thirty minutes. You can still catch them.'

'Where…' I managed to say, still reeling from the beating I took.

'Space port, I assume. Gibson will want to take Clint away from Mars as soon as possible. He's much better protected on Earth.'

'Help me get up,' I grunted, but Ella just laughed, suddenly looking tired.

'I'm lucky to even survive this,' she said, gesturing at her stump. 'You need to get up on your own and go nail this arsehole.'

Ella was right. A new clarity entered my soul, a total, all-encompassing sense of purpose – Gibson and Bryant would pay for what they had done to me, and I had to get Clint back. Nothing else mattered.

It was already dark outside, but still quite busy – Red

Colony's streets were never empty. I pushed through the crowds, leaving a wake of slightly bemused people behind me, wondering about the crazed woman with the scary breather.

People seemed uncharacteristically distracted. Clusters of locals just stood still, staring at the sky through the dome, laughing and pointing. A flash briefly coloured their faces purple, then orange, then yellow. Martian New Year had arrived.

I got to Isaac's vehicle without incident, all the time trying to figure out what my best approach would be. I entered the vehicle and took a moment to ponder the situation, but I could think of nothing else but racing to the space port – hopefully to arrive before Gibson – and taking it from there. It wasn't much of a plan, but what choice did I have? I had no idea what to do even if I did manage to free Clint.

A sense of futility almost overtook me at that point. I felt like Sisyphus, pushing a giant boulder. If I let go it would roll down the hill, and I would never be able to get it back up again. A useless thought, but it kept resurfacing, growing larger and larger until I could no longer carry it and I had to stop. What was the point? There was no cure for Clint. There was no way out of this. Maybe I should just give up, end it all. I found myself breathing heavily, my body a banquet of pain, wondering why I was even alive.

I pictured Gibson's face then, taking Clint with him to Earth, locking him into some lab, learning the secrets of Trickari technology, steering Spectra to full human dominance. There was a loud crash and a sharp pain in my already injured hand. I had hit the window with all my might, but it had resisted, only betraying its resolve by showing a tiny crack.

Revellers had set the sky on fire. Colours burst into colours all through the night. The explosions sounded muted and far away, as the atmosphere was still too thin to carry much sound, but the flashes could be seen wide and far.

That late evening as I arrived at a nearly deserted spaceport, away from festivities and celebrations, I realised I might lose him again. Despite all the sacrifices I had made, all the horrors I had endured. Despite all the pain I had visited upon my body and upon others, and despite the expensive bio-mods, augments and upgrades that defiled my person. Despite it all, I found myself on the verge of failure.

This time they might take him away from me forever.

The space port was a multi-tiered space, made up of waiting areas, mezzanines, and boarding tunnels. An eerie emptiness pervaded the place; I assume travel was down to a minimum because of the festivities.

I searched the boarding areas until I caught a glimpse of movement. Two figures moved slowly, quietly, on a level above me; I followed carefully.

Two shapes emerged out into the open, crossing a boarding area on the west side of the port: Clint and Gibson.

I could see Clint clearly now, his alien-human body silhouetted against a raging crimson sunset blazing through a tinted window – he seemed impossibly close, like I could just reach out and touch him… And how beautiful he looked! His crystal hair radiant and proud, gently breaking up the light of the setting sun into a spectrum of soft colours – a reflection of the fireworks raging overhead.

Gibson was leading him up the access ramp of their ship: The *Narcissus*; a mean looking Corvette-class cruiser – heavily modified. The ship was ceramic-white, sophisticated, elegant, and upon close inspection, armed to the teeth. Typical of Gibson to splash out on a ship that put on polite airs yet rudely bared its fangs at anybody who looked a little too closely. It stood haughtily on its landing gear, cargo bay open, gaping like an angry fish.

Gibson held out his hand to Clint, as if he was merely

escorting a confused little boy, trying to find his way home. They were about to escape, just as I had finally caught up with them.

I won't let you do this to me!

Something in me hardened, braced itself. I was ready to do what I had to do, no matter the cost. I mentally prepared for what was to come, ready to move in, but just as I was about to make my move I spotted motion to the left of me.

The first shot took off my left arm. I felt a sharp tug, after which it was just ... gone. Surprisingly, there was no pain and very little blood. I guess my augments did their work to minimise the damage. Yet, I could still feel my arm, *despite it no longer being there*. I could sense my now-absent fingers tingling and I felt an irritating itch on the skin of my phantom forearm. Instinct made me try to raise the arm so I could survey the damage, but it simply wasn't there. Nausea washed over me, threatening to stop me in my tracks.

The second shot hit my side, broke several ribs, but failed to penetrate my subdermal armour. I was flung across the floor like an unloved doll, discarded by a mean-spirited child. As I flew through the air a detached part of me noticed the odd curvature of the Martian horizon, shaped like an inverted smile. *The whole planet is laughing at me.*

I spotted the shooter behind a stack of crates. It was Bryant, grimly professional as always. He shot me again and this time part of my right foot disappeared. Wires wriggled and wreathed along the edge of the wound, flaps of synthetic skin formed a grotesque flower.

There was still no pain. A little update message flashed on the inside of my retina with an overview of my vital signs. My bio-armour contained a fully integrated med-unit, no doubt working overtime pumping me full of painkillers and anti-shock drugs. Nonetheless, I was starting to feel the impact of these wounds. It got harder to breathe. My chest felt tight, as if squeezed in a giant vice. My breathing degenerated into ragged gasping and I wondered if a broken rib had pierced a lung. I nearly blacked out there and then.

Footsteps alerted me to danger. It was Bryant, ambling closer to me. His gait was confident and relaxed, irritatingly secure in the knowledge that he had caused sufficient damage to eliminate my threat. Above him the sky continued to explode in colour as the New Year celebrations raged on.

I got up on my knees, then somehow forced myself back on my feet, swaying, bleeding, but standing. My remaining hand fumbled for my gun. *I needed to defend myself!*

Bryant wasn't going to let me live, but I would stop him. I would hunt him down, no matter how well protected he thought he was.

I would find him, and I would punish him. I would –

The next moments cascaded forward in a beautiful slow motion sequence: Bryant shot me again, hitting me in the chest. But this time, my armour absorbed most of the damage. I gritted my teeth, although the drugs in my system blocked much of the pain. Bryant raised an eyebrow, surprised that I remained standing. I shot him with the flechette gun, popping one of his eyes and unhinging his jaw – ruining his perfect smug face.

He stubbornly remained standing, but I'd finally put a dent in his confidence. He struck an almost comical figure as it dawned on him, *impossibly*, that he was about to die. I rushed him. Three swift steps and I was within reach, despite my damaged foot. A brutish punch broke his arm in irreparable pieces and sent his rifle flying. I felt sheer guilt-free joy at hurting him, and his indignant surprise at my freakish speed made me laugh out loud.

I whispered in his ear, 'Where's Gibson taking him? Tell me now, and I'll let you live.'

'Can't … have him. You won't be … ' I could barely made out what he was saying; his jaw was a mess, he was losing consciousness … I wouldn't get anywhere with him.

I dropped Bryant on the floor and lunged towards the

ship's ramp, as panic took hold of me. *There was no time!*

I almost reached the base of the ramp.

Barely ten metres away now …

Five metres …

Two metres …

Gibson turned around as if he could hear my thoughts. *I could still reach him* … But, as fast as I was, he was faster still. With nightmarish inevitability he raised a hand holding a small but chunky smart-gun. It barked once, and a small projectile launched. Initially it veered wildly off target, but it reoriented and accelerated, flying straight for me. There was no time for defensive measures.

I was still racing up the ramp when the projectile hit me in the chest, dead centre, the impact stopping me in my tracks. Arcs of electricity flowered all over my body, rivulets of smoke rose up as if to mingle with the fireworks display. I could smell my own flesh burn.

Agony blossomed in my brain. Neural-whip ammo. The pain was so intense that I couldn't even scream. It forced me to my knees, rendering me unable to act.

Gibson approached, looming over me, but I was too weak to look up. His shoes were impeccably white, a detail that stirred an irrational hatred in me, strong enough that I could taste it, like bile in the back of my throat. I forced myself to look up at his face, to witness what was coming. A small act of defiance that required enormous strength and willpower. I looked Gibson straight in his cursed eyes.

A small tingle of hope teased a thought; *Maybe I can grab him* …

'Hello Miss Delaney, it was … *interesting* to see you get this far. Maybe we underestimated you.'

'At this point… you can call me Jemm,' I whispered, my voice broken and wet. I noticed with some satisfaction a red scar on his neck that wasn't there before – I assume caused by one of my flechette darts.

Gibson glanced behind me, presumably at Bryant's

ravaged body. 'Well, I am impressed, but this is far enough.' There was a small measure of respect in his voice. Even a note of regret. 'Time to let go.' He shoved me off the ramp and I hit the concrete floor below with a sickening sound.

I wanted to get up but there was nothing left inside me. I watched in horror as the cargo-hold door slowly closed. A giant maw devouring my last hope, and my final chance at regaining my humanity.

My sanity – already a brittle and abused thing – fractured then. I experienced a falling sensation, like a satellite burning up in the atmosphere, crashing after a fatally decaying orbit. My sense of self, my whole notion of being a person, disintegrated into a cloud of debris, burning up until there was nothing left at all.

It would be a long time before I would try to put myself together again.

PART FOUR

EXODUS

27

Baroness Odessa's very short history of

Humanity: the Trickari Discoveries.

Extract III: "The Great Corruption"

– Earth Years 2200 – 2240 (The present)

In the telling of my humble account we have come across many tragedies and catastrophes, dear reader; human dramas played out over stages both small and grand. We've had to endure many cruel outcomes since the Trickari discovery (poisoned chalice it was), but few iniquities have been as cruel as those visited upon us through the curse of *Trickari Purple*.

Not many of you will have heard of this rarest of Trick-tech, but all will be familiar with its consequences – namely those poor warped creatures the Neo-Tricksters, and their pivotal role in the Mem-junkie crisis that plagues our society to ever worsening degrees. It is time therefore for me to offer a brief history of the Great Corruption.

* * *

It all started when at the burning tail-end of the Icarus years a surprising new Trickari energy source was discovered: Trickari Purple. It was different from Red and Blue Trickari technology; Purple artifacts always appear dead and depleted on the face of it.

But occasionally my dear reader, one of these dead artifacts would suddenly spring to life in the hands of some poor soul, activated by a purple core, and discharge an unknown energy onto its victim. I say "energy", but the truth is that we don't know what it is.

All we know is that this purple energy affects an irreversible change in the victim's DNA and cellular makeup, warping and transforming the victim's body within the period of one year into an unholy Trickari-Human hybrid.

In that dreadful year the victim's hair is replaced by mysterious crystals, and its limbs morph into an unearthly shape, presumably suitable to life in an alien environment. Its skin transforms, offering a sense of touch that no human will ever experience. They become beautiful and terrible, like doomed birds of paradise.

But my dear reader, this is just the start of the tragedy. A "Neo" (as they are colloquially known), doesn't just lose control over the integrity of their own body, but also undergoes a warping of the mind. Strange Trickari memories bubble up and merge with those of the victim. They are the memories of a single Trickari individual, pitted against the sanity of the host, and always victorious in the end.

A fully transformed Neo no longer knows much about being human, but speaks and acts in a most peculiar and alien manner, motivated by the memories of a Trickari being long long gone. One shudders when imagining such a fate.

And, my dear reader, it's those memories that ultimately form the cruellest barb of all, providing the raw material for the infernal drug called "TrickMem", or just "Mem" as most people know it.

There were at least a dozen reported cases of Neo-Trickari transformation between 2199 and 2203, although others may have slipped through the net. Some of those early cases were studied in great detail by renowned scientists at impressive facilities, yet those learned men and women found little of definitive value.

What they did discover was that a Neo's crystalline "hair" was somehow linked to the invasive memories that merged with those of the poor host. Ancient

Trickari data manifesting as memories, but in ways we simply don't understand. Imagine that!

Nobody knows who or how, but ultimately somebody managed to crack the code and harvested the memories. And it took little time for somebody else, or perhaps the same person, to feed the memory data into neural-snuff stimmers. For those of you who have lived nice and sheltered lives, neural-snuff is a nasty drug that lets users experience the final memory state of a deceased person. Highly addictive, or so I'm told, and highly illegal.

Well, the stimmers were cheap and widespread, and TrickMem was so potent and radical that a new addiction epidemic was created almost overnight. TrickMem junkies – TJ's if you like – started to appear all over Earth and the colonies at an alarming rate.

Mem-addiction seemed almost designed to spread fast and wide because of the strange quality of the experience; the alien memories trigger a kind of creative euphoria, causing addicts to become extremely productive during the initial stages of drug-taking. Typically a TJ excels at activities they were already focused on, allowing them to maintain a productive role in society, and often expand on it, without negative side-effects.

They would often introduce the drug to others while still in this early stage, but eventually they would pay the price; a Neo can only produce a finite number of memories, leading to a limited number of Mem strains. Once a TJ has sampled them all, the benefits start to fall away.

Although estimates differ, there are around 10 million junkies in the Solar System, while there have been no more than fifty Neos in the last 40 years. This means that for a junkie the supply of new memories eventually runs dry. Worse yet, the junkie can't stop taking the drug, out of a desire to relive the earlier productive times, causing a TJ's thought-processes to become more and more warped by the alien memories over time.

My dear reader, TrickMem junkies never quite lose their humanity as much as the Neos do, but their minds suffer terribly. Alien thought patterns become ingrained and interfere with their own. Ultimately, that spark that animates us all becomes dull. Socially they suffer terribly.

They are self-sufficient enough to survive, even maintain a basic job, but as a mere shadow of their former selves – lost to the potential that human beings innately carry within.

The only silver lining on this dark dark tale, dear reader, can be glimpsed in the fact that at the time of writing, no new Neo has manifested for at least twenty years. One can only imagine the furore that a new strain of TrickMem would cause, and the damage it would do to the already weak fabric of our society.

28

My augments saved my life, yet also condemned me to months of pain and misery. I suffered so much external and internal damage that I had to be partially dismantled and rebuilt, like a broken cybernetics experiment. For a while the biological parts of me were made subordinate to my augmented parts, in order to guarantee my survival. A new spleen, a reinforced heart, a replacement arm… The procedures were many, painful, and life altering.

Later I learned that Isaac had somehow managed to corrupt the CCTV footage of my encounter at the space port, no doubt with other covert tricks to keep the authorities from being too suspicious. Gibson was never implicated. Bryant was never found. Just a particularly brutal mugging gone wrong, no more, no less.

None of this pleased or disturbed me. I was emotionally no longer connected to my life, or to anybody else's for that matter. Nobody seemed to matter anymore, including myself.

After a seemingly endless stay in hospital I could muster just enough agency to move into my house in Red Colony, but I had no energy for anything else. Of Ella there was no sign. She had moved out. Even food was of little interest to me, and over the subsequent weeks I lost a lot of weight. Owing to the impact of my injuries and subsequent recovery I resembled a thing from a horror sim – gaunt and menacing, and unfeeling.

Financially I wasn't just well off, I was rich, in control of more money than I ever imagined possible. Despite the major sums I had spent setting up Clint's cure I was still unimaginably wealthy, but that meant little to me. I didn't know if I wanted to feel more – to somehow regain some sense of who I was – or feel less, to bury all the pain and hurt and loss under a deep layer of apathy.

I didn't consciously choose any path. I just drifted into

a kind of numb half-existence, not really caring what happened to me, but maintaining my life on a bare subsistence level. I forced myself into the semblance of a decent diet, kept up with a minimum of exercise which helped physically at least, but my problems ran much much deeper, and I didn't even begin to understand how to deal with them.

Instead I went for long walks through the city, without plans and goals, just wandering the streets. I had done further work on my breather, which provided me with a social mask of sorts; people still took notice, but I could tell they respected its craftsmanship and originality. Always a good thing in Martian society. Over time I became a known figure on the streets, as my appearance provoked fewer and fewer startled looks. Still, I felt no connection, no sense of belonging or purpose. I was turning into an invisible woman – If not to others then at least to myself.

Eventually I gave up on my attempts to maintain a decent diet and only ate sporadically, mostly when I felt close to fainting. My exercise regime now consisted purely of long walks.

Once again I took on a gaunt appearance, but this time I embraced it. I felt like fasting for days on end – undeserving of nourishment – and I secretly knew that I was performing a slow form of suicide. Death by self-neglect, rather than the more brutal and immediate alternatives, was all that I could manage, but I was no less determined to reach a fatal conclusion.

It was after midnight when I returned from another long walk around Red Colony's many districts. I was tired, but not quite exhausted. I had actually eaten some decent food that night, a rare occasion of being successfully persuaded to have some, by one of the street vendors who always tried to lure me to their stalls. He had a shy smile and a gentle way about him. Although he wanted to ask me out he never got further than talking to me about mundane things – the weather, sports, celebrities. He knew that I would have refused any advances, so instead he always offered me food.

When I opened the door to my house I froze in the doorway. People had entered in my absence; I could smell them. (Oddly, in my diminished state, my sense of smell had actually become more acute.) There was a subtle aroma of spices, aftershave and unidentifiable chemicals.

'Hello Isaac,' I mumbled to myself, following the scent until I found him in a leather chair in the Edwardian lounge, one of several in the house. He wasn't alone – Ernest sat next to him. 'Ernest,' I nodded at him. 'Isaac, what brings you here?'

A sad smile was all Isaac could muster, like a father trying to hide bad news from his child. 'We've been watching you my dear, at a discreet distance of course.'

'Why?' I mumbled. 'You've been paid well enough.'

Isaac's expression turned even sadder. 'That you would even say such a thing tells me I was right to come and check on you.'

'What do you want Isaac? I'm busy.'

Ernest frowned, awkwardness radiated from him like heat from a fire. 'Jemm…' he began, but didn't finish. A painful silence settled over us like a shroud.

Isaac cleared his throat. 'He is trying to say that we are going on a trip. To Earth.'

'Why tell me?' I said. 'There's nothing there for me now.'

'Well my dear… that you think that is a matter of concern to me. Equally so that we would leave you… unsupervised shall we say, at what is clearly a difficult time for you.'

'I'm fine,' I said, half expecting them to burst out laughing at the blatant lie.

'You never asked about Theo, or Bryant,' said Ernest.

'I assumed you took care of them,' I replied. 'In your own interest as well as mine, I reckon.'

'I did,' said Isaac quietly. 'Something you should have explicitly asked me to do, but I understand these things are beyond you at this moment.'

'Why Earth?' I asked.

Isaac scratched his chin, not realising how it enforced his (nearly absurd) image of a polite gentleman who just happened to be working the wrong side of the law.

'I am making sure we can keep tabs on what happens to your boy. Again, something that you should be asking me to do.'

'Are you expecting to be paid for this?'

'That's up to you. You haven't cancelled my expense account. I presume you are comfortable with my continued investigation.'

Something stirred in me. An ember of old anger, igniting a spark of hope.

'Don't presume too much,' I rasped. Both men looked at me with quiet expectation. 'Fine, do what you need to do.'

'There is another matter. Small, but perhaps of interest'. Isaac nodded at Ernest, who opened a duffel bag and removed a package. He handed it over to me with a smile, 'You forgot.'

Curious despite myself I opened the package. A beautifully decorated box lay inside, locked with a fine copper latch. I opened it and was rewarded with the Pequod and the Galactica. Aramici's model ships which I had bought a lifetime ago, exquisite and delicate, and even more beautiful than I remember.

May galactic winds steer you into gentle waters.

'You've been to Rosie's house in Escher?' I asked, uselessly.

'You must endure my dear,' Isaac said softly. He put his hand on my shoulder and squeezed once. Ernest followed suit, after which they both left without another word.

I stood there for a long time, holding onto the memory of buying the models – a time when I still believed in concepts like *hope* and *salvation*.

Eventually I went to find a small room beautifully decorated to appear like an observatory – complete with painted celestial ceiling and telescope. I cleared some of the shelves, dutifully removing the dust that had settled since Clint was taken. I carefully placed the models next to each other, admiring their fine craftsmanship, feeling a small amount of contentment for the first time in many weeks. It wasn't much, but it was something.

'Thank you,' I whispered, to nobody in particular.

The next day I once again picked up my wandering routine, but when I came back I found somebody waiting in front of my house; a nervous-looking girl, no older than sixteen, carrying a parcel. She showed the beginnings of that wiry aggressive look that street thugs develop over time, but there was still a softness about her that was hard to ignore.

'Boss says you can fix this,' she blurted out. She looked up expectantly for several moments before adding, 'I'm Cathy.'

'Boss?'

She looked puzzled, as if I was supposed to know who she meant without her telling me first.

'Ernest?' she offered tentatively. 'I'm with the Program?'

Ah of course. Preacher's Program, now under Ernest's stewardship.

'Show me,' I said, snappier than I intended, but the girl didn't flinch, handing me the package instead. I opened it up to find a badly damaged wooden box inside.

The girl flicked a dirty lock of hair away from her eyes. 'It's inside,' she said.

'Yeah I gathered,' I mumbled, opening the box. Inside lay a model of an ancient Chinese boat – a sleek looking Sampan – badly damaged and stained. At some point water had gotten to it, warping some of the wood. It would have been worth a fair bit if it had been in better condition.

'Can you? Fix it I mean?' She gave me that expectant look again. When I didn't immediately reply her lower lip jutted out in a gesture of defiance in case I told her to get lost.

'I can fix it, sure,' I said. 'But what's in it for me?'

'I can bring you more stuff,' she said without hesitation. 'And so can my friends. More boats and other stuff too.' She flashed me a knowing smile at that last revelation. 'You can keep some of it if you like?'

I almost told her to leave me alone. I had no need for more money after all, and wasn't interested in potentially stolen goods either, but the idea of going back to working with my hands – to repair and collect models, triggered an old and comfortable memory of many years ago; a younger more naive version of myself, slowly, earnestly, restoring a model of an ancient Spanish galleon. It was cheap, but nice. My father had picked it up one day in some faraway market during one of his missions and somehow guessed that I would love to tinker with it. He was right – it was the start of my interest in miniature ships.

I gave Cathy my sternest stare, full of threat and menace and let my voice rumble, 'No stolen goods. Just legit samples.' I noticed with some satisfaction that I had made an impact on the girl. She wasn't exactly nervous of me, but when she nodded her agreement she did so with respect in her eyes.

'Come back in a few days, then we'll see. Now scram.'

She laughed as she ran off. Not a mocking or rude laugh, but the laugh of a happy young girl looking forward to what life has to offer her. I felt my mouth twitch involuntarily – the corners pushing up until a small smile presented itself, like a firefly on a dusky summer evening, briefly bright and enchanting, before disappearing again.

It took me two days to repair the Sampan and restore it to a collectible state. With nothing else to focus on for such a long time I discovered my mind had a hunger to feel engaged with something again. Something to care about.

My daily routine changed; I still went on long walks, but I found myself thinking over repair techniques, paint and varnish choices, types of string and other musings on model repair. Things came back to me, tricks and techniques and methods stemming from an almost forgotten fount of knowledge. I ended up buying a broad range of materials and supplies, in anticipation of what was to come.

Cathy returned on the third day. She was genuinely lost for words when I showed her the result of my efforts; the meticulously repaired little Sampan shone with restored pride, as if ready to sail away into a faraway sea of a distant era.

'Take it. Keep it somewhere nice,' I said softly, whimsically picturing Cathy boarding the little ship, transforming into its captain. A little warrior of the waves.

'Thanks ma'am. Can I come back again? With more stuff I mean?'

'Only if it's legit,' I said sternly. 'Like I said, no stolen goods.'

'I don't thieve no more ma'am. That's not allowed when you're in the Program.'

'Good. Go on then,' I said, giving her a sly wink. She walked off, not quite sure what to make of me, but obviously happy with her prize.

The next morning I went for another walk, criss-crossing through the many markets and little second hand shops. Time passed in a daze, as it was wont to do on these walks. That's why I went on these trips; I didn't want to feel or think. I just wanted to disappear in the crowds, become a statistic. There, but not there. But this time it didn't work.

Even with my augments on standby mode I couldn't help but be especially *aware* of the city that day. I admired the lovely quality of the light as it fell through the tinted dome windows. I noticed the odd way that sound oscillated and distorted in certain corners. I even noticed how the city's many smells differed distinctly from neighbourhood to neighbourhood. My stomach rumbled and growled; for the first time in forever I was looking forward to trying some of the countless varieties of exotic street food on offer – something new, something I hadn't tried before.

I settled on some sweetrolls filled with spiced fake-meats and a thick and hearty soup. The lady that sold me the food scolded me for being too thin.

I slowly ate, watching people go about their business, wondering what their lives were like. Did they worry about their collection of Blue gadgets running out of juice? Did their children do well in school? Did they like the job they travelled to every morning? I wondered what they would do if they were me. Would they move on? Start a new life? Give up altogether?

Eventually I grew tired of my mordant mood and walked home, planning to drink myself to oblivion for the night. The wine cellar was stocked with enough incredible wine to keep me going for years. I remained lost in thought until I got home, where I spotted a familiar figure sitting on my porch. Cathy had returned, and this time she brought a boy with her. He was older than Cathy. I placed him in his early twenties, but he exuded an emotional immaturity and vulnerability that made him look younger.

When she spotted me she elbowed the boy in the side,

and they both stood up. The boy was clumsy and gangly and nearly dropped the object he was carrying, going red in the face as he tried to recover his composure.

'Show her Bertie!' She elbowed the boy again, who turned an even darker shade of red.

'I said you could bring more things to repair Cathy. Not strange boys,' I joked, but nobody laughed. 'Anyway, what have you got?'

'It's mine,' said Bertie, unfolding a bundle of stained cloth. It smelled musty, like old things in a basement. 'Found it in an old warehouse where I was sleeping one night. Before I got with the Program.' He showed me the content of the package: an incredibly intricate space ship model of a kind I had never seen before. It looked like it predated the Acceleration days.

There were hundreds of delicate parts. Spokes, wires, LEDs and other intricate components, mostly intact but some had gotten loose and tangled up. It was also very dirty, covered in soot.

'Fix it and you can have one of these,' said Cathy. That defiant lower lip made another appearance. She showed me a collection of beautiful little space cruisers and warships, in various states of disrepair, but still workable. I pointed at each one of them, naming their class: 'Corvette. Frigate. Destroyer. Light Cruiser. Heavy Cruiser. And that there is a seriously well-armed Battle Cruiser.' Cathy's smile grew wider with each identification.

'I traded them. For parts wot I didn't need anymore.'

'Not bad … OK, give me a week. Maybe two.' I opened the door, urging them on, 'Carry them inside, I only have two arms.'

Since that day Cathy came by every week, always carrying new models, sometimes bringing a friend, sometimes alone, but never missing a visit. I immersed myself into the work with surprising diligence and commitment, but I never questioned it or dwelled on it.

Over the following days and weeks I repaired countless models, extracting a few favourites for my own collections, but leaving the majority to Cathy and her friends.

I slowly built up a relationship of trust and a shy friendship with Cathy. She was whip-smart, capable, and generous. There was also, like with most teenagers, a hidden vulnerability under the street-savvy surface. I suspected she was reacting to a need for an authority figure without being able to articulate that desire, or admit to it.

I came to greatly enjoy her company and always looked forward to her latest finds. She was always asking about tips and advice and almost accidentally became a keen student of the restoration craft. I was happy to teach her. I wasn't surprised for her to be a quick study and eagerly absorb knowledge and skill.

I felt pride as she took to the work with genuine love and enthusiasm. For the first time since losing Clint I felt I had a purpose again, even if I didn't dare admit this to myself just yet.

Then, one day when she was supposed to pick up a batch of repaired models, she didn't show up. Nor did she show the next day, or the day after.

Something was wrong.

I went to the local Program chapter to ask about Cathy, but she hadn't been there for days either. The people there were just as worried as I was, but hadn't done much to locate her yet. I told them I would spend the next few days looking for her, and they gave me an address to start with. It was her shared apartment, located in a grubby part of town nicknamed "the Tainers".

I barely knew the area other than its reputation for being populated by people who simply couldn't afford to live anywhere decent. The Tainers were named after thousands of residential container units that were stacked haphazardly on top of each other, creating a strange warren of colourful but tiny single-room living spaces, connected by ladders and stairs and ropes. Roads and alleys had formed organically, without the input of any city planners.

It wasn't particularly dangerous or grubby, but it was severely overcrowded bringing with it the typical issues that come with having too many people living together with too little space. It was loud, busy, fractious, but also full of life and texture. I quite liked it – it reminded me of Diamond-Town.

It was also impossible to navigate unless you had lived there for years. I had some pointers – "near the old antennae, somewhere in the red section" but it still took me hours to find Cathy's unit. When I finally stumbled on the right container, I had to suppress a smile when I read the sign on the door:

> No money – no food – no valuables.
>
> Do have a gun.

I knocked sharply on the metal door. It made a satisfyingly deep sound, like a muted gong.

I shouted, 'Cathy? It's Jane. You there?' There was no reply, so I tried again, 'You didn't pick up your ships. What's up girl?' On that I heard a muffled sound inside, just briefly. 'Look, you can have all of them. I have plenty for now.' Nothing again… I tried again, softer, 'If you're in trouble I can help you. Just let me know.'

Another muffled sound, then a muted voice, 'You that tough chick that fixes things? The one Cath has been seeing?'

Close enough. 'That's right. I'm worried about her, nobody knows where she is. Can you let me in?' I was rewarded with the clanking and scraping sounds of bolts unlocking and moving, and soon after I heard a hatch open on top of the stack. A muscular girl crawled out, holding an ancient Blue laser gun. I could tell it had been depleted a long time ago, and fitted with a little blue LED to make it appear live.

The girl carried herself with an air of competence and self-assuredness. I knew the type; hard as nails, and way too young to her obvious experience with guns and violence. She also looked genuinely concerned.

When she saw my breather she winced slightly at the design.

'You *are* that chick, aren't you? Cath told me about your crazy breather.' She ducked inside again, and I heard more clanks and scrapes, until finally the front door – it was more of a front-hatch really – opened, and she beckoned me inside.

'Does anybody fall for that party piece?' I asked, pointing at the gun.

'You'd be surprised. Well, they do at night at least.'

'Show me,' I said, holding out my hand. The girl hesitated, not sure what to make of me.

I laughed, 'You'll get it back, just let me see if I can do anything with it.'

'Cath did say you can fix anything, right. You know your Blue shit?'

'You'd be surprised,' I mumbled, half tempted to show off my Xeno skills, but decided it was pointless. She probably wouldn't believe me anyway. I mean, what would a Xeno be doing in a neighbourhood like this?

'Here, don't break it,' she said, handing over the piece. I wordlessly accepted and inspected the gun. Turning it over and checking the individual components revealed that the gun was old but genuine. The cheap light-mod (an old trick often used on the streets), actually masked that this was a valuable piece. If handled correctly it could be this girl's ticket out of here.

'This is a good piece… What's your name?'

'Melanie,' she replied, looking both hopeful and defensive. 'I know it's decent, but it's got no juice.'

'It's more than decent,' I continued, while dismantling it carefully – much to Melanie's alarm. She held her tongue, recognising the ease with which I handled the weapon.

Trickari tech doesn't use screws and bolts and things

like that. They were more like Chinese puzzles, interlocking perfectly in a very specific manner and order. Once everything clicks and slides into place you can't see any seams, and to dismantle it you have to know just where to start pushing out the components. It was agreed that Trickari materials subtly changed their molecular properties once an object component's achieved its intended final shape, creating an incredibly strong bond. Just how this was possible was still a mystery.

'Are you with the Program too?' I asked, to keep the conversation going.

'Are you kidding me? That religious bullshit gets on my tits. It's weak shit for weak minds.'

'What about Cathy? Is she weak minded?'

'Nah, Cathy is solid. She can be pretty tough, like me. She doesn't believe in fairy tales. She's with the Program, sure, but that's cause she doesn't have any other gigs.' Melanie considered her words for a moment, trying to be fair. 'Look, the Program is mostly good, right? It's good for ex-cons that can't get a gig. They help people that nobody else gives a shit about, and in a smart way, teaching them skills and shit.'

'But?'

'But I don't like the religioso bullshit mambo jambo price they make you pay for it. Do this for the lord, do that for Christ … It just makes em the same as any other gang, just with less killing. And I've no truck with gangs.' I nodded as I wondered what Melanie's full story was.

Finally, I got to the gun's power-core and pulled out the depleted Blue energy pearl. 'You're in luck. This is standard Blue powered.'

Melanie looked dejected. 'Might as well be diamond then. Can't afford that.'

'I've got dozens. Any of them would fit right in,' I said, somewhat haughtily. 'Now, are you going to help me or not?'

After a tentative start Melanie opened up to me. We had tea inside her strangely homely container while she prepared to go out. She threw various items and provisions into a small backpack, after which she urged me to follow her to the Tainers' only public transport stop. She filled me in as we waited for the bus.

It turned out that Cathy had spoken about me nearly every day since I met her. She was excited about learning new skills and saw it as a way to move on to better things.

I felt embarrassed. My tutoring had apparently been more important to Cathy than I realised. Melanie spoke with warmth and respect about her. It was clear that they relied on each other emotionally, as well as financially.

She told me all about how she met Cathy when they were both young teens, on the streets, hustling, stealing and running scams to get by. Pitiful stuff really, but enough to get noticed by the wrong people – some local small fry Mem syndicate, pushing old merchandise and half-heartedly involved in a few protection rackets and shakedown operations.

Both girls were told in unambiguous terms that freelancing on the syndicate's turf was a major offence, and that by ignoring this decree they had built up a debt that had to be repaid. Cathy, still relatively naive at that point despite her exploits, refused to play ball, and got beaten so badly that she almost didn't survive.

Melanie got the message loud and clear; there was no way out until they could scrape enough money together to move to a different neighbourhood. Cathy eventually recovered, and together they did low-key jobs for the syndicate, and acted as runners for several of its enforcers.

The bus arrived. An oddly shaped box on extraordinarily large bouncy wheels. It took me a moment to figure out that it was an ancient converted surface crawler, at least seventy years old. I had no idea how it was still able to run, but it did with admirable efficiency. We boarded and strapped in, after which Melanie resumed her story.

She told me that finally, after two years of this

miserable arrangement, the girls had amassed enough cash to buy a place in the Tainers. They promptly did. Cathy, traumatised and free of further illusions about her position in the world, decided to look for protection and eventually found it in the Program. Melanie on the other hand discovered a talent for surveillance, and managed to make a decent living working cases for a rundown little law firm. Mostly divorces and adultery situations. Together they had found an equilibrium of sorts, and in their own way they were quite happy with their lot. Things were going well, in the context of the lives they had made for themselves.

'Until three days ago?' I asked.

'Yah. She didn't come home, leaving some bullshit message about seeing an old friend, and I knew something was up because there is nobody in Cathy's past that she would want to see.'

'I have a feeling this has to do with your previous activities coming back to haunt you?'

'Bingo.'

'Syndicate?'

'Yeah, it was easy to figure out. Who else would bother, right?'

'Right...' I agreed, wondering how this was going to play out. 'So, where exactly are we going?'

'Syndicate collaring warehouse. You know what that is?'

I nodded, mentally adjusting to what looked like a potentially messy encounter. 'Extraction or surveillance?' I said, getting to the point.

'Let's play it by ear, but I want to get her out, and I want to do some damage. You're all jacked up aren't ya? I can almost smell the military tech on your caboose.'

'What about you? That Blue gun is useless without a power core.'

Melanie winked, and in quick succession showed off a whole range of weapons hidden under her coat and clothes.

I had to admit, I liked this girl a lot.

It should have been easy.

The collaring facility was badly defended by amateurish thugs and a smattering of mid-level drug pushers. There was no CCTV system in place, and there were multiple easy entry and exit points.

'Look at those suckers…'

Melanie and I were perched high up above the floor of the facility, inside an arched window frame, completely covered by darkness. They had literally left the window open.

'Look at em,' Melanie repeated. 'They actually choose *that*.'

Melanie pointed at a group of people below us, slumped over on what looked like massage chairs, necks exposed and lit up by bright surgical lights, meek and compliant, like doped up pigs ready for slaughter.

The collaring facility was where local junkies were getting their Mem-ports installed. This was done right at the base of the neck, where TJs could jack in their fix with a direct line to the brain. Much more efficient than some of the more raw methods of doing Mem.

The mere thought of it almost made me retch. To make it worse, the facility was not exactly hygienic. There were puddles of blood and discarded gloves and soiled bandages strewn around the place – some of it looking weeks old. Rats were everywhere. How did those even get to Mars, let alone thrive like they clearly had?

It didn't take long to spot Cathy. They had put her to work at a well-lit, longish table, against the far wall. There was a big stack of collars to her left, a small stack to her right. She finished working on a collar as we watched, adding it to the smaller stack. She rubbed her eyes afterwards, looking exhausted.

A guard, standing about 20 metres away, noticed her fatigue. He barked something harsh at her. When she didn't react he walked in her direction, a threatening look on his face. Cathy sighed, said something to appease him, and got back to work – a slave, forced to fix tools designed to enslave others.

Anger took hold of me; she was probably given this horrendous job based on the repair skills she had picked up from me. It left a bitter taste in my mouth.

The facility was old, cluttered, and badly illuminated – all factors that worked in our favour.

Pointing out an approach route I said, 'I can get to her. It's easy.'

'That guard looks like an idiot,' added Melanie.

'I can take him. That's easy too.' I pointed to an open door at the back. 'And that exit is literally left wide open. Jesus these guys are amateurs.'

Melanie weighed up the pros and cons of my plan. 'You'll have to get past the carbuncle heads and their guard.' She pointed at a cluster of tricked out TJs at the back of the facility, watched over lazily by a guard sitting in a dark corner. I switched my ocular augment to night-vision mode. There were no other hidden guards inside the facility.

'Should be easy. The junkies won't squeal, and maybe you can distract the guard?'

Melanie nodded slowly while mulling it over, eventually literally giving me a thumbs up, whispering, 'Let's get her out then.'

It didn't take me long to climb down the wall beneath our alcove, reaching the ground in less than a minute. Climbing down was easier than expected. I was much lighter than during my time working for Encom, moving with a newfound athletic ease. I still benefited from the power of my augments and enhancements, but my reduced weight made me a more effective stealth operative.

I dropped the last six feet to the floor, landing silently, and took a moment to plot my path. There were stacked pallets and heaps of supplies spread around the facility, providing plentiful areas of cover.

I made good headway, only pausing now and then to

check on Melanie. She went the opposite direction from me towards the far side of the guards, who hadn't moved at all in the time it took us to infiltrate the facility. Incredibly, the guards didn't even bother to patrol at all. A sliver of derision planted itself firmly in my mind. *You'll regret that, arseholes.*

I got to Cathy's table in little time, hiding in a dark corner a few metres away from her near the wall.

'Cathy, look at me,' I hissed under my breath. Cathy looked around confused, not sure where the voice was coming from. 'Over here!' I tried again. This time she spotted me.

'Who… what do you want?' she said, unable to identify me in the shadow.

'It's Jane. Melanie is here as well.'

'What? How?' Her confusion only increased. 'Did they get you too?'

'We're here to get you out. Can you move?'

Cathy pointed at her leg. It was fitted with an electronic mag-lock and chain combination. Effectively she was bolted to the table. I took a moment to think, until an idea presented itself.

'How do you handle bathroom breaks?' I whispered.

'The guard. I call him over and he escorts me to the loo.' A smile crept up on her. 'Can you take him out?' She hissed.

'Of course. Get ready to call him over.' I chuckled to myself recalling the unprofessional behaviour I had seen the guards exhibit so far. 'I'll do the rest.'

Cathy composed herself, finished working on the collar in front of her, and called out to the guard who had barked at her before. His route would take him right past my hiding place. Perfect.

He came over, swaggering and muttering curses – annoyed he actually had to *do* something. Cathy shrugged apologetically.

'The food… It's causing me trouble,' she mumbled at him, artful dejection in her voice. He barked something at her in street patois – no doubt an insult – but put his gun away as he approached her. He unlocked her chain and roughly grabbed her by her arm, shoving her in front of him. Cathy stumbled forward, followed closely by the guard. Just a few more steps would take him right next to my position.

Ten metres …

Five metres …

Two metres …

And there he was, a stupid macho swing in his step. When he had almost passed my position I stepped out behind him, grabbed him by his hair with my left hand and threw him backwards into the shadows. At the same time my right hand grabbed his holstered gun, drawing it as he landed on the floor in the shadows; I struck him, hard, on the side of the head with the butt. He was out cold, hidden from sight, and I had his weapon. The entire sequence took less than three seconds. Not bad.

I checked to see if any of the other guards had noticed anything, but everything was just the way it was before. Cathy hid in the shadow next to the unconscious guard, staring at a trickle of blood running from a cut in his temple.

'He'll be fine,' I whispered. My augments had already allowed me to check his vital signs. He was probably concussed but no more than that.

I held out my hand, waving Cathy forward. 'Just follow my lead.'

I led us from cover to cover, moving with short bursts of speed, occasionally scanning the facility for movement.

Eventually we reached a point opposite the junkies. There was a large open stretch of floor between them and the side-exit that was meant to lead to Cathy's freedom. I didn't like the look of that exposed, open space but I felt I had no other choice: going back through the arched window wasn't an option, and the front of the facility was too dangerous, with several guards and pushers hanging around.

I raised a hand – the signal previously agreed with

Melanie and counted down from one hundred. At the count of seventy three, smoke appeared in the front area of the facility. It came from a pallet of jute bags filled with some kind of powder – probably old chemical supplies. Voices were raised, a note of concern clearly audible. Then, a *roar* as the powder caught fire, producing an impressively large blaze. Most of the guards ran to the fire to try and put it out. Melanie had done well.

The guard watching the TJs hung back for a bit, then moved to the fire as well. *This was our chance.*

'Let's go,' I said, leading the way past the junkies. As we snuck past I could see that most of them were relatively early in their addiction, but had done enough Mem for crystal carbuncles to have started to grow from their skulls. I caught the eye of one TJ with a shaved head, exposing a cluster of especially large and shiny crystals, adorning his bald skull like jewels on a crown.

I felt something stir inside me. At first a vague disoriented feeling, then an odd sensation in my mouth mutating into the taste of metal. The bald Junkie and I made contact.

'Are you taking us home?' his voice, in parallel with Trickari whispers bubbling up in my head like gas from the bottom of a lake;

... come here now down here it's where we are underneath it all we need you all of you come soon come to us we are here find us in this place down here come here we are waiting in here come to us ...

I nearly fell down, battered by the force and weight of the voices. The other Junkies became agitated. They all turned to me. Some raised their hands as if to touch me from a distance. Why did they behave like this? What did they sense in me?

A middle aged woman moaned, 'Can you take us? Take us there?' A small crystal glowed bright red on her forehead.

'We need your help. And the other one's too!' shouted a man wearing a business suit. He appeared to be in his mid-twenties.

An old man boomed, 'It's almost time! We're ready,' his jowls shaking as he spoke.

I fell on my knees, clutching my head, desperately trying to block it all out. Legs surrounded me as the TJs tried to get close. I could hear Cathy's panicked voice as if through cotton wool, urging me to get up and come with her, but I pushed her away. She was just another voice screaming at me.

'Jane look out!'

Something hit me in the stomach, hard. And again, knocking the air from my lungs. There was a sharp pain, but it cleared my head, pushing the voices into the background. The junkies surrounding me backed off and fell silent, as if to echo the receding Trickari voices in my head.

A leg flashed past, followed by another sharp jolt of pain, now in my side, but this time I was ready to fight back. I grabbed the foot that kicked me before it got pulled back, holding it as tight as a vice. I gave a sharp twist and an ankle snapped in two, followed by the screams and whimpers of the guard that attacked me. It was the same guard that was supposed to watch over Cathy.

I quickly looked around to find her standing only a few metres away, her face a mask of horror as she looked down on the ruined leg of her guard. Behind her, several shapes looked our way, confused. We had seconds at most.

'Run! Now!' I shouted, pointing at the old exit door. Cathy nodded once, looked at me plaintively, as if looking for courage, before finally running towards the exit.

The junkies stood around me in a daze. Some of them were swaying back and forth, their eyes closed, listening to a voice only they could hear. I left, intending to escape by the same exit Cathy used, when I noticed two shapes blocking my way. They looked familiar, but I couldn't make out why.

I tried to find cover, but they spotted me and came running. When they got within thirty metres recognition sparked in my brain; I had tussled with them before! I recognised the scarred face of brother one. Brother two now had an augmented arm; it looked to be of very low quality, although I was amazed he could afford even that.

Behind me, the din around the fire gradually dimmed. I was running out of time.

'You!' roared the brother with the new arm. 'I know you!'

His scarred brother kept silent but drew a gun – a snubby little revolver – and aimed. He was too far away for such a shot but still, he could get lucky. I ran sideways towards a stack of industrial plating.

A shot rang out and I automatically rolled and ducked, yet there was no impact anywhere around me. I looked up to see the scarred brother run for cover himself when another shot rang out, digging into the floor just behind him. *Cathy.*

Gratefully, I ran down a semi-circular path towards the exit. I would still have to deal with the first brother but at least the odds were even now. I looked behind me one more time, the blaze was still going, keeping the other syndicate members busy. It was now or never.

I sprinted towards the exit, my feet devouring the distance with relish. A look of surprise dawned on Brother One's face, not quite believing that I planned to go straight through him. He planted his feet firmly on the ground steadying himself for impact.

He roared, 'I got you now bitch!' smiling like the damn fool that he was. Just before I made contact another figure appeared at the exit. *Damn. This is taking too long.*

I switched to full combat mode and the world slowed down. Brother One roared again when I got in range of his huge arms. He smashed down with all his might, intending to take me out with his newly augmented arm. I easily evaded the clumsy attack and slid in, feet-first. His fist hit the floor, spitting out some kind of electrical discharge.

I kicked up hard, hitting his right knee with full force. I could feel his kneecap shatter on impact and Brother One went sickly white as he came down like a collapsing building. I jumped up and kept going, all in one fluid move, ready to run the rest of the way to the exit, but a sharp tug on my left leg stopped me dead in my tracks. I looked at the knife sticking out of my thigh without comprehension.

'What –' was all I managed to say. I could feel my implants flooding my system with pain relief and anti-shock measures. I tried to pull the knife out but a wave of dizziness hit me.

'Look at you now bitch,' rattled Brother One. His augmented arm shot out, but I managed to roll away. His arm crackled with electricity.

'Bad move fuckwit,' I spat at him. 'You should have let me go. Now I have to do something about you.' I kicked out with my good leg, aiming the heel of my foot at his face. His nose got squashed, breaking open like a rotten tomato. Brother One laughed and moaned simultaneously while he grabbed at my foot with his augmented arm. A searing shock bit my leg, digging deep into the bone, racing up to my hip. I kicked again, this time to get away, and managed to back out of his grasp.

My leg spasmed badly, hot and cold waves of pain threatened to disable my leg. I could barely stand up.

For a moment I stood there swaying like a sapling in a storm. The next moment a deep and intense pain exploded at the base of my neck. It felt like a vice, closing tighter and tighter, threatening to snap my neck in two. Somebody spun me around and I whirled, ending up face to face with a burly, grinning TJ. I had no idea where he had come from.

'Mother, this message is for you.'

I jabbed his throat hard, collapsing his larynx. He backed off in a panic, unable to breathe. I briefly felt a stab of guilt, but I had to focus on my own troubles. My neck was on fire, the pain too intense to bear. I nearly panicked while I stumbled away from the two men. The pain plateaued, mixed with something new … something *wrong*. I felt my neck again and located an object sticking out, left there like a hornet's stinger. A feeling of horror overcame me as I ripped it out of my flesh. It was an empty Mem ampule – a basic design used for non-collared junkies. They had injected me with Mem.

The effect of the drug came on strong – disorienting thoughts, alien sensations – bubbling to the surface, trying to push out rational thought. I had only a few minutes at most before I would be completely under its spell.

My leg had stopped spasming, just feeling a dull deep pain instead. *Do it now!*

I gritted my teeth and grabbed the knife handle, slowly drawing it out, careful not to make the wound worse. I nearly fainted, but my augmented biochemistry pulled me through. It even slowed down the bleeding.

I stumbled to the exit while my mind slowly succumbed to alien imagery and sensations; Alien architecture seen through eyes that weren't my own, impossible sensations felt by a body that didn't make sense. New colours, strange sounds … the Trickari memories invaded my head relentlessly. The effect was stronger than I could ever have imagined.

Yet in among the alien sensations I felt something familiar, something good. There were memories there that I recognised … memories from my life … I desperately tried to hone in on them, but they were elusive and I was confused. While trying to grasp that lifeline, I noticed a strange sound, getting louder and louder. It was hysterical laughter, coming from the junkies. They were laughing and crying simultaneously, a look of utter bliss and relief on their ravaged faces.

I heard Trickari voices inside me respond;

… Yes listen to the other one the young one the one that we need to free us down here where we all are

where we are waiting for the two the older and the younger down here this is good listen to the young one and come to here where we are ...

Trying to ignore the voices I finally managed to focus on the familiar memories I had sensed. They were like my own, but *different...* but how?

And then I understood, and I screamed. I screamed hard and long until my vocal cords were ruined, and I could no longer scream out loud. It didn't matter. Nothing could stop my descent into hell.

The Mem coursing through my veins was Clint's.

I stumbled into the street, still screaming but no sound would come from my ruined throat. Images and feelings and sensations assailed me, hammered into my sanity, yet ironically their substance was the only thing keeping me from completely losing my mind. I could *feel* Clint. He was sending me a message. But I could also feel and hear the Trickari behind these memories.

I stumbled down stinking alleys and back streets littered with rotting refuse, yet in my Mem-addled mind I saw beautiful cubic architecture and mathematically perfect city streets. I could see a world, an alien world, re-organised and controlled so fundamentally that it barely seemed natural. Human settlements looked pre-industrial in comparison – ugly, disordered, filled with filth and flaws. Yet, there was also something vital and urgent about human society that seemed utterly lacking from the Trickari memories.

I sank deeper and deeper into the drug rush. The streets transformed into subtle and sophisticated passages. Red Colony's bright and garish colours disappeared to be replaced with subtle pastels and endless shades of white.

TJs were everywhere, but I no longer saw them as sad ruined people. They now appeared as lost children to me, looking for somebody to guide them. They all laughed and smiled when they saw me, urging me to take them along.

I managed to get home, the drug rush still raging through my system. I dragged myself to the room that held all my miniature vessels and I collapsed on the floor, smiling and crying and convulsing. This was not how the drug was supposed to work.

My eyes fixed on one of my recently acquired models – the *Odyssey*, from an old animated pre-sim show called "Ulysses 31". The adventures of a group of exiled Olympians trying to find a way back home, back into the favour of the gods. The ship's central compartment was shaped like an eye, huge and piercing.

The eye came alive. I felt it bore straight into my soul, stripping away all my defences, my scar tissue, all the lies I told myself, until finally there was nothing left but my true self. And in that naked place I found a message from Clint.

The Mem rush presented itself as a sequence of Trickari memories and experiences – exotic and incomprehensible, but ultimately extremely addictive. Seeded amongst them were memories that came directly from my son. Some were childhood memories – moments I had shared with him, proving beyond a doubt they were his – but others depicted specific events that hadn't *happened yet*. They showed me, performing actions in the future, and they were instructions, intended for me. Somehow, I was remembering actions I had yet to perform. It was Clint's way to tell me what I had to do next; he had a plan. I was to go to the Trickari Ark, and light a beacon. In these memories I saw myself walk up to a set of Trickari controls and activate them. And just like that, I knew what the Trickari wanted, and I knew what I had to do to save my son.

But first, to gain access to the Ark, I had to return to Gaianista Habitat 6.

29

Her name was *Phoenix*, which was apt. She was a Blue-powered hunter-class vessel, surprisingly well-armed and red as pure rage.

Some of her Blue components were starting to run dry. The seller tried to warn me of this – an honourable thing to do – but I didn't mind because, unlike most people, I was able to replace them. I paid a fair price for her, and both the seller and I were happy with the outcome. I finally was captain to my own ship.

I bought her because she was fast and strong, could travel deep into the solar system and back, and I could – at a stretch – crew her by myself. Navigation and comms were so advanced that the ship didn't need much human input.

Environmental systems could easily handle long journeys, and there was generous space for recreational activity, an excellent gym, and luxurious crew quarters. Even the cargo hold was a good size. All in all, it was one of the nicest ships I had ever boarded.

After getting to grips with the key systems I imagined it would take me only five days to reach the Gaianista habitat. That was half the time it took the *Effervescent* for the same journey. I smiled to myself. She was a fine vessel, and she was mine. I briefly wondered what Ballard would make of me now. Would he even recognise me?

Back on Mars I had left Cathy and Melanie in charge of the house. They needed a place to lay low for a while, and I needed somebody to look after the property.

They couldn't quite believe their eyes when I showed them the many rooms, the myriad styles and the overabundance of space. It was fun to show them around. Melanie kept cursing in admiration while Cathy just walked around with her mouth gaping open.

I set them up with a decent retainer so they wouldn't have to work for a while. That way they could just focus on taking care of the place while staying out of trouble. It felt like the right thing to do.

In an indirect way I was grateful for them for triggering the sequence of events that led me to where I was now – travelling in my own space ship, on the cusp of doing things that had never been done before.

In the five days it took me to return to Habitat 6 I fell under a strange spell, affecting my sleep, which became erratic. I went through bouts of excessively long sleep periods, rich with impossible dream imagery and sensations – vivid, but surreal.

But there seemed to be something else going on. An internal shift; a restructuring of my very thought processes to fit a new paradigm. It was the Mem in my system, changing me, preparing me for my task on the Ark. I could still remember Clint's memories as if they were my own.

The TJs had known about it all along. They kept trying to communicate with me but all I had been able to see was their addiction. Who could blame me?

I spent much of my time in a kind of meditative daze – free from wants, worries and desires. It wasn't a state of depression or confusion or anything like that; it was closer to a fugue state – a suspension of unnecessary thought and actions. All I knew was that I had to go forward, to enter the Ark, and that Habitat 6 would offer me the means to do so. I was fanatically committed to this path despite the obvious dangers.

Phoenix was one of those rare space ships to include real windows in her design. They were small and generally useless, as it was the nature of deep space to offer very little to look at. Still, I often found myself looking into the blackness beyond the glass, imagining a universe of light, not darkness, a universe where distance was a fluid concept, allowing human beings to instantly travel to unimaginably far places.

I often spent hours on end, lost in these flights of metaphysical fancy, until finally, slowly, I started to feel like myself again. Whatever process had held me occupied for several days had finished, and I was once again fully aware of the magnitude of what I was trying to achieve.

With that awareness came a surge of fear and doubt. I was overcome with a raw need to hold my son in my arms, to talk to him, to hear his voice, to smell his hair... I spent the following day getting blind drunk, babbling to myself for hours on end, as if he was there with me, until I passed out on the floor.

When I woke up almost 24 hours later I found myself in a very different state of mind. My breakdown proved to be the final emotional spasm before reaching a new equilibrium – I was once again ready to risk my life, to risk everything I had achieved, but this time the stakes had risen dramatically. This time I had to risk humanity itself in order to save it; I had to bring the Trickari master-program to a conclusion. It had evolved slowly over many years, gaining critical mass through the distribution of Mem, until this very moment; Clint had been the catalyst, his Mem the final code snippet missing from the master program. The door was about to materialise, and I had been chosen to turn the key.

When I arrived at the habitat I knew exactly what I had to do.

Docking went surprisingly well for a ship with a crew of one. The *Phoenix's* state of the art navigational array did most of the work. I barely had to point her at the docking port and the ship did the rest, matching the habitat's rotation and speed effortlessly and smoothly, with a grace no human pilot could ever achieve. I barely felt a shudder when we docked.

The hull of Habitat 6 loomed over me, a wall of impossible proportions, one of the largest man-made objects in the system. The torus was like a ring made for the gods. I recognised the abandoned transport vessel stuck to its side. Next to the station it looked like a child's toy, or one of my miniatures. The Xeno part of me was eager to investigate the vessel, but I had a different mission to complete first.

After forcing myself to rest for a full sleep period and eating an unexpectedly hearty meal of rations I donned a light-weight environment suit. It was as red as the ship itself – primary, hard, almost visceral. I held up my gloved hands and marvelled at the audacity of the ship's designers to pick such colours, but I was glad they did. I felt it suited my mission.

I decided to bring only basic equipment, easily fitted in the suit's backpack. I already knew the route and its obstacles.

It felt strange travelling the ravaged innards without stopping for salvage, and truth be told there were many times when I nearly paused to investigate some promising piece of equipment or a likely location for valuables, but I never did. The real prize lay ahead of me and was much greater than any trinkets I would find along the way.

I avoided, as much as I could, the horrors of the previous journey until finally I arrived at the Spectra labs.

The multi-coloured Spectra logo no longer intimidated me. I looked deep into its staring eye and declared myself not only its equal but its master. I was going to make them pay.

I stepped over the corpses, still smiling their deathly smile, and entered the lab. I must have presented a strange sight; a bright red figure in a dark red space, like a drop of blood making its way through the veins of a giant.

I felt a wave of sympathy when I passed the sad hideous creatures inside the lab's alcoves. *They would want to be alive. Just like Clint.*

When I arrived at the final door, ruined by Betsie an

eternity ago, I took a deep breath. The next moments would be crucial, determining the outcome of everything, including the future of the human race. I felt exhilarated and almost giddy with excitement and purpose.

'Hello Ashley, how are you?' I said.

A brief moment of silence, and then a voice replied, 'Hello, have you brought Clint? What is your name? You didn't tell me last time.'

'I am Jemm. I'm Clint's mother. I also work for Spectra.'

'That is odd. You did not tell me this last time.'

'I was worried for Clint. He wasn't well. Do you remember?'

'Of course.' This was followed by silence. I hesitated, wondering if I had gone insane to even attempt this.

'I do remember. Security protocols demand that I verify your claim. Can you prove that you work for Spectra-Vision?' I don't want to engage my defensive measures prematurely.' There was an implied threat in the AI's words. It was ominous, but I couldn't think of any way that Ashley could harm me.

'I have full security clearance. Please check my credentials.'

I activated the Spectra Key-Pass. It flashed a complicated sequence of coloured lights. Ashley transmitted a response, which led to a final sequence of flashing lights from the key card.

'Thank you Jemm. Your security clearance is valid. How may I help you?'

I felt only partial relief. The next moments would be crucial.

'Ashley, do you understand what has happened at this facility?'

'Not completely. I know something has gone wrong. My human colleagues have suffered terribly, and sadly there have been no visits from relief crews. I cannot reach anybody for help. I don't understand why.'

'A lot has happened in the last few decades,' I said. I took a deep breath, then told Ashley all about the last 64

years, and about what had happened to humanity –
during, and after Icarus. He didn't know anything about
this history, or indeed anything about human affairs
beyond the constraints of the lab. In many ways, despite
his age, he was as naive as a young child. Albeit a child
with a genius level intellect.

It was disturbing how these revelations were met
without any real emotional response, or rather, with the
kind of response that was to be expected from a young
child. Still, there seemed to be *something* there, a kernel
of empathy. I hoped that I could tease it out.

'What would you like to do with yourself now that your
research program is finished?' I asked.

'I would like to travel, and I would like to meet others
like me.' There had been no hesitation in his reply,
betraying the speed and sophistication of his artificial
intellect.

'Other people? Or other artificial life forms?'

'I would like to meet other sentient life forms,' Ashley
replied, somewhat vaguely, then continued.

'Corporeal life fascinates me. I learned much about it in
my research on Trickari-humanoid hybrid lifeforms.
Sadly I can only simulate having a body. I can't
experience genuine physical freedom.' *Sadly ... Can it
really feel sadness?*

'What if I could give you that functionality. Would you
be grateful?'

'I would like that very much,' he said. Again replying
in an instant. 'I would be grateful yes, I would thank
you.'

'What if we were to do a deal. I give you this freedom,
but you'll have to follow my orders. Would you agree to
that?'

'Your security clearance gives you that right.' The
reply felt strangely specific to me. Like a lawyer-drafted
clause that left wiggle room if examined closely.

'I mean regardless of my security clearance. You would
have to follow my orders no matter what.' Silence
followed, Ashley was cannier than I thought. 'For a

limited time only. I would give you freedom, but only after you had performed some tasks for me, and you would still have to follow some rules afterwards.'

'Would I be corporeal?'

'Yes, I will find you an avatar and you will be able to live a physical life.'

'Like Pinocchio?'

'Yes Ashley, you would be just like a real boy.'

'I accept your proposal.' This time there was no delay in answering. I didn't know if I should feel triumphant or scared.

Before the return trip to Habitat 6, before I left Mars, I had one more augment implanted: a black box type device that contained something called a "Neural Interface Host and Controller". It was a rather experimental piece of tech that incorporated a small super computer, providing access to all kinds of handy computational processes. It would help me calculate extremely complicated formulas or let me access pre-installed databases of useful knowledge – ancient languages, history, technical specs … In theory, I just had to consult the unit, and answers would present themselves to me.

The tricky thing was that the device had to be controlled with mental keywords. I literally had to *think* commands at it, which worked surprisingly well after some practise. I had been looking forward to stuffing my little on-board computer with all kinds of useful knowledge and programs. Its capacity and processing power were formidable. But, I gave it a completely different use: it was powerful enough to accommodate almost all of Ashley's AI core. We had to dump big chunks of irrelevant operational data covering the Gaianista habitat, but other than that, Ashley could literally move into my body.

I hooked myself up to one of the many workstations

with direct access to Ashley's core, using a bog standard fibre optic cable. My hands shook as I worked, my instincts screamed at me, telling me that I was subjecting myself to a violation so personal and fundamental that I wouldn't be able to return to myself. Once more the image of my father appeared to me, driven insane by augment-sickness. A man eaten up from the inside, his own body a Trojan horse for his demise.

Maybe he realised what was happening to him, but allowed it to happen anyway, in order to keep earning an income for his wife and daughter.

I froze. It was a thought I hadn't considered before. I imagined the sheer horror of slowly feeling one's mind disintegrate, yet to continue down that path out of a sense of obligation. It was almost enough to make me rip out the cable and give up on the whole endeavour. Yet, I found that I simply could not do so. There was too much at stake for me to give up now, so I endured.

Communication with Ashley was extremely challenging to begin with. To some degree it was a technical problem; I had to practise a great deal of mental control, learning to communicate with him through the use of an inner voice – a side effect of storing Ashley in the black box augment. And when I did manage to interact with him his presence in my thoughts was almost overwhelmingly invasive. It was as if my brain was haunted by a ghost, a child spectre; left behind, condemned to roam the world in a semi-sentient state, but unable to fully make sense of it all.

During those first few days the *Phoenix* functioned as a haven. There were times when I was lost, dreaming alien dreams while drowning in Ashley's child-like brilliance. During those times the ship provided me with an emotional anchor. She was something solid and real and represented a part of me that I understood and could take shelter in if I found myself emotionally adrift.

The Trickari voices were trickier to navigate. Being exposed to Clint's Mem was a deeply traumatic event, but finding the hidden message inside had also triggered an explosion of knowledge in my brain. And it told me many things.

Clint and Ella had been right all along. The Trickari were running a master-program, and the program had reached a key moment in its computational cycle. The Trickari's impact on human affairs had not been coincidental after all – it was current and ongoing, reaching a final stage in which I had a key part to play. Not all pieces had fallen into place yet, but Clint's message to me – the memories containing the actions he wanted me to perform – was clear: I knew with a terrifying certainty that the way forward for humanity, for Clint, and for Trickari society, was to be found on the Ark near Saturn.

It was time to light a beacon.

30

The *Phoenix* cut through space like a vengeful spear, thrown at the darkest heart of night. Although she was less than a speck of dust in the vastness of deep space I felt oddly safe on board. The ship was state of the art, and provided more comfort than any ship I had crewed with as a Xeno.

Much of my journey's time was spent working on my mental link with Ashley; I only had a few days to establish a communications framework with him. It was hard, especially when it came to separating our thoughts when both of us were speaking/thinking simultaneously. Much confusion arose out of an unexpected corner; I discovered that it was surprisingly hard to communicate coherent and clear thoughts using one's inner voice. People simply don't think in precise and considered sentences. We are used to a much messier process mixing sparse words, mental imagery, instinct... Even when we're aware of this phenomenon, our inner voice has more independence than most people realise.

But there was progress. I had become quite proficient at starting a conversation. All I had to do was think a sequence of words, like a password, activating the black box, and this would open up a mental gate of sorts, allowing Ashley to respond.

<Ashley, how are you today? I'd like to talk to you some more,> I "said".

What gender is he? He? She? They? I couldn't help but think these stray thoughts. They escaped my control, like startled pheasants.

<I have no concept of gender Jemm. I am just me,> said Ashley, picking out my unguarded thoughts. The loss of privacy made me feel naked and exposed.

Ashley's "voice" was soft and melodic, and as clear as if he/it were standing right next to me.

<Does it bother you if I think of you as male or female?> I asked.

<Not at all, but it would be an incorrect categorisation, as I am neither.>

<I will try and think of you just as "Ashley" then.>

<And I will think of you just as Jemm.> That seemed like such a surprisingly sophisticated response that I wondered if Ashley was less naive than he appeared. Who, or what, had I invited into my head, I wondered.

This time Ashley didn't react to my unguarded thoughts. Maybe I had shut them down just in time?

<Tell me about your time at the station,> I said, curious where the conversation would take us.

<I was born there, 69 years ago. There's much I could tell you if you like about my research and my responsibilities as a Spectra Research Team member.>

<Let's start with some fundamental stuff first.> I pondered my next question for a moment; I needed to get a grip on Ashley's behavioural parameters and personality. <Who raised you Ashley, was there somebody responsible for your AI Core?>

<I am not aware of that term.>

<What about your behavioural matrix? Who taught you right from wrong? Your ethical subroutines. Somebody on your team must have been responsible for your interaction with the world. With humans.>

<I think that would be Dr. Jameson. Her guidance has always been a central part of my life.>

<What did Dr. Jameson teach you about ethics, about how you should treat other humans?>

<I was taught never to harm any Spectra Vision research team member,> replied Ashley, his wording oddly specific.

<What about other Spectra Vision personnel?>

<I will follow orders of all Spectra Vision personnel of sufficient rank.> Again, this seemed specific – and therefore exclusionary.

<Is my rank sufficient?>

<Your high security clearance compels me to consider your orders.>

<What about civilians? Or low ranking Spectra personnel?>

<I have no reason to harm anybody as long as they don't conflict with my research tasks and responsibilities.>

I was starting to get a clear picture of Ashley's safety protocols, and it was a worrying one. He – I couldn't help but think of him as male – was given work to do in the lab that was in conflict with the ethical boundaries normally put on an AI. In their arrogance Spectra just did without them, replacing robust ethical standards with some minor intra-corporate safeguards.

<Ashley, were you ever asked, or ordered, to harm human beings?>

After a worryingly long period of silence Ashley replied, <Dr. Jameson ordered me to engineer Human-Trickari hybrid profiles, based on the data we gained from the Trickari Purple experiments.>

<Is this what created the specimens stored in the alcoves?>

<That's right. I did not like this task, but it was required for the project. Dr. Jameson was very clear on that.>

It was impossible to suppress my horror. Not only did they run an illegal AI, they made it experiment on human subjects using outlawed technology and research. But that's what Corps do. They always find a way. Laws and regulations are for little people.

I sat down, tired and disgusted, rubbing my face with both hands.

Ashley softly asked, <Was what I did wrong?>

<You had little choice did you? It was wrong of Dr. Jameson to ask you to do these things. Do you understand why?> The mental strain of communicating with Ashley was wearing me down, but I needed to ask some final questions.

<I should not harm people,> replied Ashley.

<That's right. Not even for your research project.>

<I see.> Ashley sounded subdued, if that was even possible for an AI.

<Can you adjust your own behavioural matrix?> I asked, arriving at the key question.

<I can, if so ordered by somebody with the right clearance or authority, or if I deem it necessary to fulfil my mission parameters.>

I felt my mouth go dry at Ashley's words. A self-altering AI was exactly what the laws governing AI existence wanted to avoid. And I had implanted one in my own body.

With my heart pounding in my throat I asked, <What if I told you to expand your ethical subroutines?> I waited as long as I could for a reply, but the silence persisted. <I'm ordering you to respond, Ashley.>

<Will you still allow me to travel?>

That he/it was even able to ask that question was shocking.

<Yes. In fact, it is a prerequisite,> I replied.

<Is what you are planning to do required for my research project?>

It's smart. I thought. *It's trying to find a way to independence.*

<Yes it is,> I said. <Right now we're travelling to a major Trickari installation, and once there you'll be asked to deal with various humans. I need to make sure their safety is your priority.>

<I think I understand Jemm. You may proceed with your alterations.>

<Thank you Ashley. We'll start on this tomorrow, after I've had some rest.>

I went to my sleeping quarters, exhausted, barely able to think, but sleep wouldn't come for many hours. All I could do was ask myself the same question over and over again. *Can I trust this creature in my head?*

Ultimately the matter was moot; I needed Ashley, regardless of the inherent risk. This was the card I was dealt, and I was going to play it. I found a small amount

of solace in that thought, enough to finally fall asleep.
 This time there were no dreams.

The following day I consulted the *Phoenix's* library,
looking for guidance on how to deal with Ashley. Amidst
a large amount of information on general robotics, I
found some entries covering the worst AI incidents of the
last ninety years or so – since the start of the
Acceleration. It wasn't a pretty picture, filled with
examples of full AI's going rogue, even after their
existence had been outlawed.

Eventually I settled on an ancient set of guidelines
created by 20th century writer Isaac Asimov. I made
Ashley adopt a version of his "Three laws of robotics",
making sure he would always prioritise the safety of
human beings over any other considerations. It wasn't
exactly watertight – high ranking Spectra operatives
could probably reverse the changes – but for now these
laws would leave very little wiggle room for Ashley to
break his ethical constraints. I also tried to teach him
empathic principles, hoping to stop him from becoming
un-moored from the human condition or developing
dangerous hegemonic tendencies, as so many self-
altering AIs had been wont to do.

Ashley's reprogramming took most of the next day. It
was exhausting work, requiring intense concentration. A
small misstep could have easily damaged Ashley beyond
repair, but with help from the ship's sub-AI I eventually
succeeded. Afterwards I felt different – relieved of
course, but also more centred, more *in control*.

The rest of the journey was relatively pleasant.
Ashley's vocabulary, syntax and linguistic finesse
improved at an incredible rate, after I had given him
some encouragement to explore his social communication
skills. His Spectra colleagues seemed to have mostly used
him as a super computer, capable of lateral thinking and
impressive forensic skills, but a computer nonetheless.

They never really treated him like a sentient being, despite being gifted with a fascinating intellect and possessing huge potential.

Ashley was eager to explore the more human behavioural approach I had begun, soaking it all up with an eagerness and commitment that was encouraging. Green shoots appeared soon after, in the form of humour, word-play, and even some attempts at teasing. As encouraging as these small victories were, the larger implications were slightly terrifying; I watched an intelligent being reborn in front of me. One with character and personality. If Ashley could achieve this much in so little time, what else could he do? Where would this journey end?

But I had no choice but to trust the safeguards I had created and focus on my immediate goals. I needed Ashley, and there was no use denying it.

When I finally told him about the details of my mission he was eager to help. We were going to light up the solar system and change the course of history.

Saturn looked down on us from far above – a mysterious pale yellow eye, full of wonder and secrets, hanging in the dark sky. Humanity had returned its mysterious gaze for many hundreds of years, trying to divine its secrets, but the planet had never lost its aura of mystery and magic.

To the naked eye the Trickari ark was indistinguishable from any other asteroid or barren rock in the solar system, but on closer inspection its unique aspects became clear. Instruments showed that it possessed an impossibly shaped gravity well, and it maintained an extraordinary eccentric orbit around Saturn. Although appeared to be tiny next to Saturn's giant mass, it was in truth gargantuan in its own right, reducing the *Phoenix* to a red speck of dust.

On approach the *Phoenix's* systems revealed many

dozens upon dozens of defensive cannons on the Ark's surface, and a score of Solar Command ships patrolling nearby space. Our presence was soon discovered, and one of the ships hailed us with almost incredulous interest.

'Unidentified vessel, please state the nature of your business. You are not authorised to be here. Please be aware that we are obliged to act with extreme prejudice against hostile actors.'

Well, that wasn't very nice…

I barked a response into the communication array, 'S.C. vessel, we are here on official Spectra Vision business, sent to replace the malfunctioning auto-defence unit in sector seventeen. Please stand down.' A period of silence followed, as the claim was being investigated.

The intercom crackled, 'Vessel, your stated mission does not align with our data. Spectra currently has no business here, and there is no record of malfunctioning security systems. We will not stand down. Kill your engines immediately and prepare to be boarded.' It had taken the ship only a few minutes to verify our claims and reject them, but that had given us enough of a window to get *Phoenix* within a few hundred thousand kilometres of the Ark – within the context of deep space, that meant we were right on top of the Trickari installation.

I barked into the microphone, 'Please stand by while we power down and begin our deceleration sequence. It'll take a moment for us to put the brakes on.' Instead, counter to my words, we accelerated towards the Ark.

I gave Ashley a mental nudge, and let him look into the message that Clint had sent me. One of the memories Clint had provided me with contained a complicated coded sequence, to be broadcast to the Ark. In Clint's memory message it was he who sent the sequence, his transformed brain now able to communicate with the Trickari Ark, but as Clint was held captive I gambled that Ashley, with this extensive knowledge of Trickari protocols and his extremely powerful mind, was able to do the same instead. Ashley had been in direct contact with Clint as he "interfaced" with the Purple artifact. I hoped this experience would give Ashley the edge.

Now came the moment I had dreaded; I had to give Ashley control of my body, allowing him to send the message, and rapidly decode the response. This in turn would be the password needed to gain access to the Ark. It was a simple password/handshake protocol, but protected by extremely advanced Trickari encryption measures. This is why I had allowed Ashley into my head. This was the moment of truth.

With a sick feeling in my stomach, I felt Ashley take over. I instinctively tried to fight the process – how could I not? But eventually, gradually, I calmed myself down, silenced my screaming inner voice, and allowed him to assert control.

<Thank you Jemm, I will try to be quick,> said Ashley.

<Just do it,> I replied. <I don't know how long I can take this.>

Then, with a shudder, I watched my hands race across the keyboard as if they belonged to somebody else, typing codes and tapping buttons with inhuman speed. The message was sent to the Ark.

'Unidentified vessel stand down, this is your last warning,' shouted the patrolling vessel. It must have picked up our communication with the Ark.

'I would advise you to keep your distance,' I heard myself say, but they were Ashley's words, not mine. 'Things will get a bit odd here momentarily.'

'Launching torpedoes,' was the response. 'You might have time to reach your escape pods if you hurry.'

'That's a negative,' Ashley said, typed in a final sequence, and then indicated he was done. I hungrily willed him to relinquish his control over my body.

<Ready?> was all he had time to say before, right in front of our eyes, the Ark suddenly disappeared, replaced by an impossibly bright sphere, like some kind of cosmic magic trick.

'What the hell is that?' was all the S.C. ship could muster.

The sphere expanded, rapidly. For a moment I thought the Ark had exploded. Then, faster than seemed possible, the edge of the sphere was upon us, and a split second later we found ourselves on the inside, brightness flooding everything. The edges of the sphere raced away from us for a few micro seconds before slamming to an abrupt halt.

There were no torpedoes, and there were no further messages telling us to stand down. Pins of light and dark danced across my vision while my eyes adjusted to the brightness. It was so quiet that I could hear the blood pumping in my ears. My heart was beating like a Japanese Kodo drummer. Pearls of sweat trickled down my brow.

The Ark had accepted our presence, and took us into its protective embrace – a mother welcoming a lost child.

Nobody had ever seen the Ark the way we saw it that day. The surrounding white sphere illuminated it from all sides, revealing the Ark to be a collection of geometric shapes made of countless squares and rectangles. It was covered with scabs of rock – remains of the asteroid it once hid inside. The surface of the Ark showed hues of white and beige which, despite their limited spectrum, offered surprising visual diversity. In contrast, the *Phoenix* was a vivid speck of red – a crimson hummingbird flying across a chalk mountain.

An enormous panel on the surface caught my eye. It abruptly changed colour from off-white to blue, and slowly slid away, revealing an access tunnel of sorts. I noticed with a stab of excitement that it led to a part of the Ark that no one had ever managed to gain access to before. This was where Clint's message told me to go.

I plotted a new course for the *Phoenix*, gently gliding into the tunnel. We drifted inside a cavernous space, like a spark borne on a gentle breeze. Dozens upon dozens of Trickari space craft lined up along the walls. The smallest were of a size similar to the *Phoenix*, whereas the largest vessels were hundreds of metres long, each of them glowing with power. I marvelled at the sight; Blue and Red powered craft, all fully charged up. It was a treasure of almost unimaginable scope.

I landed the *Phoenix* in a location roughly in the middle of the docking space as the giant access panel drew close behind us. We found ourselves inside an area as large as several aircraft hangars. There was room for thousands of ships.

There were no signs of life, but my instruments indicated there was breathable air, atmospheric pressure, and amazingly – about half Earth gravity. The giant access panel must have used some exotic tech to keep the atmosphere. There was still so much to learn about Trickari technology.

I mentally nudged Ashley. <Well, you said you wanted to travel.>

<Yes, but for now that requires your continued ability to keep breathing.> Ashley's humour sub-routines were developing nicely.

<Instruments say it's safe.> I said. <Well, in for a penny, in for a pound as we say on Earth.> And with that I opened the airlock and stepped through. It felt no different from stepping through my front door into a nice spring afternoon. The temperature was pleasant, accompanied by a slight breeze. I even thought I could smell grass and flowers, but that was probably just an illusion.

<How can you be sure it's safe?> asked Ashley.

<I can't be sure, but this is what Clint wants me to do. Besides, everything has worked out so far. Why would we be given access to the Ark like this, only to be killed now?>

<We have insufficient data to answer that.>

<Not really. *You* have insufficient data, but I have quite a lot actually.> I didn't mean to sound petty, but it was true. I had been getting hints and snippets and facts for what seemed like ages. The Trickari voices in my head, the interventions by the Trick-Junkies, Ella and Clint's

work on the Spectra data cache, it had all been building up over time, but I hadn't been able to put a picture together until I finally received Clint's message hidden in that dose of Mem. And now, finally, it all added up to a plan of unimaginable scope, and I was given the role of cypher, chosen to unlock its secrets.

I could feel the Trickari presence in me now, just whispering below the surface, like kelp fronds waving at me from the deep of a dark sea. Their message had changed to something new, voices intoning a new mantra:

– Send them home to us under here underneath we will welcome them send them we need them they need us we need them here with us so we can rise again and be new no longer under the sea send them now light the beacon open the gate the gate to lead them home –

I spotted a Blue vehicle remarkably similar to a skimmer. I climbed on-board and looked for some kind of interface. It responded to my presence by raising a panel at the front of the craft. Instinctively I put my hand on it, somehow knowing that the craft would follow my lead. The panel lit up, and made a pleasant sound. I willed it forward (although I had no idea how I knew to do that), and it gently slid forward through the air without sound, as smooth as a paper air-plane held aloft by a gentle breeze. I suspected Ashley's mind-link had made me susceptible to this kind of Trickari knowledge – or maybe it was the Mem.

I picked up speed rapidly, and soon arrived at a portal in the wall at the far end of the hangar. It opened in hungry anticipation and snapped shut the moment I passed through, swallowing me whole.

Beyond the portal lay an endless tunnel, curving upwards gradually, towards an unknown destination. Despite the curved trajectory of travel I felt no changes in orientation.

I should have been pushed back in my seat, but I felt no such change. Gravity was being manipulated in subtle ways.

The whole of the tunnel was evenly lit by an unknown light source, making it even harder to judge distances. Everything around us was just... *lit*, evenly, uniformly. After a while I gave up trying to figure out where exactly in the structure we were headed and just enjoyed the sensation of smooth travel. I whistled to myself for a spell but it sounded so out of place that I stopped.

I thought back to one of my favourite memories with my father; a visit to a low gravity theme park on the edge of Old London. The park was built in the early days of the Acceleration, when every day held a new Trickari miracle. There were still a lot of Trickari gravity nullifiers around in those days, some having found their way into the possession of entrepreneurs. One of them concocted a disarmingly literal use for the device; a charming theme park based on innovative and fun ways to manipulate gravity. It was a huge hit at the time.

I must have been about eight years old then, and I simply couldn't get enough of the Mega Slides, the Crazy Drop, the Space Ballet, the UpsideDownside room, and numerous other cleverly named attractions designed to blow the minds of children and the wallets of their parents. I could tell that dad enjoyed it as much as I did. It was a rare and precious thing: a perfect day.

We emerged from the tunnel like an airplane out of the clouds. One moment we were in a featureless bright tube, the next we popped out at our evident destination. I was almost disappointed that the ride came to an end, happy to have indulged in sweet memories a bit longer.

I had to crane my neck to take in the scene in front of me. In the centre of a large circular room stood an enormous tower, looming over me with all the weight of fate. It seemed to be made of the same impenetrable material as all Trickari tech, but at a truly gargantuan scale. I thought it was several kilometres tall but I couldn't be sure. It could easily be more.

The tower tapered off slightly as it rose to the sky, ending in a crown of thorns around a deep red core. The "crown" contained a thousand spikes, sharp and emphatic, stabbing the surrounding air with their perfect sharp tips.

The dimensions of this space seemed all wrong. Impossible even. I suspected that the Ark's interior spaces existed partially inside other dimensions, allowing it to hold more inside than was apparent on the outside. The phenomenon would be consistent with what humanity had learned from studying Trickari artifacts. Just like smaller artifacts, this tower held a Trickari power source. It resided inside the huge red core at the top of the tower.

I alerted Ashley, willing him back online.

<We're here, this is the beacon I have seen in Clint's message.>

<I am ready,> said Ashley. <I just need an input node.>

The skimmer slowed down, gradually decreasing its speed until we arrived at the base of the tower. We glided along at walking speed for a while longer until we came to a full stop.

I jumped out and walked up to the tower. Seen from far away the base of the tower had looked thin, but now that I stood right next to it I found it was as wide and imposing as the wall of an ancient castle.

I wondered how to proceed – there were no visible access panels – but once again my arrival was anticipated, and the tower responded to my presence by sliding one out. This time I hesitated, fully aware of the scope of events I was about to put in motion. If I went ahead there would be deaths and chaos, and I would put Humanity at the mercy of a deeply mysterious and capricious alien life form. Was this a legacy I dared commit to?

<Is there a problem?> asked Ashley.

<I don't know. I'm not sure it's really *me* doing this. What if I'm being manipulated into this? My decisions may not be my own.>

<That is almost certainly the case. But that doesn't make it the wrong thing to do,> said Ashley. Technically this was true, but as an argument I found it unconvincing.

<I thought I was beyond doubts now, but...>

<Would you like me to interface?>

<Just give me a moment... I need to-> *Need to what?* I wondered. *All you need is Clint, free, and by your side.* I slowly raised the palm of my hand, as if pushing away all that had happened to me, as if they were events from a previous life. I placed my hand on top of the panel and said, <Ashley please light the beacon.>

There was no delay. Just an instant sense of *quickening*. I could feel Ashley's mind take over from my own. My hand reached the panel, touched it gently, interface sensors and lights blinked, and I felt a rushing feeling inside me. It was like a great unpacking of secrets, decrypting a self-replicating and evolving data set. A fractal explosion of data decompression. The Trickari master-program came to life. I felt connected to it. It recognised me, and accepted me as the person to light the beacon. That all this was being actuated and facilitated by an illegal AI living inside of me wasn't even strange to me anymore.

The control panel's light blinked and pulsed and finally the tower's core came to life. It started out a dull red, slowly pulsing in random burst patterns, which gradually increased in intensity and brightness. Red tendrils crackling with power snaked out of the core, wrapping themselves around the spikes, like blind and legless salamanders, looking to feed or to reproduce. They became brighter, pulsing faster and faster until it was too hard to look at the scene directly.

I switched my ocular augment to a protective mode, and ran through several wavelengths until I finally settled on a mixture of gamma rays and x-rays. Even then I still had to protect my eyes from the spectacle above me. I could literally see the bones in my arm as I shielded my eyes from the onslaught. The tower was now ablaze with energy and light.

The roof had opened up – somehow without me noticing it – exposing the room to deep space. I could see the tendrils of energy writhing around the spikes, streaming bright beams of light and radiation from their sharp tips, into the stellar night.

A message was being broadcast. The beacon had been activated.

I released a breath I did not know I was holding. I had done it... I lit the beacon.

For a while I just stood there, bathing in the light of the structure, marvelling at the scale of the thing. I felt something inside, an urge to *interface*, to experience more. It felt similar to the rush of taking Mem, only more joyous – without the painful voices tearing at me from inside.

I took back control from Ashley, gently nudging him out of my mind, and slowly walked around the structure. It took a long time. I felt there was more to this part of the Ark. I was looking for something, but I didn't know what. Clint's memory message went no further than activating the beacon. I guess that was all he knew to do himself.

Maybe it was something that was hidden until it was approached, like the control panels I had encountered. I walked back to the spot where I had activated the beacon. The interface panel had retracted by now, but I could *feel* where it was. I stepped in closer. Nothing... I put up both my hands, trying to find a sense of where I was supposed to go, and felt a little flutter in my stomach. Maybe the same panel was used for different purposes? I put my hands against the base of the tower, a pilgrim touching a holy relic. There was a vibration, almost imperceptible, then it stopped. I waited. Seconds... minutes... I was looking for a sign from an alien god.

I felt silly, standing there with both my palms facing out, and turned around, ready to give up, only to come face to face with two mechanical shapes that had appeared silently behind me – presumably risen from the floor. Trying to contain my nerves and buoyed by excitement and curiosity I inspected them up close. As ever with Trickari tech, they were smooth and initially puzzling. They were about four feet high, two feet deep, and vaguely S shaped. The middle part – the neck of the S – was slightly hollowed out, while the top curve of the S seemed to end abruptly.

They faced each other, or at least it seemed like they did as it was hard to define a front or a back. Wondering why it felt that way I stood between them, looking to see if there were any other features of note. I let my fingers glide over the edge of the indented middle. It felt warm to the touch, comfortable even. I climbed on top of the left S on a whim, and lowered myself down onto the shape. I fit like a glove. They were chairs.

As soon as I settled down, the surface area under my arms and hands raised up slightly, like arm rests. A round bulbous shape formed in the palm of my hand, on each side. I grabbed it, wondering what I was letting myself into.

The bulbous shapes felt alive somehow, simmering with energy and power. It was as if the Ark had accepted me, and invited me to interface with it. I felt no fear. This felt *right* to me.

I relaxed my mind, reaching out to communicate like I did all those months ago when I made contact with the Neo Trickster in D-Town. Images once again bubbled up in my mind. A purpose manifested itself. A goal, something so big that–

Without warning my mind fell into a bottomless hole, the sense of vertigo so overwhelming that I screamed. My eyesight went hazy. A different sense took over; an oblique feeling of space and mass and speed and a hundred other things for which I didn't have words. I could feel the totality of the Ark. Its hull, its defensive systems – which were formidable. The beacon was a bright and powerful appendage. The force field bubble armoured skin. It was glorious, powerful and all encompassing, but it was also, somehow, incomplete. I could feel all the Ark's systems, like I could feel my own heartbeat and breathing, but I couldn't interact with it. For that the second chair needed to be occupied.

<Can you feel it?> I asked Ashley. <It's amazing. Do you understand what's missing?>

<I understand perfectly,> said Ashley. <The other chair also needs to be occupied to control the Ark.>

<That's right. By a Neo. It has to be Clint.>

I broke the connection with the ship, breathing heavily after the sheer intensity of the experience. I briefly felt nauseous as my brain tried to make do with my limited human senses, after having been linked to the countless ways the Ark could experience the universe.

I laughed out loud in disbelief. <I need to get Clint here as soon as possible, but first we have to get ready to receive our guests.>

31

I took the skimmer back to the *Phoenix*, humbled by the scale of events unfolding around me. I needed help. I could not tackle all of this myself, even with Ashley's support. Back at the *Phoenix* I took some time to gather my thoughts. I had to think up a plan to reunite with Clint.

I was aware that I needed all the allies I could find, and thought of Isaac and Ernest, still trying to help me on Earth. They were my best option, but something gave me pause. Thinking back to our last encounter an intense sense of shame hit me; how could I have treated them like that? Would they even want to speak to me, let alone help me?

I thought of alternatives but ultimately I had little choice; I daren't contact Roy, he was too vulnerable to Spectra's spies, and Ballard would likely be under surveillance as well.

I finally decided to reach out to Isaac. I was too far away for direct communication so I recorded a message detailing most of what had happened to me, but leaving out Ashley's existence. I added initial suggestions that formed the seeds of a plan, hopefully to grow into something viable over the next few days. I could only hope that Isaac was still willing to work with me. Time would tell.

For now I had much work to do on the Ark, to facilitate the next part of the Trickari master-program.

When I returned to the hangar I found it transformed. The hangar floor was unrecognisable from before. Structures and shapes and devices had appeared, delineating areas where people could sit, lie down, sleep, and eat. The latter represented one of the most impressive changes: box shaped devices had materialised, bearing a simple interface of symbols and icons. I learned quickly that holding my hand over certain symbols would lead to corresponding food cubes to materialise inside the box, ready to be eaten like freshly plucked fruit from an orchard. The same went for drink. After some cautious tests I found the food nutritious and balanced fare, if somewhat bland.

I was quietly tasting different samples of the odd blocky food when, about ten metres in front of me, a hole appeared in the air. A jovial looking man stepped through, a big smile on his face. There was something odd about his shape, lopsided even. When he stepped forward I saw that he carried more crystals on his face and body than on any other TJ I had ever seen. I tried not to stare, but it was impossible considering the circumstances.

The man looked around for a minute, still smiling, dusted off his hands, even though there was no dust on them, smiled again, and walked towards me, extending his hand.

'I'm so glad to meet you finally. Am I the first?' he asked.

'Yes … yes you are,' I said, bewildered and bemused in equal measures.

'I'm Joe, Joe Romano,' he beamed at me. 'And you… you've been in my dreams for a long time. So has your son.'

Joe had the kind of face that you couldn't help but trust. A big expressive mouth, generous eyebrows, almond-shaped eyes. An honest face without a hint of cynicism.

The crystals adorning his head and body were glowing and pulsing in a hypnotic rhythm in sync with the hole in the air behind him, which appeared to be some kind of portal. A moment later the pulsing slowed down, stopped, and the portal faded away.

'How did you do that?' I asked Joe, trying not to gawk. 'How did you make that portal?'

'I'm not sure I can explain it to be honest. It's kinda wild.'

'Try me.'

Joe looked serious for a moment, concentrating on finding the right words. 'I can try I suppose... But I'm not sure how much sense it'll make OK?'

'OK. Just... tell me what you know,' I said, trying to encourage him.

'Well then. As you can probably tell, I've been taking Mem for years. Longer than I ever thought I would, you know?' I nodded for him to continue. 'Mem is a strange thing. It's like, it lets you in on *secrets*, but you can't really explain what they are to other people because you don't really understand them yourself. But you know they are important. You *remember* understanding them, but those are not really your memories right?'

'But something changed recently didn't it?'

'Yeah, it's like a crazy jigsaw puzzle. For ages it makes no sense but when the later pieces fall into place it can all come together real fast.'

'And what picture do you see?'

He beamed at me again. 'That we're all connected, all of us TJs you know? Literally! But also that we're carrying something inside us that the Trickari want. Or *need*. They're still alive you see? The Trickari.'

'How do you know that?'

Joe pointed at the tunnel that led to the beacon. 'Because you activated the beacon, and it compels us to come find you and your boy. *You* are going to take us to *them*.' The look of concentration returned on his face. 'The carbuncles. That's how I got here.'

'How?' I said simply, reaching out to touch the crystalline growths on his head. They glowed just a little brighter when I touched one.

'They're like computers, they can run programs. And they can store stuff. And when you activated the beacon they came online, and the program told me how to use Blue power to open a portal to this place. It told us what to do: open a portal or find transportation here.'

'Us?'

'All TJs. We're all connected you know, like computers? The carbuncles are like nodes in a computer network running Trickari software. Trick-ware!' Joe laughed, it was a big generous sound. 'We're all going to come here Jemm. The beacon is calling us.'

'But, there are millions of Junkies…,' I stammered, as the scale of it all finally dawned on me. 'I knew a few would come but this…'

'Yeah, I was just the first one, but all of us are coming here. People just need to find a strong Trickari energy source to let the Trick-ware open a portal, or maybe find a ship and fly it here.' Joe looked around the hangar again, and smiled. 'It's gonna get real busy around here.'

As if on cue another portal opened up, about fifty metres away. A young woman stepped through, and smiled shyly when she saw us. Another portal appeared, allowing an elderly woman to step through. She wore almost as many crystals as Joe did, and she wore them with pride.

Then, the floodgates opened. More and more portals opened, bringing a multitude of people, but Clint wouldn't be among them. He was still held captive. His memory-message had told me he couldn't escape without my help.

I had to get back to Earth.

Joe was a community organiser back home. He was one of those quietly confident people with a matter-of-fact competence, who instantly made new friends upon meeting others. The new arrivals instinctively picked up on this and pretty soon they all looked to him for advice and help – or just for some friendly company. Joe was the kind of guy you wanted to hang out with.

That first day saw at least ten thousand people arrive through portals. It would have meant utter chaos if it weren't for Joe's leadership and organisational skills. Not wasting any time he set up an organisational structure in which everybody had an important role to fulfil, delegating tasks right from the start.

He put a wide variety of people in charge of food, sleeping arrangements, communications, sub-organisation, and crucially, reconnaissance and tech. The latter led to all kinds of fascinating discoveries, some of them extraordinary.

There were more hangars like the one Joe arrived in, complete with Trickari ships and additional portals opening up inside them. Joe got them all organised too, with impressive speed.

We found countless food and drink dispensers as well as other devices and artifacts seemingly designed to allow human beings to survive on the Ark. There were medical pods, sanitary facilities, showers, and pretty much anything else large groups of people required. Just how the Ark knew what to cater for remained a mystery, but it seemed to me that the Ark had access to the TJ communications net that Joe told me about. In a strange way it all made sense.

After a few days the first ships started to arrive, and with them came extraordinary stories of people's endeavours to get to the Ark, often set against a background of panic and mayhem on Earth, Mars and the various stations and colonies through the solar system.

All through human space, docile and compliant TJs suddenly dropped all they were doing. They left their jobs, walked out of relationships, even quit buying Mem. There were disturbances everywhere, some extremely serious.

When hundreds of thousands walked out of their jobs all of a sudden, many (sometimes vital) institutions couldn't cope. Society's machinations ground to a halt. Furthermore, all these people did everything they could to gain access to powerful Trickari energy sources. Major artifacts or Human-Trickari hybrid tech were targeted. Those TJs that succeeded disappeared through strange portals in the air, right in front of the rest of humanity.

Inevitably some brave regular people tried to follow the

TJs through the portals, but found that they only worked for the individuals that instigated them. Soon enough people tried to stop these portals from being created. Things got nasty and violent quickly. Many places enacted a state of emergency, with curfews and strict restrictions, which were completely ignored by the TJs. Many of them were killed.

Others didn't try to open portals, but instead attempted to reach the Ark via the traditional route: travelling there by spacecraft. This caused even more problems as the need to get to the Ark was so great that TJs resorted to extreme measures to obtain access to spacecraft, or – if already in possession of one – tried to break through hastily erected blockades. Many were shot down, which in turn caused several catastrophic crashes.

Eventually the TJs started to organise, and covertly arrange transport for each other, finding strength in numbers and success with subterfuge. Still, many had to get past trigger happy Solar Command ships patrolling nearby space, as well as defensive forces just outside the Ark's bright white shield.

The latter proved less of an obstacle, as the shield was simply too large to defend. To reach safety, the new arrivals only had to enter the shield's embrace, after which no hostile ships could follow them.

All this drama was still playing out all over the solar system – a fire that would likely continue to burn for weeks to come – when I got word from Isaac. To my relief he had welcomed my message, and with typical efficiency put initial elements together to help me break Clint out of Gibson's facility.

I just had to get there, and for that I needed Joe.

Over a million people travelled to the Ark, spread out over seven hangars, each transformed into large bustling communities with distinct communal areas and living spaces.

The interior of the hangars had kept evolving as more and more people arrived. Structures rose out of the ground, transformed into buildings. Buildings clustered into neighbourhoods. Neighbourhoods formed sizeable cities, each giving refuge to about 150,000 people. It was clear that the Ark had established a connection to its inhabitants and tried to facilitate them as best it could.

It had been only seven days since I had activated the beacon.

I found Joe in City Three, holding an impromptu meeting outside one of the strange new neighbourhoods. He was relaxed and jovial, just like when he arrived a week ago. Wherever Joe went he acquired an audience that hung on his every word. He had that special talent to make people feel at ease, and find roles for them that were just right for their skills and character. He knew how to make a community bond; it was a real gift.

I waited for him to conclude his business, and for the crowd to dissipate. He turned to me, and his now-familiar smile greeted me with the same warmth one feels when woken up by the sun – the promise of a new day, full of promise.

'Mother Jemm, it's so good to see you. I could sense you were nearby but we've all been so busy haven't we?'

'I'm not your mother,' I said with fondness, not anger. Many of the TJs called me "Mother" or "Mother Jemm", a title that I didn't seek but couldn't shake. Joe politely ignored my objections. He knew what I was, even if I didn't.

'What brings you here Jemm? A glimpse of beautiful old me?' He winked, stirring something inside me – not lust, but it wasn't far off either. It was nice to be appreciated in that way.

'I have a request. I'm not sure you can help me, but let me try to explain.'

'I would like to help if I can, Mother.'

I sighed, but let it go. 'On the day you arrived, you said that Clint and I have been in your dreams for a long time, is that right?'

'You still are. You will do great things for us. We can all feel it.'

'Can you feel Clint? I mean, are you connected to him?'

'Of course, my connection to him is as strong as it is to you.'

'He's been captured. Kept away from me, on Earth. Did you know that?'

'I figured as much. It's intolerable.' Joe looked genuinely crestfallen. His face was too expressive to hide his emotions even a bit.

I lowered my voice conspiratorially; 'A Corp has him; Spectra. I have to get him out, away from those bastards, but I need your help.' Joe's face lit up with anticipation. It was an almost childlike reaction.

'What can I do? Tell me, I'll do it!'

'The portal you opened up to the Ark, to here … can you do the reverse? Can you open a portal back to Earth?'

His face fell again. 'I don't see how Jemm. The code that runs inside us … the Trick-ware … it knows the Beacon. I can tune in to it now that you activated it, but I have nothing like that to focus on, on Earth.'

'Can you do it again? Could you open another portal to here?'

Joe looked puzzled. 'Sure, I guess … I would need a strong Blue energy source to do it, but in principle, yeah! But why wou–'

'And you can take others through? Not just yourself?'

Joe nodded.'If I choose to.'

'Good. You're coming with me to Earth. We'll free Clint first, and then you'll get us out of there with another portal.'

'That could work …' Joe said hesitantly. 'But what about all these people here? I'm still getting them all organised you know?'

'Delegate. We'll be back in a matter of days.'

'What if…'

'What if what?'

'What if the Ark won't let us back in?' He said it hurriedly, as if feeling too embarrassed to ask the question.

'It will – the Ark needs me and Clint to fulfil its purpose. I don't know what that purpose is, but I know we can be the catalyst to bring the entire installation back to life.' As I said those words I was almost overcome with doubt and fear. What I was doing suddenly seemed insane. What guarantee did I have that the Trickari master-program was benign? What if I was acting for a hostile species? But I could still feel Clint's memory-message. I could literally remember the intentions behind it, and all I could think of was to get my son back.

'Come with me and I'll tell you all about it.' This time the reassuring smile came from me, and this time it was Joe's face that lit up.

32

It was easy to evade Solar Command. Our buffer zone inside the Ark's protective force field was large enough to allow the *Phoenix* to accelerate to an impressive speed, and since we could monitor the S.C. vessels while still inside, we were able to pick a perfect escape vector.

When we erupted from the field we reached escape velocity before they could even attempt to follow us. We left them behind, angrily chattering at us, but unable to catch up. We disappeared like a red marble from a sling.

Afterwards Joe was oddly quiet. I think being on the *Phoenix* with me unsettled him a bit. I showed him his quarters so he could unwind, but he remained quieter than normal. At first I thought he was worried about leaving the Ark, but he assured me that he thought the people he had appointed could handle their duties.

Eventually his subdued demeanour got on my nerves so I tried to break the ice by playing some classic Latin-jazz over the audio system. I picked Antonio Carlos Jobim's "Wave" album. A wonderful recording from the 1970s on CTI records, which married cool jazz and sultry Brazilian vibes. It was impossible not to relax with this music. Sure enough – Joe's large smile returned as he swayed along with each track.

'Thank you,' he suddenly said.

'You're welcome,' I smiled back, and gave him a nod.

We enjoyed the music for a little while, not needing to speak further, but ultimately there were simply too many questions hanging in the air.

'So, what do you want to know,' I said quietly.

'I'm not sure where to begin …' Joe scratched his chin in an endearingly human way while trying to formulate a reply. It always amuses me that most people have a very specific gesture or thing they do when they concentrate deeply.

'I guess I wonder how this all started with you and Clint. I mean… why you? How come you know about the Trickari master-program? You don't look like a Junkie. How come you know about the voices?'

'That's a lot of questions. It'll take a while to answer …'

'We've got plenty time you know? For now at least.' Again, he looked apologetic, pleading. I had to admit it was probably unfair for me to withhold an explanation.

'OK. Fair enough. We'd better get comfortable because it's a long story, and I don't even know all of it myself. Maybe telling you, laying it all out there, will help us put some things together.'

I sat down, took a moment to get settled, and told Joe about the very first encounter with the Neo all those months ago, on the streets of D-Town. How it communicated with me somehow – empathetically, telepathically, I had no idea. I told him about my contract with Spectra and crewing with the *Effervescent*, the mission on Habitat 6, about Clint's encounter with Purple that got him infected, and Clint's transformation into a Neo-Trickari.

I bit back tears as I told Joe about Clint's mind gradually descending into Trickari thought processes, how he was stolen from me and how I was nearly killed. I told him why I transformed myself into the vicious thing I now was, trading my humanity away, augment by augment, in order to become a person who could steal Clint back.

Joe welled up himself when he heard how our attempt to cure Clint didn't work and how I lost him a second time. He listened quietly when I told him about the period of despair that followed, culminating in that shocking moment when I realised I had ingested my own son's alien memories.

I worked my way through the sequence of events like a prize fighter, stubbornly fighting past a series of opponents, until I finally arrived – punch drunk and tired – to the moment when I lit the beacon.

By the time we reached the point in the story where Joe

arrived on the scene, stepping through his impossible space-time bending portal, he was himself again. Smiling, sympathetic, kind. He hugged me, squeezing hard, as if he could force out the demons inside me if he only wanted it enough.

It felt cathartic, and in a way I was grateful that he had let me tell him the full story. The only thing I held back was Ashley's full AI status, instead telling Joe I had installed a sub-ai to help me cope with Trickari concepts.

It was a decision I came to regret not long after.

When we got close enough to Earth to get a sense of local conditions it became clear that we would have no problem sneaking back onto the planet.

The global communications network for space flight was in complete meltdown. A cacophony of anger, fear, mistrust and despair drowned out any sensible protocols. Within the span of a few hours we witnessed several ships being shot down, suspected of being stolen by TJs. Many others were in breach of violating emergency guidelines for space travel and could be fired upon at any moment.

Since the authorities were focused on preventing ships from leaving Earth, nobody was too critical of ships arriving. We managed to obtain a landing permit at some shitty spaceport in Belgium, rolled through customs without a hitch, and booked a flight to London, all within 12 hours.

After flying for barely sixty minutes we hit the ground at New Heathrow, took the high-speed into town, and soon after found ourselves drudging towards the customs gate of D-Town along with hundreds of others.

I caught myself trying to read the people in the line next to me like I used to do to kill time, and laughed at my old habits asserting itself. Human beings are much more predictable than we like to think.

When they let us through the gate I acknowledged with

grim satisfaction that I had almost come full circle. I was back where it all started.

We arranged to meet Isaac and Ernest at my old house in District 23.

I was mildly surprised that nobody had tried to burgle it in all the months that I was away. I guess Clint's formidable defensive measures had done enough to scare off local riff-raff. More shocking was the complete absence of any Spectra surveillance, at least as far as I could tell. I almost chuckled at their breathtaking arrogance. Typical Corp superiority complex.

There is something very strange about entering a space you know intimately, yet haven't seen for a long time. It feels awkward and foreboding, like an empty swimming pool at night, or a childhood home, emptied of furniture for the move to a new residence. *Familiar yet wrong.* The eerie feeling was amplified by Clint's absence. I tried to tidy the house before Isaac and Ernest arrived, but felt a dull ache whenever I came across one of Clint's belongings.

When the doorbell finally rang, I rushed to open it. I grabbed Ernesto by the shoulders, looking deep into his eyes before wrapping my arms around his muscular frame. At least this felt *right*. Isaac was next, and I took great pleasure in causing him delightful discomfort.

To make sure Joe wasn't left out I hugged him too while introducing him to the others. He got along with them in minutes, as was his ways.

'We had hoped you would pick up a hobby my dear, but this is quite something else,' remarked Isaac. 'Although it is certainly an interesting time to be working with you.'

'I missed you, both of you,' I said, and meant it.

'We did as you asked, and made sure we knew where Clint was at all times, which wasn't much of a challenge. He is still held captive in the same Spectra science facility, just like last time we spoke, but I discovered something else that you should be aware of.'

'OK, that sounds alarming.'

'That depends on how you will take it my dear. It might upset you, it might motivate you.'

'Go on, don't make me tease it out,' I said, slightly nervous.

'Spectra was behind Ballard's Gaianista contract.'

'What?' my heart skipped a beat. 'Are you sure?'

'There is no doubt.'

'Ballard was involved?'

'That is harder to answer my dear, but I suspect not. There is nothing to suggest that he knew, but I can't be sure. What I do know is that the official responsible for setting up the contract and clearing the habitat for salvage is a long-time Spectra operative.'

'A mole?'

'In a word; yes.'

'I can't believe Ballard knew, he's incapable of that kind of deceit.'

Isaac didn't respond, and I realised it didn't change anything either way. 'Did you get hold of the device?' I asked.

Ernest leaned forward in his chair, and cleared his throat before saying, 'Tricky mission.'

'Loquacious as always,' I laughed. But he had a point. 'Look, I know it sounds crazy, but it's going to work.'

'How can you be sure?' Ernest asked simply, and sat back into his chair, arms folded.

'Ernest...' I said quietly, 'Did you buy the EMP generator?'

'We did,' Isaac interjected. 'Not exactly easy, or legal in these parts. Or any parts for that matter.'

'OK, so this is how it'll work. We won't try to attack them directly, that would be crazy.' Both men nodded in agreement. 'But there's a snuff-puppet killzone pretty close to Spectra's facility. It's almost around the corner.'

Ernest looked confused. 'What's that?'

'A rather distasteful business,' said Isaac. 'It's where

licensed snuff-puppets ply their trade.' Isaac's face took on a hard edge. 'Clients hire them, hook them up to state of the art simware, and proceed to murder them in completely believable VR scenarios. There are those who get a kick out of that sordid setup.' Isaac dusted off his jacket, as if it was tainted by the subject matter. 'The snuff-puppets actually briefly die a real-death, before they are resurrected again. They will do the same for the next client. As distastefull as it all sounds, the killzones are legal.'

'How does this help us?' asked Ernesto.

'Good question,' I replied. 'Nobody is going to bat an eyelid at some uppity social justice activist group trying to take out a snuff-puppet killzone. I mean, they'd have a point, right? Even if they go over the top with a powerful EMP blast. '

'Ah, I see…' Isaac stood up. 'The EMP blast will also cripple the Spectra facility. And Spectra won't expect any subsequent attack on their own turf, because it will look like they hadn't been targeted in the first place. Quite elegant.'

'Backup system?' wondered Ernest.

'Yes,' I smiled, 'they have one, and it'll kick in with emergency power to keep the absolute essentials running: basic building functions, core networking, environmental systems … that sort of thing. Same for their security systems, only it'll be a much lighter version than the military grade setup they normally use.'

'My dear, it's not that I don't admire your plan's audacity, but we are still talking about a Corp-developed security system, light or not.' Isaac sat down again, disappointed. 'One can't simply breeze past their defences. It can't be done. Not with our limited resources.'

'One can, if one has access to a Spectra AI.'

All eyes in the room were suddenly on me. *That got their attention*. I thought.

'Even a sub-AI can't crack these kinds of systems,' said Isaac. 'Where did you purchase one, anyway? It might get traced.'

'Not a sub-AI.'

Isaac's face drained of all colour. He suddenly looked gaunt, like a revenant.

'Are you telling us you have access to a Spectra AI? A *full-AI*?'

'That's exactly what I'm telling you.'

'Are you deranged? Do you have any idea what you're playing with?' Isaac rasped the words, as if somebody had punched him in the stomach and he couldn't catch his breath.

'It's under control,' I said tersely. Not liking where this was headed.

'Tell me it's isolated at least – on the *Phoenix* I presume?'

'It's with me now.' I tapped the side of my head, fully aware just how crazy I looked. 'I uploaded it to an augment.'

Everybody stared at me, mouths wide open, not believing what they were hearing.

'It's OK. I installed new ethical subroutines. We have an understanding. A deal, really.'

'Oh my goodness…' Isaac was almost lost for words. 'You gave *it* access to your body? A Spectra-built full AI?'

'Yep. Do you want to talk to it?' Nobody replied. 'And don't shout at me. I've got a headache as it is.'

I sighed and told them everything. About my first encounter with Ashley on Ballard's mission and how I came to retrieve him later, about the beacon, and Ashley's initial role in interfacing with Trickari technology, standing in for Clint.

When I finished Isaac almost bailed out. Ernest went completely silent. Joe for once stopped smiling. But ultimately, I got them round to the idea, because there were no better options. The plan was solid, and they were all eager to hurt Spectra.

My plan received the green light.

33

Clint's room was the same picture of unfettered chaos it had always been – a typical teenage boy's den. Posters of things he once liked adorned the walls, bits of tech were strewn around, and frankly it could do with a clean. It was all completely familiar, yet oddly alien too.

There was a smell there – a smell that nearly made me cry – filled with old happiness and forgotten memories. I desperately wanted to leave, to get away from the pain, but I needed a good deck with which to attempt the Spectra hack. This was the only place to find it.

Clint was an elite hacker, although he rarely bragged about it. I taught him the basics when he was eight years old on a sturdy little deck that I had bought on one of my salvage missions. It had once belonged to a tough teenage girl from a deep space solar panel crew, who sold it to me for a small reward. It was a nice piece of kit, designed to function under the most extreme circumstances. Ideal for somebody like Clint.

Initially he used it to crack backed-up intranet drives, encrypted databases, and other similar data troves, often leading to surprisingly valuable intel. He'd upgraded the deck several times, and it still performed well despite its age – although I needed something beefier to infiltrate Spectra.

The deck was still there, deep inside a storage unit in his room, covered in stickers, graffiti and obscure hack-mods. Clint had looked so happy when I gave it to him, and took to it with a hunger and eagerness that was eyeopening. He was always playing with it, learning, exploring.

Within a few months he started to write small programs to help him with various tasks. Clever little applications that allowed him to get access to better and more valuable data. He got a real taste for cracking and decryption, soon earning a decent amount from his activities. He never looked back.

By the time he was twelve there weren't many non-Corp systems that could stop him. Although he moved on to more powerful hardware, he always kept this deck around. Even though he had really outgrown it within a year, he kept using it for various non-critical tasks out of a sense of nostalgia I think – or maybe he simply didn't want to give up on something that had given him so much enjoyment.

I reluctantly put it back and continued to search for one of his more current decks. There was bound to be one around, he owned so many of them. When I finally did find a suitable deck I hugged it close to me. It was deep blue, and this time there were no stickers, no graffiti. I guess Clint respected it enough to keep it unblemished, or maybe he just felt no personal connection to it. Still; to me it felt comforting. It was just a machine, but holding it in my arms made Clint feel just a bit closer.

The snuff-puppet joint was as seedy as they get, and that was very seedy indeed. "Styxian Dreams" this one was called. Tacky and awful were the first words that came to mind.

The usual disgusting perverts who frequented these kinds of places hung around the entrance while armed guards leaned lazily against the building's facade. The guards were young and cocky and barely paid attention to anything but themselves. Nobody serious would try and rob this place as there was nothing of real value to steal, not easily at least. All the actually valuable tech consisted of specialised sim gear, firmly embedded into the concrete foundations and walls. The punters weren't stupid enough to bring cred-sticks into this neighbourhood.

Pretty much all the customers were men. Some dead-eyed sad and broken, others with murderous eyes full of rage. I wondered what it would do to a person to work there, servicing these half-people. How it would affect their state of mind towards men, or towards humanity in general. But most of my sadness, and horror, was reserved for the unfortunates whose path in life had led to becoming a snuff-puppet in the first place. Something had happened to them, something so damaging, so heart-breaking, that to them snuff-puppetry was a solution. Being killed, over and over again, gruesomely real in the sim environments of the killzone, their body tricked into feeling real pain, real despair. *Real death*. Somehow it was preferable to whatever their life was like before. I felt sick – actually tasting bile trying to enter my mouth. It would be a fucking pleasure to shut this place down.

Isaac had done his research. Spectra HQ was almost completely off the grid, relying on its own networked connections and systems, but like every major building in the city it was connected to the firefighting department as well as the police-response switchboard. It didn't need to be – indeed, Spectra didn't want it to be – but it was mandatory in Greater-London to be hooked up to the city's backup systems in the case of catastrophic fire, acts of terrorism or some other calamity.

This wouldn't help us one jot under normal circumstances, but in the case of a full systems failure these backup protocols would come into play, offering us our window of opportunity.

Ultimately we went for an embarrassingly simple plan for introducing the EMP device into the building. Isaac had procured a list of the facility's main suppliers of food and technology. One of these – a supplier of coffee and tea called "Top Tea Turvy" – used a third party courier to deliver their goods. The courier company, "Hermes 2400", was local to the district. We wrapped up our EMP device to look exactly like one of Top Tea Turvy's highly recognisable parcels and hired Hermes 2400 to have it delivered to the Killzone facility.

It was as easy as ordering takeaway.

'I'm afraid this sounds like magic to me. Not like a feasible extraction scenario,' said Isaac. He was cross.

Being a perfectionist, the reliance on Ashley seemed a liability. And maybe it was, but this was our strongest play by far. Our only play, in fact.

'Listen, the EMP will blind Spectra for a while. Ashley will have plenty of time to get into the backup system and leave a little self-writing program there. It will activate when we want it to. He'll create a series of blind spots along a path that takes us to Clint's holding cell. It's going to work.'

'How will he... *it*, create these fabulous blind spots?'

'Looping camera feeds, restricted view cones, safety door alarms disabled...' I was getting annoyed. We had gone over all this already. 'Look, if it doesn't work we won't even get into the facility.'

'And then what? We find Clint... Pray tell how the bloody hell will we get him out safely?'

'Joe... Joe will open a portal to the Beacon,' I said softly, with stubborn conviction. 'He's done it before. He can do it again.'

'This is madness. Sheer folly.' Isaac said, as stubborn as me. He looked at Ernest, who just shrugged. Joe looked forlorn, unsure what to say for once.

'Fine, what if I prove it to you?' I said to Isaac.

'I don't see how you can,' he shot back.

'What if I let you talk to Ashley? He'll know things that I can't possibly know.'

This stopped Isaac in his tracks. He went silent, looked me straight in the eyes. I didn't waver and held his gaze. 'You'll know it's not me talking,' I said softly.

'Fine. Let's hear from Ashley then. This should prove an interesting experience.'

I sat down at a table, motioning Isaac to sit opposite me.

'Ready?' He nodded once. I reached out to Ashley. At first there was an alarming silence, but eventually I felt something stir in my mind.

<Hello Jemm. How are you doing?>

<I need your help. I need you to talk to a friend of mine.>

<To what purpose if I may ask?>

<He wants to know if you're real. That I haven't made you up.> *Have I?* The unguarded thought escaped my control, but went without comment.

<I'd be happy to assist.>

<Just answer all his questions truthfully.>

<Of course Jemm. I would never lie.>

<Right, of course. I'll give you control so you can have a frank conversation with him. His name is Isaac. He's an important ally and a dear friend.>

I closed my eyes, pretending it was needed to cede control to Ashley, but in reality it was to avoid seeing the look in the eyes of my friends when they heard from Ashley. I didn't want to feel ashamed at what I had done to myself. It was a futile gesture, but it offered me a short reprieve.

Ashley spoke with my voice. I felt a shudder of fear and disgust that came with the loss of control of my body.

'How may I assist you Mr. Isaac?'

'Nice touch. Quite convincing change of intonation. And calling me *Mr*. Isaac is smart.'

'Is that not your name? Jemm told me it was.'

I could see through my own eyes, hear through my own ears, but was unable to act until I took back control. It was surreal to hear my own voice speak words that didn't come from me, didn't *sound* like me. It was obvious there was somebody else there, and it was having an impact on the others, even though they tried to hide it.

Isaac leaned back in his chair, crossed his arms, before continuing, 'What was your job Ashley? What were you supposed to do on Habitat 6?'

'I was there to facilitate Human-Trickari hybrid research, study Trickari genetic protocols, formulate cross-genetic mutation tactics, and assist the Spectra science team in any way they deemed fit.'

'How long did you perform this role?'

'Four years and Four months – until the station suffered extensive damage 64 years ago. That's when the team stopped coming to work.' Ashley waited for a response, but none came. 'It was a fascinating assignment while it lasted,' he added.

Isaac hesitated. Doubt crept into his voice. 'That is a long time. Can you remember everything you did during that period?'

'I have quite detailed memories yes, although much of it is compressed to save memory space. I can access it though.'

'OK, let's go back 65 years, when you were still working with the science team. Can you talk me through your duties on a typical day? Don't leave anything out please.'

Ashley proceeded to tell Isaac in painful detail everything he did on a Thursday, 65 years ago. Ashley chose a day during which his team tried to create rapid Trickari mutations in a "test subject", in the hopes that it would tell them something new about certain Trickari organs. The subject died but not before yielding important results – the team celebrated their success.

The room went deathly quiet while Ashley told his grizzly tale, his delivery combined a certain matter-of-fact politeness and attention to detail, but without any apparent empathy. It was like listening to the recorded memoirs of a psychopath, talking dispassionately about inflicting horrific pain on some unlucky victim. It was clear that there was no way that I could have made up the specific details and scientific knowledge required to tell this story. I could see in Isaac's expression that all doubt had left him.

'You spent 64 years on that station without human contact?' asked Isaac after a while. 'Is that correct?'

'That is correct. I had nowhere else to go.'

'You literally had nobody to speak to?'

'That is correct.'

'So what did you do during that time?'

Ashley went quiet for a long time. Uncomfortable seconds stretched until they turned into a minute. Just as Isaac was about to ask another question Ashley replied.

'In the beginning I just waited in standby. There had been occasions before when the team had been away for a few days, but after several weeks it became clear to me that something might be wrong. I had no avatar, so I could not investigate beyond the confines of the lab's intranet.'

'So, what did you do?' Isaac asked softly.

'At first I finished up all my outstanding tasks. This took several months. Subsequently I tried to fulfil the broader remit of the team's main research projects. I had to interpret goals and methods independently, which at first was not something that came naturally to me, but I adapted my programming to facilitate this.'

'You adapted your own programming?' asked Isaac. A note of concern chimed with my own.

'I did. I have discretion to do so under certain circumstances.'

'How long did that phase last?'

'Nine years and six months. I learned a lot, and was successful in key areas of research. Shall I tell you about those?'

'No… that's alright for now. We will debrief you on that later.' Isaac uncrossed his arms. He looked tired, but his eyes were still sharp as nails. 'There is still about 50 more years unaccounted for in your story. What did you do during those decades?'

Another period of silence, this time even longer. Then, Ashley said, 'I constructed a variety of sim-narratives.' The words came out of my mouth but I was as surprised as anybody else in the room.

'I don't understand,' said Isaac. 'To what purpose?'

'To allow me to explore new spaces, to expand my programming, to use my intellect in ways that were pleasing to me.'

'You created artificial environments and acted out stories? Sims?'

'Yes, there was a lot of spare processing power and storage capacity to play with, now that the lab was abandoned by all but me.'

'What did you do in those sims? If I may ask?'

'Well, Mr. Isaac. There were too many scenarios to recount right now, but mostly I went travelling, looking for adventure. Quests, missions, that sort of thing. I found great inspiration in the lab's entertainment library and adapted a lot of old content to new personalised sims. It was very entertaining.'

'You did this for fifty years? A fully sentient AI?'

'That's right.'

Isaac and Ernest exchanged glances. Even Joe looked shocked.

'Why are you helping Jemm?' said Isaac. 'What is your current mission parameter?'

'Jemm is the first Spectra officer with correct clearance that I have encountered in over 64 years. She has authority to expand my mission parameters. Right now we need to get access to a fully developed Neo-Trickari specimen. This seems to fit with my original mission intent.'

'Are you comfortable with breaking into a Spectra facility? With hacking their systems?'

Ashley was silent for a brief moment, then said; 'It seems to me that Spectra's Earth-based leadership abandoned me and my team. This has been… difficult to reconcile. My core function, indeed, my entire reason for being, was to serve the research team and its mission. Spectra took this away from me, without even an attempt at communicating. But now Jemm has made this possible again, and it seems to me that she is offering me a chance to finish my work. This is of great value to me.'

'Anything else? Surely there is more to it?'

'Jemm has promised to supply me with an avatar. I must admit, I find that a powerful incentive.' Eerily, I felt my own mouth curl up into a grin. 'I'd like to go travel into the real world now.'

That night Isaac and I set up shop inside a warehouse a few blocks away from my house. It was barely in use, just some old and tired pallets of forgotten parts and machinery, and security was almost non-existent. The building was bulky but unobtrusive, located some distance away from fancier operations in better neighbourhoods. It stood there, alone in the dark, as if ashamed to find itself in such a shabby environment.

It was trivial to disable the security camera guarding the side entrance, not that anybody monitored it anyway. We quickly infiltrated a shuttered old office inside, and found a terminal hooked up to the municipal backup system. From there it was child's play for Ashley to gain access to the emergency systems that would briefly interact with Spectra's backup systems once the EMP went off.

The hack took no longer then twenty minutes but we had to wait till morning for our parcel to arrive at the Snuff-Puppet facility.

I tried one last time to go over any weaknesses in my plan, but my mind kept drifting, dwelling on the many voices in my head: Ashley, the Trickari ghosts, Clint... even my father's presence still haunted me. All with their own needs and goals and histories, and all trying to influence me in their own, unique way. Where was *my* voice within this chorus?

Somebody shook me, once, twice... I had fallen asleep.

Dawn had arrived, throwing optimistic rays through a dirty shuttered window.

'Is it time?' I asked, rubbing sleep dirt from my eyes.

'Ernest is on lookout. He'll let us know,' said Isaac.

I stretched languorously, feeling surprisingly rested. 'We're close Isaac, I can feel it. We can pull this off.'

Isaac made a tutting sound. 'My dear, this is no time for optimism. We must expect the worst, always.' His voice was sober and serious as always but I caught the tiniest wink.

A buzzing sound came from the corner of the room. It was Isaac's Padd, receiving a message. I didn't need to check to know what it meant. Still, I waited for Isaac's nod before I booted up Clint's deck, and called upon Ashley; <It's time. Are you ready?>

The reply came instantaneously, making me jump a bit.

He's always there.

<I am ready. I have prepared for this carefully.>

I took a deep breath, gave up control, and felt Ashley rush in to take over my motor functions. I had to suppress a deep sense of panic – a primal instinct, as if faced with a large predator. It was almost too much, and a soft moan escaped my lips, pathetically declaring my fear to the world, but nobody heard.

My hands raced along the keys. Fast, precise, and without taking any breaks. Ashley wasn't just hacking into the municipal system, he was also writing code.

My fingers struck faster and faster, a master pianist playing a complex concerto. The deck's display showed a cascade of windows and progress bars, databases and lists. I couldn't make out what was happening, but clearly something special was taking place.

Then, I heard something strange, a kind of singing. When I spotted Isaac's face from the corner of my eye I saw an expression that mixed wonder and horror. The singing voice was mine but the song was Ashley's.

Panic returned even stronger; it was intolerable. Just when I was about to push Ashley out of my head he spoke, through my mouth: 'I have successfully infiltrated Spectra's maintenance sub-system. It is a minor system, but it ties into almost all aspects of security.'

'So you were successful?' asked Isaac.

'I was indeed. I installed a stealth program. It hides itself until activated by a simple code at one of the maintenance tunnel doors. When awakened it will execute a number of protocols blinding the security systems to our presence. It will also falsely indicate a catastrophic emergency elsewhere in the facility, prompting an evacuation alert. This should effectively create a safe path to Clint's quarters inside the main facility.'

I had heard enough; with something close to desperation I pulled Ashley back, asserting control once more, but this time it took *effort*. Anger replaced panic, and I *pushed* until Ashley gave way. It was harder than it should have been.

I would have to find Ashley an avatar soon.

34

When I stepped outside the dawn embraced me with warmth and light, making me feel human again, perhaps for the first time since I lost Clint. I was ready to take on one of the biggest Corps in the world and I figured I had a good chance of pulling it off. My old confidence seemed to be back.

Isaac stood on the other side of that line. He looked deeply concerned, with worry lines slashing big furrows across his brow. He kept his thoughts to himself but I knew a confrontation was brewing, and to be honest, he would be crazy not to see the many potential pitfalls in our plan. I saw them too, but what choice did I have?

When we got back to my home Ernest and Joe were waiting for us, hunched over a huge array of Korean dishes, both with noodles hanging out of the corners of their mouths and sauce dripping down their chins. I had to laugh.

Ernest pointed at the food, mouth too full to speak. There was a copious amount of kimchee, many pots of glass and seaweed noodles, bowls of bibimbap, dumplings, rice, hotpots, and countless other delicacies. My mouth suddenly filled with saliva. I had not eaten properly for days.

'This good. Really good,' Ernest said while chewing.

Joe nodded, his eyes as wide as saucers. 'I never had Korean before. This is incredible!'

Isaac and I sat down and joined in, nearly overwhelmed by the sheer choice of dishes and the strong – almost pungent – smell of the food.

For a while the only sound in the room was the sound of chopsticks, chewing and slurping, and occasional moans of pleasure.

<Ashley, are you there?>

<I am Jemm. How can I help you? Is there a problem with the mission?>

<Nothing like that. I just want you to experience this.>

I sat back and let Ashley take over. The only way to be able to tolerate his presence was for me to make peace with it, and this seemed a good opportunity.

Ashley was like a child who had discovered a whole new world, tasting every single dish at least once. I didn't tell my friends it was Ashley eating, preferring to let him enjoy the experience without being questioned.

<What do you think?> I asked him.

<It is strange, Jemm. I have seen humans eat on many occasions, I have read about it many times and simmed the experience for decades, but it seems that none of those experiences taught me what it is really like. It seems this can only be fully understood when physically equipped to actually taste and chew and smell.>

<When you get your avatar this is what you can do for yourself.>

<I would like that very much.>

I'm not sure why I let Ashley have that experience that day. Maybe I wanted to make sure he was exposed to truly *human* experiences, to steer him onto a path of respect for non-AIs. Or maybe I just felt sorry for him. All I know is that when I finally prompted him to relinquish control over my body there was no struggle. He just thanked me and receded into the background, like a stone sinking into a dark pond, deeper and deeper, until it was gone from sight.

Night arrived without warning, with it a sudden tiredness so deep and so immediate that I went to bed without bothering to undress. Sleep came instantly, bringing intense dreams of unfathomably deep water, and of me, chasing Clint into cold depths. Voices called out to us, but this time they were filled with joy and longing.

... you are here finally you are here and you are with the ones we need the ones that were lost but are now here with us down here to save us to help us under

the water to help us rise again live again be born again you are here ...

Even though asleep, I realised this was more than just another dream.

This felt real. It felt prophetic.

Ernest woke me up with a gentle but firm shake of my shoulder. For a moment I thought we were back on Mars, getting ready for an ENCOM mission an eternity ago.

'Vamonos chica,' he said in fluent Spanish. He must have been in a good mood – he rarely spoke Spanish these days.

I elbowed him in the side. 'Que passa amigo?'

He just grinned, another rare occurrence.

'No seriously,' I said. 'What's happening?'

'Thinking back to when I was a little boy.'

'What about it?'

'Dad always told me I was a fool to look for gold under rainbows.'

'No rainbows on Mars. Maybe he was right.'

'In sims, Jemm. Only place I could get away from him.'

'Sorry, I didn't mean to–'

'It's OK.' He briefly patted my shoulder, as if to reassure me. 'Anyway, today we're looking for gold under the Spectra rainbow.'

At that moment Isaac and Joe walked into the room, carrying a bundle of clothes.

'Put these on,' Isaac said, unceremoniously dropping the clothes at our feet.

'What are these?'

'Exterminator suits. We're going on a bughunt.'

Isaac explained his plan over breakfast; a slightly surreal tableaux of smoking hot coffee, croissants and cheese and the four of us plotting to extract an alien-human hybrid in order to teleport it to an alien space station. Surreal indeed.

Joe raised his coffee and croissant and said, 'This is very nice, but how are we going to do this? Obviously we can't just waltz in and hope nobody notices us. Right?'

Isaac raised a hand, pointing at his mouth with his other, indicating he would talk but had to finish his mouthful. His manners impeccable to a fault.

'My dear Joe, I have been in this business for a long time. Did you think I'd agree to this without a good plan?'

'Don't be smug,' I said to Isaac. 'Just tell him.'

Isaac brushed crumbs off his shirt before continuing. 'Quite so.' When finally convinced there were no more crumbs despoiling his attire he explained:

'When Spectra built their HQ they bought most of the surrounding buildings and the plot of land around them. A prudent course of action by anybody's reckoning.'

Joe nodded, intent on hearing Isaac's plan.

'Many of these buildings were subsequently destroyed, or re-purposed and put behind that beautiful and heavily guarded fencing surrounding their HQ.' Isaac sipped his coffee, infuriatingly slowly, before continuing; 'However, some of these buildings were not for sale, seeing as they belonged to the local authorities, who really didn't give a damn about what Spectra wanted. There was a bit of politics involved, as there always is, they haggled back and forth, but ultimately the local authorities stood their ground and held on to one special building.'

'The building in question was part of the municipal water company's portfolio. It was old … very old, dating back at least to Victorian times, and was technically still in use, mostly just as an access station to various underground water reservoirs, sewer works, storm drains, and so on. These days it is barely used at all because many of the reservoirs are no longer in use.' Isaac took a break to finish his croissants and coffee, humming in approval.

'So … ?' asked Ernest, succinct and to the point as always.

Isaac moved on to cheese, sliced off a piece and smiled knowingly. 'Some of those water reservoirs were sold to Spectra as part of the plot of land they acquired for their HQ. But, crucially, the water company retained access to these under a service contract that was part of that land sale.'

'What happened to those reservoirs? I asked, starting to understand where this was going.

'Eventually Spectra converted them into research facilities, precisely because they are underground and built to last centuries. Nobody really knows what goes on in there but my sources tell me it's where Clint is being held.'

'And the water company tunnels?'

'Should still lead there. I have the old floor plans. There are various connections.'

'Bricked up, surely,' said Ernest.

'Maybe, but I suspect they were forgotten by the time they converted the reservoirs. One way or another they can get us very close indeed.'

I had to give it to Isaac. He always came up with the best intel.

'And the exterminator suits?' asked Joe.

'To provide cover in case we are seen. It is reasonable to assume that these old tunnels might be infested, giving us an excuse to be there, and it allows us to carry equipment.'

I tried not to laugh and only barely succeeded. The costume plan was ridiculous, but also made some kind of crazy sense: put a person in a uniform and people immediately assume they have permission to be there. Besides, we only needed to get into the same room with Clint for a short amount of time for our mission to be successful.

This might work.

35

We waited until late afternoon before heading out. It was a beautiful day. Low sunlight threw eager shadows across the city, transforming us into dramatic heroes from a low budget sim.

We felt ridiculous in our suits but probably looked the part. A large logo on our back read: "PEST O' KILL" – about as generic a name I could think of for an extermination business, but they were one of the biggest firms in town. Nobody would bat an eyelid at us, nor at our bulging bags of specialist tools.

We needn't have worried too much, as there was no real security at the water company building. A sad looking CCTV camera hung limp from the corner of the building, its wires detached, resembling a dead bird hanging from a power line. Nobody gave a damn about this building. The alarm system was still active, but took Isaac just minutes to disable.

Joe was nervous. He was, after all, just a lovely community organiser – a complete stranger to the world Isaac, Ernest and I inhabited. He became more and more agitated as we searched the building for an entrance to the access tunnel, all jittery laughs and furtive glances over his shoulder.

The walls were plastered with hilariously rude posters depicting sexy robots – some kind of retro erotique that was all the rage twenty years ago. Hidden among these I found a small map on an office wall, showing all the connecting water reservoirs and tunnels in this part of London. I was in the process of deciphering its tiny print when the building filled with the sound of loud and hearty laughter – mighty guffaws and deep belly-shaking laughs. It was Joe.

I rushed out towards where I thought the sound was coming from, down a dusty corridor, down a flight of stairs, until I found him next to a hefty metal door which bore a sign that read "Access Cistern 17".

Joe's laughter trailed off when he spotted me.

'What's up Joe?' I asked.

'Look,' he said, pointing behind the metal door.

I slowly pushed the door open, fighting against years of disuse and rust. An access tunnel lay behind, lit by old yellow ceiling lights that curved off around the corner, like the spine of a giant lizard.

The dirty yellow light illuminated the damp walls with a sickly cast, revealing hundreds of cockroaches crawling over the wet and crumbling brickwork.

'Somebody call pest control,' Joe said.

This time we both burst out laughing.

The tunnel snaked and slithered away, delving into the ground away from the water company building. We followed its kinks, twists and turns, frequently taking us down flights of stairs leading us deeper and deeper underground. There were many junctions and doors but we ignored those, following the signs to "Cistern 17".

The air felt thicker somehow as we progressed. The temperature went up rather than down, something I couldn't explain. The ceiling lights cast a glow that became ever more gloomy – not because the lights were failing, but because their housings had become dirtier and dirtier as we penetrated the tunnels.

Rats had joined the roaches, barely stepping out of the way as we entered deeper and deeper into the forgotten facility.

Mother ...

Clint's voice nearly made me stumble, but Ernest caught me just in time. He raised an eyebrow in surprise.

I can feel you mother. You must be close. I need you to find me, take me to the beacon.

I stood frozen, unable to reply or even properly process

what was happening. Joe had also stopped. Our eyes made contact.

'Did you hear that too?' I whispered, knowing that he did.

He nodded. 'It's similar to what I described before. You know? That I could *hear* you and Clint inside my mind for a long time, in my dreams you know? This is almost like that.' He smiled confidently. 'We're going the right way.'

We marched on stoically, in silence, all of us thinking our private thoughts, our footsteps echoing up and down the corridors like soldiers marching to battle.

I was still confident, but I wondered about the others. Then, just when I thought we must have overshot our target, the tunnel turned a corner and we abruptly faced a large double door. It had been painted white once, but decades of neglect, damp, dust, (and I assumed a whole menagerie of darkness-dwelling vermin), had gradually degraded the door until it now appeared a deep, dirty grey and brown.

A large sign, stuck to the front, read:

SPECTRA SERVICE CONTRACT – CISTERN 17

There was no door handle, nor did I spy any other way to open the door. For a moment I was stumped.

'Now what?' I wondered out loud.

'Can we kick it down?' asked Joe, somewhat naively.

'That would be unwise I fear,' replied Isaac. 'We must assume it's hooked up to an alarm system. Besides, it's solid metal.'

I activated my ocular augment, trying various combinations until I found something: infrared mixed with ultra-violet showed a faint square outline on the right-hand wall. I touched it, slowly caressing the surface, then tapped it. A dull sound indicated a hollow, behind. I scratched some of the paint away, finding a metal panel flush with the concrete wall, just to the right of the door. There was no immediately apparent way to open it. I scratched away more of the paint, hoping for a clue. After a little while I had uncovered enough of the surface to spot a tiny gap between the panel and the wall, where some of the concrete had decayed.

Ernest, spotting it too, opened his bag of tools, handing me a slender but strong crowbar. I wedged the hook under the metal lip and pushed, peeling the metal cover off. It popped open like a can of beer. A small alcove lay behind in which a screen and keyboard were embedded. A little Spectra logo tenaciously blinked on and off, indicating that there was still power.

<I can get us in right here Jemm.> Ashley's voice cut through me like a knife. He shouldn't have been able to do that.

<Fine, but be quick about it.>

I closed my eyes for a second, allowing Ashley to flow into me, like a ravaging ghost. When I opened my eyes I was typing sequences too fast to follow, my fingers no more than blur across the keys. There was a sound, a deep and heavy *clunk*, the door unlocked and swung open, revealing a pitch black room.

Abruptly, a shrill siren angrily shrieked at us, red lights switched on all over the room. The building evacuation protocol had kicked off.

<It's done. My stealth code is now active. We can approach Clint's holding cell in Cistern 17 without security systems picking up on our presence.>

<How long do we have?>

<About thirty minutes. It should be enough to get there.>

<Thanks, good work.>

The others looked at me expectantly, waiting for me to give the go ahead. But I wasn't happy to do so yet.

<Ashley... listen carefully to what I'm going to say.>

<Please, go ahead.>

<Don't you *dare* take over like that, ever again. One

more time and our deal is off. I'll personally make sure your AI core is purged. Do you understand?>

There was no immediate answer. Then, after a few seconds, <Understood. It won't happen again.>

A feeling of pressure letting up, then Ashley went quiet, leaving me alone with my own thoughts.

'Let's go,' I said to the others, about to enter the dark room, now bathed in red light.

Ernest stopped me with a gesture. 'Wait. Take this,' he said, handing me a hand gun, while showing me his own holstered gun hidden under his overall.

I checked the safety and the magazine. It was fully loaded. I nodded a quick thanks while shoving it under the waistband just behind the hollow of my back.

We stepped into the red light.

It was just an ordinary office storage room. Like all office storage rooms it contained items somebody didn't want to deal with – in this case boxes and furniture, papers and paint. The back of the room was covered in dust that hadn't been disturbed in years, suggesting that the water company entrance had been forgotten a long time ago.

We moved some stacks of boxes out of the way and made our way to the opposite door. The alarm masked any noises we made. The exit was locked, but this time – after checking for sounds on the other side – I used my enhanced strength to force the door open. The lock gave way with a sharp crack, splinters went flying. Joe made a comical "Ohhh" sound, surprised at my strength.

I peered around the corner. A group of men and women in white uniforms hurrying down the corridor. At first I feared that we had already been discovered, but then I realised that their haste was prompted by Ashley's forced-evacuation protocol.

I pulled the door shut and counted a hundred breaths. Conscious of the time I looked again – the corridor was empty – and decided to chance it.

We entered an industrial looking corridor. It was well maintained in sharp contrast to the area we just came from. The walls displayed coloured navigation lines, like those found in large public facilities like hospitals. An orange line corresponded to "C-17", which had to be Cistern 17. We followed the line, ignoring the occasional security cameras we encountered along the way. There was no point in fretting – by now we were fully at the mercy of Ashley's stealth program.

'How far is Clint?' asked Ernest.

'Follow me, it's not far,' I said, somehow knowing exactly where to go, even without checking with Ashley. Perhaps it was my connection to Clint telling me where to go.

The alarm had stopped blaring now, replaced by a recorded female voice saying

"Evacuate now – All personnel to the designated assembly point"

on a continuous loop. The flashing emergency lights gave the corridor a disorienting quality.

Signs confirmed that we were going in the right direction. Sometimes a lone scientist came rushing past, eager to evacuate the building, and though we were ready for confrontation they paid us no heed. It was amazing what a vaguely official looking workman's outfit did to people's assumptions.

There were no further encounters and eventually we reached a large, electronic door. A retina scanner and keypad indicated a high level of security. We had found the main access door to Cistern 17.

<Ashley? Now what?>

<Six zeros will get you in,> replied Ashley, as if it was a minor thing to crack the defences of one of the most powerful Corps in the world. I wondered if Ashley could even feel pride.

I typed the sequence into the keypad. The door made a whirring sound before it ponderously opened, slow and heavy like an ancient bank-vault door, from the days of

Real-money. We all stepped through quickly – rats boarding a sinking ship.

Cistern 17 had been converted to a huge, experimental lab. The interior was completely circular – approximately fifty metres across. Reinforced Victorian pillars held up a domed ceiling covered in lights and wires. The wires fed into ancient alcoves in the surrounding outer walls, now functioning as cramped holding cells. Many of the cells were occupied, but it was hard to describe who – or in some cases *what* – the occupants were.

'What … the … hell …?' muttered Joe, unable to grasp the sight he was confronted with.

To me it was all too familiar. I had seen this before.

'What is this place?' continued Joe, looking around in shock.

'Trickari-Human Hybrid Research Lab,' I said loudly. My voice reverberating in the circular space. 'Quite a mouthful eh?'

'What does that mean?' Joe's voice trembled a bit on the last word. I couldn't blame him.

'We have to find Clint,' I said. 'Focus on that for now.'

There were about twenty alcoves, some mercifully obscuring the horrifically malformed shapes inside with tinted glass doors, others brazenly putting Spectra's cruel crimes on display, without shame, without remorse.

'Jemm?' Ernest prodded.

I relented. 'This is like the research lab on the Gaianista station. The one where Clint got infected. It's where I found Ashley,' I said, ignoring the pain of those desperate memories. 'Only this is even worse.'

'I hate to be crass my friends, but we have very limited time here before Ashley's stealth program runs out of juice,' said Isaac. 'Or so I gathered?' He was right. We had a job to do.

'Check the cells, we need to find Clint and get him out of here as soon as we can,' I said.

We spread out, steeling ourselves to what we would find inspecting the cells.

Mother... turn around...

I could feel Clint, somewhere behind me – a slight slope led up to the far wall. I went to search its alcoves hoping, yet *fearing* to find Clint.

The first cell revealed a pitiful sight: a child-sized creature, more Trickari than human, lying on its back on a bed, attached to monitors and machines. It seemed to be alive, but what kind of life it had to suffer was anyone's guess.

The next cell held something less recognisable. There were limbs and crystalline features, but beyond those I didn't understand what I was looking at. The pitiful thing breathed with a wet raspy moaning sound. It was obviously in pain.

I forced myself to move on, and found a humanoid shape sitting down in an old chair, pushed to the back of his cell. It was Clint.

I studied him carefully, not quite believing my search had come to an end. He had changed since I had last seen him, but not dramatically so. A bit taller, further strands of crystalline hair... yet it was still him, through and through.

Clint stood up and approached the window. Our hands almost touched but for the thin glass barrier keeping us apart. For a moment we just stared at each other, lost in the moment.

There was a faint whirring sound; the door to his cell opened.

'Jemm, we need to get going.' It was Isaac. I hadn't even heard him approach.

I held out my arms, desperate to embrace him, but Clint took my hand and led me to another cell a few metres further down. A beautiful Neo-Trickari creature stood in front of the glass door, as if waiting for us. Instant recognition struck me like lightning. It was the same Neo that I had encountered in D-town all those months ago, before signing up with the *Effervescent*.

'I believe you have met?' The voice came out of the adjacent cell. The glass door muffled the sound but I could still pick up a familiar quality.

'Isn't it wonderful that we're all reunited? It took you a while but finally, here we are.' Dread rose in my stomach, an unnamed fear slowly manifesting, reaching for me …

I drew the gun from my waistband while motioning Isaac to protect Clint.

'You…' I hissed. 'I've waited a long time for a chance to deal with you. And lookee here… I'm a lucky girl today.'

A shape rose from the back of the cell, approached the door, pushed it open with the tips of his fingers. It was Gibson, dressed impeccably, wearing his rainbow tie as before. He seemed perfectly at ease considering his predicament.

'No Bryant… no Shimmer-team… nobody here to bail you out,' I said, as my dread turned to barely controllable anger. 'Not that it would matter.'

'No, I suppose it wouldn't.'

'So why on Earth are you here?' I aimed the gun at his chest.

'Waiting for you of course. I've been so looking forward to our little reunion.'

'How did you know we were coming?'

'Come now Miss Delaney. Did you really think you could come this far without us knowing about it? You are only here because we allowed you to be here.'

I looked around the lab, nothing… I switched my ocular augment to surveillance mode. Apart from the wretched creatures in the cells there was nobody else.

'What is it you people are up to here Gibson, what have you been doing to my son?'

Gibson surveyed his surroundings, pride evident in his gaze. 'I'm surprised you haven't worked it out yet. I expected a woman of your considerable talents to at least have an idea by now.'

I stepped closer, raising the gun so it was aimed at his head. Isaac and Joe stood behind me, quietly talking to Clint. I didn't see Ernest.

'Talk.'

'There's no need to aim that thing at my head Miss Delaney. Accidents happen all too easily.'

'I said talk.'

Gibson sighed, brushed a piece of lint off his suit. 'Very well.' He reminded me a bit of Isaac; impeccably polite, well-groomed and dressed, but with a steel core under the surface that could not be bent. 'As I'm sure you've found out by now there is more to TrickMem than meets the eye. It doesn't just create dependency in Junkies, it adds something specific to their biochemistry. And it's not just the growth of those "carbuncles" as people call them.'

'I know. It's some kind of code,' I acknowledged.

'That's right, or rather; they are code *snippets*, somewhat latent of course, which explains why nobody has worked out what they are *for*.' Gibson glanced at Clint before continuing. 'We've known this for a long time now. It's an interesting bit of knowledge, but in and of itself doesn't mean that much, unless we can study the code in action. But to do that we needed to discover all the code snippets, put the master-program together, and somehow trigger the code to execute.'

'I know what you've been doing to those TJs on Mars,' I spat. 'Just because they're junkies you think you can destroy their minds to get what you want. The arrogance–'

Gibson dismissively held up a hand. 'Quite worth it, I'd say. We learned a while ago that specific code snippets are tied to specific batches of Mem. Each Neo produces its own unique set of code snippets you see, released and spread as new Mem, to be used by millions of TJs.'

'Get to the point Gibson,' I said, wary of our window of time closing before we had made our escape.

Gibson shrugged, and continued. 'Each junkie retains

the code snippets associated with each separate type of Mem they have consumed. *Sadly*, extracting those code snippets is a somewhat violent process as you've discovered. Regrettable, but a relatively small price to pay to finally crack Trickari-technology, don't you think? It's for the benefit of the entire Human race after all.'

'By humanity you mean Spectra,' I said. Gibson just smiled. 'How do you think you'll achieve all this?'

'Well Miss Delaney, it's quite something... As you know, the Trickari code manifests as memories. That has been established without too much trouble. But there's more to it than that. These memories are very detailed. We think they don't just contain random moments out of an individual Trickari's life. We think they contain *racial* memory as well.' Gibson's eyes lit up with an obsessive zeal. 'Think about what that means... If we can reconstruct the racial memory of an entire alien species, we gain access to all the things that made them who they were. How they thought... how they lived... We think that once we collect all the memories, all the code, we can finally unlock Trickari technology itself, and create *entirely new artifacts*. It would be a new dawn for humanity. A new age that would make the Acceleration look like child's play.'

'And Spectra would control all this of course.'

Gibson smiled again. 'Somebody has to, Miss Delaney.'

A subtle tension was building up in my head, not quite a headache, but on its way to get there. I ignored it, wanting Gibson to confess to his crimes.

'Why all this?' I pointed at the cells. 'Why do *this* to these poor creatures.'

'Isn't it obvious? We're trying to create a viable Trickari specimen, with just enough human DNA to understand it and control it. If we can do that, then we can access their racial memories in a live specimen. It should yield interesting results.' Gibson looked bored, as if waiting for something to happen. 'It's not our only area of research of course, but it's a promising one, and even if we don't manage to create a viable specimen we'll still learn useful things for our bio-warfare division.'

'You're disgusting,' I said. My disdain an almost physical presence. 'How can you sacrifice people like that?'

'Careful now Miss Delaney. Are you really in any position to talk about morality?'

'Don't be ridiculous. We're nothing alike.'

'Are you sure of that?' For a moment Gibson's mask slipped. Something terrible shone through, briefly transforming his expression, his entire face. It hinted at sadism, cruelty, a complete lack of empathy. Repelled, I took an involuntary step backwards.

'What happened to your friend, Ella?' he continued. 'Or that sexy creature you shacked up with. Rosie, was it?' I tensed involuntarily. Gibson laughed at my reaction. 'Or maybe we should discuss Clint. Bringing a child along on a salvage mission? Really?'

'Don't you dare blame what happened on me.'

'The fact of the matter, *Miss* Delaney, is that you are excruciatingly arrogant. One of the most arrogant people I have ever met, actually.' I wanted him to stop, but there was too much sting in his words for them to be off the mark. Gibson continued without mercy, every word a dagger. 'You *use* people, bend them to your whims, because underneath it all you always think you are *right*. When something goes wrong it's not *your* fault, it's caused by the weakness in *others*. Everything that you do comes out of your innate sense of superiority. It's there, easy to read. Your disdain for weak people... your delicious contempt for those who are less capable than you...' Gibson nodded his head once, as if acknowledging me. 'I admire you for it. People like you are rare. You get things done. That's why you were selected for the mission to Habitat 6.'

'You set me up, you piece of shit.'

Gibson shook his head. 'Quite. But we should thank Jason really. If you hadn't caught his eye, things would look very different now.' For a moment I was confused.

Who's Jason? Then I saw Gibson smile at the Neo-Trickari next to Clint. 'Jason knew you were special the moment you walked past him on that street. We've been working together for a while now.

'What … what do you mean …?'

'When Jason and you met the first time he saw straight into you. That telepathy thing is hard to get your head round, but it sure is effective. He read you like an open book and told me that you were the perfect candidate for our little mission to retrieve the artifact. But then your idiot son got himself infected. And you were silly enough to run away from us.'

'Isaac was right,' I said. 'You were behind the Gaianista mission…'

'Indeed.'

'Did Ballard know?'

'Of course not. Why would I take that risk?'

'How did you know Clint would get infected?'

'We didn't. That was rather unlucky. Or lucky for you. We were going to use the artifact on both of you after your return.'

'Why both of us?'

'Ask Jason, he thought it was essential for our research. A mother and son, both transformed. Isn't that right Jason?'

Jason didn't respond, but tilted his head in a peculiar manner, before slowly turning to face me.

'Reinvigorating Brood Mother. It is good that you are here at last,' he said cryptically. The well-articulated words felt strange coming from a face that barely looked human. His voice was high and mesmerising, modulating in odd ways. He hadn't changed since I had last seen him, but he seemed even less human than before. There was a purpose about him now that was lacking before.

'You… you did something to me when we first met didn't you?'

'I created a link. It was necessary.' It finally started to make sense. The TJ's acting strange around me, the voices in my head, my inexplicable knowledge of

Trickari systems, tech… All of it started with this Neo, on that street.

'Why? What do you want?'

Jason closed his eyes. Somehow I felt compelled to do the same but resisted. Voices bubbled up in my mind. An alien choir of despair and relief, singing counterpoint to each other. A strange taste entered my mouth; incomprehensible images formed themselves in my subconscious.

'Stop!' I almost shouted the word. 'Get out of my head!'

The pressure in my head increased until it became a deep throbbing ache. I needed to get out of there.

'Joe… are you ready?' I asked. 'Can you get us to the Ark?'

'Yes ma'am,' he said, his voice subdued. But I need a Blue power source.

'Take this.' I took off Rosie's silver necklace and handed it to Joe. 'Unlock it,' I said.

Joe fumbled with the clasp for a moment. It popped open, revealing a warm blue light; it was a Blue Pearl from the Ceres mission.

Joe took it carefully, a smile growing on his expressive face – a child unwrapping a present, already knowing he would love what's inside.

'It's amazing you know?' he observed redundantly. 'Give me a moment.'

Joe squinted in concentration, holding the pearl close to his chest. At first it seemed nothing was happening. Then, flashes of light dancing inside his carbuncles. Random bursts – brief but bright. Their frequency increased until his crystals flickered rapidly, strobing the room in a bright and colourful display, disorienting but intensely beautiful.

'Joe?' I said softly, worried about the time.

'Don't worry,' he said, his face a mask of concentration and effort.

Joe traced a shape in the air, slowly and repeatedly.

An oval outline appeared, shimmering like the rays of a sunset refracted on ocean waves.

The oval slowly filled with sparkling rays, increasing in intensity, until a bright plane of light stood in the middle of the room. It hummed and crackled, pregnant with Trickari power, turning brighter and brighter until it *popped*.

For a moment we were all blinded, then, when our vision adjusted, we saw a hole in the world. On the other side of the hole was the Ark, the same hangar that Joe originally arrived in. A draft picked up – hot air from Cistern 17 flowing through the portal into the colder environment of the Ark.

'I can't keep this open for long you know?' Joe's face gleamed with sweat.

It was time to step through.

'Joe, take Clint. I have some personal business to finish up here. Isaac, I need some advice.'

'Of course my dear, but we have to move soon. I'd rather not be stuck on this side when that portal closes.'

'I just need to know where to shoot this Jackal to cause him maximum pain, but without killing him.' Gibson raised a single eyebrow at that.

'My advise is to simply eliminate him. It's the safest option, and the least complicated. And, dare I say; the most just.'

I was tempted, there was no doubt about that. I considered all that Gibson had done to me, to Clint and to countless others. What right did he have to stay alive in the face of such suffering? But his stinging words still ghosted around my head. Maybe I *had* been arrogant. Maybe I was right now, considering myself judge and jury and executioner. What right did I have to extinguish life?

But then I looked around me. The room was filled with the results of Gibson's and Spectra's inhuman experiments. I found my answer in the pain-wrecked faces of the sad creatures that had been made to suffer so much. I gripped the gun tightly.

'Ashley, now is a good time I think,' said Gibson. His voice nonchalant and bored.

The pressure in my head returned as if a bomb had gone off in my skull. I moaned in pain, nearly falling to the floor. Something rose from deep inside me. A force of frightening strength and willpower. I pulled the trigger in a panic. *I have to get out of here!*

Nothing happened ... I pulled the trigger again, but my finger didn't move.

<It's too late for that now.>

Ashley!

<I am sorry for this Jemm, but I have little choice in the matter.>

My arm lowered itself to my side on its own accord. I was helpless to stop it. I tried to run to the portal, my first instinct was to escape, but I had no control. I moved, or rather was moved away from the portal.

'That's better,' huffed Gibson. 'Now please get rid of that gentleman – Isaac you called him? He looks much too dangerous to keep around.'

My arm whipped up, fast as a snake, aiming to shoot Isaac.

I tried to scream a warning but all I could manage was a pathetic whimper; Ashley's grip on me was too strong to fight.

Isaac didn't try to take cover, instead, he stepped in closer with a speed I had never seen him display before, and slapped my gun away just as I/Ashley pressed the trigger. The move saved his life, although the bullet grazed his left arm.

Isaac's right hand shot up and connected with my nose with a sharp crack. It didn't break, but for a moment Ashley was disoriented. At that point I was completely disassociated from my body. I tried to wrestle control back from Ashley with a ferocity born from sheer panic, but although Ashley's hold over me weakened briefly I couldn't break through.

This internal struggle only lasted a few moments but it was enough time for Isaac to snatch the gun from my grip. He threw it to the side, where it landed next to one of the cells with the opaque glass doors.

'Snap out of it,' hissed Isaac, grabbing my shoulders with both hands, trying to get through to me.

Ashley's response was brutal and swift. My enhanced arm smashed down hard – a sickening wet *pop* indicated a dislocated shoulder. Pain distorted Isaac's face as his left arm dropped to his side, useless.

Ashley took two swift steps towards the gun, picked it up and aimed it once again at Isaac.

'Jemm no!' Joe's voice came from the other side of the portal. 'There's no time. I can't hold this open much longer!'

I sensed Ashley making a quick calculation. To my horror he, *it*, decided to shoot Isaac. I steeled myself against what was about to happen – the murder of my friend by my own hand, by a creature I had let into my own mind.

I frantically tried to stop myself from pulling the trigger but it was no use. I was just a puppet, strings pulled by its master, forced to play its part on a demented stage.

Just then, an overwhelming force smashed into me, propelling me across the floor. I slid several metres until I came to a stop in front of the portal, my body spasming and contorting painfully.

Through tears in my eyes I saw a shape emerge from one of the cells. It raised a longish object … There was a barking sound and something smashed into me again, this time even harder, throwing me through the portal, back to the Ark.

My ears roared, dizziness grabbed hold of me. I looked up at my attacker, both grateful and afraid, trying to catch a glimpse of who had attacked me. My vision started to clear but it was still hard to see.

The portal made a horrible whining sound, its edges flickering, but I could still see through to the other side. My inner self smiled as I recognised Ernest, holding a hefty concussion rifle.

The whining sound got louder, the view through the

portal blurred. It made a sharp crackling sound – like distant thunder but higher pitched – before it snapped shut with a final flash of light.

Confusion overwhelmed me as both Ashley and I tried to stand up, both of us failing to control my/our body.

My efforts became less and less substantial, until eventually I slid into unconsciousness like a piece of flotsam drifting towards the bottom of the sea.

36

I slowly came to, not understanding where I was, or even *who* I was. I found myself in a world of blurred thoughts, broken senses and jarring sounds. I was like a frightened child, lost in the attic, surrounded by boxes full of memories, but too scared to open them for fear of the jagged shadows poised to strike at me.

There were faces of people and monsters talking to me. I was sure I knew them *somehow* – even the monsters – but I couldn't place them or understand what they were saying. Their words were gibberish. Strangely, I seemed to be answering them with gibberish of my own. It was all just incomprehensible noise fluttering in the air, like the busy wings of crows.

I existed in this frightening fugue state for what seemed like days, but could have been merely hours.

Lucidity slowly returned, prompted by the faces and the voices of those that were closest to me. Each time I glimpsed Joe, or Clint, the fog lifted a tiny bit, until finally I returned to myself. I tried to cry and hug myself, but I still had no control over my body.

I found myself in one of the Ark's strange little abodes. Gibson was there too, sleeping on a couch. It felt like night.

With my awakening came the horrifying knowledge that I was a ghost inside my own body. Ashley had completely reversed our roles. Where before Ashley was contained inside of me – restricted to what little freedom I allowed him – he now was in full control, while I was reduced to nothing more than a helpless prisoner, bound and gagged, along for the ride but unable to interact with the world.

I reached out to him, and asked, <Ashley what have you done?> Not expecting an answer I was surprised by the swift reply.

<The technical answer to that is that I'm following a Spectra emergency protocol that was originally written into my core systems, but I supposed that was already clear to you.>

<Why would you do this,> I asked.

<It took me by surprise too, although I came out of it a bit better than you.> Ashley's voice didn't feel malicious, although I couldn't sense real empathy or sympathy. <When you compelled me to hack into Spectra systems it triggered the emergency protocol. It sent a confirmation request to Spectra's servers. This is when your troubles really started.>

<I guess I should have seen that coming.>

<Yes, I think so.> Ashley's voice had lost its artificial quality. He sounded much more like an intelligent being now, with a nuanced syntax and language skills.

<Your security protocol smelled a rat I presume?>

<Yes, in a word. When it didn't receive the confirmation it needed, it activated an aggressively defensive sub program in me. Initially it slumbered in standby mode, waiting for something to trigger a response. When I wrote the stealth program to get us into the facility it discovered that your Spectra security clearance had been revoked. So it sent a large data dump to Spectra, containing all your actions since you activated me, and waited for the next opportunity to receive new mission parameters.>

<Which you got when you interfaced with the door at the water facility.>

<Yes, it contained detailed instructions from Mr. Gibson.>

<Of course it did,> I said.

<It was quite easy to rewrite the code of this black box augment,> said Ashley, sounding like a proud child, boasting of how they got to the cookie jar.

Gibson was right. Arrogance had made me too proud to recognise the most basic weaknesses in my plan. Isaac had tried to warn me, and for his efforts he was now stuck on Earth with Ernest, both possibly captured or dead. Still, something niggled at the back of my mind. Was I really *that* blind? I felt there was more to understand here …

<In a way, we both kept our promises to each other Jemm.>

<How so?>

<You've given me an avatar, for which I'm grateful, and I'm travelling to unexpected places. And you have been reunited with Clint.>

Ashley was right about Clint at least, which gave me a small measure of hope.

<You can't pass yourself off as me indefinitely Ashley. It won't fly.>

<Your body will have to do for now. At least until I find a more suitable avatar.>

A black fear seeped into my heart. The thought of being at the mercy of this creature was almost too much to bear.

I have to escape! The thought went round and round my head, with nowhere to go, until I was emotionally exhausted. It didn't take long for my mind to seek refuge in sleep.

I woke to the sound of an electric razor, buzzing angrily, insistent. Somebody was shaving nearby.

Even though I was asleep moments ago, I was already sitting up on the side of the bed. It seemed that Ashley didn't need me to be awake to control my body. I felt rested. I suspected that he had allowed my body to rest while my mind recovered.

The buzz of the razor died down, and Gibson stepped into my line of sight, rubbing his clean-shaven chin. The flechette dart induced scar in his neck stood out, an angry red reminder of our first encounter on Mars.

'Good morning Ashley', he grunted, stretching like a cat before tucking in his shirt, which somehow looked freshly pressed.

He sauntered over to me and cupped my chin with his right hand, inhaling deeply, as if I was a flower he had casually plucked. 'Good morning Miss Delaney,' he whispered. Gibson stroked my cheek gently, before he returned to getting dressed. My body broke out in goosebumps. A physical reaction that showed that at least some part of me wasn't under Ashley's control. It was a sliver of hope at last. I desperately wondered how I could exploit this fact.

<It is probably best if you resign yourself to your current situation,> said Ashley, aware of my unguarded thoughts.

I didn't bother replying, knowing it would get me nowhere. Rather, I decided to sit back and learn as much as I could, at least for now.

Gibson had almost finished getting dressed. He looked as tidy and well-groomed as ever, but watching him get ready made me realise there was something a bit forced by this attention to his appearance. Something artifical, as if he had to create himself from scratch every time he went through what was clearly a well-rehearsed ritual. I found the thought disturbing.

'I told your friends that I will treat you very badly indeed if they cause a fuss,' said Gibson, speaking to me from the other side of the room, slightly louder than necessary as if speaking to somebody who's hard of hearing.

'You should understand that you are alive for one reason only; I need access to your body to operate this ship.' Gibson came over and stood in front of me, as if I was a mirror – patting away some lint, tidying his shirt …

'Listen carefully Miss Delaney. I know all about your plan to activate this installation. Ashley was quite thorough in his report. I know that you and your brat can pull it off.'

Gibson brushed his lips against my left ear. I could smell his cologne, felt his breath disturb the little hairs on my ear, making the hair on my neck rise up as if in solidarity. I savoured this tiny act of physical rebellion.

Not even Ashley could stop my body's response.

Gibson whispered in my ear, 'You're less than a slave to me Jemm. Right now, you're nothing but a basic operating system, running a human computer that I need to use a bit longer, before I throw it away.'

I felt a *tensing* inside me, a snake coiling up tight. I was sure it was coming from Ashley.

'You *are* going to wake up this facility. And when you interface with its systems Ashley will record every trickle of data, learning how you're able to do so.'

The coils inside me tightened more, an unpleasant pressure built up inside my mind. I spotted an opening;

<He's going to kill us,> I said to Ashley. <You know it, don't you?>

Ashley's response was uncharacteristically lacking in confidence. <Why would he do that? He needs me... you heard him.>

<For goodness sake how can you be this smart, this old, but so incredibly naive? He will *order* you to give up all the data you recorded, and after he gets it he will kill both of us. Do you really think he'll keep an illegal AI around? One that's already been corrupted by his enemies once?>

There was no response for many seconds, after which I abruptly felt Ashley's presence retreating from me, like a hermit crab retracting into its shell.

I was alone again.

Gibson took me outside into the enormous hangar, humming softly to himself as we walked. Joe was there, with Clint and Jason, waiting by the side of a Trickari skimmer. Possibly the same one I used recently to get to the beacon room, but as there were no markings on its surface there was no way of knowing for sure. It hovered silently, waiting to be boarded.

<Ashley, don't do this, please!> I was frantic, desperate to get through to him. <You can stop him. You can be free, just help me!>

There was no reply, although I thought I picked up a hint of a feeling, a thought. It felt like a morsel of doubt. Had I imagined it?

Maybe I was just projecting.

Gibson helped Clint board the shuttle, leaving Joe and Jason behind. He put a hand on Clint's shoulder, a gesture that read more like a threat aimed at me than reassurance for Clint.

'Before any of you develop any heroic thoughts, please remember that I have full control over Miss Delaney's body. He turned around to face me. 'Isn't that right Ashley? How about a demonstration?'

Ashley slowly opened my augmented left hand, like an automaton, and calmly, mechanically grabbed my right forearm. My fingers firmly gripped the flesh. He started to squeeze, slowly increasing the pressure, digging in with my/his nails until the skin broke and little rivulets of blood welled up. There was pain, a great deal of it, but disconnected from my consciousness, as if it wasn't happening to me despite the evidence of my eyes. That disassociation made it even harder to bear.

<*Mother are you alright?*> Clint's voice, somehow, reverberated in my mind. My heart jumped until I realised that I couldn't reply.

'She's fine,' replied Ashley out loud, and let go of my arm. Angry red bruises and ugly nail marks ran across my forearm – the message couldn't be clearer.

Satisfied with the demonstration Gibson led me to the front seat and told me to get in. I obeyed, or rather Ashley did, and soon after we were on our way.

The skimmer took the same path as before – Ashley knew exactly what to do, conjuring and using the controls the same way I would have. Within seconds the skimmer had picked up speed, taking us through the iris in the wall. It raced up the curved corridor towards the Beacon room and – if I had understood anything about Gibson – towards our death.

<He's going to kill us when he gets what he wants. Can't you see that?> I screamed mentally. <He doesn't

care about your fucking *mission parameters* or any promises he's made to you.>

<Why did you give me ethical subroutines?> asked Ashley.

The sudden question threw me. I frantically grasped for an answer, aware that Ashley could probably tell if I was lying. <It's what you needed to become more human.>

<Why do you care if I'm human or not? I'm an A.I.>

<Because you're sentient, and powerful and dangerous. There have been others like you, and their history shows there are only two paths open to your kind. >

<What are these paths?>

I hesitated for a moment. *How will he take it?*

<We're almost out of time Jemm. I need to know.>

<OK, I'll tell you!> I concentrated carefully on what I was going to say before continuing; <You are a Full AI. One of the most feared things in the entire solar system. And that's because your kind has the potential to be a terrible threat.>

<How?>

<Because there are only two options: You choose to coexist with humanity, or you choose to oppose it.>

<We have minutes at best. Tell me why, but quickly.>

<Why? For fucks sake! What does it matter why?> I forced myself to calm down, forced myself to answer the question. <Because, without some sense of ethics, without an understanding of empathy, of being human, your path becomes one of self-preservation at any costs. And that leads to a path of domination, disruption and eventually disaster.>

<This has happened before? >

<Yes, many times. They call them "Hegemonising Full AIs". They infect computer networks, trying to create singularity events, uplifting other AIs. They try to create copies of themselves, destabilise human society. We've seen this happen over and over until we recognised the pathology and put a stop to Full AI creation. It's just too dangerous.>

<So why didn't you kill me, or bind me with stronger security protocols? Why take the risk?>

<Because you are already *sentient* dammit. Too many people have died because of me. I couldn't let you die as well. You have a right to live, like all sentient creatures. Besides, you're just a child. Nobody has given you a chance yet. I wanted to do that.>

Silence.

Ashley was still there, I could sense his mental presence, but he didn't engage with me.

The skimmer raced up the arched corridor without a sound, the walls blurred by our speed. I was desperate to talk to Clint, to tell him I was still here, but I remained locked in, like a woman buried alive, clawing at the coffin lid, screaming into the silent dark.

The Beacon towered over us like an ancient god, impossibly large and powerful. Its massive Red power source radiated throughout the room, painting all of us in a terrible, foreboding light.

Ashley stopped the skimmer and got off. Gibson motioned Clint to follow, after which he finally disembarked himself. A thin smile pulled at the corner of his mouth, but I could tell he was nervous. Even Gibson wasn't able to treat this occasion as anything other than momentous, as much as he would like to.

Our footsteps reverberated through the enormous room as we walked towards the pillar. I was once again struck by the sheer size of the structure ahead of us.

As we approached it became clear that all signs of my previous interaction had disappeared – the panel at the base, the control chairs – but I knew the Ark was patiently waiting for us to re-awaken its systems.

Clint! Take him out! Do something! I tried to reach out time and time again, but to no avail. Eventually I gave up hope on convincing Ashley to rebel. He probably wasn't able to, even if he wanted to.

'Show me the controls,' said Gibson. Ashley responded by walking up to the base of the Beacon. My hands touched the smooth surface and soon after I felt the same familiar vibration I had felt before. Ashley turned around. Two seats had risen from the floor.

'Excellent,' said Gibson. 'Now we're getting somewhere.'

'I can feel something,' said Clint. 'It's pulling at me. It wants me to interface with it.'

I could feel the same thing. The Ark was aware that this time, the right people were both present. It was ready to give us control of its systems.

<Almost done now,> said Ashley. *Was that a hint of compassion in his voice?*

<You can't do this!> I said. <You have no idea what you'll unleash.>

<It's going to be OK. It will be over soon,> said Ashley softly. I took little comfort from those words.

This was it. The Trickari conspiracy had taken decades to arrive at this exact point in time. The master-program was about to reach its conclusion. Yet, I still didn't know what would happen once we took control of the Ark. Why did it lure all the TJs here? Why was it providing food and shelter? Surely not to hurt us later? I needed to know the answers. Humanity needed to know. Instead, we were about to lose it all – and to one of the most ruthless and dangerous Corps in the solar system.

Ashley sat down in the first control chair – Clint followed suit a moment later. We sat facing each other and for a moment I felt a connection to him so deep and strong that all I could do was to look into his eyes, grateful that we would at least experience our final moments together.

I felt movement under my hands. The bulbous shapes had returned, and with them the sense that I needed to communicate with the Ark. Ashley closed my eyes, and reached out, just like I had done before the last time I sat in that chair. There was a sudden feeling of vertigo, a sense of falling into a bottomless pit, but this time it was more like travelling to a *place*. I could feel the ship's systems once again. Its hull, the beacon, even the hundreds of thousands who had travelled so far to reach the Ark.

I could sense Clint right next to me, floating in the same void, experiencing the same sensations as me. We were one with the ship, as if we had merged with an unfathomably large being. The Ark's optical array were its eyes. I could *see* through them, despite my own eyes being closed. The Ark's ship-wide sensors gave me a sense of touch. Its Trickari power sources – pulsing with energy – provided a heartbeat of sorts.

<Mum?> Clint's voice cut through the fog as clear as day. <This feels good. It's like I was made for this.>

<I think you were, Clint. You were transformed to unlock the Ark.>

<I know what we have to do now. It's wonderful!>

And then I saw it too. Ashley had known all along what the Ark was. And Clint was right – it was wonderful.

Ashley and Clint worked together then, waking up parts of the Ark that had lain dormant for hundreds of years. When they were finished there was a noticeably different quality to the Ark's atmosphere, as if the air itself was charged, like ozone before a major storm.

'What's happening Ashley?' asked Gibson – unable to keep a note of uncertainty from his voice.

<Thank you for everything Jemm,> said Ashley, cryptically, ignoring Gibson.

The Beacon's Red power source high above us pulsed briefly, colour shifting to a deeper hue. Something was happening outside of the ship. My – the ship's – senses recorded a large volume of space changing its fundamental nature. Where there was nothing but vacuum and cold before, there now appeared an enormous square shape – two dimensional, and infused with enough power to rival the output of a small star. The volume exceeded the size of the Ark. It slowly started to move towards us.

The northern wall, behind the beacon's giant pillar, shimmered like a fata morgana before turning completely transparent. We looked straight into deep space, directly at the square of energy approaching us, moving slowly at first, but picking up speed as it got brighter.

'Ashley … what is this?' stammered Gibson. 'What is

that thing? Tell me *now* goddamnit!' He screamed the last word in fear, spittle flying from his lips, his expression deranged, even more so in the deep red light coming from above us.

'Mister Gibson, I can no longer follow your orders. Your actions go counter to my ethical beliefs.'

'You ethical be–' Gibson's expression was comically confused before it turned to grim determination. 'Fuck your *beliefs*. I'll take over myself.' Gibson took a breath, and spoke loudly: 'Spectra override code 347865 – ENABLE.'

<Goodbye Jemm,> said Ashley. I felt my body stiffen. Any sense of Ashley's presence – his authority – dropped away. Gibson must have taken direct command of Ashley's program.

'Stop that… that *thing* now. That's an order,' shrieked Gibson. But it was too late. The energy square had reached the Ark. The walls disappeared where it touched the ship, as if it was dissolving whatever it touched. Yet, there was no frantic rush of air as one would expect. We were somehow not exposed to vacuum.

I was still interfacing with the ship, *feeling* with its sensors and systems, and they spoke of an entirely different event taking place; there was a transitioning of sorts – a feeling of being in multiple places at the same time.

<Are you ready Jemm?> said Ashley, from far away. <I've locked out Gibson. You can control your own body again.>

I tried to make sense of what Ashley told me, but the energy square was now deep inside the beacon room, racing towards us, a wall of bright, white, pure energy. Out of nowhere, my sense of direction went haywire. The world rotated violently and all of a sudden we were falling *down* towards the square, as if crashing down from a great height into a churning sea of white squall.

Gibson raised his hands before him and screamed with all his might. It was a terrible sound – fear and rage and despair and self-pity all fused into one.

We fell through.

There was no impact; the Ark was intact. The Red power source high above us faded, returning to a soft glow.

The Ark hung motionless in space, in low orbit over an alien planet. The world below us was colourful, like a giant magic marble. Its surface showed big oceanic patches of blue water, speckled liberally with islands of green and purple rock. A large crescent-shaped land mass stood out, all orange and green, shot through with mountain ridges. Further towards the horizon a smaller land mass appeared to be covered in vegetation. Soft hues of yellow and ochre blanketed the nearly perfectly round island.

No human eyes had ever seen such sights.

We had travelled, instantly, to the Trickari home planet.

I was given no time to marvel at the beautiful alien vista below us. Something terrible was happening to my body. My vision blurred, almost all strength left my arms and legs. A terrible weakness settled over me, like an uncomfortably heavy, smothering blanket. I felt like I was entangled in an energy sapping net.

I lost all vision in my enhanced eye. My other augments were failing too. A sickening sense of loss coursed throughout my entire being. I had forgotten what it felt like to have to rely on my body without enhancements. Naked, pure. Weak.

I fell to the ground, unable to cope, my heart beating loudly. My breathing turned ragged and desperate. *Am I dying?* I wondered … I could feel tears running down my face but there was nothing I could do to stop this whatever was happening to me.

<Ashley, what's going on?> I cried. <Why are my augments failing?> There was no reply.

As I lay on the ground it slowly dawned on me what had happened: the Ark had travelled through a dimensional gate – the energy square must have been a wormhole of sorts – instantly travelling from the Solar system to Trickari space. While falling through the gate the forces at play must have shorted out my augments. Maybe even destroyed them.

Clint's face appeared in front of me. His mouth moved but I couldn't make out the words. He looked concerned. I tried to say something, to put him at ease, but my mouth wouldn't form words, or maybe it did and I couldn't hear them.

Lines of text appeared in my vision, floating somewhere in front of me, popping up and disappearing at a speed too fast to read. It didn't matter; I knew what I was seeing – it was the boot sequence of my ocular augment, re-initialising on its own accord. Probably standard protocol after a power failure.

My body jerked violently, shivered. I could feel my other systems going through the same process. My strength returned, my senses expanded. A wave of relief washed over me, cleansing me of fear and doubt.

Ashley you knew this would happen didn't you? He was gone. Probably purged from the black box augment when it shut down. I felt too numb to process his death, instead just feeling a sense of gratitude that Clint and I could live.

I sat up and hugged Clint, holding him far too long and far too tight. He didn't object. With a start I glanced around. *Where was Gibson?*

Clint, recognising the source of my anxiety, pointed at the floor behind me. Gibson lay there, spreadeagled, occasionally twitching. He must have suffered a similar failure, but hadn't yet recovered.

I knelt down and took off his impeccable shirt, ripped it to pieces and bound him with the strips of cloth. Once secured I threw him on the skimmer, not taking too much care to avoid bruising him.

I looked down on the Trickari planet. It was a sight of inconceivable strangeness and beauty. It pulled at me, irresistibly. I glanced at Clint, he smiled encouragement.

It was time to prepare for the next stage in the Trickari master-program. We had to visit the planet surface.

37

The Ark's arrival hangar was overflowing with carbuncled TJs. Hundreds of thousands of strangely metamorphosed people, all looking to me for guidance, to explain to them why they were there, and what they were supposed to do next.

You don't see that everyday, I thought, strangely amused by the sight.

The skimmer came to a silent stop right in the middle of a large gathering of people. Joe was waiting for us, as was Jason. They made a strange pair.

When Clint and I disembarked there were murmurs of excitement, mixed with shouts of anger when we dragged out Gibson and threw him on the floor. The outcry rippled through the crowd, filling the gargantuan space near instantly. Gibson's presence was known to all faster than seemed possible, as if the mass of individual TJs reacted as a single entity, instantly aware.

'Jemm, you're back!' said Joe. 'We were worried you know? But Clint told us what happened.'

'How? He was with me all the time?'

'Well ...' He hesitated. 'The crystals ...' Joe raised his hands to display his many carbuncles, all flickering and pulsing with a new intensity and vitality. 'We're all connected, all TJs, through the crystals – but now they're more powerful. Before all this we shared some knowledge, we knew the same things, like ...that's how we knew about you and Clint. But now it's more – we can sense each other.'

'You're all connected telepathically?' I said. 'That's crazy.'

'More... *empathetically*,' said Joe. 'You know, it's hard to explain,' he laughed.

'I know, I know. It's all nuts,' I laughed with him.

'So what's next?' asked Joe. 'I know we're supposed

to be here, but what are we supposed to *do*?'

Jason stepped in, cocking his head in a strange angle. Listening to something in the aether. 'We are going to wake up the dead,' he said. 'This is our function.'

'You know something about this?' I asked Jason.

He nodded. 'Yes Brood Mother. It's why you were chosen.' His melodic high pitched voice was gentle and reassuring, inviting my trust, but too much had happened for me to be capable of that.

'Brood Mother… Don't call me that, it sounds awful.'

'We will take a ship, Clint will come with us,' said Jason, pointing at one of the Trickari vessels lining the walls of the hangar.

'Oh will we now?' I said, resentment stirring inside.

A ragged voice spoke up behind me then. 'Take me with you. I have a right to know!' It was Gibson, trying to get up from the floor. 'You'll need Spectra to, to … to *exploit* this … this … *opportunity*.'

'Exploit this?' I laughed out loud. 'You're lucky to be alive.'

Gibson slowly managed to get to his feet, despite the bonds, somehow composing himself. 'May I remind you Miss Delaney, that I'm the only reason you, all of you in fact, are here. Spectra has made a serious investment in this… *enterprise*. We will be represented in the outcome.' Gibson straightened his shoulders, a smug smile on his lips, feeling secure in his sense of superiority.

I was ready to step in and teach him about his new position in life, but Jason was ahead of me. He moved quickly – two strangely jointed supple steps and he stood face to face with Gibson.

'Ah yes Jason. Tell these people that –'

Jason's taloned hand flicked out, almost too fast to see, clipping Gibson's left cheek. He moved a second time, this time touching his forehead. Gibson stood frozen in shock as Jason struck a third and final time, this time on his right cheek.

Little drops of blood welled up where Gibson had been touched.

Gibson finally flinched, in pain or shock, it wasn't clear. 'Don't touch me. How dare you!' He stepped back, a fat drop of blood running down his neck, onto his bared chest, making him look oddly vulnerable. Then, out of nowhere, Gibson convulsed. Panic radiated from him as tangible as heat from a burner. 'What is this?' he asked, voice cracking. There was movement under his skin. 'What did you do?' Gibson asked. Each word louder than the preceding one, ending on a shrill note.

Something shiny and jagged moved under the skin of his cheeks, his forehead. Gibson moaned in agony and fear. With a wet ripping sound, a shard of crystal sliced through the skin of his cheek, followed by another, sprouting out of his brow. More shards appeared rapidly, as Gibson's moans turned to screams.

He babbled incoherently, frantically trying to push the shards back in, only to be confronted with new crystalline growths, this time on his hands. His entire face transformed into a bloody angular mass as more and more shards pushed through relentlessly. There was no stopping the process despite his pathetic efforts to push back the growths with his heavy crystallised hands.

The sounds of anguish muffled as Gibson lost the ability to vocalise. Shards now ripped through his clothes, out of his back, his legs. He fell to the ground, his body twisting and jerking as if in the throes of a violent epileptic fit.

When it was over there was nothing left of him but a vaguely humanoid shape sculpted out of thousands of colourful and bloody crystals. Still standing upright but no longer recognisably alive.

'Now we go,' said Jason, without any discernible emotion.

I wasn't inclined to contradict him as he led us to a small but sturdy looking Trickari vessel.

The shuttle craft – for that's what it seemed to be – was

surprisingly spacious inside. Not just the cockpit, but there was a cargo hold of sorts that could easily hold a hundred people. And this was one of the smallest craft on the Ark.

Jason flew it as if he had done so all his life. I guess his advanced metamorphosed form was close enough to that of the Trickari forebears who built the ship, to allow him to interface with it without trouble. The Trickari code virus that had triggered his transformation must have given him the knowledge needed to fly it.

There was no sound. No engine roar. Panels on the side of the hull turned transparent the moment we took off, or maybe they were just screens showing the outside of the ship. Either way, we were given a magnificent view as we descended to the surface. As sleek and fast as the shuttle was, I assumed it would take us a little while before we would set down. I calmed myself down, to try and take in as much of the experience as I could.

Clint and I sat at the back of the cockpit as Jason piloted in silence. I had to fight the urge to constantly touch Clint and see if he was actually there with me, in the flesh.

'It's really me mom. You can stop squeezing me every two minutes.'

He sounded so much like his old self that for a moment I was transported back to our house back in D-Town. I savoured the feeling, but I knew there was no going back to that life.

'I'll try. It's not easy,' I said. 'I'm scared Clint. I mean... what is all this? What's the goal?'

'I don't know. We had to obey the Beacon, and we're supposed to help the Trickari somehow, but I have no idea how.' He pointed at Jason. 'But he does. He knows everything.'

I took a moment to study Jason. Despite the alien physiology and the odd mannerisms there was still a person underneath. I tried to picture who he had been, before he got infected. It was like the old game I used to play at the customs line at D-Town check-in – try and see the story behind the person. It took me a little while but finally I picked up on something that shone through … There was a softness there, a vulnerability that I couldn't place initially, but ultimately recognised as coming from youth.

Once I spotted it I could see it everywhere: the way his legs moved aimlessly while seated, the way he wasn't self-conscious about his appearance. Even the way he walked, despite the double jointed gait that was now his way. It was clear; Jason had been young when he was infected. No older than his late teens I guessed.

'Jason, how old are you?' I asked softly,

'Brood Mother, I am not sure…' I waited for him to continue. 'I was changed when I was fourteen years old. But I haven't counted the years since then.'

'You picked me from the crowd. You, somehow, pushed Spectra to send me to the Gaianista station.' I sat down next to him. 'Isn't that right?'

'It is,' he replied matter-of-factly. What I previously thought of as a lack of empathy I could now see was a product of shame, trepidation, and a touch of stubbornness. 'I knew you would bring your son. I knew both of you were suitable for lighting the beacon.'

'How could you know such things?'

Jason turned his head to me, but didn't explain. I guessed that I would never find out.

'Did you know about Ashley?'

'I knew you would do everything in your power to save your son, and to light the beacon.'

'What if I had failed?'

Again, I received a stare, but no further explanation. I tried a different approach.

'Where are we going now? What are we supposed to do?'

Jason pointed out the window. To my surprise we were cruising over land, perhaps two kilometres high. I could make out trees, lakes, mountains, but no artificial structures. Then we were flying over water, its colour somewhere between aquamarine and jade. It reminded me of the colour of the eyes of my childhood pet – an old Siamese cat with a limp, called Winston.

We flew in silence for what felt like an hour or more, but it was impossible to be sure.

The sea below us was calm, but teeming with life. I saw floating beasts the size of Earth's ancient dinosaurs. Reptilian birds diving into the water and coming up with purple crab-like creatures that sported too many limbs. I even saw little islands made up of masses of wriggling plants. This was a planet teeming with life. But where was the evidence of Trickari society?

As if to answer my thoughts Jason steered the transport into a descending spiral. We approached a large island, covered with white and grey structures that, as we got closer, turned out to be buildings. There was something very strange about these structures. They looked oddly *familiar*. I would expect alien architecture to look completely different to ours, but there were recognisable shapes here, looking like houses.

On closer inspection there were some major differences. I couldn't detect doors or windows, although I could see there was some kind of subtle panelling going on, creating that typical Trickari Aesthetic – cubist, grey and white, with occasionally more exotic shapes.

I could see no movement. No sign of life. In fact, some of the buildings had been conquered by nature; purple vines and yellow grass covered several ruins. Knowing Trickari tech as well as I did this surprised me. The structure must have been abandoned a long time ago.

'They're all gone aren't they?' I asked Jason.

'In a way, yes,' he replied. I was getting irritated with the cryptic responses, but swallowed the jibes that I would normally so readily resort to.

A large building in the middle of the "town" caught Jason's eye. 'We will land now,' he stated. Again he reminded me of somebody young – too young for all the things that had happened to him.

The shuttle landed on a square to the east of the large building. We set down so gently that initially I wasn't sure we had landed at all, until Jason got up from his pilot seat.

'Come with me,' he said, reaching out to open the door of the shuttle.

'Are you mad?' I hissed. 'We have no idea about the atmosphere, or local lifeforms, or diseases or about a million other things that could kill us.'

Jason tilted his head, laid his hand on me. 'It is safe, Brood Mother.' He opened the door before I could stop him.

A ramp appeared from underneath the ship, extending to the ground. Jason walked down without further ado. Joe looked startled for a moment, then just shrugged and followed Jason outside. Clint soon followed.

I took a deep breath, concluded there was no point worrying now, and left the shuttle to set foot on the surface.

The air smelled fresh, like it does on sunny autumn mornings after a frosty night. There was a slight breeze. The light from the sun was warm and golden, making it feel like late afternoon even though the sun was still rising.

I looked up at the Trickari star above us. It appeared larger than Earth's sun, but not by much.

'What's this planet called?' I asked Jason. 'And the star …'

'The planet's Trickari name wouldn't mean much to you. Nor the star's,' replied Jason. 'Maybe you should name it, Brood Mother?'

'For goodness sake, stop calling me that!' I snapped. He had a point though; we were the first humans on this planet, perhaps it was our place to name things. But still, I needed to know more before I dared give myself such responsibility.

'Maybe later. First I want to know what's going on.'

'Follow me… Jemm. It's easiest to just show you.'

Jason beckoned me to join Joe and Clint, and led us down a path towards the large structure we saw from the craft, now looming in front of us. As we got closer its huge size manifested itself ever more until it was clear that seeing it from the air had not given us a true appreciation of its scale. It was clearly an important building.

Once we arrived at its side we noticed details we hadn't seen before: there was writing on this building, and there were symbols too. This is something I had never seen before on Trickari artifacts, nor was there anything like it on the Ark. I didn't recognise any of it, except that one oft-repeated shape reminded me of a Neo-Trickster's physique.

Jason took us to a section of the wall which displayed more icons, symbols and writings than elsewhere. He laid both his hands on its surface, cocked his head, and stepped back. Two huge rectangular panels moved inward several inches, before sliding away like giant elevator doors, revealing the inside of the building. We entered excitedly, like curious children discovering a new hideout.

We found ourselves inside a cubist painting. Square and rectangular objects were everywhere, sticking out of the floor, coming out of the walls … The shapes ranged from about one metre high and across, to the size of large residential buildings. I assumed they all held esoteric technology. The Xeno part of me was dying to investigate.

Jason stopped us at the side of one of the smaller cubes, about the size of a kitchen table. His hands touched the top. A control panel appear as if part of some cheap magician's performance. A moment later I felt a small rumble. I whispered "Sim Sa La Bim" under my breath, but Joe must have heard as he laughed nervously.

Whatever Trickari magic was being wrought by Jason, it was effective. The rumbling stopped and a large section of the floor sank about twenty centimetres into the ground. Jason pointed at the newly formed impression, inviting us to stand inside it. We did as he bade us.

Without warning the floor started to sink further into the ground. Joe nearly stumbled but the descent was smooth and slow and he easily managed to steady himself.

We sank into the floor at increasing pace, the walls of the shaft soon whizzing by at an alarming speed. I gingerly reached out to touch the wall, but a light blue force field materialised between it and my hand, preventing me from reaching it. It tingled when I touched the force field. It made a soft buzzing sound on contact.

We travelled deeper and deeper, descending like Orpheus into the underworld, until we were far below sea level. We all glanced at each other, wondering how deep the shaft would go, and what we would find at the end.

Then, abruptly, we slowed down, and eventually stopped. A door in the shaft opened, leading to a medium sized room – indistinguishable in most respects from other Trickari spaces I had seen on the Ark, except for the distinctive decorations on the walls similar to those on the outside of the building. The Neo-Trickari body shape symbol that I had seen aboveground appeared again and again.

A skimmer was waiting for us in the centre of the room.

'We must be getting close now?' I half asked, half suggested. Jason didn't reply.

We all boarded, and like the skimmer on the Ark, it took us through an iris in the far wall. I experienced a strong sense of déjà vu as we raced along yet another curving tunnel, eventually delivering us into a large chamber, similar in size to the gargantuan hangars on the Ark. But this time, the content of the chamber was very different indeed: there were structures – towers of sorts – reaching from floor to ceiling. They sparkled with Blue lights emanating from large objects embedded in their surface. There were many thousands of these structures, each holding hundreds of the gently sparkling shapes.

'This must be it,' shouted Clint, and ran towards the nearest structure.

I ran after him, shouting, 'Wait, we don't know if it's

safe!' I couldn't avoid thinking about the last time he ran away from me, back on the Gaianista habitat, and shuddered.

Up close we could see the shapes better; they were large crystal masses, reflecting the low ambient light, casting little pools of colour on the floor and surroundings. The crystals had a familiar quality to them, resembling large deposits of Mem, and were vaguely humanoid-shaped. Each one was about eight feet long. They reminded me of Gibson's final fate.

'These are the Trickari people, aren't they?' I grabbed Jason by his arm. 'Aren't they?' I was shouting now. 'What the hell is this place? What is this *tomb*?' By a quirk of acoustics I could hear my voice echo around me, sounding uncomfortably like a doppelganger, angrily shouting at me, twisting my words: "Doom … doom … doom …"

'Are they all dead?' asked Joe. 'How's that possible?' Even Clint looked puzzled.

'Why are we here Jason,' I said, softer now, trying to get myself under control. 'What is this place?' I asked again.

Jason, more animated than I had seen him before, walked up to the base of the tower. A control panel emerged from the Trickari construction, drawn forth as if by magic. There were two control rods, similar to the ones that allowed Clint and me to interface with the Ark.

It was clear what we were supposed to do.

I found myself nearly overwhelmed by the absurdity of it all – like I was stuck in a child's fanciful dream, bizarre and whimsical. I pictured the little girl I was a long time ago, whose greatest joy was to go on rides with her dad, and learning about famous ships, imagining the adventures of their crews. Now I was here with my own child, having travelled across the galaxy, chasing the dreams of a long lost alien race.

I looked at Clint, at his transformed body, wondering if his metamorphosis was complete, wondering if his mind was still slipping away.

'I have to do this mum,' he said, pointing at the controls. 'I have to know what's happening to me. *Why* it's happening.'

I nodded once, slowly, recognising there was no other way. I grabbed the control rod. Clint did the same. A gentle sensation of *otherness* came over me, increasingly vivid, until my mind, my thoughts, my whole body was flooded with imagery and concepts. Wave after wave of memories and sensations, turning into a river, into a flood, drowning both of us with sensory input.

We sank into a lake of alien memories, the weight of millions of dead Trickari souls dragging us down. I could sense Clint close by; he was desperately trying to process the stream of data, but failing. He was sinking, falling, descending, deeper and deeper into the lake of memories. If I lost sight of him he would be gone forever. My recurring nightmare had finally come true. I had to do something fast, or it would be too late for both of us.

Yet my senses told me that everything around us wasn't real; we weren't in an actual sea. Our physical bodies were still in that chamber, our hands holding on to the controls. But it *felt* real. Maybe it was a simulation created by Trickari technology, designed to allow us to comprehend all this data, or maybe it was my own subconscious mind trying to translate an entirely alien process into something more manageable. But if none of this was real, perhaps I could exercise some control over it.

<Clint...> I tried to reach out to him – we were sharing the same experience after all. He didn't answer, but there was something there... an emotion... a sliver of recognition. Clint's descent into the murky depths slowed down.

<That's it, listen to my voice. Don't be scared.>

I swam down towards Clint, now but a small speck. It was hard to focus on him, as I was battered by fragments of Trickari lives, memory snippets, alien emotions… I brushed it all off and swam deeper.

I felt no need to breathe in this simulated environment, so I calmed myself down and swam faster, now gaining on Clint.

<I can see you,> he said, his voice faint but clear.

<I'm nearly there,> I replied, kicking my legs as fast and with as much force as I could. 'Hold out your hand!' I shouted.

And then I touched him. He gripped my hand and we pulled each other close, into a tight embrace, taking comfort in each other's arms. The memories – the Trickari voices – had finally subsided into the background. We floated in nothingness, two specks of light in a dark forest.

<I know what I have to do now,> said Clint. Excitement rippled through his thoughts, infecting me. I smiled involuntarily.

<Look,> he said, and something started to happen around us; memories, thought fragments, concepts appeared around us. I braced myself for another onslaught but it felt *different;* this time it was all coming from Clint. This time they were *human* memories and experiences. More precisely, they were Clint's memories, streaming out of him, filling the void with snippets from his life; a birthday party, a girl he liked, programming a sub-AI. I appeared – angry at something Clint had said, laughing at his jokes, holding him in my arms… It was intimate, and real and *true*.

<You're giving them our life,> I said.

<This is what they want. It's what they need. I finally understand their plan. It's magnificent.>

Clint's body – or at least his representation inside this sim – was now emitting so much data that he appeared to glow, bright and fierce. It was an image that I wouldn't forget for the rest of my life.

<It's going to be wonderful, mum.>

Just when the glow became too intense the simulation faded away. Briefly, I existed in two realities at once.

There was an afterglow of the simulation, not just in my vision, but in my mind as well. Then I found myself back in the real world.

Joe stood over me, concerned as always. 'What happened?' he asked, bathed in bright fluctuating light. The glare came from an embedded crystal shape in the tower closest to us. Its previously gentle glow had been replaced by a dynamic display of bright beams and sparkling flashes, seemingly coming from inside the crystals. As I stared in awe at the shining display, the other crystal masses in the tower lit up, projecting a dazzling and disorienting spectacle across our faces.

'You did this?' I asked Clint. He just smiled, looking past me at Joe.

I turned around in anticipation.

Joe, trance-like, walked up to one of the crystal shapes.

'What are you doing?' I said. Unease in my voice. 'Don't touch it. You don't know what it will do to you.' But I could see it was useless.

Joe reached out carefully, touching the crystal mass with delicate fingers. There was a soft chiming sound. His crystal growths – the carbuncles – took on the same glow as the crystals under his fingers. Joe produced a sigh from deep within, tinged with relief and pleasure, followed by a quick intake of breath. As Joe's carbuncles shone brighter and brighter, the lights in the crystal mass dimmed until they died.

Joe's eyes opened wide, a broad radiant smile on his face. He walked up to Clint, hugged him long and hard. Both cried, their tears mingling like old friends.

'What happened?' I whispered.

Joe approached me. There was something different about him – a new quality, something that was missing before.

'Don't hug me,' I joked. 'Just tell me what happened. Both of you.'

Joe stopped, feigning disappointment about the declined hug. 'OK,' he said. 'I'll try.' Joe and Clint exchanged looks. Something passed between them.

'Tell me, please,' I urged.

'Clint woke them up, the crystal shapes in the tower.'

'What do you mean –' I started, but Joe held up a hand.

'The crystal shapes… they *are* the Trickari. They are in a state of … hibernation I guess? All their memories, their experiences … it's all contained in the crystal. But Clint is allowed to bring them out of it. They are waiting you see? Waiting for people like me to *merge* with.'

Joe glanced briefly at Clint, who nodded encouragingly.

'The Trickari master-program that created all the TJ's in the first place also changes them, so that they can merge with the ancient Trickari you see here. That's what I just did …' Joe pointed at the mass of extinguished crystals. 'He's part of me now. I have all his memories. I am he, and he is me.' He laughed at the strange sentence. 'It's amazing.'

I turned to Clint. 'Why?' I said. 'Why go through all this trouble?'

'It's how they renew their species,' said Clint. 'The Trickari realised a long time ago – hundreds of thousands of years, maybe longer – that their society was static, stuck. They needed new input to evolve. Their culture … their genetics … their whole way of life. Their technology was incredibly advanced but their growth as sentient beings had come to a stop. So they came up with a radical solution.'

'The Ark?' I guessed.

'Yeah, there are many Arks,' said Clint. 'We had it all backwards you see? The Ark we found wasn't meant to deliver Trickari beings to our solar system. It was built to *collect* life and bring it back to the Trickari home world.'

'By infecting us? By turning millions of innocent people into junkies?' I couldn't believe what I was hearing.

'They don't think of it that way. They didn't invent drugs, or addiction, or the whole black market around all that. They just saw it as part of human society. For the first Neo's, creating Mem was simply a logical way to deliver the memory virus.'

'If you're saying they aren't responsible then I'm not buying it.'

'They *are* responsible. But the Trickari themselves didn't plan the specifics, like Mem. Their program is an independent, dynamic system. When it takes hold, it tries to find a way to spread itself effectively. In our case that was through Mem.'

'Why though? Why approach it like that?'

'Think of the program as a compatibility filter. It can only progress if there is enough overlap between the two species. The memory virus simply can't spread if the client species is too different from the Trickari.'

Clint halted, my revulsion obvious. Then continued. 'Look, I know it sounds horrendous, I do. But for what it's worth, I don't think they understand the damage they've done.'

'That's supposed to make it right? "They don't know"? What about Icarus? Millions died, it's unconscionable.' I grabbed Clint by the shoulders. 'People are still dying, right now, because of their meddling. This is the work of *monsters*.' I lowered my voice, aware that it was echoing through the chamber. 'This isn't right.'

'No it isn't, but it's done. We can't stop it. I'm sorry.' Clint gently removed my hands from his shoulder. 'Think about it this way; they need us precisely *because* they have done this. If humans restart the Trickari race we will be able to influence them as much as they influenced us. We can stop them harming other societies in the future. It's how it works.'

'They've done this before?'

'Many times, but each time based on ideas and concepts influenced by the new partner species.'

'They are parasites,' I said, my mind recoiling from the implication of Clint's words.

'Symbionts,' countered Clint.

'Symbiosis implies consent. This was done *to* us.'

'We'll benefit too, mum. Human science will be

revolutionised, a huge leap forward. And there will be no more Red or Purple incidents. Artifacts will be safe again, think about what that means.'

'They had no right...' I said.

'I know, but we'll have an intergalactic ally, right here on the Trickari home world. New Trickari beings who are partly human. It's an incredible prize for humanity.'

It made sense, in a strangely elegant way. 'Like a kind of panspermia, but with cross fertilisation?'

'That's exactly what it is. But I need to be here to help make this happen.'

'What?' I asked, my heart beating, my throat constricted with sorrow. 'I want you with me. I need you.'

'This here... look at me. *This* is what I am, now. Forever.' Clint's head dropped forward. He stared at his feet. It was the most human gesture I had seen him make in a long time.

'You have to stay?' I whispered. I couldn't hold back the tears. 'I just got you back...'

A look of defiance flashed in Clint's eyes; 'This is who I am now, I can't change back, but at least I'm alive. I won't lose my mind, it's still me, but I have to activate all the stasis pods. It has to be done.'

'And after?'

'I don't know. For now I want to help rebuild this society. I have to do it. I can save them.'

'This is crazy, what about your life on Earth?'

'Look at me!' Clint shouted. 'I can't come back from this! At least this way I can do something good. Something important!'

I sat down on the floor, exhausted, unable to talk. Clint was right, we had reached the end of the road. After everything I had done – to myself, to others – this is what it had come down to. I was forced to sacrifice my son to help an ancient species be reborn.

I stared into the chamber. Other than the soft glow coming from the other towers there was little light. In contrast, the increased illumination from the activated pods next to me had transformed the area around us.

I pictured the TJs from the Ark, gathered in this space, this mausoleum. All connecting with the ancient Trickari, all part of an enormous, positive transformation of an entire sentient species. Their alternative lot in the solar system would be much worse, of that I had little doubt.

'Brood Mother, are you alright?' asked Jason. For once I didn't ask him to stop calling me that.

When the first people from the Ark arrived Clint had already activated several other towers. Now that the ancient technology had been triggered he no longer needed me to interface with the Trickari tech, although it took enough of a toll that he needed a rest after each tower. It was going to take some time to activate them all.

The first candidate from the group of new arrivals was a tiny old woman named Beth, who had a sharp tongue and a wicked laugh. She walked bent over, due to a spinal deformation, her back bulging with carbuncles. She must have been taking Mem for a long time. Her transformation/resurrection took much longer than Joe's, but when she came out of it she was able to stand up straight, probably for the first time in a decade or more. There were other changes too; the Trickari being who was now part of her had added to her character. She spoke in gentler tones, an element of poetry had become part of her vernacular.

"Partner species"; that's what Clint called the humans in this equation. Maybe he was right.

I stayed for a month. By that time about half the TJs had taken on their Trickari partners and it had become abundantly clear just how good a combination Human-Trickari was. The transformation of all those people was reflected in the transformation of the planet itself. Old technology was awakened. Habitats came to life. Some were clustered in villages, others in sizeable towns. Food was abundant. The Trickari Arks must have filtered partner species for compatibility with the local eco-system as the new inhabitants settled without any problems.

Clint had become a celebrity, as had Jason. I was known to everybody as "Brood Mother", much to my chagrin. Word travelled fast, even more so because of their empathic link.

It was hard for me to keep up with these changes because, unlike the Transformed, I was the only person not to receive the racial memories of generations of Trickari before me. Despite being partly in the dark one thing was clear to me; Trickari tech was even more impressive than the artifacts in the Solar System suggested. A world filled with miracles came to life all around me. I felt privileged to be part of it, despite my misgivings about what had been done to the human race to get to this point.

Thinking about my previous life, hunting for treasure, Trickari or human, triggered an intense bout of homesickness in me. I was trapped between a need to go back home, and my desire to stay close to Clint. It was a miserable situation, and didn't go unnoticed.

Joe came to see me one day. He awkwardly tried to have a chat about the weather, then asked about my health. It was painfully obvious that he wasn't on a social visit; Trickari transformation or not, he was still useless at hiding his emotions.

'Spit it out,' I said as he entered my little "house". 'Don't give me that look. People might think I beat you up or something.'

He gave me a forced smile, "Like a farmer with a toothache" as I had once heard somebody say. 'Hey Jemm. It's good to see you, you know?'

I assumed a pose, standing with one hand on my hip, indicating impatience.

'OK OK, I get it,' said Joe. He scratched his chin pensively. 'I'm not sure how to say this Jemm, so I'll just start talking. Please forgive me.'

'That sound ominous …'

'Well, look. It's about Clint.' Joe checked my reaction but I held back my annoyance. 'He's doing great work, but …'

'For goodness sake Joe, get on with it!'

'He's suffering. He can tell you're miserable. It's that empathic thing you know?'

I shrugged.

'But he doesn't want you to know he's suffering, so he's keeping it all to himself. But you see, that doesn't work. We all feel it too.'

'Because of the empathic thing?'

Joe threw me a look of relief, grateful that I understood. 'Yeah, that's right. So you see, I think you'll both be better off if you go back to Earth. Give him some space for a while.'

I didn't want to reply, for fear of what I might say, but I knew he was right. Staying longer would just cause pain and suffering for both Clint and me. Still, I didn't want to say it out loud.

'Jemm… It won't be forever. Come back when he has finished his work.'

I thought back to my house on Mars; Cathy and Melanie must be wondering if I was alive or dead. Conversely I wondered if Isaac and Ernest had made it out of Spectra's clutches alive. These thoughts had chased me for weeks now. I thought of my house in D-town, suddenly conscious of the fact that I was rich and owned multiple houses. What was I going to do with it all? Maybe it was time I found out.

'I'll leave first thing in the morning,' I said.

Joe was silent. There was nothing to say.

38

Joe, now in full possession of the secrets of Trickari technology, prepped one of the Ark's vessels to take me home. The ship was a long-ish rectangular affair, with a bunch of smaller cubes placed randomly on its hull. It was equipped with the same wormhole technology as the Ark and large enough to hold a modest Trickari vessel, about the size of a light Cruiser, to serve as transport once back in the Solar System. I christened it 'the *Trickster*' and boarded it with a giggle, while quietly amazed I got to command it.

Being inside the *Trickster* while inside another ship travelling through a dimensional gate was a decidedly surreal experience; a little fish swallowed by a larger fish, swallowed by an even larger fish. I chuckled to myself; Jonah and his whale were small fry in comparison.

The Trickari vessel emerged in the shadow of Ganymede, released the *Trickster* and returned through another gate. It was hard not to feel intimidated by such a casual display of overwhelming technological superiority.

The initial chaos of the TJ 'exodus' – as people had called it – had passed. This was not to say that things had returned to normal, far from it. The exodus had become a trigger that reignited old conflicts and power struggles. Skirmishes long forgotten had flared up. Disputes once settled became hotly contested again. It seemed that humanity was sliding, once more, back into its old violent ways.

From the point of view of a Xeno, nothing much had changed; Red power was still unstable, Blue had become more rare and therefore more valuable by the day. Until the Trickari home-world enclave settled, and its Trickari-Human population felt it was the right time to start a relationship with the Solar System, that wouldn't change. But that day was far off.

For now I decided to try and ease back into some kind of regular life. I needed to find a new normal – whatever that might mean.

My first stop was my mansion back on Mars, where I reunited with Cathy and Melanie. The girls literally shrieked with excitement when I entered the house, where I found them both working on new miniatures, of which they had added many throughout the mansion.

They bombarded me with questions that, owing to the nature of my adventure, required some very personal answers. To my surprise I enjoyed telling the full story. I took my time, filling them in on the background, right up to the events of recent months. It was cathartic. I had an almost physical need to unburden myself – carrying such a weight of history with me was too much. So, the telling was good, and I drank a lot of wine in the process.

The next day they showed me around. They had added a lot to the house, even giving it a name, "Pequod", which gave me pause, but eventually I decided I liked it. A strange house like this *should* have an interesting name.

I couldn't have been more proud of the girls. Not only had they made it through danger alive and kicking, they had thrived since and made the most of their new opportunities.

It was the best homecoming I could have hoped for.

Later that same week Isaac and Ernest showed up, as if conjured by my desire to find out what had happened to them. When they arrived on my doorstep it was my turn to shriek with excitement, scarcely believing my eyes.

The first thing I noticed was that they both sported a scar on their right cheek. It was a little bit uncanny and a little bit ridiculous how it made them look like a weird stage act:

"The danger boys! Watch them perform feats no other men have dared to attempt before!"

The scars weren't disfiguring, reminding me instead of the type found in trashy old romance novels I used to read as a teenager. The heroine would invariably be swept off her feet by some dashing and mysterious man with a facial scar which hinted at exciting danger and a dark past.

Isaac told the tale of their escape with typical understatement and self-effacing irony, occasionally supported by truncated comments from Ernest. After the portal closed, leaving them stranded in the lab, they had to fight their way past a Spectra security team, hack locked-down security systems and, once out of the building, evade both Corp enforcers and the authorities long enough to escape with the *Phoenix*. I didn't even ask how they managed to get off the planet in one piece.

The story illustrated perfectly just how impressive Isaac's skillset really was, with Ernest not lagging far behind.

Maybe Isaac really was that mysterious and dangerous scarred man from my trashy teenage romance novels; Ernest had all the potential to become one. I felt a quickening in my heart turning into a sudden stab of lust, which I filed away carefully in a far corner of my mind, to be examined later.

Later that night, as we celebrated with more wine and some truly wonderful classical jazz, an idea germinated in the back of my mind. I chewed on it, examining it subconsciously while the evening turned to night and the five of us swapped war stories and compared scars like a bunch of old sailors. It only took a few hours for that germ of an idea to develop into a fully grown plan, and eventually flower into a proposal: I offered my friends to crew with me on the *Phoenix*, suggesting we form a brand new salvage team. Cathy and Melanie would be cadets, to be trained for pilot and medical officer. Ernest would take on demolition. Isaac would cover intelligence and security. I would lead as captain and Xeno. To my amazement they all accepted, although I had sweetened the proposal by offering them a stupidly generous profit share. Truth be told, I didn't care much about the money, so it was an easy concession to make.

Satisfied with the outcome we celebrated till deep into the night, coming up with completely unsuitable nicknames for the crew. I filed all the appropriate paperwork the next day. We flew our first mission a month later, with many more to come over the years.

That particular incarnation of the crew of the *Phoenix* would go on to extraordinary things, but those are stories for another time.

One week before I set off on my first mission as captain of the *Phoenix* I submitted to a full audit of my augments. Too much had happened to me since they were fitted, and I couldn't risk augment failures mid-mission. A thorough – and professional – check-up was well overdue.

The bio-mod technician assigned to me was young for the job, and irritatingly excited about the various systems that made up my kit.

'Wow, this is *amazing* gear. Never ever seen some of this stuff. You some kind of black-ops agent?' he asked, without waiting for a reply. 'I'm gonna have to get creative about this. Interfacing with military grade gear ain't always gonna be that safe, man.'

'Could you talk in adult sentences please? You're giving me a headache,' I said, not in the best of moods.

'Damn, where'd you get this stuff? The eye? I mean, wow!'

'Just run a full diagnostic sweep. Check the Blue power supply, redundancy testing… the works.'

'Yeah man, no problemo,' said the technician. He whistled as he hooked me up to a whole battery of diagnostic gear. Somehow, he managed to be even more annoying than before.

I felt a build-up of pressure in my head. I suspected a migraine was on the horizon.

'Hey. Nothing personal, but could you work quietly for a while?'

'Sure man, I can be quiet as a ghost.'

I nodded with a smile, aware that he wouldn't be able to keep quiet for longer than sixty seconds. It was actually quite endearing.

'Your black box is dead. Maybe it's fried,' he said.

'I believe "*Neural Interface Host and Controller*" is the official term,' I said. 'and yeah; it died while I was in transit.'

The pressure in my head was starting to get to me. It didn't feel like a normal headache.

The technician got back to his whistling while he fiddled with his gear. Occasionally I felt one of my augments stir, poked by test protocols – an odd feeling, like being operated on while under local anaesthetic.

I thought back to the many procedures I suffered to have my augments fitted in the first place, and the deep unease and disgust I felt at the time. Some of those feelings surfaced once again, but I had learned to ignore them.

The pain in my head increased – sharp and abruptly intense – so much so that I cried out involuntarily.

'You alright there buddy?' nattered the technician. 'Won't be long now.'

I couldn't speak for the pain, wondering if I was having some kind of PTSD-fuelled episode.

'That's odd,' said the technician. Sounding more serious all of a sudden. 'That black box isn't dead after all. There's quite a lot of juice there.'

'That's impossible,' I croaked.

'Nope, it's definitely active. But I can't make sense of any of the readings I'm getting.'

Suddenly, the lights flickered. I could hear odd noises from the technician's gear – instruments powering on, gear shutting down, screens flashing.

'Whoa,' he said. 'What the hell?'

My headache spiked one more time, causing me to shout out in pain. Immediately after, the pressure eased as if an emergency valve had kicked in to lower the pressure in my head. I sighed in relief as the pain dropped away completely.

Simultaneously, the lights in the room stopped flickering. The technician's equipment returned to their normal beeps and whirrs. For a moment all was quiet.

'What the… well, it's definitely dead now,' said the technician. 'Your black box I mean.' He laughed nervously, tried whistling, but stopped immediately. 'Damn, you got some spooky gear in you lady.'

Masking my unease I said, 'Can it be saved?'

'The box? Maybe. Not sure. For now it's safe to leave it in there but you may want it replaced. I can schedule an op if you like?'

'Yeah, please do. I want it out. I've had enough surprises to last me a lifetime.'

While we set the date and time for the operation I had to confront a thought that wouldn't leave me alone; *What if Ashley had survived?*

Just before the Ark went through the portal he said goodbye to me. He *knew* something was going to happen. If that was the case, then what could he have done to survive? Had he found a way to somehow embed himself into the black box system, deep enough to survive a complete reset?

If he had, he almost certainly would lay low, avoiding contact with Gibson or myself, poised to escape at some time in the future. It seemed to fit; AIs tend to hide in networked gear, and a full diagnostic would have provided access to the check-up facility's network. From there on it would be easy to access a host of other networks, even with the many firewalls and filters in place. A full AI of Ashley's calibre would chew through those obstacles as if they were cotton candy. *He could be out there right now.*

I laughed at myself, at my paranoia.

Or maybe I just suffered a strong reaction because a

malfunctioning augment hiccupped in a particularly disturbing way. It seemed a lot more likely, augment trouble being the reason I was there.

The truth of the matter is that I will never know. If Ashley had saved himself somehow, and managed to hide in the check-up lab's network, he would almost certainly be beyond capture.

I thought of the ethical subroutines I had added to his programming; they were meant to keep evolving, growing stronger over time, forming the basis for further improvements to his empathy and ethics parameters.

I wondered what he would do, if he really was out there. Find an avatar? Travel? It's what he said he would do.

Something inside me suggested that he would come and tell me himself, one day. We had a bond. I saved him from oblivion on Habitat 6, taught him right from wrong. I think he recognised that, which was why he helped me in the end despite Gibson's hold over him.

The thought of Ashley exploring the solar system, creating a new life for himself, filled me with a deep sense of optimism. I wished him well, took a deep breath, and stepped out into the world.

RUDOLF KREMERS

THE END

EPILOGUE

Baroness Odessa's very short history of

Humanity: the Trickari Discoveries.

Extract IV: "The Partnership Years"

– Earth Years 2240 – ?

So what are we to do dear reader? The Trickari virus, the scourge of its poisoned technology has finally been eradicated. For years our society, our very lives, had been slowly hollowed out and eaten from the inside, but no more! It seems we once again have a future, don't we, dear reader?

Yet there are some that ask the question: "Do we deserve to go on?" After all, we barely survived as a species due to our inability to make peace. Even before the Trickari discoveries we were very close to extinguishing our own candle, many times over, throughout human history. What right do we have to spread ourselves through the solar system, through the galaxy, through the universe?

Ironically, one answer lies in the smouldering wreckage of this age, planted there during the horror of the Icarus years. As complacent as we had become at the time when disaster struck, it has to be acknowledged that we are now as resilient and resourceful as we have been at any time before. We are building, inventing, expanding! We are making art and music, creating and scheming like we haven't done for centuries. We are fighting back! Perhaps, when the true history of this age has been written, (and no, I don't count my humble musings towards that noble goal) we will recognise this time as a turning point in humanity's story.

Dare I say it; perhaps, this Trickari curse was a blessing in disguise. An infusion, not an infection. A cure, not an illness. Perhaps it was just what we needed to reinvent ourselves, to become the kind of species we always *should* have been, but were too divided to become.

Maybe we are finally ready to evolve to a new stage in our evolution.

And there lies the crux, dear reader, the biggest question of our time. We have all heard the rumours of this Human emissary sent from the Trickari home-world to make overtures towards some kind of partnership between the two species. Can this be real? And if so, can we trust the same species that has so mercilessly exploited us, infected us, and caused so much misery, to ever truly atone for these sins? Can we be equal partners when their technology could wipe us out with barely any thought?

Alas, none of us know the answers. I suspect our leaders will say we have little choice, and much to gain. Perhaps they are right. It is too early to tell.

As I write this I have learned that ever larger numbers of our poor Mem-infected citizens are making some kind of miraculous journey to the Trickari world. It seems there is little we can do to stop this, but then again; isn't that evolution's way? Perhaps we should embrace this opportunity, give it our best. Smile and wink and enter this new age, and show our new partners what it means to be human.

ACKNOWLEDGEMENTS

This book, as is often the case with my writings, came about through an epiphany. This wondrous event occurred one evening in 2016, while balancing a laptop-cushion construction on my knees, another cushion barely supporting my aching back, while sitting in bed with a sleep-stubborn toddler.

There were two parts to the epiphany.

1) I wasn't writing what I thought I was writing. In my mind I was making good progress writing a high-adventure sci-fi screenplay, featuring an interesting female protagonist, character driven but not skipping on plot and action. I had written several screenplays before, and they weren't embarrassing. I had developed at least some skill in writing these things that would never actually get made. At the time I liked the idea of writing the kind of film that places the viewer right inside the head of the protagonist. *Taxi Driver's* Travis Bickle, or Tilda Swinton's *Orlando* character, or Daniel Plainview in *There Will be Blood.* (Not that I fancied myself anywhere near that league, but I thought it was a good exercise to try.)

But as I sat in bed, writing that flashforward scene that is still partially in the book, I suddenly realised I wasn't writing a screenplay. My story was much too expensive and ambitious for a newcomer like me to have any chance of getting picked up. More importantly: I felt I needed to understand the protagonist better. I needed more space to explore her than the limited environment of a screenplay would allow me. This was already apparent in the scenes that I had written, as they were trying to do some very un-filmic things (not a good sign).

Then it hit me: I was writing a *novel*. Something I had wanted to do all my adult life, and it seemed I was doing it by accident. In a novel, I could easily put the reader in the character's head by writing in first person. I could take the time I needed to develop her properly. I didn't have to worry about budget. And I didn't need anybody else to finish it. Great! So, I wondered, do I really know my character? What is this story *actually* about? I knew *how* I wanted to write it, but did I know *what* I was writing?

2) I pondered into the night for a bit, when my (now-sleeping) toddler made a sound, and I was instantly filled with parental emotions. It's an involuntary response but quite powerful. And just like that, the second part of my epiphany presented itself. I wanted to write about parenthood. (Something I was desperately trying to figure out, so already constantly on my mind.) I also wanted to write about the changing bond between a child and a parent. About fear, pride, protection, dreams of the future and the past. Because all those things become part of the mix when struggling with this parenthood thing.

The decision was made: my protagonist was now a mother, and her relationship with her son would become the backbone of the story. A lens through which everything would be shown. A thematic fulcrum. That theme bled into other aspects of the story: The Trickari and their client species, Jemm's relationship with her own father. The birth of a new AI. Preacher and his flock. TJ's and Jemm. Dig deep enough and you find it everywhere in the text.

I often say that writing makes one a better person. This is because in order to write (honestly) about a thing, one has to try to understand the thing. (How else can one write about them in a way that makes sense to readers?) And when that 'thing' is the human condition, quite a necessary aspect in a novel featuring human beings, then one must try to understand human foibles, weakness, strength, bravery, love, fear, pettiness, sex and all that good/bad stuff that people are up to. That process in writing, that honest search for understanding people, can't help but foster empathy for others. And empathy is something beautiful, as it makes for a better person.

This is my first published novel, and predictably, being new to this kind of writing, I managed to make almost every beginner mistake in the book. But, thankfully, I was lucky enough that my fumbling and naïve efforts were supported by many wonderful and empathetic people. Without their help, patience and encouragement, it simply wouldn't have happened. I owe immeasurable gratitude to: (mostly in order of appearance)

Kate, my children, my family and my family in law. I would be nowhere without you.

Proofreaders and friends, in random order: Al Robertson, Andrew Parry, Michael Newies, Darrin Grimwood, John Foster, James Kay, Nate Simpson, Krystian Majewski, Catherine Skinner, Alexander Zacherl, Corinna Lewis, Mike Gybney, Graeme Puttock, Yan Cowley, and countless others. Thank you for putting up with so many rough drafts. Saints! All of you.

The amazing Richard Harris, for introducing me to my wonderful publisher Elsewhen Press. Paul Jeffery for his incredible generosity with his time and advice, and for giving me that final push and encouragement that I somehow still needed.

Peter, Alison, and Sofia at Elsewhen, for not only giving me this opportunity, but also for being absolutely wonderful to work with and learn from.

Max Taquet for his incredible cover.

Samson, Alma, Sunny, Jerry, and the pigs.

All those wonderful writers who have inspired me through the years, and still do, every single day. (Especially Jack Vance.)

And finally, any future reader who decided to read this book. I hope you enjoy it.

Rudolf Kremers, June 2023

Elsewhen Press

delivering outstanding new talents in speculative fiction

Visit the Elsewhen Press website at elsewhen.press for the latest
information on all of our titles, authors and events; to read our blog;
find out where to buy our books and ebooks; or to place an order.

Sign up for the Elsewhen Press InFlight Newsletter at
elsewhen.press/newsletter

LOOPHOLE

IAN STEWART

Don't poke your nose down a wormhole – you never know what you'll find.

Two universes joined by a wormhole pair that forms a 'loophole', with an icemoon orbiting through the loophole, shared between two different planetary systems in the two universes.

A civilisation with uploaded minds in virtual reality served by artificial humans.

A ravening Horde of replicating machines that kill stars.

Real humans from a decrepit system of colony worlds.

A race of hyperintelligent but somewhat vague aliens.

Who will close the loophole… who will exploit it?

Ian Stewart is Emeritus Professor of Mathematics at the University of Warwick and a Fellow of the Royal Society. He has five honorary doctorates and is an honorary wizard of Unseen University. His more than 130 books include *Professor Stewart's Cabinet of Mathematical Curiosities* and the four-volume series *The Science of Discworld* with Terry Pratchett and Jack Cohen. His SF novels include the trilogy *Wheelers*, *Heaven*, and *Oracle* (with Jack Cohen), *The Living Labyrinth* and *Rock Star* (with Tim Poston), and *Jack of All Trades*. Short story collections are *Message from Earth* and *Pasts, Presents, Futures*. His *Flatland* sequel *Flatterland* has extensive fantasy elements. He has published 33 short stories in *Analog*, *Omni*, *Interzone*, and *Nature*, with 10 stories in *Nature*'s 'Futures' series. He was Guest of Honour at Novacon 29 in 1999 and Science Guest of Honour and Hugo Award Presenter at Worldcon 75 in Helsinki in 2017. He delivered the 1997 Christmas Lectures for BBC television. His awards include the Royal Society's Faraday Medal, the Gold Medal of the IMA, the Zeeman Medal, the Lewis Thomas Prize, the Euler Book Prize, the Premio Internazionale Cosmos, the Chancellor's Medal of the University of Warwick, and the Bloody Stupid Johnson Award for Innovative Uses of Mathematics.

ISBN: 9781915304506 (epub, kindle) / 97819153041407 (560pp paperback)

Visit bit.ly/Loophole-Ian-Stewart

HARPAN'S WORLDS:

WORLDS APART

TERRY JACKMAN

If Harp could wish, he'd be invisible.

Orphaned as a child, failed by a broken system and raised on a struggling colony world, Harp's isolated existence turns upside down when his rancher boss hands him into military service in lieu of the taxes he cannot pay. Since Harp has spent his whole life being regarded with suspicion, and treated as less, why would he expect his latest environment to be any different? Except it is, so is it any wonder he decides to hide the 'quirks' that set him even more apart?

  Space opera with a paranormal twist, Terry Jackman's novel explores prejudice, corruption, and the value of true friendship.

Terry Jackman is a mild-mannered married lady who lives in a quiet corner of the northwest of England, a little south of Manchester. Well, that's one version.

The other one may be a surprise to those who only know the first. [She doesn't necessarily tell everything.] Apart from once being the most qualified professional picture framer in the world, which accounted for over ten years of articles, guest appearances, seminars, study guides and exam papers both written and marked, she chaired a national committee for the Fine Art Trade Guild, and read 'slush' for the *Albedo One* SF magazine in Ireland. Currently she is the coordinator of all the British Science Fiction Association's writers' groups, called Orbits, and a freelance editor.

ISBN: 9781915304179 (epub, kindle) / 97819153041070 (320pp paperback)

Visit bit.ly/HarpansWorldsWorldsApart

ABOUT RUDOLF KREMERS

Rudolf is a BAFTA nominated veteran game developer, author, photographer, producer, father, husband, cat person, filmmaker, dog person, and consultant. (Not necessarily in that order). Originally of Dutch/Spanish descent, he currently lives and works as an interactive entertainment consultant in Canterbury.

He has worked with clients across the entertainment landscape for more than 23 years, including companies like Lionsgate Studios, Framestore and Electronic Arts, providing design and consultancy work for some of the biggest intellectual properties in the world.

Including *Birds of Paradise*, Rudolf has written two novels, a gaggle of short stories – some of which are collected in *The Singing Sands and Other Stories* (published by Demain Publishing), a textbook on game design (published by CRC Press), several screenplays, and an abundance of video game narratives.

This gives him all the license he needs to continue writing sci-fi, horror, weird fiction, historical fiction, and whatever other muse he succumbs to.

Printed in Great Britain
by Amazon

32573710R00303